NORSEMAN RAIDER

By

Jason Born

WORKS WRITTEN BY JASON BORN

THE NORSEMAN CHRONICLES are:

NORSEMAN RAIDER

NORSEMAN CHIEF

PATHS OF THE NORSEMAN

THE NORSEMAN

THE WALD CHRONICLES are:

WALD VENGEANCE

WALD AFIRE

THE WALD

COPYRIGHT

NORSEMAN RAIDER. Copyright © 2014 by Jason Born. All rights reserved. No part of this book may be used or reproduced in any manner without written permission.

ISBN-13: 978-1500861971
ISBN-10: 1500861979

DEDICATION

James M. Miller

ACKNOWLEDGEMENTS

Thank you often feels unsatisfactory when it comes to praising the partners that were involved in getting a book from my head into the hands of faithful readers. Nonetheless, I hope these few words of gratitude I offer are read by many fans so that it is clear that any success I've been fortunate enough to garner is chiefly due to my associating with patient and talented individuals.

I have read some historical fiction authors who've said that they choose not to put any maps in their work or to use only the bare minimum. They have sound reasoning, for these men and women believe it is their job to create the settings with words alone. For this, I commend them and support their endeavors. My approach is a little different. I believe that maps can only enhance the readers' experiences with the characters and their actions. Maps can help explain context, proximity, and borders more than my feeble words are able to do on their own. Such maps can be used as quick references whether the book is in physical form or electronic.

Making his sixth appearance here is Mike Brogan, our master cartographer. If you've stuck with me throughout, you know that I cobbled together some sort of pictures on my own that I insisted were maps in my first novel. They left much to be desired. Thanks, Mike, for your partnership and for enduring my six a.m. emails chock full of "clarifications."

Nathaniel Born, too, provided a few of the maps this go 'round. If you recognize his last name, that is because he is my son. At just thirteen, he did a marvelous job. Thanks, Natt.

My co-workers at Camelot Portfolios, LLC and Munn Wealth Management deserve praise. They consistently bear my lunchtime disappearances as I bolt to write a page or two at the local park or restaurant. Tolerating my proclivity to bring up the history of almost any situation during our investment committee meetings takes certain fortitude. My friends at work exhibit such strength in spades.

Michael Calandra continued his string of marvelous covers. His best work comes when I shut up and allow his imagination, pencils, and brush to do the talking. For this cover, I began rambling about the action sequences in *Norseman Raider*. Within moments, Michael had his pencil sketching out what he saw in his mind's eye. His talent deepens continuously! Thank you, Michael.

Finally, the most challenging of all positions on the team is that of proofreader and editor. Debbie Long, despite a multitude of deep commitments, makes time to take the sometimes messy pages I give her and form them into something that readers want to read. Similar to our cartographer, Debbie tolerates emails containing "just one more scene" or "an improvement" to another even after I've sent her my "final" draft. Though I end up reading each book I write about a dozen times, I am so much more confident in their eventual release because she offers her attention to detail and experience. I thank Debbie for her time and expertise.

NORSE WESTERN EXPANSION

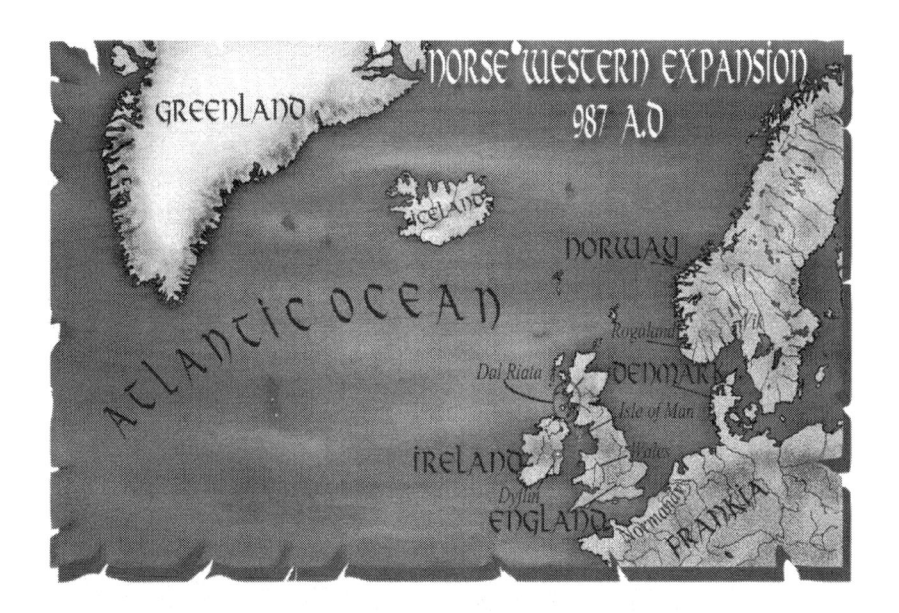

GODFREY'S RAIDING AREA

RAID ON ANGLESEY

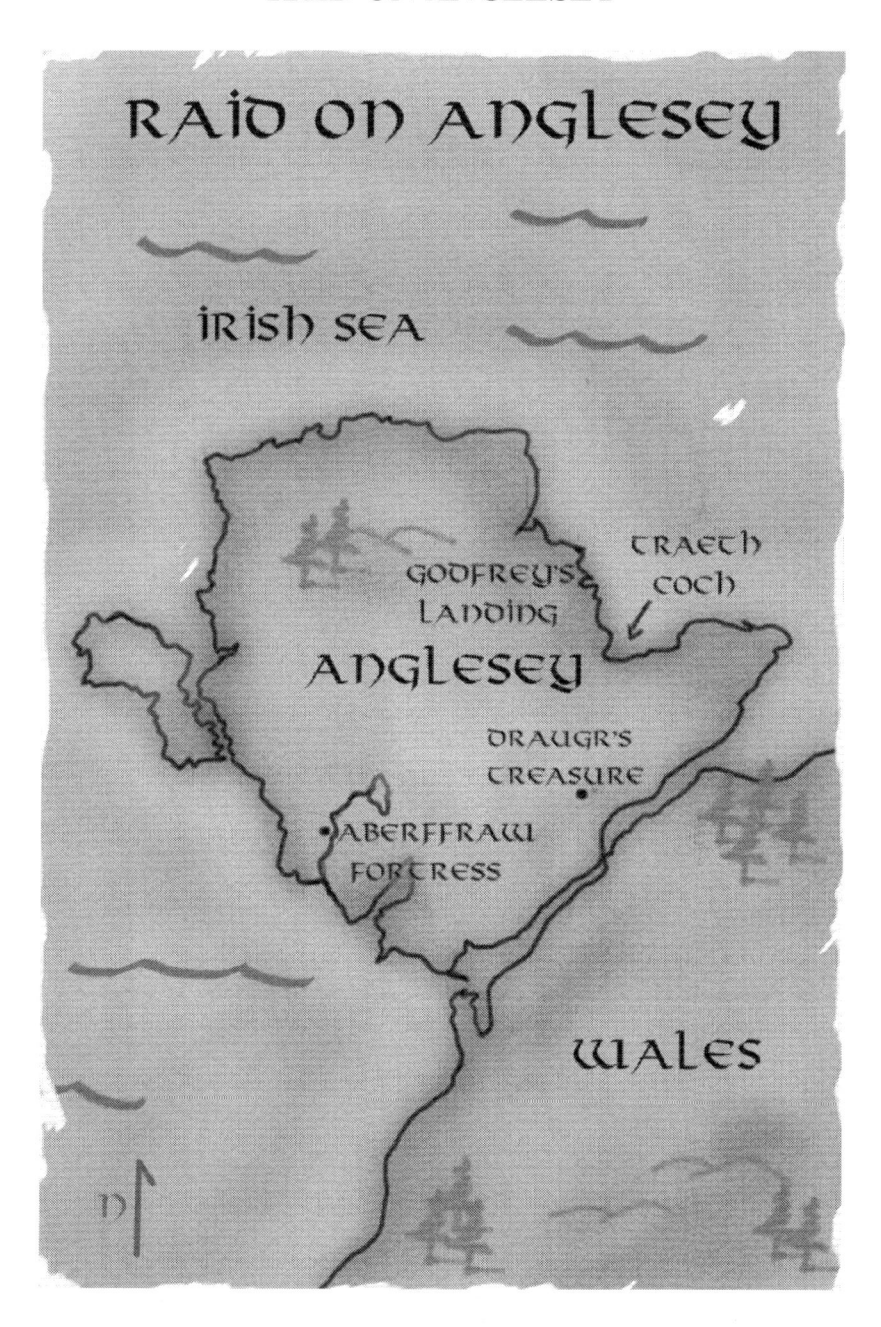

RAID ON WATCHET

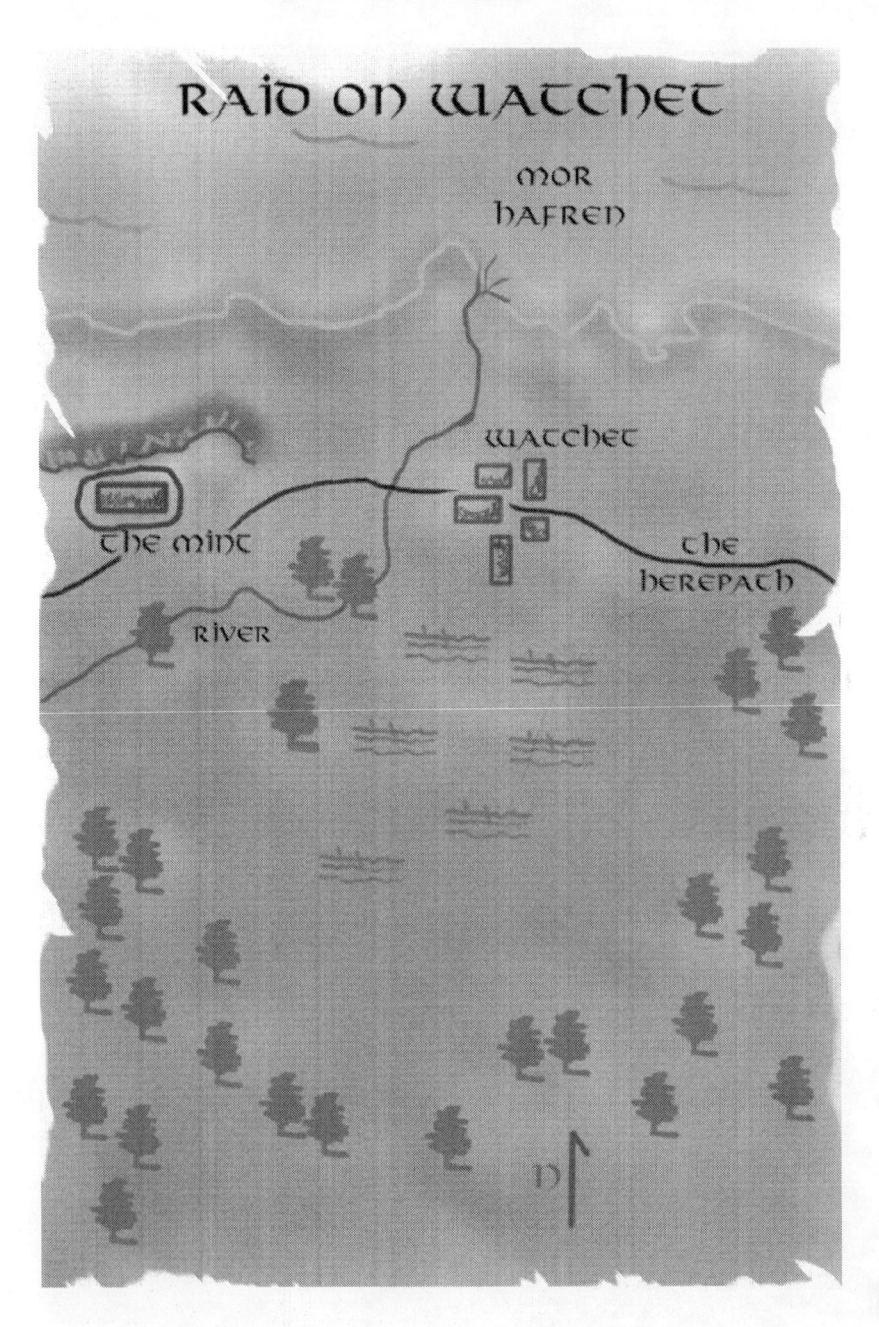

RAID ON DUNADD

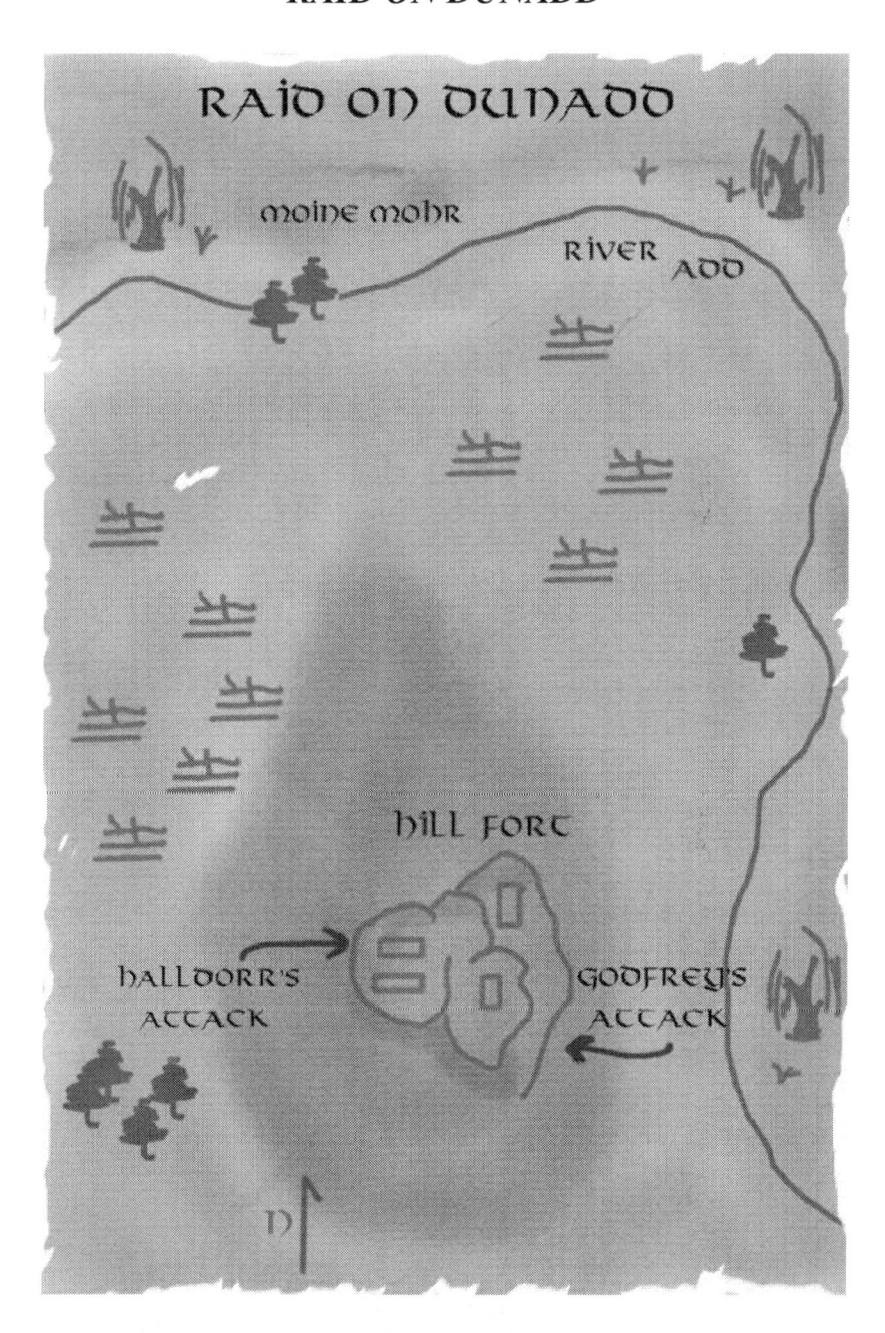

PROLOGUE

Fate goeth ever as she must. ~ Beowulf – J. R. R. Tolkien translation.

986 A.D.

The sometimes-king splashed through a winding ditch. Veritable fear was etched into his face as he crawled up the sloppy mud of the far bank. His shield, his bark, was gone. It lay in a heap of more shields. He felt naked without the armor.

Randulfr offered a hand down and helped hoist the king up. The two compatriots' worried eyes met. The king offered a grateful nod. On through the scattered trees they trod, not certain whether or not they were pursued any longer.

The thicket to their right rattled. The king reached to his belt for his sword. His hand grabbed air. That's right, he remembered. The sword was gone, too. It was not on the pile of shields. The bishop down at Lismore would save that prize. The man would clean the blood of his fellow Dal Riatans from the blade and have it mounted above the hearth as a forever reminder of his victory over yet another would-be sea king.

Randulfr held his sword at the ready. He tried to shove the king behind him with one of his strong arms. The king pushed through it and stood planted next to his lieutenant. Together they would meet the threat.

A small priest punched through the thick mess of thorns. His robes were shredded and covered in blood. He held a sword that was equally drenched in crimson. Only the torrential rain that fell with thunderous rapidity washed the splattered red from the priest's face enough to make out his dark features. He saw Randulfr and the king. "Praise God!" he said, resting his hands on his knees while sucking in swaths of wet air.

"Are there others, Killian?" asked the king.

The priest looked over his shoulder. "A few, I think. We should get you to the ship. The men know where to go, lord."

"I'm not leaving them behind. I mean to be a real king, not some pauper. If I want men to follow, I need to give them a reason. This disaster," said the king, pointing back the way they'd come, "certainly won't help."

"Neither will your death," said Randulfr.

King Godfrey chuckled like men in nervous situations do when they are afraid to admit their gravity. "You've got a point," was all he cared to acknowledge. He scanned what they could see of the countryside through the forest. "That hill." The king was shouting now in order to be heard over the slapping rain. "We'll flee to the hill and wait. That's a natural place to assemble. Once we have the men, then, and only then, will we run down to the ships."

Randulfr and Killian exchanged glances. They decided not to argue. The king was already bounding up the oozing slop on the hillside, reinvigorated that he once again had a plan.

Once at the top of the rise they peered east. The rolling land was open in that direction. In front of them and extending north the green terrain was dotted with white. Sheep ignored the rain and tore at the grass. Lambkins sullied their nascent wool by chasing one another and rolling through the mud. At the south edge of the pastures was the town they'd assaulted with the monastery at its center. The townsfolk with a brigade of buckets brought up from the sea along with the windless rain had already put out the fire that Godfrey had started. The king and his two followers crouched in the rain watching for a sign of survivors from their ill-fated mission.

"We'll have to leave most of the fleet behind, King Godfrey," said Randulfr. He said it quietly and wasn't sure the king even heard him over the din.

He did. Soon, the king was shaking his head, no, but that wouldn't change the facts. "I know. If we could sail most of them back, that would be something good, something we could salvage from this debacle."

"It's not your fault," said the small priest. "For all we know it was that bastard, Horse Ketil. He is curiously absent from this raid. He sits and plots and drinks in your hall whenever plans are made. Runners come and go from his presence. Ketil is . . ."

"Ketil is my cousin's husband. He and his family still hold sway over half of my island. No amount of hoping will change that. I needed a victory here. Now I still need one."

"I shouldn't have let you do this," said Killian, changing tack. "It was a misguided . . ."

The king cut him off a second time. "It is not for you to *let* me do anything."

Killian knew when his king was malleable and when he was not. It was time for the priest to shut his mouth. He had no real fear of Godfrey. The king wasn't overly cruel as some men of power could be. The priest bit his tongue because he actually respected Godfrey's authority – most of the time.

They heard sucking footsteps slowly working their way up the hill. Killian and Randulfr didn't bother to draw their weapons, for the noise was the plodding sound of defeat, not the heroic resonance of pursuit. They watched a handful of their brethren, their fellow warriors, straggle up the hill. Two of the men carried a third between them. The man in the middle had a wide gash across his belly. His thick leather mail was splayed as was his flesh. Each step of the men who held him aloft, each pattering raindrop caused him to wince. Rain-diluted blood ran down his back and legs and onto the other two. Brandr and Loki set the man against a moss-covered elm whose roots stood up sideways. The magnificent tree had been toppled by a storm years earlier. Stagnant, brown water filled the leaf-strewn pit left behind by the uprooted tree. Loki swore and kicked at the puddle, splashing its rank contents onto the other men. They didn't notice the extra wetness.

"How many more?" asked the king. He didn't look back at his men. There was activity in the town that caught his attention.

Brandr said, "The six of us. I saw another batch run off into the woods, but haven't seen them since we left the town. They should find their way here." Brandr was shoving his hands into the wounded man's belly to staunch the blood. Other men came over and offered rolled up pieces of cloth to help. It was no use. The man's breathing stopped. His head slumped. Loki again kicked the puddle.

"There should be more of us," grumbled Godfrey. He moved his eyes from the train of villagers moving out from the town's north edge to where the main battle had taken place. The dead bodies of his men littered the ground. Godfrey made an attempt to count them from the far distance. After getting to thirty, he estimated the rest. "Eighty or one hundred dead, perhaps," he mumbled. "But that means we should have another hundred fifty, at least. Where are they?"

"There," said Killian. The priest pointed to the growing string of people winding out into the pastures.

Sheep skittered out of their way. Townspeople carrying the farm tools that had been their weapons in the fight walked among Dal Riatan warriors who, by happenstance, had been sojourning on the island when Godfrey landed. Normally, Lismore was the weakest of soft targets. It had no soldiers, no forts. That is why King Godfrey was a frequent raider of its people and church. Not this time. Fate! Fortune! Happenstance! Or, as Killian thought, it was Horse Ketil's treachery.

"Thor's beard," whispered Godfrey.

In the center of the throng of people were his missing men, their feet clumsily shuffling through the meadows. They were bound. Their long hair was dripping. Their heads hung low. Coagulated blood was caked around their ears where someone had systematically beaten each of them with a club.

The bishop, Godfrey didn't know the man's name, led the procession. Killian had told him the bishop's name once or twice, but the king didn't care. Lismore was to be a source of wealth for Godfrey's kingdom-building ambitions. The monikers by which the island's leaders were known were of no consequence to him. It was forever a soft place, tucked in a thin, deep fjord. Until today, the king reminded himself. It was a hard place today.

The bishop stopped next to a great field oak. The tree was majestic and lonely as it stood in the center of the pastures. Its great boughs had been trimmed so that farmers and their sheep could walk under its shade in the summer. He pointed at a stout, low branch and barked orders to some soldiers. A thick rope was soon slung over the limb. It was tied off to the yoke of an old horse. The beast was a grey, dappled thing that might have been pretty fifteen years earlier. Today, its back was deeply swayed. Its bony hips protruded. Yet it was more than adequate for the job at hand.

The first prisoner was shoved over to the rope. A noose was cinched around his neck. At the bishop's command, a farmer led the horse forward, slowly lifting the Norseman off his feet. His hands were bound behind his back. The man's feet kicked, trying to find ground that was no longer there. He flexed his chest and neck to keep the rope from choking him. He held his breath. His face turned red. That's when he realized his beating feet weren't helping. The man calmed. That is how he hung for fifteen full heartbeats.

With a whoosh, breath raced from his lungs. His struggling began in earnest. He gurgled. He tried to curse the bishop, but couldn't find the wind. Spittle shot from his mouth. Tears streamed down his cheeks. Both feet were kicking in time so that his body undulated like a mermaid dancing in a longship's wake. His entire body shook, nearly vibrating. The rope shuddered. The tree branch bobbed. Piss mixed with rain-soaked trousers.

The man died.

The bishop nodded. The farmer eased his old grey back. Two soldiers carried the body twenty paces away and flopped it into a mountain of sheep dung. A frightened rat was dislodged and bound through the soaked fields. It ran through the villagers who jumped out of the way until one of them used a wooden shovel to kill the foul beast. Another Dal Riatan warrior prodded the next raider into place.

He was slowly killed by the rope.

They were dying in their own filth. The incessant rain beat them, keeping the stench of their shit at bay. It was a bloodless affair, but Godfrey knew that each of the warriors being hanged would have rather died from a gaping battle wound if it meant they'd enter that final round of sleep with a sword in their hands. Instead, they died a death gruesomely impish even in its relative peace.

The king and his followers on the hill watched three more executions in total silence. Only the constant patter of the rain made a sound.

A few more of the survivors climbed the hill. An older warrior led them.

"Good to see you, Turf Ear," said Godfrey quietly; resigning himself to the fact that he was a king in name only.

Turf Ear put a hand to the side of his head. "Eh? King I can't hear ya with the racket made by the rain."

Godfrey walked over and set a hand on the man's shoulder, but didn't bother offering his greeting a second time. Turf Ear plopped down in the mud, not asking again for the king to repeat himself. His name advertised his affliction. Turf Ear was used to missing most conversations. But the king didn't want Turf Ear along for his ability to sycophantically repeat all that Godfrey said. No, Turf Ear was there because he could fight six other men when the terror of the shield wall materialized.

"We should go," said Killian, who stood behind King Godfrey.

Godfrey didn't immediately answer. "We could assault them," he said glaring down into the pastures. "We send a few more of the Dal Riatans to death. Send them to Hel's icy depths. Send more of us into Odin's hall. It would improve the day."

Randulfr and Killian looked at one another. "We could," said the priest.

"Or, King Godfrey, we could save the men we've got. We're no cowards. We don't flee out of fear of death. But why not fight when we know we can win?"

Godfrey looked back at his lieutenant. Randulfr had been with him for years. And the king knew the man was no coward. Randulfr was closest to the king because he was trustworthy and had his heart chained to the king's determination. They were one in purpose. He'd always done whatever was asked of him by Godfrey or Godfrey's queen. If the king gave the order to attack the Dal Riatans in the field around that oak tree, Randulfr would lead the charge.

One-by-one, the king studied the exhausted faces of his men.

"Yes. We go," said Godfrey at last. "But we don't leave until we've seen all of our men sent on to the next world. We owe them that."

Killian moved to stand by the king. "That's a fine idea. You know Providence, the One True God, has a plan for all of us. This may just be a challenge that you face not unlike Job's. He moved on to more prosperity after his tragedies, you know."

Godfrey crossed his arms at his chest, his eyes not deviating from one of his Danes who was dying on the tree. The king forced a grin. It was his way of compelling his mood to change, to affect the future. "Oh, I have no doubt that I will again rise. Our Christian God will send us deliverance in his time. But our old gods will send us the warriors we need in our time."

And they did.

PART I – *Anglesey!*

987 A.D. – Early Summer

CHAPTER 1

The battle had raged since the dawn.

It had been characterized by waves of activity. Like the ebb tide, periods of low consumption, cursing, contact, and collapse were quickly followed by violent episodes of the flow tide where men rammed trés, elbows, and fists into the faces of their opponents. Men and blood ran. Ale flowed. The old men watched, reminded of the splendor of their youth. The children pointed, laughing, the boys hoping to one day become captains on the field, the girls hoping to marry one of those future leaders. The young maids congregated together like hens, clucking, giggling, and feigning indifference, all the while keeping a sharp eye on us as we strutted and fought. The battle, though the participants were exhausted and long since drunk, would rage to the gloaming and through the morrow if we couldn't end it soon.

Our band of Norsemen, who hailed of late from Greenland and were considered foreigners on this Isle of Man, had formed one side for the ongoing knattleikr contest. The island's king considered the game something of an initiation for us. We were Leif, Magnus, Tyrkr, me, and twenty or so others.

Our opponents were made up of the experienced men of Godfrey's small army. How a man remained a king with only a few dozen armed men at his disposal was beyond my understanding at the time. I knew this, however, about his followers: they were full bodied, muscled. I was the largest among the members of my team. I was a head taller than any man I had ever met. Yet my girth could not compare to those hardened raiders of Man. Their legs seemed like the trunks of trees that sprouted stoutly from the ground. Their arms were the size of a man's waist. At least it seemed so that day.

They had spent the morning pummeling us on the field of sport. The grounds were paced out south of town on a high, flat shelf that dropped off in a series of rocky crags down to the Irish

Sea. A spear with a waving rag tied onto its shaft was rammed into the ground to mark off each of the four corners of the field. We had no boundary lines because we knew we could count on the exceedingly drunken spectators to argue among themselves and keep us somewhat honest when a man or the wooden ball tumbled out of bounds.

As it was, ten of our Greenlanders were already strewn about the edge of the playing field, their exhausted bodies further delineating the sidelines. They laid there with contusions or broken limbs. It was not by choice that they now sat out, nursing their battle wounds with more and more ale. Our opponents were hard men and they picked out one of us at a time to purge, to painfully relieve us of our chance at play.

Yet we continued on, for if we had any hope of becoming integrated into their society, we'd have to demonstrate as much tenacity as them. We'd arrived only weeks before after Leif and I had been exiled from Greenland for the massacre of our countrymen. We didn't kill them, of course. Our women, children, and fellow men fell during a battle with the shrieking skraelings. Leif and I were blamed for starting the fight in the first place. As a result, and to appease village elders, Erik had banished us for thirteen years – one year for each one of our townspeople who'd been killed. Erik was the jarl of Greenland. He was also Leif's father and my adopted father.

Godfrey's warriors had tried to eliminate Leif first. He was still the smallest among us and they assumed he would be the easiest prey. It was yet a few years before Leif would find the broad-shouldered body he'd have throughout his adult life. His red whiskers were only slowly beginning to fill his face. Godfrey's man, Brandr, clasped a large hand on Leif's jerkin and yanked him off his feet. Brandr used his other arm to swing down the trés, which was a long thin club made from oak. The trés was supposed to be used to bat the oaken ball down the field from man to man, however, in practice and all-too-common it was employed as a weapon. We used it thus. So did Godfrey's men. They were better at it.

But at that moment Leif proved to be too quick. He gave a single tug on the leather straps that were tied at the top of his jerkin. They loosened and he released his bat, lifting his arms up, so he could slide his entire body down and out of his shirt. It happened so quickly Brandr couldn't adjust for the reduction in weight at the end of his arm. The same arm that now held a dangling leather jerkin, shot up into the air. Brandr's own trés, instead of knocking out Leif, crashed down onto his arm with such force that Brandr was the first casualty of the game for Godfrey's men.

The Manx warriors had lost no others since. They gave up on the crafty Leif and took us down one by one until it was our dozen against their twenty-something. Their success was just beginning to take its toll, however – on them. You see, every time the men from the Isle carried the oak ball across the end line after a maximum of five bats, it was considered a score. A young maid would step forward to keep track of their points so that our opponents had fourteen maidens lined up on their side. We had only four young lasses. I say their ample scoring was beginning to catch up with them because with each maid stepping forward, the scoring team had to drink a pot of ale – each man had to drink a pot. We took no time for rest or food all day; so that even the most experienced drinkers among them were beginning to falter on wobbly legs.

Randulfr clutched the oaken ball. He was their best batter and after he took his allotted four steps, I knew he would whack the wooden sphere down to where his men were already running. Though it was a little terrifying, I ran straight toward him to what we called the silly spot. More than one of our team had found his way to the sideline after Randulfr batted the heavy wood ball directly into their noses. Godfrey's lieutenant took just one step. He saw that my intent was to ram my trés into his chest and steal the ball before he could hit it. Randulfr immediately stopped, leaving three of his steps unused. He lightly tossed the ball into the air. It was a short toss because he saw me coming quickly. I was tired of losing all day and had vowed to, at last, make a game of it. I lowered my head and stuck out the club.

He hadn't thrown the ball high enough. We both knew it instantly. It sank down to the green sod before he could bring the bat around. Randulfr then made the same decision I would have. He carried his swing right on through, knowing that on I came. His trés connected with the fingers of my left hand so that I released the bat. Though I knew that at least two of my digits were broken, I decided that the injuries were minor enough. My blood was up. I ignored the ball that hit the ground with a great thud and went headlong into the mighty batter of Man.

Randulfr seemed surprised that I hadn't clamored after the ball as I had all day long. It was time to take the game they played back to them. I drove my forearm into his neck. Because he was off balance from his swing, he fell back and I landed on top of his chest. I heard gasps and cheers and shouts from the crowd. An old man teetered on the side of the field and began shouting a host of obscenities. In a rasping voice he called, "Damn Odin, you puke child. Why don't you shove that trés back up your ass where it came from? You wouldn't know knattleikr if it bit you on your manhood!" I still don't know for which side he cheered.

I rammed a knee onto Randulfr's arm, pinning it and the bat it held to the ground. With a great balled fist, I rapped his cheek with my right hand. Then, because I was enjoying a few moments of success, I forgot about the throbbing pain in my fingers and balled the left hand. I don't need to tell you that as soon as that hand rained down onto his other cheek, I instantly recalled the pain. I howled and rolled off on top of the ball. Randulfr spun toward me and used the bat like a whip. First, it hit my ribs, then my arm.

All of a sudden Randulfr's head was jerked back. His body was forced to follow. I looked up to see that Tyrkr, our German thrall, had seized Randulfr's long hair. Tyrkr had the fingers of both hands wrapped amid the strands and used all his strength to heave the man up and off me. It was Randulfr's turn to scream. He winced. I think I saw a tear jump from one eye. Yet he held onto the bat and began using it to blindly swat the chest of the dedicated German slave.

A true melee began. Loki tackled Tyrkr. Our man, Magnus, in turn, piled on Loki, using his thumbs to press into Loki's eye sockets. Man after man, more of theirs than ours since the teams had become so lopsided, leapt onto the pile. Even Godfrey, the unrefined King of the Isles joined in. I kicked a man in his sack. I had hoped it was one of our opponents, but later that night I saw Tyrkr cradling his crotch like a new mother holds her firstborn. Someone stepped on my already broken fingers. The crowd cheered. Even the old women, some were as old as forty-five, I think, shouted with glee at the action.

Randulfr had somehow wriggled free of Tyrkr's grasp. He crawled through the scrummage and found me, mostly where I had been left. Randulfr gave me a wicked smile. It looked so thoroughly frightening that I thought he meant to kill me. He reached down. I threw up my hands to guard against the knife I was sure he had hidden beneath his shirt.

He didn't have one. He stuck his hands under my back and flopped me over. "Where's the ball, lummox?" Randulfr shouted. He was a smart player, using the ongoing brawl to move the ball down the field. I laughed in relief.

"What's so funny?" Randulfr barked as he scraped his hands through the grass.

"I felt the ball under my back a moment ago," I said as I crawled to my feet at the edge of the fight. "You can't find it?"

"It's not here!" Randulfr was swinging the trés in my direction to keep me at bay. I heard it zip as it passed my face.

"Well, where is it?" We both began scanning the ground amidst the pounding feet and falling bodies.

A shrill whistle tore through our deep throated shouts. Our struggle paused. I heard a smack as a combatant got in one last punch. We all turned to face the headland of the field where young Leif held the wooden ball in one hand. He took one step over the end line to score a point for us, the first since midday.

"Too many steps!" cried Loki, pointing his finger at Leif. All of our opponents and their supporters claimed likewise. Pots of ale were hurled onto the field, empty pots.

Leif smiled and gave a playful shrug. "Are your rules different than ours?" Leif pointed to the pretty maidens lined up on the sidelines. "Had these beauties seen an infraction, I would have been called long before I reached the headland. Yet, here I am, scoring a point and a drink for my men." Everyone knew that the crowd had been focused on the skirmish near centerfield. No one had paid attention to the smallish man who had stolen the ball from under me and trotted down to score. The men of Man began furrowing their brows and tightening their grips on their trés in order to renew their attack.

Leif had merely produced a brief pause in the battle with his score. It was Godfrey's turn to put an outright halt to the fight. The king gave a belly laugh. I looked over to him. His lithe frame wiggled. Blood trickled down from his nose and from a short, but deep, laceration near his temple. He didn't bother wiping it away. King Godfrey Haraldsson waved his bat down the field toward Leif and then toward me. "I'd say these men know how to make a play when the odds are against them!" He planted one end of the bat into the ground like a cane and casually leaned on it. Godfrey waved his other hand. "You won't win the day, Greenlanders, but you've won my respect."

He balled his fist. "Now get your ale! We won't fall for that one again."

• • •

We lost the knattleikr contest, badly. It would have been worse had the ale not slowed down Godfrey and his men while simultaneously soothing our wounds, dulling the pain they'd dished. As it was, when the sun had long since fallen and the burning torches lingered, throwing their undulating light across the grass, the number of maids standing in Godfrey's line was four or five times the number in ours. Our men were exhausted and whipped. We had lost the game badly, but we had entered the brotherhood of Godfrey's men boldly.

I was the last man standing for our team. In truth, even I wasn't standing. I ended the game flat on my back, my chest heaving for air, one of my eyes swollen shut, my broken fingers three times their normal size. I stared up at the blackness of the sky and saw the bright belt of stars that ran from one end to the other. Below the rocky crags at the meadow's edge the surf from the Irish Sea pounded in its incessant manner. It had done so since before Ask, the first man, and Embla, the first woman, had been sprung from the trees. I was not yet a follower of the One

God in those days. So back then, I knew the waves were created by Jormungandr, the serpent that coiled itself around the entire world. His breathing stirred the waters where they started as mere ripples until the wind and rains forced the waves to blossom into the behemoths that crashed into the dominions of mankind. The sea and her sounds had long been a comfort to me and hearing the proof of the gods that night brought a reprieve from my physical agony and fatigue.

Words from a man broke my mind's peace. I would have beaten whoever it was had I been able to move. I turned my good eye toward the sound and saw that Godfrey was extending a hand. His bloodied face showed great pleasure. Of course it did! His men had just spent the past day and night in near perfect revelry, drinking and carousing, drinking and thrashing Norse Greenlanders all the way through.

"Thor's beard!" Godfrey said. "I hope you're still alive. What a waste to have lost a specimen like you before I even took you into battle."

"Aren't you a Christian?" I mumbled. "Shouldn't you curse your own god?"

Godfrey laughed while crouching down. In the dim light I could see that one side of his face was swollen and blue. The King of the Isles didn't seem to notice any pain. He clasped a hand around my upper arm and began hoisting me up. His thumb accidentally found a bruise of which I was not aware. I grunted, but let him sit me upright. "Christian, yes. I straddle the two worlds I must. Many of my subjects are Christian." He spat out a wad of blood-laced phlegm onto the sod and wiggled a loose tooth with his tongue. "Ireland is Christian. England is Christian. Much of the wealth sloshing around Man's and Normandy's ports is from Christian lands. If I want my isles to trade, to do business with Christians, I must show the steps to being a good Christian. Many of their kings and even traders enforce such a prime-signing." He winked. "I have become one. I have my own priest. My father dabbled in their faith. There's something to it, you know."

My head was slowly clearing from its battering. I was starved, for I hadn't eaten since the night before. My belly was sour. I moaned. I was not prepared for a discussion of my old gods, let alone this new, One God. I nodded to Godfrey and placed a hand on his shoulder while he steadied me. With another tug, I stood on my feet.

The field was clearing. Leif's men were limping off after Godfrey's. I saw that Greenlanders and Manx alike were chatting with one another. Laughing split the late night air. They relived their favorite parts of the game. We had entered their society.

The maidens had left. Other than the dying torches, Godfrey and I were all that remained. "*Their* faith? Isn't it yours?" I asked as I walked with heavy legs next to the king. The village, tucked behind its palisade, was spread out before us.

"Yes, but no." Godfrey's eyes sparkled even in the darkness. His mind always hid more thoughts than his words said. "My father was the first in our line to become Christian. He thought it would relieve the trouble he was having with the sons of Rollo and Longsword in Normandy. My father wanted allies and thought it would help. It didn't help with that, for he still had to flee Bayeux." Godfrey gave a large sigh. "It did help him win my mother, though. She was Irish, which means that, of course, she was Christian." The king chuckled. "My priest would tell me that my father's marriage proves the goodness of God's Providence. It shows that gain can come out of any situation." Godfrey shrugged while we ambled. "When my father died I thought more about his old gods, Thor, Odin. I thought I'd give them a try. Just because I'm a Norseman who's never been to Norway, doesn't mean I don't think of home."

"How does that work, following both sides?"

"I'm a king, am I not?" he slapped my back on the spot where Loki had driven the end of his trés early in the game. "The truth is that the men who follow the old gods are the best fighters. They see the grandeur in the task itself. There is no fear of death, for it brings with it endless revelry and war. They want the silver and treasure, they want the women, too, but they understand that how they carry themselves in battle is the true prize." Godfrey abruptly stopped and tugged on my sleeve. He examined my face. "Now, you mustn't repeat that to anyone.

I'll deny I ever said this. I've got Christians among my men who fight like their devil and I want to keep them. But the Norse, the Swedes, the Danes, those men, especially those who follow Thor, fight." He looked ahead to the palisade that surrounded the village. The open gate was guarded by two sentries. Watchmen stood high on a raised platform behind the wall, pacing and looking to the sea and inland, but especially the sea, for that is where the danger forever lurked. "They fight." He said the last as if he would choke up, but fought through his emotions and forced a smile.

I sighed and wondered what I would do in a real, full-scale battle. I had killed men who were lesser fighters than me. That had always been in self-defense, in the normal scraps of life. But how would I stand when the steel was truly thick? I hoped I could make King Godfrey think of me the same way he had just thought of his men, with welling pride. I sighed again and realized how tired I was. I looked down to the quay. "I'm going to the boat to sleep," I huffed.

Godfrey slapped his hand on my back again. I winced. "No, you're not." The king suddenly had a resurgence of energy. He marched off toward the gates. "I've called a Thing. After we've decided whose chickens are whose and after we've said which oxen belong to this man or that, we've got an army to rebuild. The Dal Riatans will pay." Godfrey disappeared into the shadows beneath the gate.

I limped after the king. "Who are the Dal Riatans?" I mumbled.

• • •

Though the Dal Riatans were foreign to me, I knew what a Thing was. It was common among my ancestors and was as much a part of life as the hunt. Two or three times a year free men and women gathered in a sacred place where a leader or the lawgiver guided us through the proceedings. Disputes were solved. My long dead father had taken me to them in Norway. I had attended them along with Erik, my adopted father, in Iceland. As a full free man in Greenland, I'd gone to the Thing that was, by then, led by Erik himself. In fact, it was at such a meeting at Fridr Rock, Peace Rock, in Greenland that the skraelings attacked and killed the thirteen members of Eystribyggo, hence the thirteen years of banishment for Leif and me. Their assault had been blamed on us for reasons that stray from this tale.

I say that Things were held in sacred places: groves, glens, valleys, dales, mountains, stream sides, meadows, or forests. It made sense that we did this because the spirits dwelt on such hallowed, natural ground. How else could a man hope to resolve problems peaceably without the favor and active intervention of the gods? Otherwise, man's nature, certainly mine, was to thump a man, to rap him with my fist, a club, or to pierce him with a spear until he and his family relented. When the last happened, a man could get what he wanted. But inevitably such success unleashed the flood of the blood feud, a blood for blood, life for life, death for death exchange that spiraled on until one family overwhelmed the other or a larger, stronger family came into the picture to overwhelm the first two. So I ask again, with such proclivities, how could we hope to end problems without first being in a sacred meadow?

In Iceland the Althing was held next to the River Axe, a strange name until you understand that men hurled their axes into the flowing waters at the start of the assembly. Weapons were not permitted and the act of throwing them into the river was a solemn promise that blood would not be shed during the discussions. Heated debate often led to arguments. Arguments mixed with ale and steel brought on blood. Since there was no way to eliminate drink, long ago a wise man decided to forgo weapons.

The scoundrel-turned-jarl Erik mimicked this when he began holding a Thing in Greenland. Each year, he'd march from Fridr Rock to the pebble-strewn shingle and hurl a great war axe into the fjord that bore his name. It was a peaceful, happy gathering, that is, until the last one with the skraeling attack. But, I've said to you, that is for another time and another writing.

The men of Man were strange to me. To start, they called the assembly the Tynwald. In practice it was a Thing which was why the king had said as much. Why his followers called it Tynwald, I know not. Beyond the odd name for the meeting, the men of Godfrey and the people he ruled appeared foreign in dress and custom. They looked like me in most regards. Many had blonde hair or red hair. Many were fair of skin. I wore baggy, woolen trousers. Their men wore better fitting, lighter linen pants. But as we walked to the Thing, Tynwald, I reminded myself, I could think of nothing else but how peculiar it was to head into town, rather than out. I did not understand how a Thing could be held away from the trees and grasses of the gods but instead in a tightly-packed longhouse.

  A great fire burned outside Godfrey's hall. Its light illuminated a kind of town square in the middle of the walled city. The face of the remarkable hall formed one edge of the square. The king had paused and I was slowly catching up to his shadowed back. Separately, we looked at his hall's short side, with the peak of its long, thatched roof running away from us, away from the village square. The gable end, or rake, was adorned with long planks that formed an 'X' at the peak and extended up into the dark sky like the antlers of a great beast. Along the surface of the planks, carvings of swirling, vine-like designs adorned. I had seen the motif before on the Isle of Man and had become used to it, though Godfrey's hall was the only one in the town that resembled any of the styles of building with which I was familiar. His was constructed of timber. The rest were made of stone, something foreign to my original homeland of Norway.

  What struck me that night was not Godfrey's hall. What was truly weird was the combination of disparate images that made up the right and left sides of the square. On my right was a Christian church. In the middle of a community made of former Norsemen, Danes, and Swedes was a building honoring the One God. The One God! Many of my new brothers-in-arms were Christians but it was clear from the church's prominence that Godfrey paid not a waving tribute to the new faith, but actively supported it.

  "A church?" I asked dumbly while I limped around the fire.

Godfrey was having fun at my naivety. Glancing over his shoulder, he laughed at me as he had a half dozen times since I met him. "How can I, a Christian or a raider king as the case may be, attack and steal from churches in Wales, Scotland, England, and Ireland while I pay for one right here?"

"Uh, huh," I grunted while scanning the boring stone building. There were no animals carved anywhere.

Godfrey stopped and pointed to a dark, shadowed area in the corner of the square between his hall and the church. "Do you see those markers there? They are graves. The men of Man haven't burned their dead for many centuries. Do you see the markers? No, look. They are Christian crosses. Some of those men died four or five hundred years ago and do you see? They were Christians. I support this church because as I told you I'm a Christian, mostly, well sometimes. But my people, the natives of this island, too, are Christian." He began strolling to the doors that sat closed at the end of his hall. "And my men, my army, what's left of it, Christian or not, do not mind one bit if we take treasure from someone else's church to enrich our own. It's a world where the strongest will kill or enslave the weakest."

The truth of his last sentiment, I knew to my core. Life was a constant struggle until a man died and entered Odin's hall, where the warrior-poet god would entertain him.

Godfrey puffed out his strong chest and plunged into his hall where the sound of a hundred men's voices echoed off the walls. I stayed behind and studied the church and her cemetery. It was a strange faith, I thought. Admittedly, I knew nothing of it at the time. It was foreign and I never considered for a heartbeat that I would one day be a Christian, helping another zealous king convert his subjects to the One God. Yet those days would come, later. That night, I teetered my way around and looked at the side of the square opposite the church. Across from the church were images I could understand.

Someone had erected a tall, flat stone in front of a small grove of misplaced trees. I say misplaced because, though they grew from the ground like all life, to have them inside the walls of a palisade was odd. The rock was turned so that I could see an edge and part of one face where the square's firelight danced across it. The edge had the familiar thin etchings that were Norse runes. I knew each of the letters, but I could not read then, not even my own language. So I didn't know what great man's name was carved from one side, up and over the rectangular top, and down the other. I only knew that those letters formed words. The image I could see in the light was immediately recognizable.

It was Odin, his one, good eye staring out at me. His presence would mean that the small grove of trees behind the stone was a sacred place, artificial, perhaps, since it was in town, but one where the power of the old gods could be found. There was comfort in that. On Odin's shoulder sat one of his messenger birds. I thought it might be Hugin, the raven of thought, though why it could not be Munin, the raven of memory, I do not know. From where I stood, it looked like the pair, Odin and Hugin, was under a square roof of some sort. I hobbled closer and saw that in one hand the chief god had a spear and was thrusting it down into a wolf. Aha! It was Fenrir, the wolf of the Ragnarok, the finale of the world. At the end of the gods' time, the world would finish in a fiery furnace of destruction, with the sun and gods themselves disappearing. As I meandered closer, a sense of pride welled up inside my chest. Though I knew that the mighty Odin and Thor and all the gods I loved would meet their deaths at the Ragnarok, seeing Odin fight off the beast Fenrir, who had already swallowed a part of his leg, was an inspiration. To lose a battle while struggling valiantly was no disgrace.

I stepped in front of the stone's face so that I could see the rest of the inspiring carvings. The square roof under which Odin stood was not a roof at all. It was not a building or longhouse or other dwelling. It was the horizontal piece of the Christian cross. Odin was at war with the events of the Ragnarok under the unmistakable watch of the Christian symbol. The stone seemed to say that the One God was in charge of it all. Impossible, I thought with a smug shrug. On the other side of the cross, under that horizontal section was the carving of a different event. At the time, this scene was unfamiliar to me. A man carried a book in one hand. In his other he carried his own short cross. From this smaller cross dangled a long fish. And beneath all that, under the man's stomping feet, was a dying serpent.

I couldn't look at the images any longer. They unsettled my stomach. It could have been the sour ale that did its work on my belly, but it felt like the events on the stone shook my foundations. The carvings clearly showed that whoever commissioned it believed that the fall of the old gods would usher in the rise of the One God. I shuddered.

I turned, frowning. With a grunt to get myself moving, I awkwardly sauntered toward the hall where the rumbling of multiple conversations and songs inside rose and fell. I pushed the church and the stone to the back of my mind. Soon Godfrey would begin his Tynwald.

• • •

Everything was foreign. My life was in the lurch. I pushed my way into the hall and wedged between the broad shoulders of warriors, fishermen, and farmers. Free men and free women sang and drank. A couple grunted atop a mead table. A thin blanket half-covered them as the young man mounted the drunken woman. She continued drinking, ale spilling while he rutted like a mountain goat. I saw Leif's men, those who had volunteered to come with us on our exile, and felt comfort. I walked to them and found a seat. Their bruised faces gave me weak smiles and nods.

"Let's see if this king can rebuild a Norse army," said Leif. He was eager, seemingly unfazed by the countless changes that had occurred in his life since we left our homes. I was envious of the way he glided from one situation to the next without a care.

"A Christian Norseman army," I corrected, unable to stop thinking about the Christian dominance over the old gods from the stone.

Leif smiled. Like Godfrey had, he played with a tooth, loosened from the day's battle, with the tip of his tongue. Fresh blood seeped into his saliva when he dislodged a miniature clot. "Either way, Norse and Thor or Norse and the One God, I've told you I mean to lead men. I mean to be a wise, moderate, and fair leader of my people. By the time we return to Greenland, it will be my turn to be jarl in place of my father."

"Do you think Godfrey is the one to teach you all that?" A small, waifish girl came by with mugs of ale on a platter. We each took one. The barefoot little thrall gave me a snarl and walked to replenish her load.

In answer to my question, Leif flashed one of his knowing smiles. He'd done this ever since we became true friends. It was like he knew something I didn't. Perhaps, since his birth, Leif had been able to feel confident about the future no matter the situation. But I always attributed his self assurance to the night he spent sitting atop a barrow mound – awake on a barrow mound! I say the last with emphasis because as most men know, though you may not, the spirits of the gods grant a man the powers of divination once he has spent an entire night unspoiled by sleep while perched on a man's grave. Leif was always sure – even when the circumstances seemed to demonstrate otherwise – even when I was not. He was even more certain since that night on the grave.

Leif glanced over to where Godfrey was kissing his wife, Gudruna. The woman was pressing her lips hard against her husband's, knowing that he had bruises and wounds from the game all over his face. Both of her hands clutched the back of his head, pulling it tightly to hers. Gudruna giggled while she toyed with her man. To pay her back the small pain she caused, Godfrey fished his hand under her brightly colored tunic and into her brown dress. He pinched one of her nipples. Gudruna yelped and slapped him on the cheek.

Godfrey and his woman stepped back from one another laughing. They snatched up their half-empty mugs of ale and finished them in one, long draught. Leif looked back to me and pointed to the King of the Isles with a tip of his head. "Probably not the one to instruct me in the ways of wise leadership, but it will be fun."

Fun, I wondered? Or, would following the fool king lead us to an early death?

• • •

Godfrey was still laughing with his woman when Killian, the village priest, stepped to the fore and raised his hands to calm the crowd. "A Christian priest acting as the lawgiver, leading the Thing?" I asked, aghast.

"They call it the Tynwald, Halldorr," said Leif as if that were enough to answer my question.

"Free men and free women of Ballaquayle, Kirk Braddan, Knock y Donee, Ramsey, Andreas, Balladoole, and Ballateare welcome to the Tynwald," began Killian.

"And Doarlish Cashen!" shouted a large women with an angry face and stern brow ridge that would make any warrior afraid enough to stop dead in his tracks.

Killian was not cowed by the woman's bluster. "I was coming to that Lady Edana!" She was far from a Lady in the traditional sense. Killian chose his words wisely, like a warrior chooses his weapon based upon the nature of his opponent and the coming battle.

The village priest was diminutive. He had dark eyes and black hair to match. I did not know the man, but had heard that Killian had a reputation for fighting, in both the traditional meaning and with words. Apparently, he did not back down from any argument. The story went that Godfrey decided to keep Killian alive when the former first invaded the island just because he admired the priest's tenacity. Since then the two had developed a deep friendship based upon a mutual respect for strength. Godfrey appreciated Killian's mind. Killian enjoyed the protection and brawn offered to the island by Godfrey's might. "Had you given me but a moment, I was prepared to introduce your cause to the Tynwald first. I'm now of the mind to push off your business to the last, but since this is a congregation of free men and women I'll leave it to them." Killian scanned the crowd, which had fallen silent at the prospect of a raucous argument between the two.

"I'll not be last!" Edana huffed. "I've waited since the last meeting of the Tynwald to plead for my divorce from that!" She pointed with a thick thumb to the lump who must have been her husband. He had long since passed out in a corner near the thrones. He still hugged a cup of ale. He'd wetted his trousers.

Loki found a spot next to our group. He appeared as battered as were we, but chatted like we were long friends. He leaned in and whispered. "The king and Killian can't permit a divorce," he explained. "Her husband is something of an important person. He was a minor chieftain on the island at Godfrey's arrival. So I guess he's a noble. He may even have relations in a powerful Irish or Scottish clan. Edana is our king's cousin. Godfrey offered her hand in marriage to keep his back secure. Godfrey doesn't want to disappoint men like Ketil who can build an army while we are without one. So Killian and the king delay to keep the truce in place."

"Why not just say, no?" I asked.

Loki grinned. "This way is more fun."

"There's a reason you wait," said Godfrey over the waiting crowd. The king had a saex drawn and now spun it on its tip atop a thick table. Godfrey looked at the knife, not the woman. "The priest runs this assembly with the approval of our people. You'll abide by the decisions just like the rest." Edana's husband rolled over, groaning. I swore that I saw his eyes open and aware as he went.

"Who exactly is he?" I asked.

"Horse Ketil," Loki said. "He's mostly worthless. The king lets him nip his ale all day and all night. Once in a while Ketil awakens enough to go a-Viking with us. The drunken ass forever wants treasure to fall into his lap. Godfrey always feels obligated to let him come, since it was Ketil who helped negotiate the peace between his family and Godfrey. The politics of the Irish Sea, don't you know." Loki rolled his eyes. I didn't know politics, but I knew that a man that felt he deserved something for nothing could be dangerous, especially if he sobered up.

Edana scowled at her cousin, the king. Killian didn't wait for Edana to protest further. "All those who hope to delay hearing of the Lady Edana's divorce petition until the Tynwald next meets, answer with aye."

"What happened to going last tonight?" barked the thick-armed woman. From one side of her head her drab brown hair stuck out like the quills of a hedgehog. The other side appeared as if she had just rolled out of bed since it was matted and stuck to her temple. Just looking at her made me pull out my walrus tusk comb and run it through the hair of my beard. Though we often had to wade through filth, most respectable Norsemen and our women prided themselves on cleanliness. Not so with this creature.

"Aye," answered nearly every voice in the room. Many of them were in some way kin to Ketil. Hushed chuckles followed.

"And so by unanimous consent, the petition will be heard when we next meet," said Killian with a firm, dark stare. I noticed that the priest didn't bother asking for any dissenting opinion.

Edana had experienced this same setback before. She pushed her way through the crowd and, with a massive paw, punched open the doors at the end of the hall. Several retainers, unarmed like the rest of us, followed her out. Horse Ketil stayed.

The gathering remained oddly quiet until the door slapped shut. Then a round of laughter and chattering erupted. I later learned that neither Edana nor Horse Ketil was considered insufferable by the citizens of Man. The free men and women at the Tynwald did not give any thought to the personalities of husband or wife. Those gathered, like men and women far and wide, did not care a whiff about the politics at stake. Godfrey merely tolerated the pair, waiting until a better option came his way. The king exploited the indifference everyone harbored for the couple and pushed off his cousin's divorce petition again and again. It kept the peace on the island and made for a terrific sideshow. The latter is why people came to the Tynwald in the first place.

Leif leaned in. "You see, Halldorr? This is just like home. A Tynwald is run no different from a Thing." He was right. Arguments, disagreements, ale, happy petitioners, angry participants, sex on tables, it was all part of every Thing I'd ever attended.

"What were all those arguments about?" asked Tyrkr. He was Leif's thrall. Actually, he was Erik's thrall, but he'd volunteered to come into exile with us in order to protect Erik's son. Tyrkr's native tongue was German. He had learned Norse later in life after a group of Danes had captured and sold him into the frigid north. We considered his accent humorous, his inconsistent comprehension more so.

Though he was a slave, I liked Tyrkr very much. Our crew treated him as nearly an equal. But he still understood his place when it came time to sharpen blades, prepare the morning meal, or to slosh out a dung bucket. I decided to lie to him, for fun. I spoke slowly so that he could get a better grasp. "That woman who just stormed off wants to marry the man in the corner over there," I said pointing to the drunken husband. "But it seems they have a tradition that one of the man's kinsmen must sleep with her first. She's upset that no one volunteered."

"Oh," said Tyrkr with an understanding nod as if what I just told him made any real sense. "I suppose I could do it." The thrall held out his hands wide and swayed his hips as if he was humping the large woman right there. Leif gave a chortle. Tyrkr shrugged with a devious grin. I smiled and shook my head, slightly disappointed that my ruse didn't go further.

"Settle yourselves," scolded Killian after he had let his meeting ramble. "We've much work to do. All our exertions tonight result from the transactions of man, but we must perform them as if we do so for Christ. Let us labor well." I was really not sure of this Christ person. He was somehow related to the One God, though he must have been in many ways even more important since the Christians were named for him and did many of their daily tasks in his name.

A string of people and animals were trotted before Killian and the king. There was an argument about a bride-price for an upcoming wedding. The father of the bride said that twelve ounces of silver had been agreed upon. That was the standard price at the time and most of the rumbling from the crowd began to side with the father. After taking one look at the bride and her family, though, Killian easily surmised that no bachelor in his right mind would have offered more than eight ounces silver. The priest didn't bring the matter to a vote or consult the king. He used his own authority to levy a decision. Godfrey waved his approval, though Killian didn't seek it.

There was the case of an old farmer, nearly blind, who complained that a neighbor had slowly been moving his land markers further onto his land so that his crop of barley shrank every year while the neighbor's grew. The aged, crusty man had waited five seasons, he said, in an effort to be neighborly before he reported the crime. With narrowed eyes, Killian accused, "It is widely known that you can barely see a hand stuck in front of your face, you have no sons left, no wife to support your allegation. How is it that you expect to make such a claim and have it believed?"

The old man pinched one side of his lips together, squinted one eye, and scratched his tanned neck. "Father," he began. "When the night has long since fallen and your fire is nothing but cold, dark embers, and your lamps and candles are out, when your bladder reminds you of your humanity, how do you find your way to the door?" asked the weathered farmer.

Killian was quick-witted, faster than me. He studied the old plaintiff and the young defendant. "I find in your favor, old man. You've walked those fields for two lifetimes. You know the number of steps and paces from one end to the other, sight or not. Anyone who has followed a horse for just one day knows the distance from one headland to the other. Tomorrow three of Godfrey's men will return with you to your farm and replace the markers where they go." The crowd murmured their admiration at the quick decision making.

Godfrey silently nodded his consent while gripping the rump of an English thrall who stood next to him. He'd bought her in Dyflin. She was pleasing to the eye. The woman stroked the king's back.

"It's a good partnership they have," Magnus, who was our longtime helmsman, whispered. He referred to Godfrey and Killian not the king and his thrall.

"Like Halldorr and me," said Leif with a broad smile.

I began nodding and then wondered if Leif was saying that he was the brains, like Killian, and I was the brawn, like Godfrey. When I frowned, Leif began laughing. I rapped him on a black and blue knot that he had received from the knattleikr game. It was his turn to frown and my turn to laugh, though I suppose I had my answer as to who played which part.

Cases, claims, and petitions came through like a string. It was fun to watch all the problems and disputes of others. It helped me forget my aching bones and all the turmoil I had felt just a few weeks earlier when we first arrived. Killian took each problem seriously, though not in a morose manner. He gave the ancient proceedings a dignified air. With each new complaint, he attacked as if it was the first. Even when two shitting heifers were brought into Godfrey's hall so that the owners could show the differences and similarities in their ownership marks, Killian executed his duties faithfully and honestly. He hiked up his plain vestments and stepped right through the dung, not mocking, not feigning disgust. The more I watched the priest, the more I liked him. I could see why Godfrey had kept him around.

"Now our king would like to raise the issue of an army in order to renew our strength and the very safety of this island," called Killian when the line of petitioners was finally empty. It was late into the night, possibly morning. It was the first time that one of the priest's actions caused a disapproving grumble from the crowd. Godfrey heard the mumbling and sat up in his chair, ready to fight, but Killian steadied the king with one hand. With the other hand, the priest scratched the thick, dark stubble that was coloring his own face more with every passing moment. The priest's touch calmed the king. Godfrey slowly stood. His English pet backed away. His wife beamed.

"My brothers," King Godfrey bellowed, "we've suffered of late. Men of Norse, Dane, and even Manx descent have run to God's heaven before their time or they've entered Odin's hall. We care not where they've gone, only that they died serving us." Godfrey held up a wooden mug. "Let us drink in honor of our fallen." We joined the king in draining our mugs. Cheers rang out, but an undercurrent of murmurings persisted.

The king shared every detail of his Dal Riatan raid the previous year. He told of their approach to the village from the west. The king said if he did it again, he would slide right under their noses and slice the monks at Lismore. Godfrey told of how they were vastly outnumbered by a host of warriors who happened to be there. It was poor timing, the king said, no more. It wasn't any specific part of a vast tapestry woven by the norns who spun out our lives from their dwelling under the Yggdrasil tree. It wasn't his fate to lose that day. It was a temporary setback. Man was to be at the center of an up and coming kingdom.

I remember how I felt when I heard Godfrey's tale. It was a turning point in my life. Perhaps it was *the* turning point. He convinced me that my brothers, none of whom I had ever met, died in that rainy pasture just outside the monastery. I was livid. I was furious, indignant. I was also young which goes hand in hand with foolishness.

The tiny Irish thrall walked by again with more ale. I snatched another cup. The wicked little thing gave me the same snarl that she'd given me before. Leif took note and prodded my ribs. "She likes you," he said. I made a drunken face at him and the girl.

By the time I heard about the wicked Dal Riatans, my passions were up from swilling Godfrey's ale all day. It was fine ale. In truth, I was totally drunk. Add in my lingering anger at being banished from my own home by my adopted father. Toss in being penniless for having spent two weeks dropping what pathetic amount of coins I had left onto the tables of the mead halls each and every night. Add in my youth. With all of it you get a powerful army of raw emotions. When Godfrey, king, told the assembly the tale of my brothers dying in their shit under a dark sky, I rammed my balled fist into the heavy oak table. The cups of my equally drunk friends bounced, spilling some of their contents onto the sticky, wet wood.

"We kill them!" I shouted over the king's words. I said the phrase as if killing men who didn't want to die was as easy as stepping on the back of a mouse in the thrush.

King Godfrey stopped. He smiled. The hall fell silent.

If anyone with whom I sat had any sense that night, the conversation would have ended right there. Leif or simple Tyrkr or some maiden with hips broad enough to make children and perhaps a mind equally as thick could have pulled me aside and instructed me of my folly. Magnus should have dragged me out and put me to sleep on our ship.

I suppose since I take the time to write this story which took place back in my young days, you already have guessed that none of us had even an ounce worth of brains. My friends all pounded the table too. They furrowed their brows and sloppily drank another swig of ale so that much of it found its way into their beards. What did go down their gullets clouded their minds as much as mine. "Kill them! Kill the Dal Riatans!" they shouted when their cups, that had been so full of courage, again slammed into the table.

I am now an old man, well beyond my ninetieth winter. I recall with my mind's eye today that my companions looked fearsome then, for they were bruised and battered from the day's events. My friends had not yet become raiders. I couldn't have called myself one at that point. But each of us was raised in the harshness of life in the frigid north. We, my friends and I, were north men. We were Norsemen. I had been born in Rogaland, Norway. After my father was killed, a rapscallion named Erik Thorvaldsson took me in as his own. I followed him to Iceland and then to his discovery and settling of Greenland. Like Erik and his son I had fought and killed along the way for mere survival, not glory. My friends around that mead table, young Leif among them, had done the same. So we weren't raiders, yet. But we were hungry, young, and so full of life that we still thought we could freely decide who should and would receive death.

King Godfrey was pleased. He basked in our bravado. His queen studied us with a curious eye. Her gaze lingered on Leif. She reached forward from her throne and gave her husband's hand a squeeze.

Looking back, I suppose it all makes sense. Those one hundred forty men who died under the soggy tree of Dal Riata were Godfrey's men. They had been his crew, his army, his hungry young men. They were the warriors, the thought of whom, caused the king to choke up. He looked at us around that mead hall table and saw the beginnings of a new army, a fresh batch of his men, sent to him by the old gods.

To the king's side, Randulfr and Brandr folded their arms as they dubiously studied us. In the corner, drunken Ketil rolled over again. It looked like he scratched notes on a piece of parchment, though I was drunk and could hardly believe all that my eyes showed me.

Damn. As I scratch out the tales of my youth on vellum made by my own worn hands, I shiver. I shake in the evenings of summer even though I huddle under two great hides brought to me by my little Skjoldmo. Getting old is a curse, I say. The other men of the village where I live say otherwise. They say things like, 'Getting old is a blessing from Glooskap.' Or they say, 'How much more of a blessing is age when you can see your children become men and women of the tribe?' If any of them knew what a horse was, I'd tell them they are full of horse dung. None of my current people has ever seen a horse. I haven't seen a Norseman in many years. But all this is beyond the tale. Well, it is part of another tale which I have written on another page of vellum that sits stacked up somewhere in my smoky hovel.

I tell myself in my aged feebleness that had I known the entire story of those hanged men, my brothers whom I never knew, and their gory deaths, that I would have moved on and not chased after the glory of war so quickly. I tell myself that had I known the truth and not been so drunk, I would have thanked Godfrey for buying my ale that night and returned to the *Charging Boar* to sleep rather than pounding the table, spewing vitriol and nonsense. Those are the things I tell myself. They are delusions, in truth. They are no different than the fat, ugly jarl that weds the seventeen year old maid, the fairest in the village, and deludes himself into believing that she married him and not his power or the heaps of hacksilver he had stored under his bed. They are my own fantasies. They are the songs I make up in my head about my life's events. Like a skald is asked to make his lord into a hero in every song, I do the same in my mind.

The truth is that I probably did know the full story even in my drunkenness. I was a foolish youth, but not stupid. I could see that Godfrey was a typical king, like every one of whom I'd ever heard – Harald Fairhair or Gorm the Old. He was

King of the Isles – exactly which isles changed with the day as opponents' fortunes ebbed or flowed. What made him like all kings and men, for that matter, was that Godfrey wanted more, more gold, more land, more ships, more women, in a word, more. And it was the pursuit of more that got him and his one hundred forty brothers into trouble in the first place.

"Look at these fine men," exclaimed Godfrey. "They are new to us, fresh from the sea and yet they understand our cause. They will lead us to our final revenge over Dal Riata and they will take us to our rightful place among the kingdoms of the earth."

One of the Manx citizenry sidled next to me. "Lad, you're a fool." Godfrey talked on, but I listened to the whispers in my ear. "The king up there already had his revenge last year. On Christmas night, the time you heathens call Yule, our fine king slunk into the church at Lismore. His sword cut the bishop. It sent the abbot's blood spraying against the wall. The story goes that thirteen monks were butchered. Monks!" the man scoffed. "What kind of man bothers killing monks?"

I turned to defend the king I didn't really know, but the man had slipped back into the crowd. When I again turned to face the king, the Manx gossip was crouching down talking with Horse Ketil who had sat up against a low wall.

"So you Greenlanders will be mine! We'll take your oaths soon." King Godfrey was pacing with excitement. "I'll need more native Manx to join our army than I've ever had before. It will be some time before we can count on Norse transplants to arrive. In the meantime, let us show the world what you men of Man may do with steel in your hands."

Horse Ketil shook his head, clearly indicating, "No." The man who had been whispering with him climbed to his feet and moved through the crowd. He quietly encouraged a cautious course for the assembled men.

No one ran forward to volunteer, confirming two things: that even when drunk, Horse Ketil held sway and that we were young, inebriated fools for having so quickly joined Godfrey.

"I hear some griping," said Killian. This time it took the priest's hand and Gudruna's slender hand to calm the king.

Godfrey sat back down to see what inspiration his priest could provide. The king crossed his legs, sinking low, and pouting on the throne. He wound a stray shock of his beard around a finger.

"What? Is it fine to have our Norse and Dane warriors battle the swells of the seas and fight our enemies in order to keep us safe? Is it acceptable to let them weaken the Welsh, Scots, or English so that those brigands cannot attack us? Is it satisfactory to have the men, who a few generations ago were complete foreigners to us, provide us security and return with treasure, riches, and plunder? Wealth, I might add, that finds its way into all of our homes in the form of goods imported from Frankia, England, Ireland, and even the Mediterranean? If so, perhaps the ancestors of these Norsemen were correct. Perhaps we Manx are docile sheep to be penned, shorn, and kept. Perhaps without them we would be taken by the wolves."

"Stop saying we, Irishman!" shouted a man's voice from the crowd.

A wrinkly smile curled amid Killian's dark features. "As you wish," said the priest, now pacing like Godfrey had done. "Though I've been preaching the gospel among you for fifteen years, you wish to view me as foreign. That suits me, because then I do not have to include myself or my ancestors among the pets of Man, who are all-too content to let Norsemen and a small Irish priest be their shepherds. I will volunteer to be a part of our king's next army. I will return to Dal Riata with him and exact retribution for what they've done to our men." Killian looked accusingly at Horse Ketil, but said nothing to him. "I, a lowly Irishman, a peaceful Christian priest, will come back to this place, my home, with treasure for the benefit of our church and our poor and the rest of you cowards."

Killian kept up his pacing. Godfrey and Gudruna scanned the crowd expectantly, clearly hoping that the priest's goading would have the desired effect. Volunteers would always fight better than conscripts.

I drank more ale, trying to forget all my promises from just moments earlier. I studied the swirling grain in the table, rather than accidentally meet the king's eye. Was it too late to sneak off to sleep in an alley?

"What's the pay?" came another lone voice. Killian smiled. The priest was making headway, he thought. He turned to Godfrey who sensed the small shift and eagerly jumped to his feet.

"Plunder," shouted Godfrey, cutting to the core. His voice echoed among the rafters and high, peaked roof. "The monasteries, churches, and towns of Dal Riata are filled with riches. We take them. The monks pay us a ransom to give them back. It is so much more profitable than outright thievery because we sell the same item time and again. Every man who comes will get a portion. Even those who fall and do not return to their homes will have his share go to his widow."

Killian gave his king a nod. The Irishman was clearly pleased. "Very Christian of you, good king," said Killian.

I suppose it was, though at the time I did not even know what that meant.

The king waited for the first of a flood of volunteers. An older man with a deformed ear stepped forward. He fumbled with his hands.

"Speak, Turf Ear," said Godfrey.

"Huh?" asked Turf Ear.

"He said speak," shouted Killian.

"Oh. I'm no man of Man according to many of these. I've lived here for many years, but count myself as a Norseman, so I am no coward like some. But there's a problem, King Godfrey. It's that your call for an army will be difficult to fill. Another assault on Dal Riata is nothing short of tough. We lost many fine men in the rain last year. It is in my memory, for you know I was there. I was wounded and crawled away in the rain. Like you, I saw our men hanged as I curled up on the distant hill. It will be tricky to get even a kinsman to join, if you had one, that is, when the payment is plunder on the come, with no guarantee of silver." Turf Ear took a step back, still nervously playing with his hands.

"Good speech," said Godfrey. If he was angry, he now hid it well. "So you will not be with us when we avenge our fallen heroes and return victorious?"

Turf Ear threw his arms to his sides and again stepped forward. "I didn't say that!" He was shouting so that he could hear himself. "I'll not miss a chance to thump the soft head of a Scot! Toss in the head of a Welshman and I'll be a happy man. What else do I know other than fighting? Should I farm like the old blind man?" Several men laughed at the thought of Turf Ear settling into domestic life.

Godfrey was pleased with his first official and public reenlistment. While Killian rested a hand on Turf Ear's shoulder, the king called to the crowd. "We have our first in a long line of heroes." He spread his arms wide and waved both hands to himself. "Now the rest of you may come. If you be Christian, Killian will lay a hand upon you to give thanks to the One God and to bless your fighting spirit. If you still follow the old gods, drink! I'm sure some of our newcomers from Greenland will happily celebrate with you." The king turned and sat down. He received an encouraging stroke on his hand from Gudruna. He patted the pale skin of her arm.

His closest guards piled their way to the front. Loki left his spot at our table. They didn't have to volunteer, for they were all that was left of his army and would follow their king in bounty or to their deaths if need be. However, they did publically enlist that night in order to spur more men to courage. Randulfr, Brandr, and Loki led the charge, followed by the rest of the crew of Godfrey's command ship. There was a smattering of Manx among them.

No others from Man came forward. They sat glued to the seats of the mead benches. Mumbling. Mumbling. Grumbling. Ketil snorted. It almost sounded like he laughed.

It was a growing embarrassment for the king. Were it not for the crackle of the hearth's great fire, I believe that the chirp of crickets could be heard from the corners of the hall. Some men stared at their boots, others allowed their eyes to nervously dart around to see what their comrades would do. The as-of-yet un-enlisted men of Man were united in their quiet rebellion. Godfrey, undermanned, could do nothing about it.

Young Leif tapped my chest with the back of his hand. "Let's help this king out."

We had already volunteered and the more I thought about the task at hand, the more I hoped that King Godfrey had been too drunk to remember my bellowing moments before. I was not a raider. I had fought in scraps. I had killed a few skraelings in Greenland, but had not experienced war. Leif, however, younger than I and more confident, would not allow the potential horrors of battle to dissuade him.

Leif stepped forward. Magnus and I locked eyes, rolled them, then walked to join our fearless, though inexperienced leader. Tyrkr, loyal to a fault, veritably bound up after his owner's son.

"King Godfrey, I, Leif, grandson of Thorvald, son of Erik, who is jarl of Greenland, who hails from Iceland and Rogaland in Norway before that, swear to bind my crew to yours." He reached his hands up and smacked one onto my shoulder and the other onto that of Magnus. "These are my captains. Though they clearly have much to learn on the knattleikr battlefield, they bring strong arms and passion to the coming fight."

Godfrey stood again. He made no great speech this time. Rather, the king walked to Leif and took his hand, shaking it vigorously. "It's the mark of true men, to take a beating like you did today. You are welcome and I thank you." The king moved to again sit down. His English thrall glided next to him and gave Godfrey an encouraging tap.

Killian walked over to us and I noticed just how small of a man he was. His ears even appeared small to me. "Are you lads Christians?"

I laughed out loud. "No. Until a month ago, I'd never met one in my whole life."

Killian didn't seem to mind my outburst. "Then Christ has just begun his work on you." Under his breath, Killian said, "Let's hope it doesn't take as long as his work on our king. Godfrey sleeps with women who aren't his wife. His wife sleeps with men who aren't her husband." Killian craned back and gave the royal pair a smile before returning his attention to us. "I'll pray for you nonetheless." The earnest priest reached a hand over and grasped Leif's shoulder. He tried to reach up to mine, but found he could not. He clutched a paw on the sleeve of my cloak and wrenched it down. Then, with me awkwardly crouching to one side, he began his prayer. "Pater noster, qui es in caelis, sanctificetur nomen tuum. Adveniat regnum tuum. Fiat voluntas tua, sicut in caelo et in terra. Panem nostrum quotidianum da nobis hodie, et dimitte nobis debita nostra sicut et nos dimittimus debitoribus nostris. Et ne nos inducas in tentationem, sed libera nos a malo."

Killian paused here and many of the men in the hall filled in the gap in unison with 'amen.' I looked around and these same men had their eyes averted to the floor, heads bowed. Even the king had done this as if such corporate prayer was common. It was strange for me. The congregants began to slowly bring their heads upright. I gently tried to straighten myself, but Killian's grip was strong and he wouldn't allow me to budge. When the priest went on, the Christians in the assembly again dropped their heads.

I did as well, but I studied the priest's narrow arm that reached up out of his vestments. It was covered in black hair and scars. "Pater, quos habuimus sub manu tua, et congregabo ea in signum. Conforta cor eorum. Robora in acquisitionem animæ. Eas ad vos." Killian paused again. This time the Christians in the hall were not duped into saying 'amen.' They waited on their holy man. The priest changed to the Norse tongue. "Father, bring these men wealth so that it may be used for your people. Allow their labors to bear fruit for your glory. Bring these Greenlanders to the faith, Lord. Give me the strength to lead them and the king in your word. Amen."

Other than the improbable requests in Killian's Norse-tongued finale, I understood none of what he said. It was in a language I later learned was called Latin. It had been spoken by an ancient culture called Rome. As difficult as it may be for you to believe, I had never heard of either the tongue or its people. My only excuse is that I was born and raised in the farthest reaches of mankind. The days of my people were filled with the activities of survival. We never had time to consider what went on far from the shores of our fjord. Of course, if you read this, you know that in the intervening years I've learned not only the spoken Latin, but also the written.

The crowd raised their heads. A man far in the back audibly expressed his relief that the prayer finally ended. I could see that Godfrey and his woman brought their heads up at the same time. The king wore a determined expression. The queen's face, turned, said that she feared for her husband and his next adventure as she stared at the side of his head. The king clenched Gudruna's hand, worried that our public declaration would bring no further enlistments from the citizens of Man.

He was right to be concerned, for the hall again grew quiet.

"It's not enough, it's not enough," Godfrey was muttering so that only those of us at the head of the hall could hear him. "What kind of king has an army of, what, sixty men in his hall? Sure I've got some sentries on the wall, but not many more."

Godfrey fretted. Sweat broke on his brow. He could see his kingdom slipping through his fingers.

• • •

Gudruna stood and broke the silence that had taken over the Tynwald. She brushed between Leif and me and mounted the stones of the hearth. I thought it was time for another speech. A strong woman could often shame men to do her bidding, especially if the strong woman was beautiful, which Gudruna was. I was wrong. "Bring in a skald!" Gudruna shouted. "When an evening is near over, when a king has assembled a brave army of retribution, Thor's Army, as the Irish would call it, it is time for song and poetry. It is time for the heart strings to be played. Now where is a skald?"

Gudruna scanned the room. A ruckus began working its way to the front as men were parting the way for a cloaked and hooded figure. Without seeing the man's face, Gudruna called, "We're in luck!" Her praise was genuine. "We'll be delighted with the words and tales of Eyvind the Troublesome."

As Eyvind completed his path toward the royals, Leif walked over to the hearth and offered a hand up to the queen. Gudruna looked down at the young man and was fixed by his green eyes. I'd seen it happen before. There were plenty of young maids in Greenland who wanted nothing more than to stare into his orbs. I had never seen it happen with a queen, though, let alone one who must have been twice his age. Gudruna gathered her senses and climbed down with Leif's assistance. Before he could step away, the queen planted a kiss on the now-delighted Leif. A jealous ripple trickled through the crowd of young men. Godfrey appeared indifferent. Killian grunted at the sight.

The enshrouded Eyvind stepped next to Gudruna. She snatched his arm and led him toward the twin thrones. "Thor's Army?" Godfrey cursed, under his breath after they had approached. "What are you doing? I have two longboats, one with experienced men, the other filled with youngsters from Greenland. That is hardly an army. There are poverty stricken pirates who can muster more men. You embarrass me."

Gudruna knelt to her husband. She clutched his knees. "There is still time before the dawn. Let the skald inspire us with his stories. Instead of begging for an army, perhaps hearing of heroes past will bring out the heroes of the present."

King Godfrey frowned, but patted his wife's hand. "I'd sooner crack the men over their heads to make them join, but I don't have the manpower even for that. The mind of a woman is mysterious to me. Have your way."

As Godfrey nodded in agreement, Eyvind the Troublesome turned around to face us and the rest of the crowd. He took a dramatic step forward and un-cinched the cord tied at his neck. With both hands, Eyvind lifted the cloak off and allowed it to drop to the floor behind him. I was already impressed, for skalds, or poets, were usually impish things, versed in words and not showmanship. Eyvind, though, was different from those traveling artists. He was mostly average in every way. His hair was sandy blonde. His beard had just a few flecks of white. His arms were strong, but not overly muscular. If I passed by him in the marketplace every day for a year, I would never have noticed him, save one thing – his manner of dress. The tumbling of the shabby cloak revealed a warrior's uniform, shining. His mail shone bright even in the low light. I could see my reflection in his recently scrubbed helmet. He wore gold and silver medallions around his neck. Arm rings decorated his upper limbs. It was all too perfect and too clean, however. Eyvind had never had to fight a feeble Christian nun over a meal, let alone survive a pitched battle. His clothes were part of his show. They were probably gifts from the jarls and kings he'd entertained over the years.

    He stepped forward again so that he was nearly on top of me. Without uttering a word, he pointed to the earthen floor. I and my comrades followed his command, unquestioningly. The entire hall obeyed and a few moments of rustling, crouching, and sitting went by. Gudruna had moved from the foot of her husband and now sat next to Leif, holding him as if they were longtime lovers. She stroked his wispy red beard. Leif wore a satisfied grin. The king had moved with the English thrall to sit next to another one of his housemaids. He grasped his ale mug with one hand and the maid's midriff with the other. Killian, too, had found a place to sit among the crowd. All grew quiet.

    Eyvind let the moments linger. Surprisingly, though the night was long and I was beaten and exhausted, I did not find myself getting irritated from the wait. My ale mug found my lips and I sipped at it gently. My broken fingers throbbed. The room and my head became mellow. I could feel the warmth of the hearth on my back. It soothed my aches and bruises.

    Eyvind began his first song at a whisper. The low volume forced me to hold my breath just to hear his words. "What follows comes from the mighty Odin, giver of the poetic arts, blameless and without blemish."

> You must climb up on to the keel,
> Cold is the sea-spray's feel;
> Let not your courage bend:
> Here your life must end.

> Old man, keep your upper lip firm
> Though your head be bowed by the storm.
> You have had girls' love in the past;
> Death comes to all at last.

That had always been a favorite of mine. It was especially popular when I lived on Iceland. After Eyvind finished the last line I heard a few guttural grunts of agreement from the crowd. All knew that poetry could grant or deny immortality. In that way, Odin's gift to man was even more powerful than the war axe, which could only kill.

Eyvind told three more well-known tales of honor and glory. With each passing moment, the hall grew quieter.

"A love poem," called Gudruna as she nestled her head to Leif's chest and her hand elsewhere. She seemed to have forgotten, or at least she no longer cared, about her original reason for calling a skald forward.

Eyvind cleared his throat. "Kormakr meets Steingerdr." I knew this one, too, for it hailed from Iceland as well.

> The bright lights of both
> Her cheeks burned onto me
> O'er the fire-hall's felled wood;
> It's no laughing matter.
> By the threshold I gained a glance
> At the ankles of this woman
> Of glorious shape; yet while I live
> That longing will never leave me.

> The moon of her eyelash – that Valkyrie
> Adorned with linen, server of herb-surf –
> Shone hawk-sharp upon me
> Beneath her brows' bright sky;
> But that beam from the eyelid-moon
> Of the goddess of the golden torque
> Will later bring ill to me
> And to the ring goddess, Eir.

To my left, Gudruna was kissing Leif. Leif did not stop her. Nor did her husband make the attempt, for he was occupied with his housemaid and the thrall, performing much the same actions with them as his wife was on Leif. Throughout the hall, men who had had the sense to bring their wives, found Eyvind's words as an aphrodisiac. Men who did not have a woman beside them curled under their cloaks and began to fall asleep. The Tynwald ended without ceremony. It ended without the king building an army. Eyvind and I were left staring at one another, the only two in the hall not thinking of amorous passion or peaceful sleep.

So it seemed that the recitations of Eyvind the Troublesome did not have the patriotic effect Gudruna had hoped. I looked again at Leif and the queen. Perhaps the effect was working out for them. I blocked out those lusty thoughts, having been rebuffed twice in a year's time by Leif's sister, Freydis. One of those times was a vast, public humiliation. I wanted nothing to do with women, even though for the first twenty-one winters of my life they are all I had longed for.

"Why do they call you the Troublesome?" I asked the skald.

He peered around the room and saw that no one was paying him any attention. He gave a knowing smile. "No one has ever asked me that before. I suppose they assume that to do so would bring trouble."

"I guess I'm foolish that way."

"I killed my mother. It wasn't intentional, you see. I was birthed, she died. Friggas saw that she was fertile, but not hardy." Eyvind sighed at that heavy thought, but quickly smiled as he pointed to where Leif's young hand groped its way onto Gudruna's rump. "My father called me Troublesome ever since."

I thought it time to change the subject. "Do you know any tales of mystery or adventure? I'm your only audience member now and I've got no woman on whom to use your love words."

Eyvind offered me a hand up. I took it and the two of us walked to one of the hall's long mead tables. I pushed a drunken man off the end of a bench. He crumpled to the earthen floor. Not once was his snoring interrupted. Eyvind sidled onto the bench opposite, between two snoozing free women. He grabbed a nearly empty pitcher of warm ale and topped off our mugs. "To Odin," he said, raising the cup.

"To poetry and tales and love and battle," I answered, though at the time I had failed at all my attempts at the first three and had never truly engaged in a full-scale battle.

"Have you ever heard of Wales?" asked Eyvind. Still at his place on the floor, Edana's drunkard for a husband farted behind me, interrupting the settling peace. He finally seemed truly asleep to me, pleased with himself for dashing Godfrey's hopes.

I shrugged at Eyvind's question. I had heard of it. I had even spoken out against the stinking Welsh when I was at the mead hall. In truth, I wasn't sure why I didn't like them or where their putrid land must be. My travels had taken me over what seemed the entire Midgard realm. It just so happened that until we had arrived on Man, most of the regions in which I had lived had very few men of any kind, let alone Welsh.

"You're an enigma, my Norse brother – a Norseman who doesn't know where some of the easiest pillaging in the Irish Sea is to be had." Eyvind shook his head. "With fair winds, the northernmost point of Wales can be reached from Man in just a morning of sail."

I didn't like being called an enigma, whatever that was. I also didn't like being told I didn't know where things were. Ha! As I now sit, old, feeble, and shivering in a smoky room writing these yarns on parchment I made last week, I laugh at my young self! Of course, I knew nothing. That night, I curled my lip, baring my teeth like a wolf to show Eyvind I was displeased.

Eyvind took what was left in his ale mug and dumped it in mine. "There," he said, "a peace offering for your wounded pride. Now there's no need to thump me. I'm a poet. You'd have me whimpering on the floor in an eye's blink. Then you'd have to explain to the king over there why you attacked his favorite skald." Eyvind appeared ready for whatever came, a beating or conversation. I rightfully laughed at myself and drank his ale.

"I travel from court to court in these Isles. I've been to Kvaran and his son, Sitric, in Dyflin. I've been to Aethelred in

England. I've even told tales to the Irish kings from the north, the Ui Neill, and from the south, the Leinster." I listened, happy I had more ale, because I understood nothing of what Eyvind said. "I've even spoken to the local ruler; he thinks himself a king, but he is under Aethelred's thumb, in northern Wales. He's called Maredubb."

"This is a boring story. Can you go back to telling me poetry?" I thought myself funny, using words rather than my fist to get Eyvind back. He kept on going. Far away, near the walls at the edge of the village, the first cock of the morning called his warning.

"Maredubb talks incessantly," said Eyvind. Horse Ketil was stirring again. He was the most restless passed-out man I'd ever seen. "He certainly talks more than what a king ought. He says this and he says that. A king ought to make his will happen without constant blabbering. At any rate, the man talks even more when he is drunk on ale and on my last visit, he was drunk on both mead and ale. His head, the next morning, must have felt like it was the size of well-laden knarr."

"This King Maredubb sounds like half the men I know. He sounds like almost all the men in this hall, mostly unremarkable." I brought the cup back up and found myself tipping it higher and higher, my head back further and further. It was empty. Just to make sure, I brought it in front of my eyes and stared down at the dry bottom. I had trouble focusing. Gudruna, the king's wife, moaned in pleasure at something Leif did with her under his cloak.

"The men in this hall, if they get toppling drunk, can say nothing of value. But a king just might say something worth noting. Maredubb told me of a great treasure."

My eyes rapidly came into focus. My head cleared. The cup went to the table and I studied Eyvind's face. "Treasure?"

Horse Ketil cleared his throat. It was apparent that he was sobering up as much as me at the talk of money. It might mean more ale for him, I suppose. Or, if he ever quit the drink, his eavesdropping could prove to be a real danger to the king and his court.

"Suddenly my tale is not so boring? Suddenly you are sober?" Eyvind yawned and stretched his arms wide. "Well, it has been a long night. I'm going to find a lightweight man to drag away from the hearth so that I can take his place by the fire." Eyvind stood, but I clasped my hand on his mail shirt and tugged him back down. He sank without a fight.

"Talk." I was desperate for money. Mine was gone, pissed away in a few weeks time as I tried to forget my banishment and console myself with merry. If Godfrey's army would be a failure and no invasion of this Dal Riata would occur, I meant to find myself some treasure. I'd make my own glory rather than following an erstwhile king.

Eyvind dove into his story quite willingly. "There was a great king who lived in Wales, on an island called Anglesey. He lived there long ago, long ago. He reined before the Jutes and Saxons came to England. This king reigned in the wilds of Wales before the Roman Claudius came, even before the Roman Julius came." There was another reference to those Romans. "Before even steel was invented, this king ruled."

"By Hel," I barked. "I understand that it was long ago. Tell me about this treasure."

"It's important that you know just how ancient is this treasure. When this king died – Maredubb wasn't able to share his name for he didn't know it, it was so long ago – he was buried in a great mound. Inside with him went his riches, bejeweled weapons and metals like copper, silver, and gold formed into magnificent works."

"If Maredubb knows all this, I'm sure he or his people have rummaged through it by now," I said with a wave of my hand at the preposterous story. I thought that I should be sleeping.

"That's just it. No one has touched it, though it stands in the open and a blind child could stumble across the mound by accident."

"I don't believe it. Why would someone not dig up the mound at night and become the new and richest king?"

Eyvind frowned. "Because the king also had one thousand of his best soldiers sacrificed and buried with him.

This ancient king humps forty of his wives so that they plow their way through eternity behind the able guard of a regiment of the dead. The mound is cursed. It requires no human sentinels. No one has touched it for thousands of years. No one will touch it now."

Gudruna yelped. Eyvind and I both looked over to where Leif was climbing out from under the queen. Her dress was bunched up around her waist so I could see her naked legs and bare chest. She wore a surprised and disappointed look on her face as if Leif had cut off their union prematurely. He was young, I thought with a shrug. The woman couldn't expect him to last very long.

The queen moved to gather up her clothes and leave, but Leif gently set a hand on her side to hold her in place. "An unguarded treasure?" Leif asked Eyvind. Gudruna looked confused. Clearly, she had been attuned to the desires of her loins more than my conversation.

"That's not what I said," answered Eyvind. "No *man* guards it."

Leif looked at me. His eyes flashed as his terrific and thoughtful mind worked its sorcery. Leif pulled Gudruna to him so their naked torsos barely touched. "And our King Godfrey needs wealth to rebuild an army to exact his revenge on Dal Riata. What better way to obtain money, than to steal it from a useless corpse?"

Eyvind and I were both shaking our heads. "Leif, you know the power of the dead," I scolded. "Think of your night on the barrow mound. Think of our encounter with the skraelings and all that brought. Death brings death. It is as sure as a man and woman, living, bring more life."

"Halldorr's right," said Eyvind. "It's a tale. I believe it to be true. I told it not to inspire action, but to entertain. I'm a simple skald, telling yarns for coin."

Leif and Gudruna were nodding their heads in agreement, with neither Eyvind nor me, but rather each other. They had already set their minds on a treasure, free for the taking. Without looking away from the queen, Leif said, "Halldorr, you were moments ago just as interested as I am now."

"That was before I found out the grave was cursed," I protested.

"And I wasn't interested until I found out it was. Men with a spear can kill us, but draugr, or specters will . . ."

"Terrify us and then kill us," I finished his sentence.

"Will embrace us as their own," corrected Leif. "We will free them from their eternal burden of vigilance. We will take the riches of the ancient king and use them for today's king to build a great land." I remember thinking that I had wanted the treasure for myself, not necessarily for Godfrey. Now we were talking about sharing it, giving it away. "This Anglesey will be part of a great kingdom, ruled by King Godfrey and Queen Gudruna."

Leif moved away from Gudruna and took a step toward where the king now slumbered curled up next to his housemaid and thrall. The queen halted Leif with a light touch. "You will propose to capture this treasure with and for my husband so that he may build a stronger kingdom?"

"Of course," answered Leif as if it was the only possible choice.

Gudruna glanced over to her husband with pride. She firmly grasped Leif's arm and drew him close. "The hour is late and the king is tired. One morning of delay will not harm the outcome." She sat back to the ground and tugged Leif down with her. "And you have work to finish for your queen." Gudruna again pulled Leif's cloak over them. Their childish giggling resumed.

Eyvind looked back to me. "It seems like your friend means to use my yarn to lead you to your death."

It wasn't the first time and wouldn't be the last. I raised my mug to offer a toast. "I thank you, troublesome skald." I brought the mug to my lips and remembered it was empty. I tipped it over my mouth and shook it until one last drop of the brew fell onto my extended tongue.

My hands slapped down on the table and I pushed myself up. I left Eyvind to find a place to sleep and picked my way through the crowd of snoozing bodies on the floor. I pushed the doors of the hall open and went out into the cool morning.

A slight ray of sun had just begun breaking over the horizon to the east. Two thralls, already starting their days, carried buckets of water for their masters. Killian, who I had not even seen leave the assembly when Eyvind finished his tales, used a wicker broom to brush off the dirt walkway of his church. Despite staying up as long as me, the priest seemed to have bountiful energy. "Good morning to you Norseman!" he called. "It looks to be a beautiful day."

I grunted something incomprehensible in return and staggered toward the great stone with Odin's likeness carved on it. I patted the image with my hand and smiled, thinking of home and my first and second fathers. The stone felt warm despite the chill from the night air. I pulled my cloak tightly around me and sat down with my back resting against the marker.

I fell asleep, my dreams turning to nightmares of draugr and warriors, death and failure.

CHAPTER 2

I awakened sometime after the midday meal and found that my back ached where it had rested at an awkward angle against Odin's and the One God's shared stone. But I was young and in just a matter of moments, the pain was a mere memory. My fractured fingers still throbbed with every beat of my heart. I could already begin to see a slit of light through my swollen eye.

Killian had taken pity on me sometime during the morning and covered my shivering form in a blanket made of the wool from the many sheep inhabiting the island. It was actually a stray, flapping fiber from the well-worn blanket that awakened me when a breeze caused the errant thread to repeatedly brush against my nostrils.

As I came back to life, I sat up and stretched. The village was alive with the activities expected in early summer. Hungry, thieving gulls raced overhead, heading inland and then back out to the shingle where fishermen were already returning with their catch. The stench of a tanner's craft wafted from a nearby street. A smith's hammer split the afternoon. So did his echoing voice as he screamed at his apprentice for working the bellows too hard and blowing his fire too high.

My belly was in the process of eating itself so it was a welcome sight indeed to see the small priest shuffle across the square carrying a platter of bread and fish. Killian wore what I had supposed was his typical priestly robe. It was white. He or a servant must have taken great care in laundering it because the color was not faded or yellowed. Instead, the robe was as white as a baby's first teeth. At the bottom hem, though, his actions of the day had already splashed the robe with flecks of dirt and mud. The sleeves of the garment came just to his hand and were wide, shaped like a bell, flaring out. The cuffs had deep violet piping at the edges. He wore a simple, but fine, white cord of three strands for a belt. The rope's ends bounced down at one of his knees as he scurried. Killian bent down and offered the food without asking whether or not I was hungry.

Likewise, without asking, I greedily snatched up the bread and tore it in half before stuffing a large hunk into my mouth. Though my mouth was parched from all my drinking, the dry bread tasted good. Killian set the plate on my lap and crouched so that he balanced on the balls of his feet. I could see his footwear for the first time. They weren't the sandals that I would later see on monks or the fancier shoes preferred by many priests. Killian wore boots much like mine. He wore woolen trousers too, also like those I wore. Beneath his royal-looking garb, Killian was a working, or perhaps, fighting man at heart.

A second enormous bite of bread slid down my gullet. I jammed a section of the salted fish in closely behind. Through my gnawing I asked, "What price is the food, priest?" I wasn't sure what to call the man. I had heard the Christians call him father, but I already pined for my first and second fathers, so I was in no hurry to add another.

Killian allowed a smile to draw upon his small face. It seemed to nearly swallow his head, it was so broad. "Young traveler, I was under the impression that you had no money left. Your man, Leif, has not been shy in telling your plight."

I actually had a few copper pennies, English I think they were, and one silver Kufic that had come to me on some circuitous trade route from a land of deserts. I wasn't destitute, but it would be only a matter of days before I would have to sell my arm ring from Erik, the brooch I used to fasten my cloak, or even my walrus tusk comb just to eat. "Then what did you expect in return?" I began eating faster in order to quickly fill my stomach in case he gave me terms with which I'd not agree.

"There's no need to gorge yourself," Killian said, tut-tutting. "If you need more, we can find you some."

"What's the price?" I asked, not believing him.

"The price has been paid," he answered.

"Leif?" I asked. "Another of my crew? I don't need any charity from them."

He shook his head.

"Not King Godfrey?" I asked.

"You are one of his sworn men now and so it would be in his interest to keep you alive so that you may do the same for him when the time comes. But no, the king did not buy you a meal." Killian plopped his rump down in the dirt. It made me cringe to think of how filthy his clean, white robes would get. He didn't seem to care. "A man who was God and was of God, long ago paid the price for all of us. I simply do my feeble best to extend his sacrifice to others. Just now, it happens to be you."

He spoke in mysteries to me. I now know all there is to know about the One True God and his only Son, the Christ, Jesus and his sacrifice for all mankind. I've read the God-inspired words of his book. I've served a holy and devout king who himself converted thousands upon thousands of my countrymen to the faith of the One True God. But that is for a different tale at a different time. Suffice it to say, I understood nothing of what Killian said that day.

He could tell. "You come from Iceland and this new land, Greenland?"

"Yes, and I've never known a Christian. My father and all his fathers before him followed our gods." I pointed to the image of Odin above my head and behind me. "He's one of them."

Killian studied me. Looking back on it now, I think the feisty, little priest saw something in me that day. I think the One God told him that with patient care, I'd be a follower of His. "I've heard how the fire and frost giants formed the world. It's hard not to hear the tales with so many Danes and Norseman plodding about. I know of your Odin and Thor. I know of your Midgard Serpent. I know of the Yggdrasil Tree."

I was impressed that he could recite some names from my Norse past. "But do you know what goes on beneath the tree, in and among the moist, dirty roots?" Crumbs were scattering down my chest.

The question was too easy for him. He had served as a Christian priest in a part of the world that had been subject to raids from Norsemen for over a hundred years. "Oh, you mean the three norns, Urdr, Verdandi, and Skuld – what was, what is, and what will be – those women who spin the thread of every man's life?"

He said it, not in a mocking way. Killian answered me in a matter-of-fact manner. I was left wondering whether he believed in the norns or not. I for one did believe. It was not so much that I believed, I suppose. I *knew* them to exist, especially the malevolent ones. The norns spun the fate of everyone, but I knew those three women were active and probably enjoying themselves as they toyed with my life. My thread, I always thought, was more akin to a coarse piece of unraveling twine, the three cords of the past, present, and future fraying, preparing to snap. The norns pushed me left just after I became comfortable gliding right. They killed my mother before I was old enough to know her. They killed my father just when I was getting old enough to know him. The norns sent me to Erik, who was a fair, but rough man. Then after I had followed him to Iceland then Greenland and just when I was convinced I would settle, serving him and raising a brood of children with his daughter, he banished me. I was an exile by accident, I thought. So, I believed in and knew the norns intimately.

"We Christians believe in those concepts," said Killian, playing with his rope belt with his fingers, "of a fashion. We call it God's Providence or just Providence. I think you'll be surprised by all that Providence has to offer you in your life."

The bread was gone. The fish was gone. I began to stir and so Killian sprang to his feet and pulled me up. He was surprisingly strong for such a little man. My back creaked like someone twice my age.

"I cannot be surprised any longer," I began.

The priest scoffed at me. "You're too young to have seen it all. Just wait."

"I haven't seen it all. I meant that nothing goes as I plan. It's gotten worse since I fell in with Leif. Nonetheless, where he goes, I will follow since I owe his father everything. I suppose it will be all the worse now that Leif and I both serve King Godfrey. The two of them together will work with the norns or your Providence to see the death of me."

"Then why wait to find out?" asked Killian.

"What?"

"While you sleep out in the street your Leif, Magnus, and Tyrkr make plans with Gudruna and Godfrey and his crew. I assumed you knew because as I left with your food, Leif was giving you credit for the plan to invade Anglesey ahead of Dal Riata."

I gave a heavy sigh. So it was true. The stories swirling in my head about treasures were not drunken dreams. "Then I might as well go find out the manner of my death. You know it's madness to attack a grave with a thousand draugr standing guard."

Killian extended his hand for the plate and said, "I think not. Remember, I go with you on this strandhogg of yours. God has much work for me yet to do, especially on King Godfrey. And since I'll be standing next to you in the shield wall and since I don't mean to die, you'll probably survive for a few more years."

I didn't believe him at the time. A shield wall filled with twenty thousand hardened Norse and Dane warriors couldn't survive a battle with ghosts and spirits. And we did not have twenty thousand. We had two ships worth of fighters, one filled with experienced men, the other filled with green men from Eystribyggo.

But we also had and an impish Christian priest.

• • •

When Killian and I returned to Godfrey's hall, the priest dropped my empty plate onto one of the great tables that were still being cleared of the remnants of last night's festivities. The dish made a clattering racket so that the king and his advisors abruptly stopped their conversation and peered into the smoky haze that drifted up from the hearth. The slaves, too, stopped their work at the commotion. The king saw Killian's and my approach and quickly returned his attention to their meeting. The household thralls, one, the snarling, grubby young girl with bare feet, again began picking up the mess scattered about.

We moved easily and briskly across the cleared floor. Just a half day earlier the free men of the village and surrounding areas had littered every ell of space on that ground. Most of them had now retreated back to their shops and farms. Actually, all of them save the large Lady Edana's husband had left.

64

Horse Ketil sat upright on a bench at the far end of the mead hall. His trousers still shone wet from his night of revelry. One leg was crossed on a knee. He sat back against a table, relaxing as if he were king. Ketil held a wide parchment in front of his chest and pointed to something on it with an extended finger. Two other men, strangers to me, talked in hushed tones with Ketil.

Killian caught my glance. "That's Horse Ketil if you don't know him." He said the name derisively. "He's a mischievous Manx. I don't trust him. I think he used contacts in Dal Riata to ambush us there. I think he'll do it again."

"Why have Godfrey ambushed? And if he did, why do you not tell the king your concerns?" I asked like a simpleton. Ketil's two companions skulked out of the hall through a back exit. The Manx noble rolled up the parchment and stuffed it into his soft leather jerkin.

The priest shook his head in disgust. "Politics of the Irish Sea. Godfrey lost most of his tiny army over the last twelve months. Here and there the raids haven't gone well. Horse Ketil could have a thousand well-armed farmers at our doors in a day. That would be enough to end Godfrey's reign."

"And so Godfrey placates him. The king is afraid of what Horse Ketil can do," I said.

"That sums it up. He treats Ketil with too much deference until the king has rebuilt his own forces. At that point I'll encourage Godfrey to push his fat cousin and Horse Ketil off the banks of this island so their heads can crash against the rocks." Killian then seized my arm, looked toward the king to make certain no one saw, and shoved a pair of bone dice into my hands. The priest stood on his toes and whispered into my ear. "Put these into your empty purse. Bring them out at the proper time."

I was about to ask him what he meant when Killian noticed my scarred and mangled ear. "What happened to that?" he asked.

I shrugged. "Skraelings." I pointed toward Leif with my nose. "Without him, the spear would have buried itself in my eye and not merely torn off half of my ear." Killian studied the ear for a moment more. He gave me a knowing glance with raised eyebrows. "Providence," he said, before quietly leading me to the conference.

We entered the circle of war planners just as Leif was finishing his second or third round of pleading for Godfrey to follow his mad plan to invade Anglesey. "It's an unguarded treasure!" called young Leif, seemingly unaware that he was shouting at a king.

Godfrey pulled the mustache of his beard to the side as he thought. "That is not what you said just a few moments ago. You said that an army of draugr acted as sentries."

"Indeed, that is what I said. But you need not worry about that since I have survived a night on a barrow mound, awake," countered Leif.

I could see that Godfrey and Randulfr, who stood to the side of the king, were nearly bent by the simple argument. Christians or not, they knew what abilities Leif had likely gained from his brush with the spirits. Gudruna gave Leif a playful wink, approving of his line of reasoning.

King Godfrey frowned. "You nearly had me there, but I'm not going to be swayed by your green eyes quite as easily as the queen. I've been to Anglesey before." The king looked to Randulfr. "What fifteen, sixteen years ago?"

Randulfr nodded with a scowl.

"And you'd think if there was anything to be had on Anglesey that I would have returned in all that time, but I haven't. I'm here to tell you that the defenses are nearly non-existent. There's good reason for that, however, since there's not much to plunder. Even their churches are poor. Poor churches! Can you imagine that Killian?"

"A travesty that a king such as you would never allow befall our fine Manx institutions," said Killian with great political deftness.

The king nodded his approval at the priest and glared at Leif. "I like your enthusiasm, young Norseman, but you don't know the area. Give me a mint. Oh, the English and their mints! That is something worth plundering." The king again looked to Randulfr. "Five, six years ago when we had our best year of looting – Wales and Cornwall and Devon and the former Mercia – what was the name of the mint?"

"Chester," Randulfr barked. He said it as a rebuke to Leif.

"That was a fitting raid. Not only did we take many pennies with King Aethelred's pretty face staring back at me, but they still had buckets of coins with the English version of King Solomon. We snatched those too." This time Godfrey went to the expert on the Bible. He looked to Killian for help with the particulars of the tale.

The priest said, "Like Solomon, King Godfrey, the English King Edgar was able to lead during a peaceful period because of all the hard work wrought by his forefathers, Alfred and Edward and all. You, I'm afraid, King Godfrey, don't have that luxury." Killian glanced over to Horse Ketil who returned the look with his own sarcastic smile. "Your father, Harald of Bayeux, was strong, but came up by more modest means. You are required to pursue a more aggressive strategy. King David may be a better model for you."

Godfrey rolled his eyes. "I wasn't looking for a model, priest." He returned his gaze to Leif. "So, I was saying there is nothing there worth raiding. We will have to attack Dal Riata with what we've got."

Ketil was suddenly behind me. "Let's go to Anglesey. I've met the ruler there," he said. He stunk of day-old urine.

"Where was your support last night during the Tynwald?" asked Godfrey. "Don't think I didn't see you spreading seeds of discontent through the crowd."

Ketil gave a playful shrug. "My support was stuck on the film at the bottom of an ale mug." He pointed to his pants.

"That's not his reason," barked Killian.

"Shut up, priest," said Godfrey. Killian shook his head and folded his arms.

"No, I take no offence from the Irishman," said Ketil. "The priest wants what's best. The truth is that so do I." I didn't believe his words at this point, but had to admit that my view of him was skewed by the priest and Loki from the night before. "I can't suggest that my fellow Manx throw in with you until you prove yourself victorious once again."

Godfrey frowned. He bobbed his head sideways, acknowledging some of the truth of what Ketil said. He returned to tugging his beard. "It's just no good."

Gudruna was shaking her head. Her long hair had been pulled back up in the braids expected of a respectable married woman. I smiled as I thought of her illicit tryst with Leif when she'd let the hair cascade over her bare shoulders. "Regardless of the Manx lack of support, husband, king, it would seem that something worth taking is on Anglesey, for Eyvind said as much in the wee moments of this very morning."

The king crunched his brow. "Is he the source for the fable?"

Leif looked at me. I opened my eyes wide in surprise, preferring to not be pulled into a verbal battle with a king, no matter how unsuccessful his latest fortunes had been. Even though both Gudruna and Leif knew the answer, everyone waited on me. "Yes."

"Then it's either a spun tale or truth. There's no in between with Eyvind. I think that is why they call him the Troublesome. You can never tell." I smiled amidst the cover of my long blonde beard since I knew the true story behind Eyvind's moniker. "Find him and bring him to me."

"He left this morning on a knarr bound for the south of England," said Killian.

"Then can we please stop talking in circles about a fortune in land devoid of wealth?" growled Godfrey. It wasn't a question.

The queen ignored her husband. "King Godfrey, there are men in this room who believe the treasure is there and that it will be enough for you to use build an army." She looked at Ketil. "Will you be more aggressive in your support of the rightful king if he comes back from Anglesey with ample plunder?"

Ketil didn't hesitate. "Of course."

"Then it's settled. Dal Riata cannot be effectively raided with two longboats worth of men, even those as fine as yours.

You'll rebuild your army from among the Manx upon your return."

"It's no good," Godfrey muttered.

Gudruna turned to Killian as she spoke. "I think we ought to seek the council of the One God as well as the luck of the old gods that these foreigners bring back to our shores. Why not cast lots and let the fate woven by the norns decide whether or not you go to Anglesey?"

Godfrey grimaced. "How will casting lots be like seeking our Christian God's guidance? Just last week our priest here excoriated us about the evils of gambling."

"This won't be gambling, husband." She patted him gently on his chest. "It will be using fortune for divination. And the best way to incorporate the One God's direction is to use dice from our local priest." Gudruna didn't wait for her husband to answer. "Leif, you advocate an attack on Anglesey. Ketil does too. Randulfr, you do as well." Randulfr appeared surprised by the woman's assertion, but obviously had, from experience, gained the sense to avoid a conflict with her. He merely nodded. "Since you three will be affected by the king's casting of lots as much as he, will you accept the course that the dice lay bare?" Gudruna finished with another nearly imperceptible wink to Leif. She offered one to Killian, who answered her by surreptitiously pointing toward me. I was utterly confused.

Randulfr and Leif gave the queen a slight bow. "We will."

Ketil simply said, "Aye."

"There you have it, husband. These men," began Gudruna.

"These men are trying to trick me and you are in league with them," accused Godfrey. "I'd sooner sail the rolling slopes of Meiti with a fieldstone as a ship than accept dice from Killian. The entire island knows that he has dozens of weighted pairs that he uses to teach lessons to those caught in the sin of gambling." The king stood and paced in front of his throne for two full passes. "But every respectable Norseman, especially those who still follow the old gods, has dice of his own. Since this Halldorr has no spear in this fight, I'll use his." It was Killian's turn to give Gudruna a secret wink.

I decided that now was the proper time mentioned earlier by Killian. I reached into my mostly empty purse, pushed aside the lone silver Kufic, and snatched up the dice Killian had given to me on the way in. Godfrey quickly snagged them for himself and walked over to the low stone wall that held up the mighty roof. As he crouched, preparing to throw the dice, I marveled at how adroitly Gudruna had helped turn the argument from certain defeat to one that would hinge on Killian's loaded dice.

Horse Ketil grinned as if he, too, already knew the outcome. Perhaps it was he who was manipulating the strings of all of us.

While we all began huddling around the king, Godfrey fished into his jerkin and pulled out a small gold cross that hung from his neck. He put it to his lips and kissed it. Then the king clutched the dice in one hand, closed his eyes, and mumbled a prayer. It started in the Latin, which I was quickly tiring of hearing, before it morphed into a familiar Norse expression that asked for Thor's favor. Before the last words escaped the king's mouth, he tossed the dice. They rattled and vaulted their way to the wall, struck it, and bounced their way back. Godfrey's head was in the way and I couldn't see the result. I didn't have to, for the king swore bitterly against his Christian God.

"Godfrey," Killian scolded.

The king swore again as he rose, kicking the dice so that they bounced off the feet of Horse Ketil. "I am sorry, father," said King Godfrey, genuinely. But then he swore again.

"It looks as though we attack a non-existent cadre of draugr in the non-existent grave of a non-existent king for non-existent wealth to help me raise what will be a non-existent army," said the king sarcastically.

Leif, Killian, and Gudruna smiled. Randulfr growled, for he had been to Anglesey and thought it would be nothing more than a chase of the mythical.

Horse Ketil turned and walked across the hall to sit back down on his bench. He snatched a stray jug of ale from a table. The Manx noble chuckled to himself.

The king clapped his hands to end the meeting.

We filed out into the sun. I remember thinking that if all those things the king listed were truly non-existent, that would be the best chance any of us had for survival.

I did not look forward to going to war with ghosts, but that is just what we meant to do.

• • •

It was quite easy for an experienced raider king to arrange and equip a short expedition of just two ships. Since we planned on a total time for the outbound and return trip in the Irish Sea to be just one full day and since we hoped to run onto the island, steal the treasure, and scurry home without giving King Maredubb time to mount an attack, Godfrey asked that only three days worth of foodstuffs be spread between the longboats. Hudfats were crammed with bread recently made over the king's hearth as well as the hearths of many of the village residents. Since the voyage was to be so quick, I looked forward to having to scrape mold from the bread for perhaps just a single a day. Several large barrels of ale were tightly secured at each ship's center around and over the mastfish. Heavily salted eel and turbot filets were packed in a trunk onboard each ship so that we didn't have to chase over the countryside and delay our march in search of meat. Livestock was left behind as I learned that for almost all strandhoggs, thievery was the preferred method of finding additional sustenance. Other than the rats in the bilge, the king's lone horse was our only animal companion.

The two warships thus packed were the small and fat *Charging Boar*, under Leif's command, and Godfrey's flagship, *Raven's Cross*, a name that I thought took the menace associated with the great, black bird and ruined it with a reference to the Christian faith. Despite the feeble name, it was a long, sleek boat with lines that looked like they could slice right through any waves that Aegir would place in the ship's path. Dangling from both hands, I hung down from the forestay of *Charging Boar*, watching *Raven's Cross* like a lustful old man watched a barefooted maiden carry a basket of eggs back into her father's house. She was a fine ship.

"You want your own boat someday?" asked Magnus as he dropped a heavy spare rope into place up on the steering deck, aft of where he would control the rudder.

I had never thought of it. Growing up, as you know, I wanted a home, a woman, a place to hunt and fish, and gaggles of children. I pushed back and forth on my dangling toes and gently swung on the forestay. "She's pretty isn't she?"

"She is," agreed Magnus. The helmsman then jabbed my ribs. "Come on, Leif has a present for you."

I dropped to my feet and rapped Magnus' forehead with my knuckles. He swatted the hand away and laughed. "Where is the little red-haired son of a jarl?" I asked in a manner that said to be the son of a jarl was a dishonor, which, of course, it wasn't. "He'd better have something nice for me since he's getting us into one mess after another." Actually, I was the one who first volunteered to be a part of Godfrey's crew. But I was drunk. You know that.

Magnus led me to the gunwale over which we leapt easily, thinking nothing of the jarring vibrations that greeted our knees when our young feet slapped against the narrow oak dock. He pointed to the shore and there I saw Leif wearing a grin that overshadowed his orange and blue striped cloak, a gift from Gudruna. He was a point of calm amidst a sea of marching warriors, servants, villagers, and thralls who put the finishing touches on the details of the voyage. Next to him stood a knobby-kneed, barefoot girl aged about six summers. It was the dirty household thrall I had seen working in Godfrey's hall. "This can't be good," I mumbled as we approached the pair.

I opened my mouth to question and protest whatever he had in mind, but Leif held up a hand. I clamped that mouth shut because even though when he cut me off like that, it sent a bolt of fury coursing through my veins, I had learned the confident lad was usually correct in what he said next. "You have no say in the matter. You were bound to my father. We were exiled together. You're bound to me." I huffed and shook my head like an ambling toddler getting ready to fall to the ground in hysterics, but Leif was correct and I didn't argue. He continued. "Someone must take care of you. Our old goddess Friggas has clearly forgotten all about you. This is Aoife. She's to take care of you."

"A little young for a bride," I said, mockingly. "You think because I'm done plowing your sister, that I've given up on it altogether." I actually would give up women for a long while. If I was decidedly chaste, I could avoid the pain women brought to a young man's heart. "You couldn't find me someone older?"

Leif and Magnus laughed at me. I punched Magnus in the chest, hard. He gasped for air. Leif stopped laughing. "I couldn't afford someone older. Besides, she's not to marry you. I suppose if you can keep her alive long enough, you may take her as your wife when her time has come. I bought her to take the place of my mother and my sister for you. Thor knows they doted on you."

"They did not!" I protested a bit too much, then thought about it. "Perhaps your mother, but never that wretched sister of yours." I called her wretched, but at the time, I think that if she materialized out of the mist that I'd have, for the third time, proposed marriage, damning the consequences. By Hel, that red-haired woman had me enchanted.

"Why me? Why her?" I asked, pointing down to the waif with hair the color of barley chaff. It wasn't the bright hue of barley after a beautiful growing season. No, her hair better resembled the plant and husks after a wet spell when the creeping, brown blight took over. It wasn't a bad color, but it wasn't radiant. The drabness could have been due to the fact that Aoife's last bath may have been a year earlier. She scratched at lice in the barley chaff on her head.

Leif shrugged. "I already told you that you need someone to take care of you." He patted Aoife on the shoulder before shuffling past me. "As for 'why her,' I think you'll see. Don't be too long getting acquainted with the girl." He grabbed Magnus by the arm and dragged the helmsman with him. The two young men giggled like children half their age. "Godfrey will be down shortly and then we run off for our first true command and adventure."

"Your command," I mumbled. "I command nothing, not even my own life." I wasn't really angry about my lack of command, but I felt like being upset about something. I peered down at the young nymph-like thrall. I could hardly take care of myself and now I had to provide food, shelter, and clothing for a little girl – all with a few pennies. Oh, that frozen bitch, Hel, and the norns were having a time that day!

I heard a ruckus from up the hill toward the village, looked up, and saw that Godfrey was coming down to the dock. Loki was next to him and carried a hudfat that was stuffed with the king's armor and extra weapons. Gudruna walked on the other side of the king, her arm locked in his. The two, husband and wife, chatted easily. The way her eyes looked up to his told me she loved or at least respected the man.

The pair of royal lovers ignored Horse Ketil who ambled confidently after them swilling the day's mead. It was as if he held court of what he thought were his Manx citizens. Men clapped his back, wishing him good fortune on *his* adventure. One woman gave him a kiss on his cheek. Only Ketil's wife, Edana, was absent. With all the fanfare the Manx noble garnered, I saw that Godfrey was truly only a sometimes-king.

"Ahem," came a high-pitched, though soft voice from below. Aoife frowned while tugging on my jerkin. By the time I looked down, the girl held her arms crossed in front of her chest. I think her foot tapped. She had to be a relatively recently made slave, I thought, in order to show her new master such insubordination.

"Now you listen to me," I started with a wagging finger.

Aoife snatched the finger in her dirty hand and held it tightly. "You listen to me," she began in passable Norse with an accent that sounded a bit like Killian's. "Out of twelve children, I'm the twelfth. My father's a man who, other than managing to keep himself alive for too many years and broadcasting his seed into my mother's seed bed with amazing proficiency, has accomplished something less than little. My mother, tired and worn, is much the same. When I was young . . ."

"Young?" I asked the six year old.

"Young. Now don't interrupt because I'll say this just once. When I was young I remember walking along the shore line to the great sea that stretches out forever into the setting sun.

My mother was with me and had just finished telling me for the fifth time that day that she and my father could hardly figure out how to feed themselves in their old age, let alone feed me. I remember looking down in the basket that I carried and seeing how it was filled with whorled periwinkle for that night's soup. To me it seemed like enough food for a king. Then my mother gasped."

"Because of a basket of sea snails?"

"No, because that very boat right there was sailing up to the coast." Aoife pointed to *Raven's Cross*. "The old woman nearly died from fright on the spot. I asked her, what was the matter, and she said that the men on that boat were pirates and would kill us all and take what they would. My mother hiked up her skirts and ran home to warn the rest of the brood."

"And you didn't," I surmised.

"Of course I didn't!" she scolded, wrinkling her small nose. "My parents had already sold off my older sister, the eleventh child. It happened right after my mother finished telling her that they could hardly afford to feed themselves. My time was coming. So I took matters into my own hands and shouted after my ma. I still remember what I said. 'One day I'll own a ship like that! She'll have lovely oars! So I'll go with those pirates and stand in the stern. I'll steer their damned ship and put into ports or slide into shore. I'll take plunder and maybe kill a man or two!' That's what I said to her before I marched down to the beach alone and confronted that man there." This time she pointed to Godfrey.

"And did you steer *Raven's Cross*?" I asked, bending to one knee to study the feisty, filthy girl. One of her front teeth was missing. The other was half grown.

"No! So it is your responsibility to see that I am given the proper authority on our strandhogg. I mean to become rich and kill a few men."

I chuckled into her face. She tugged my beard, hard, so that I yelped.

Godfrey and Gudruna stepped next to me. The king asked, "I've heard that's the kind of response you normally get when you propose to a woman." Leif and Magnus were on the dock behind me laughing along with the king. Leif had not been shy in telling all of Man about my money woes as well as my on-again, mostly off-again romance with Freydis.

"But the king thanks you for sharing your periwinkle with the crew that day, Aoife" said Gudruna. King and queen giggled and moved off with Loki and Horse Ketil in tow to chat with Leif about the last minute preparations.

I couldn't believe that the king would accept Horse Ketil as one of his soldiers. If Godfrey allowed a man who was clearly opposed to his reign or could benefit from the king's fall to raid with him, then we were in a sorry spot indeed. Loki's voice echoed in my head, "Politics of the Irish Sea." I suppose we were desperate for every man we could get.

Aoife jerked my beard again so that I faced her. I poked her in the belly with a rigid finger. It was her turn to yelp. "You should find a way to run back to your parents," I said while she was doubled over. She spat out a curse or two in her native tongue.

The little, hard girl shrugged when she gathered her composure, again standing as tall and proud as her tiny frame could muster. "Dead. Killed by King Godfrey. The aged pair could only tempt fate long enough until the reaper came through the fields and harvested up their over-ripe carcasses." I marveled at how the cold girl held her parents in such disdain while I, hardly knowing mine, held them in the highest esteem. She went on, "The raiders took a few of my brothers as slaves and sold them at the Monday slave auction in Dyflin. Godfrey kept me for sport – he said I made him laugh – until that Leif of yours paid two English pennies for me. But now that I'm yours, I mean business. I'm not waiting on Providence any longer."

I rose to my full height and snatched the girl by her ear and pulled her after me toward the boats. "Come, my little Valkyrie."

"What's a Valkyrie?" she asked, swatting at my hand.

"I'd thought you'd know since you seem so precocious. They're the women who lead men up to Odin's hall once they die. I think you'll lead me to my death so that a real Valkyrie can take over once I fall." My hand began to sting where she kept up her incessant slapping. I let go of her and allowed her to follow on her own.

I gave Leif a stern glance as I shoved between him and Godfrey, but Leif's mind had moved to the mission. "The man shouldn't come," I heard my friend saying to the king.

"I wish it were that simple," answered the Godfrey. They pointed over to where Horse Ketil had plopped his rump on a hudfat and nursed his cup. "He and his wife are of no importance by themselves. Look at him," the king derided, "I'm sure he can't fight. He does nothing of value. However, the drunkard holds sway on the north end of the Isle. It is through Ketil that I've made a peace pact so that I can rummage about the sea and not worry about losing my island while away. In that way it is better to have my enemy close so I can see what he's doing."

Killian called down from *Raven's Cross*. "I side with our newcomer. I don't trust him."

"Shut up, priest," said Godfrey.

"I won't. We shouldn't take the village drunk on this strandhogg. 'Tis bad luck," answered Killian.

Godfrey waved off the priest with disgust. "You don't believe in luck, Christian."

"Nor do you, Christian," parlayed Killian with a twinkle in his dark eyes.

Leif threw up his hands. "Then we get him gut wrenching drunk. Pour Horse Ketil more and more ale. He'll suck himself to sleep," said Leif. "We'll be to Anglesey and back by the time he wakes up."

Gudruna shook her head. She whispered to Leif, "Have you learned nothing during your time here? Those of us of Norse descent are outnumbered on Man. There are always political reasons to consider. Ketil should be treated as a full member of the crew even if it means giving him undeserved favor now and again."

I could take no more of their yapping. Their talk of politics gave me a headache. I again reached to tug Aoife's ear and pull her away. She was quick this time. The girl smacked my hand and began marching to the *Charging Boar*. "It's about time we moved on from that talk. We're adventurers Halldorr, you and me. We don't have time to discuss this alliance or that faction. We're killers, hard stone killers." Aoife took one look at the boat that was to be her transport into her first glorious battle and stopped in her tracks. "I can see I'm going to have a lot of work to do to whip you into shape." With that, she scampered up the gunwale, using the strakes and an opened oar hole for toe holds.

And I you, Valkyrie, I thought.

CHAPTER 3

Horse Ketil drank, slept and vomited on our ship. Though politics had deemed it mandatory that he come with us, the king drew the line on actually sharing a longboat with the stinking creature or traitorous bastard, as the case may be. Even the two thralls on board, Tyrkr and Aoife, appeared cleaner and gave off a better scent than his oozing, fetid stench. I'm sure he heaved, not because of the ale, which was the same ale he'd been drinking for days or perhaps years. Our boat, short and wide compared to the king's, pitched on moderate swells that day. As we traversed every bottom, Horse Ketil's face showed that he felt the weight of the sour piss that danced in his stomach. The contents of his retching splashed onto the deck planking then splattered the strakes. Thankfully, the spray from the wind and sea washed the yellow streaks and puddles away, down into the bilge where the ballast stones sat securely on the ships strong ribs.

The skies looked like a rainstorm would blow in sometime. Huh! It always rained. If Greenland had nothing but rocks and ice, rocks and ice, rocks and ice, Man had nothing but rain, rain, rain. In the month since arriving, like the regular beat of a heart, it rained one afternoon and was dry the next, only to rain the following day and repeat itself again and again. The rocky terrain of the island was the only thing that kept its inhabitants from wallowing in shin deep mud for their entire miserable lives.

It was good to again be at sea. Her waves meant freedom to me. Today they were also the highway to riches, or death as the case may be.

Magnus was at the steering oar of *Charging Boar*. I was peeved since my thrall, the girl who was supposed to be my servant, was chatting with the helmsman, asking all she could about how to guide the ship. Aoife should have been fumbling with my whetstone and nearly cutting her fingers off with every passing wave as she put a new edge on my ancient, tarnished blade. I told her as much. Instead, she was aft starboard making Magnus laugh with wild yarns. He let her hold the rudder for a moment but the power of the sea scaled right up the steering oar – long ago fashioned from a mighty field oak – and rapped her on the cheek. She was sent tumbling to the deck. Magnus laughed. I smiled and went back to sharpening my own blade as I sat on the baggage. I suppose the girl was learning something that resembled a lesson even though she disobeyed her master.

Leif snaked his way through the men who sat or lay scattered about the planks, bags, and trunks. The wind was ample, filling our red and white striped sail like water filled a bowl, and our fellow Greenlanders rested their strong backs until the time came when they again dragged the oars through the surf. My young friend steadied himself on the oars over his head. They were stacked on the T-shaped brackets at the ship's center. "I don't like it that Horse Ketil is here," he said.

I slowly slid the stone down my blade's edge. "So throw him over. Even his fat wife would believe that the drunk toppled off the side. His followers will believe the same." I held my blade aloft and tried to catch what little sun filtered through the clouds that day. Nothing. Even if I had found light, the blade was so old, so tarnished that if I slowly twisted it in a sunny meadow, I'd be rewarded with the same dull sight. It would still kill a man, but I doubted it would help us against draugr.

Leif ignored my comment. "Even the priest says he's bad luck."

"What does the priest know about luck? He knows only his Providence." A gull swooped low, overhead, its droppings peppering our decks. We were already approaching land after our short journey. "Luck or fortune comes from our norns, Providence from the One God." I tapped the side of my blade with a wide palm. "I can show Horse Ketil what his fate may look like."

"Shut up, Halldorr," said Leif, shaking his head while looking down at Horse Ketil. The stinking beast moaned continuously. His face was a mixture of blue and green, smeared with yellow spittle. "I suspect something. Ketil is more than he seems."

"You see things that aren't there," I said. The truth was that I had seen the same signs. The king had spoken, though. Ketil was a member of our army. What could I do?

My blade quickly found its way into its wooden, fleece-lined scabbard. The sheath was an old one, like the sword. It had cracks down its entire length where the countless summers and winters had dried out the grain. I set the belt, blade, and scabbard amidst the baggage and lay back, resting my head on my clasped hands. "So do we even know where this mythical treasure is located?" I asked with my eyes closed.

"Didn't Eyvind tell you?" asked Leif.

I opened just one of my eyes to study the man. "I thought you listened to everything we said that night."

Leif smiled, recalling that night. "To a point. After the queen pulled me under my cloak a second time, I lost track."

"Was she as good as Tofa," I asked laughing. Tofa was a rotund woman with pendulous breasts who frequented many a man's longhouse in Eystribyggo. She was advanced in years, perhaps thirty, and was with young Leif the morning we left for our exile. She'd been his first.

Leif smiled too. "Halldorr, you can't compare women. They're all good in their own right."

"So she was," I guessed. "To have a queen," I said wistfully.

"Aye," was all that Leif said. "Gudruna's a fierce woman. She runs the island while Godfrey is away. I'll need a woman like her one day if I am to return to Greenland and become jarl."

"We won't be going anywhere and you won't become anything unless you can come up with a plan for Anglesey. I don't think this Maredubb will allow sixty armed men to trot around his island until we stumble across just the right barrow mound. Who knows? There may be one hundred of the hills. How will we know which to dig?"

"Just ask!" Aoife had climbed up the baggage pile from the aft side and was perched behind me. I saw the distinct mark of the rudder on her cheek. One half of her stringy barley hair dangled in her face. The other side was pulled up and tied in a knot near her crown. She used her dirty toes like the claws of a marten to clamber around on the heap. "How do you think I managed to stay out of the thrall auction at Dyflin? The king says that I amuse him. Well, how would he know that unless I spoke?"

"Shut your mouth, little rat," I said. I put my mitt against her chest and gave her a playful shove. She rolled into a sleeping crewman. Her toes were soon jammed into his face as she climbed back to her place next to me. I laughed at her. She smiled at me for the first time. It was a good smile.

"No, Halldorr, she's right," said Leif. Without looking his way, I knew that his face was bright and would show that his mind was turning on an idea, an idea given him by a scruffy rodent who talked too much.

• • •

After Leif had shouted over to Godfrey on *Raven's Cross* and the king agreed to his plan, we changed course, angling to port. Rather than landing in some cove or wharf on the north side of Anglesey, we would come in from the east. Young Leif ably served as our captain on the short journey. He called to our fellow Greenlanders on board, giving them zealous speeches about war that would only sound fine to men who'd never been in a real fight.

While Leif strutted around on the small ship, Ketil crawled to his rump. The green tint of his face had waned. "You're a big one," he said.

"So," I answered.

"I bet you're good in a scrap." Ketil pulled out a rag and wiped his face.

"We'll see," I huffed.

"Not very friendly are you?"

I shook my head. "No, I am the friendliest man you could meet. I have no time for someone who works against the king to whom I'm sworn."

He clicked his tongue in his cheek. "That is a problem." He patted my knee in a condescending manner. "Maybe you should reconsider that pledge. Maybe you've given an oath to a man who isn't the king."

I craned my neck to see the king standing on *Raven's Cross*. He looked regal to me. "I don't think so." Then I glowered at the man who sat against the gunwale. "If you think you should be King of Man or King of all the Isles, why don't you just show up with the farmers who supposedly support you and physically take it while Godfrey is weak?" That would shut him up, I thought.

It didn't.

He gave a shrug that told me he knew things I would never know. "Maybe Godfrey is so weak that I can do it without a fight." Ketil grinned with one half of his mouth and slid back to the planks. He closed his eyes and feigned sleep.

I thought it foolish to keep an enemy this close. But I understood nothing of politics. I was nimble with steel, not words.

• • •

As we ate a light midday meal of still-fresh bread and ale, Randulfr called from Godfrey's boat that it was time to turn back to starboard. Soon we found ourselves on the lee side of a fat protuberance from the looming Anglesey. The swells eased when the cape halted the northwesterly winds we had used all day. Our pace slowed, but there was just enough breeze to keep us moving and since both the king and Leif wanted us fresh for whatever befell us upon landing, our oars remained stowed. Horse Ketil remained quiet.

The island began to close in around us and when we were two or three vika away from our landing beach, I became anxious. It was my first invasion. After today, I'd be a raider. My heart sped up. I chewed on my lip as I slipped my second-hand mail up, over my head. The shirt had several of the iron rings missing so that I had to use some stray pieces of metal to bind them back together. That repair work caused one side of the mail to ride higher than the other. I cinched my belt tightly about my waist. My sword and my father's saex clattered against one another, telling me they, too, were anxious.

I ran fore, intentionally stepping on Horse Ketil, and peeked around the prow that had been carved in the shape of the ship's namesake. To port a red-tan, sandy beach stretched for perhaps two rost into the distance. That beach was what Godfrey had called Traeth Coch when we shouted our final plans as we sliced through the seas. I would have called it rjodrstrandr in my tongue since the beach and waters splashing against it reflected an almost red hue. Rightward from the long beach were tall, jagged cliffs that grew straight up from the sea as if the giants had pushed them up from beneath Midgard at the forming of the world. We wouldn't be making landfall there. The cliffs were too tall and wisps of smoke told me that a village rested on the plain above. At that time I believed that we were too small of a force to go kicking in the doors of a populous town. I was wrong about this, about what a few determined Norsemen could accomplish, but I get ahead of myself and will tell it all in due time.

Instead we made a direct heading for another beach, this one smaller than the first and without the red hue. Trees hung over it in places, making it appear nearly secret. It would provide easy access to shore and hidden cover for our longboats once we moved inland. To my knowledge the small patch of sand and rocks had no name.

Randulfr guided *Raven's Cross* and Magnus steered *Charging Boar* toward the north end of the narrow bit of sand so that our grounded boats would receive a less severe battering if the swells grew with the flow tide. Straight inland, west from our landing area, the land rose gently to the plain. An eroding, rocky cliff climbed from the beach on our right.

Even when I wasn't a raider and was just a simple boy, I found the last few moments just before a longboat shuddered into the shore exhilarating. The closer the land got, the faster it seemed we went. Gulls and other sea birds dashed around our heads, making it appear as if we soared over the very tips of the surf. The water began wearing caps of white as the waves spent the last of their energy, exhausted from racing across the ocean and seas from the Midgard Serpent all the way to land. The sound of those breakers, I thought deafening as a child. There was magic in those waves and they dumped it out in sound and power onto the dwelling place of men. They also dumped me and my men out on the shore that day. I remember hoping that we would carry their enchantment with us for riches and grandeur as we pillaged Anglesey.

Our momentum kept us going as our shallow draft allowed us to skip up the shore. Finally, the ship's weight and rules of nature took over and we slammed to a halt. My feet were pressed into the decking. My hands held the prow so I was prepared. Horse Ketil rolled and bumped his forehead on a sea chest. Aoife toppled off the baggage heap and landed on the drunken ass. She quickly pushed herself up and off of him. The young, dirty thrall appeared disgusted at having touched any part of Horse Ketil. Magnus again laughed at the little imp.

I leapt over the gunwale and splashed down into the rolling surf. Leif threw me a rope that was secured to a knee in the ship. I carried it to a mangled pile of stones and driftwood and tied it off. Men gathered shields and made a clattering racket as they poured over the sides after me. The noise they made, though great, was swallowed by the incessant pounding of the surf so that unless someone saw our approach, we had still not given away our venture. Looking at the eyes of the men, I could see our Greenlanders looked ready, but nervous. Godfrey's experienced raiders appeared only ready – ready to steal and kill.

Our raid had begun.

• • •

"Tyrkr, you'll stay with the ship," instructed Leif. "Protect the supplies from the claws of Welsh children and wanderers."

"How am I to earn the wealth for my freedom if I stay with the ship? Besides, I'm a better fighter than you," protested the German thrall. He was right, I thought.

"Someone needs to protect our route out of here. Don't worry about the plunder. You'll get a fair share, just from your willingness to go." Leif turned away, finished with the conversation.

85

Godfrey, on his horse, was giving similar instructions to Turf Ear on *Raven's Cross*. He had to shout it three times. When the experienced warrior finally understood what his duty was to be, he frowned. His grumbles were exceptionally loud afterward due to his affliction, even though Turf Ear probably thought he spoke only to himself.

It was to be just the two of them guarding our ships. It was not really enough. Normally, we would have left a few more men behind to guard the boats, but we were already shorthanded. Mostly, we hoped the norns would spin us luck so that no one would look down in the isolated cove while our boats were there. Even if they were noticed, they would be safe from all but the hardest fighters. Tyrkr and Turf Ear, working in concert, could take on a dozen inexperienced men.

"Why don't I leave my present behind?" I asked, pointing to Aoife. "One look at the little urchin will send the stoutest of men for the hills."

Leif wasn't amused. "She'll either run off or, worse yet, give away the boats' position. They'll be burning by nightfall," he said pointing to our ships.

"I can only hope she runs off. I can hardly afford to feed myself."

Aoife was fuming. "I'm not here to nap on a grounded boat." She reached out her tiny mitt. "Now give me that saex of yours."

"So you can cut me?"

"So I can save your pathetic life when the time comes," she answered.

"We'll see," I said.

"We have to move," Godfrey called. The king was already inching his horse inland. The beast kicked its hooves in celebration when it walked up out of the loose sand. "We're not here to chat."

Leif nodded to the king. The young man spurred a crewman out of *Charging Boar* by smacking his shoulder. He turned again to Aoife and me. "She's coming with us. She's part of the plan we worked out with Godfrey and I trust her. You should too." I cursed my lot and stuck my paw up to the longboat. I grabbed her mangy dress. She was light and I plopped her down in the surf with one arm. The little thrall, with wide eyes, gave me a triumphant look all the way down.

Like a child myself, I stomped off after the king and his band. They were already snaking their way up the path that led to the upper lands. I grumbled to Loki, who trotted at the rear of Godfrey's force. "I'm supposed to now take orders from a thrall. I am to trust her no less. I, after having my heart tortured by a real woman, am to trust a miniature woman and thrall." I huffed. "The world is upside down."

Loki was giggling. He didn't really care about my plight. In truth, it wasn't anything more than an inconvenience. Yet, it was something foisted on me by another and that fact made me hate it. Loki glanced my way. "Don't you even have a war helmet?" he asked.

"Reindeer nuts!" I said. I stopped and trotted back past Leif and the others as they ascended the winding path on the hill.

Tyrkr was already holding the helmet in his hand when I ran up to the gunwale. "You might want this," he said as he tossed it down to me.

I placed the old, tarnished, and battered helmet on my head. Most of the soft sheepskin cap inside had long ago dry-rotted away so that the left side of the iron helm rested against my head. I had meant to get it fixed before leaving Man, but had forgotten as it was buried in my luggage. Now, a single, lucky blow from any blunt weapon on that left side of my helmet would rattle and crack my skull. I turned and ran after our war band, wondering what kind of weapons a draugr would employ. Were they sharp, dull, or ephemeral?

I fought the sand and pebbles up the beach. I mumbled and cursed. Ahead Aoife skipped. Ketil teetered. He hummed a sailing tune like he walked along friendly shores gathering shells. I was a novice raider who'd thrown his lot in with misfits. I had forgotten my helmet, worried about a traitor, and babysat a young, deluded girl.

It was not the best of beginnings.

• • •

And it would get much worse before it got better.

"Help," called Aoife as meekly and pathetically as she could. Killian had taught her the Welsh version of the word after she said she didn't know it. At the time, the priest had chastised her for not knowing another Celtic tongue that was so related to hers. I didn't know what a Celt was. The girl didn't care what the priest said. She insisted it was more about feeling than getting the word just right.

Godfrey, who was mounted on a dappled charger, had held the beast's speed back and allowed her to pace at just an amble. The king had let Leif lead our band on a circuitous path around the nearest village, giving it a wide berth, and did not want to get far ahead of the rest of his men who remained on foot.

My creative friend said he was looking for a certain sight – a lone worker – and a certain scent – human waste. Godfrey grumbled under his breath at the crazy boy to whom he had given so much power. However, the king could see, as most men could, that behind the youthful appearances of Leif, he owned a quiet wisdom that surpassed his years. That didn't stop Randulfr from occasionally speaking questions into the king's ear.

We passed by homesteads and farms where groups of men worked in fields together. Leif was careful to stay in woods or in low streambeds, sheltered from view. At last, he stopped us in a long, wide copse of trees when, in a sweeping land below us, Leif spotted a single man working in a field of green oats. It was the first time in my life I'd seen oats growing in a field. My three homelands were just too harsh for such grasses. The plants were already more than shoots, quite far along when I compared them to the grains we had ever been able to raise in Norway, Iceland, or Greenland at any time of the year, let alone this early in the season.

The farmer bent over and tugged up weed after weed before they would choke out his coming bounty. He tossed their green dying corpses into a basket that sat next to him in the field, occasionally kicking it along as he moved onto the next patch of unwelcome grasses or nascent thistle.

"Help," Aoife nearly whispered again. Leif had told her to err on the side of too soft when she called. It was best not to scare the man, he said. We all stood in a thick part of the woods several fadmr in from the meadow. Leif had found several piles of human feces, dried and crusty and had us plant ourselves among it. Godfrey, whose horse was held by Loki some distance in the woods, wrinkled his nose at the thought of standing in another man's waste. Killian made some joke about how life itself meant traipsing around in the refuse of others. Neither I nor the others laughed at it.

The farmer stood and stretched his back, pushing on his hips with his hands. He peered up at the sun and carried his basket heaping with broadleaf weeds and thin, invasive grasses to the edge of the field, closer to the forest. After taking a drink of water using a hollowed wooden cup dipped into a leaky wooden bucket that sat at the field's edge, the worker walked up the hill toward the woods.

"Help," called Aoife again.

The man tipped his head as he marched up the hill as if he wasn't sure whether he heard anything or not. He shook his head, convinced he had not. His hands went to his trousers and he untied a fraying rope that held them up. Within one stride in that copse of trees, the man pulled his manhood out and stepped behind a thicket to release his bladder. He was out of my line of sight now.

"I knew he'd come up here," whispered Leif, making a show of pinching his nose. "I smelled his morning dung. And capturing him quietly is better than rushing into the middle of a valley and having an entire village as witnesses." Leif looked down to where Aoife lay on a path just five steps away and nodded.

"Help," she called, just a bit louder.

We couldn't see the man. We could have easily chased him down and hoped that no one in a neighboring field saw us, but it was best if he simply disappeared until nightfall or the next morning when we were done with him. The worker would then be able to tell tales about being captured by dangerous Vikings and impress all the lasses of his village with his bravery. That is, once we were gone and our need for stealth had passed. So we waited.

After what seemed half a day, we heard his voice call, "Who's there?" he asked, still unseen.

Killian, who lay down behind a fallen tree trunk next to the path, whispered to the girl, "Just say your name, dear one."

"Aoife," she answered weakly. "Aoife." I chuckled to myself at just how frail the minute, but resilient, creature sounded.

"Are you alright?" the farmer asked. The voice was coming no closer.

"Help. Ankle." Aoife was completely pitiable.

"Where are you from?" the man asked, suspicious. Bandits were common in everyone's woods, on Anglesey, in Norway, everywhere.

I saw Killian bite his lip, puzzled. Say someplace too far, and the man would wonder why she was alone away from home. Say someplace too close, and the worker might ask more questions about people he knew. "Say Llangyngar. You're from Llangyngar."

Aoife repeated the conniving priest's words.

"Where are you?" the man's voice was moving closer now. I thought I could hear his feet falling on the path.

I nervously gripped my sword. It is humorous to think about now that I've been in what seems like a hundred battles. An unarmed farmer was walking into a trap with nearly sixty young and strong, armored and armed Norsemen and yet I was on edge. I'm embarrassed to admit it, even though by the time another man educated in Latin finds this parchment with my musings etched across it, I'll be long dead. Godfrey frowned at me that day and held up a hand, calming me. The king hissed, "He's no good to us dead. I think he'll succumb easy enough."

And he did – sort of.

All of a sudden he was next to us on the path, crouching down to the ailing girl, who had begun to hold her ankle and whine as he approached. I think she was even able to produce a few counterfeit tears. "What are you doing out here? You must be six miles from home if you're from Llangyngar?" he asked.

Since most people never moved beyond three miles from the spot of their birth throughout their entire lives, it was a fair set of questions.

In answer, Aoife scurried to her feet before the rest of us had even stepped from our hiding places in the woods. The eager Irish thrall latched a hand on the man's shaggy brown hair and tossed a leg over his back like she mounted a pony. She used her other hand to club the top of his head like a carpenter strikes with his hammer.

The man rose up and turned to run back toward the field. He scanned the forest for bandits while grabbing Aoife by her hair. I stepped out to cut off his retreat. The two of us locked eyes. The terrified farmer broke into a full run in an attempt to break through to freedom before his cause was hopeless. "Run!" the man screamed. He listed what sounded like a host of names and shouted again, "Run! To the king, run!" He jerked down on Aoife's head and tossed her to the side of the path so that her little form bounced and skidded against a tree, unmoving.

I don't know what it was that happened. If you ask me today, I'll say it made no sense for me to get so upset about a thrall, a girl no less! But back then, in my youth when I had something of a soft place in my heart for such things, I became enraged. I pushed Brandr from behind and shoved my way onto the path. My mind was not totally lost, however. I didn't want to kill the Welshman so I slammed my tarnished sword into its old, cracked scabbard. Just as the farmer was set to sprint past us into the field, I stretched my great paw out and snatched the one thing I could. My fingers became tangled in his shaggy hair and I gripped it, knuckles white. Then my feet became planted, almost rooted, on the packed road and I heaved with every bit of my vast, youthful strength. The farmer's feet continued running forward and then flew into the air while his head jerked back. I never let him come back to rest. Instead, I wrapped my free hand into his hair and spun him around once then twice before letting him fly. "Run! Run!" He was screaming maniacally as if someone else had been in the field with him. It was too late to worry about that. I fell backward onto my rump while he shot into the king, both men tumbling over one another into Killian, whose small body was nearly swallowed by the rolling mess of arms and legs.

Leif grabbed Magnus by the arm and the two ran toward the field to see if there were more workers. They disappeared around the curve in the path. I panted from the brief moments of excitement.

The farmer had skidded to a halt, dazed, where several of Godfrey's men hoisted him up by his shoulders. He dizzily blinked and began his rambling pleadings. Killian was crawling back to his feet, his robes torn and dirty, but appearing no worse for the wear. Godfrey lay sprawled on his back. His body was racking and shaking. I thought I had killed the king and what I saw were his death throes.

Then I heard his laughter. King Godfrey stared up at the underside of the forest canopy and roared. It was too loud, but nobody was going to tell him that and deprive him of his mirth. The entire band then looked at me and joined him when he propped himself up on his elbows. "That was one way to do it, I suppose," the king said. "When we conquer the bloody Scots of Dal Riata, I know who will be our first man to take part their games of strength. I think Halldorr knows how to throw the weight."

I still huffed from my exertion and anger and, ignoring their jest, ran to Aoife. She had managed to roll over without assistance and with large eyes the girl watched me. Aoife gathered up a great smile beneath those huge eyes. Her face was dirtier than usual. "We make a good team," she said as if nothing had happened. She even yawned.

The men now laughed at me over my concern for the girl. "He's never tried to save me like that," Magnus joked, as he walked back with Leif.

Embarrassed, I said, "She's an investment. I don't want my property damaged by a Welshman. Thralls are expensive enough. What did you find?"

"We weren't as fortunate as we thought," said Leif, walking in behind Magnus. "There was a swale where another half dozen workers toiled. They were already running in the opposite direction when Magnus and I walked out of the trees. They heard him and saw us."

"But they saw just two of you," I said. "They'll think that a simple group of highwaymen came through."

"Perhaps," said Killian in a way that meant he didn't believe it.

"We best get this man to tell us what he knows and then move," said Godfrey, losing his sense of humor. "If they saw the two of you with your long hair, mail, helmets, and swords, they know that Norsemen are afoot. It won't be long until a rider brings King Maredubb and his army, searching for a fight."

And so began our race against time.

• • •

The farmer knew what and who we were, having heard tales, especially from his relatives who lived nearer the coast, about what Norseman did when they came to visit Wales. Despite his well-justified fear, he performed ably. He led us into the heart of Anglesey, skirting many small villages and not once shouting out for help even when a mounted patrol trotted by. Our captive seemed to believe Killian when the priest promised that we would set him free once we had our treasure. He should have believed us. We, especially Godfrey's crew, were hardened men, but what we wanted more than anything from the farmer's island was wealth. Spilling a peasant's blood might be good sport for the barbaric in the world. It wasn't, however, our objective.

We walked briskly, eating and pissing on the run. Sometimes the king would trot ahead on his dappled beast and scout out the beautiful countryside which had the bountiful green life of early summer growing from end to end.

Killian took the time to educate me on the island. Anglesey, he said, was part of some ancient kingdom called Gwynedd which included the island and a part of the mainland. Maredubb tried to run it as a king of old, but faraway Aethelred of England was the true master. Gwynedd, like the other Welsh kingdoms, had ceased being a sovereign power over a hundred years earlier. Hundreds of years before that, those infamous

Romans had a base or two on Anglesey and many forts dotting the whole of Wales. Killian said he knew all these tales because the Romans left their stone ruins behind as permanent markers. This fact amazed me since every human structure I had ever seen would have rotted away and been swallowed by the mud within a few score of years. My people had no good stone with which to work. I came from a line of woodworkers.

Even more astounding than the Romans supposed prowess at building things was that all their histories had been written down. Why would anyone record the mundane events of life? I wondered it then, for I was an illiterate. But here I huddle and write and write and write. I write sentences that describe me cleaning my ears or killing a man while he evacuated his bowels. My excuse is that I am well past the years where living is anything close to exhilarating. By writing my tales, I hope to bring them back to my mind's eye. I'd relive them if I could. Why the Romans of ancient Anglesey, most young soldiers, thought to pen anything still puzzles me.

As night fell around us, Godfrey rudely told the priest and me to clamp shut our yapping mouths. Our pace slowed as we moved from woods to woods, careful to not trample crops like a herd of escaped cattle so that if our quest took us into the next day, we'd not alarm any probing, curious Welshmen. We weren't afraid of a confrontation, but we weren't certain where this King Maredubb was and what his army might look like. We were confident, however, that by morning a runner from our captive's village would alert the Welsh king and he would very soon send soldiers out to kill us. Speed and stealth were our only weapons at that moment.

The moon had risen high and bright very early in the night. Soon the few clouds that had covered the bright orb at dusk and beyond blew into the distance, leaving a bluish-black sky that was devoid of stars. It was then that the squawking farmer held out both hands and, I guess, told us to stop, for Killian immediately held up his hand. The farmer pointed out across a rolling terrain where several cows calmly chewed their cud, staring back at us. Calves obediently stood next to their mothers. In the center of their pasture was another copse of trees, like the one in which we then stood. The priest talked to our captive, back and forth.

"He says our treasure is in there." The priest pointed to the trees in the meadow. "He asks that we not take him with us if we mean to unearth it," said Killian, looking up at Godfrey. "He's pale with fright. He's heard the same stories that Eyvind shared with Halldorr."

"What did you tell him?" asked the king.

"That a Christian has nothing to fear from a draugr army," said Killian.

"Good. He comes with us." The king dropped down from his horse with a thud and handed his reins to the nearest man. Godfrey scanned the pasture for prying eyes before boldly stepping out and marching toward the dark grove of trees. The rest of us followed, careful not to clatter our weapons and tools against one another. I patted one of the heads of one of the cows as I passed. Its great tongue curled up to lick my hand. I gave it a playful pop on its snout with my balled fist. It retreated a half step and then followed me to the edge of the woods that hid the treasure. It had the sense to halt. We men did not.

When I entered the dark grove from the west end, a chill racked down along my spine. It radiated outward, even creating the visible bumps of geese on my bare arms. I shivered. I looked at Magnus who, though he had the brains to say nothing, appeared just as frightened. Leif, on the other hand, went fearlessly in pursuit of Godfrey. In moments we had reached the center of the small forest. My young friend scrambled up an out-of-place looking mound in the middle of the isolated copse of trees. Godfrey was already at the top, stomping on the ground and probing the earth with his sword to see if he could find an indication of where the best place to dig would be.

If either of our leaders, the young Leif or the experienced raider, Godfrey, was apprehensive, each hid it well. Godfrey was chuckling to himself, no doubt already counting his new found wealth and listing all the men and ships he could buy with it. The Christians with us were mumbling prayers. The followers of the old gods gripped their swords, readying for what might be their greatest quest.

Aoife dashed off around the perimeter of the large mound which was a dozen fadmr in diameter. She started at the base then quickly scaled a rim made of massive stones that rested on their sides and skirted the entire barrow. Who put the stones there in the first place had to be the giants of yore. Aoife skipped from one foot to the next and began humming a tune I'd not heard before. She disappeared around the south side of the large circle, oblivious to the fact that we were in unknown territory with ghosts and kings and now maybe giants soon to be hunting us.

"Halldorr," rasped Leif. "I don't think the king wants to chase your thrall around Wales."

"My thrall," I huffed and then immediately jumped up onto the immense stones and walked around after her.

While I chased my quarry, the king called out in a hushed voice. "We dig here." He stabbed his sword down into the very center of the top of the burial mound. The blade rang as it swung back and forth. "Take a moment to eat. Then we dig until we uncover the treasure store." Godfrey gave Leif an appreciative grin, already acknowledging the young man's part in the king's ascent.

I looked over my shoulder and though none of the Christians were supposed to be afraid of the spirits lurking in the barrow, to a man they all moved their hands up and down and across their bodies in the way Christians do. The Norsemen relaxed their grips on their swords and kissed their mjolnir amulets if they had them or simply plopped down on their rumps to eat before their backs were broken digging up the ancient monument.

Horse Ketil, who had thus far been remarkably quiet, was arguing with Killian for the priest to give him a second share of ale. "You've had your allotted dose. You drank it all!" protested Killian.

"Irish ass," said Ketil.

"Manx traitor," answered Killian.

I realized that I had walked all the way around the circumference of the grave back to where I started. That's when I panicked. This time it was not because of my love of, or care for, the little Valkyrie child, but rather I was afraid she had run off and would intentionally or accidentally warn a village or, worse yet, Maredubb himself. I thought we could fight two times our number. An army would be another story.

Without letting on that I may have just lost the girl, I circumnavigated the hill a second time. I was more careful and peered out into the dark grove of alders surrounding the barrow. Once I saw a flash of dirty white and thought it was her, but a harmless bleat told me it was a lamb, probably owned by the same family who owned the cows. I stopped on the northeast side of the circle and rested my hands on my hips. I scanned the trees, this time with my ears. A grunt and then a scratching sound reached out and surprised me from behind.

I faced the shadowed hillside. Above, moonlight shined down on Leif's and Godfrey's position as if Thor marked out the location of the riches for us. For the first time, I noticed that this corner of the barrow had a rough stone path that cut toward the center from the large stones at the perimeter. In the dark it looked like several more of the enormous stones had been stood upright and stacked onto one another in a disorganized fashion. It was like a sealed door into the heart of the mound and into the world of the spirits beyond. When the door again grunted at me, I jumped back off the stone walkway and drew my sword. I nearly toppled over. I was young and my sword shook in my hand. My head conjured images of ghosts.

Leif and Godfrey ignored me, chatting in hushed tones. I thought that I must have already been killed by the first grunting draugr who escaped from the grave. I just didn't know it for certain. I hadn't felt it when the ghost reached into my chest and stopped my heart. It was true after all, the girl had been my Valkyrie and she did lead me to my quick death. All I had to do now was find her so she could help me finish my journey to Odin's hall. I relaxed at the thought of the immortal life of revelry that awaited me around the master god's hearth. My sword steadied.

"The little lying bastard." It was my Valkyrie's voice. She'd come to lead me. My head darted back and forth. The sound came from the walkway. I peeked over the perimeter stones and saw nothing.

Aoife's tiny head squirted out from under the shadows of one of the rocks. The girl grunted and wriggled until I saw her shoulders. Then an arm shot out from under the collapsed entranceway. She carried a sputtering torch. This caught the attention of the king, who called down harshly, "Put the light out. We don't need to call attention to ourselves!"

"Oh, tell the useless king to be quiet. He dragged us all the way here for nothing," grumbled Aoife. "It'll be a long while before I get excited about going a-Viking with the likes of you."

"I said put the torch out!" screamed Godfrey as loudly as he dared.

"I'll ram the torch into your mouth," said Aoife. Before the king could even rise to his feet, offended, the thrall shouted up to him again. "There's no treasure. Unless you count part of a human skull, a few rotten wooden shields, and some tarnished copper jewelry, we came all this way for nothing. King Maredubb will chop you down tomorrow and I'll have a new owner to train." She looked at me, disgusted.

Leif and the king threw down their packs of smoked fish and barreled down the hill toward us. "Where did you get the torch?" I asked the girl.

"In there," Aoife said pointing toward the walkway. "I saw the hole and crawled in. It kept going down a passage way that widened and grew tall enough for me to stand." The girl rubbed her head. "I bumped into the torch and stepped on jasper stones. I married the two and made fire."

"How am I to believe you?" asked the king.

"Because I have a burning torch in my hand." Thankfully, the waif didn't add, "You idiot!" Her tone was sufficient.

"I warn you girl that I may easily tire of your insubordination." The king raised his hand as if to strike her face. "How am I to believe that there is no treasure without digging?"

The foolish girl didn't back down or cower. "You may dig all you wish, but there is no treasure. And I'd not dig up there," she said pointing to where Godfrey's great sword still shone in the moonlight. "Once you've wasted most of the night and moved a mountain of earth, you'll come to a terrific slab of stone that is held up from beneath by a carved, stone pillar and stacked stone walls. That slab won't be moved by you men before next week."

The king swore to the old gods and gave Leif an icy stare, taking back the praise given by his previous glance. It was Leif and the amorous Queen Gudruna who had pushed Godfrey to entertain this quest in the first place. Godfrey even gave me a dirty glance, remembering that it was "my" dice that helped him make his decision. If Aoife was correct and the crypt was empty, Godfrey risked the last of his most loyal of men and his very kingdom on a fairy tale. "The Troublesome!" the king cursed, referring to Eyvind, the skald who had told me the story just a week before. The king wanted to blame anyone but himself.

He stepped down to the mangled pile of enormous stones that covered the entranceway. "We've still got men's backs and a war charger." The king rested a wide palm on one of the cool rocks. "We can move these enough to get some of the men in to see if the girl tells the truth." Angry now and raising his voice, Godfrey shouted toward the men over the mound. "Killian!"

The priest trotted around the man-made hill and saw the concern on his king's face. He awaited orders. Killian's dark features danced on his face in the fading, sputtering light of Aoife's torch.

"Bring the men over here, now. Bring the ropes and my horse." The king was quick and efficient. Sensing the urgency, Killian nodded and ran back to gather everything.

"The girl has no reason to lie," I said, not defending her. It seemed the truth to me, for Aoife wanted glory and wealth as much as any man. It also seemed true that if there was no treasure; that meant the legend was wrong. And if it was mistaken, then there would be no draugr to fear. Though frustrated that I'd still be poor, I was more than pleased that I'd not have to fight spirits.

Godfrey dropped his rump onto the rim of stones that encircled the barrow. "Perhaps not," he said, cooling down.

Aoife set a surprisingly gentle hand on the king's shoulder. He looked at it out of the corner of his eyes. Godfrey gave a weak grin and brushed her hand with equal gentleness. "But we've come all this way. My Kingdom of the Isles will no longer exist or it will be another man's in a year's time if I can't replenish her with a real army and fleet of ships." He was suddenly grave.

Leif, reflective, moved back up to the top of the mound and sprawled out on his back amidst the grasses. Godfrey craned his neck to see what my friend was up to. I remembered the night Leif had spent on the barrow, a much smaller one, in Greenland. "It's best to leave him alone, King Godfrey. He's thinking, about our situation tonight and your predicament as king."

"I need every back working on that stone," the king protested, still bent on unearthing what may or may not be inside.

"He's still a lad. His back is weak and he'd be in the way," I said. "Besides, when left alone, Leif can solve any man's problems. Then it's just up to the man to follow through."

Godfrey opened his mouth to issue forth another complaint, but Killian came around the hill with a long rope draped over his shoulder. The other men filed after him carrying shovels, more rope, and leading the horse. They still gnawed on the last of their dinner scraps while they piled empty hudfats which were ready to receive the mound's riches. Even the captured farmer, who was now untethered, came around with eyes wide, curious with a mixture of fear and awe splashed across his face.

We went to work. Aoife crawled back into the tiny hole with her torch and caught the end of the rope that had been sent down a crevice. With her thin arm she stuck the same end out another crack. The rope was tied off, laced around an alder, and cinched across the horse's shoulders and chest. Men found a place all along the rope's length to get a grip. Several others found solid footing nearer the stone so they could help push it up and out of the way.

"Now!" the king rasped.

Every man sucked in a last big breath and heaved. Killian held the charger's reins. The small priest stepped backward. The dappled horse obeyed the silent command and the muscles of her shoulders bulged, her shod hooves pressing down into the sod that surrounded the hill. The rope creaked as it slowly stretched. Men methodically stepped and pulled. Grunting began, jaws clenched, teeth grinding. The workers themselves had moved an ell from where they started. The stone had not budged.

I remained at the stone and wedged my large frame between the mound and the boulder at an uncomfortable angle. I pressed my feet into the earth and my shoulders and hands into the cool rock. I had entirely forgotten about my earlier fears. Draugr or not, I meant to move what the ancients had placed in our way. Like the charger, my shoulders bulged, my neck strained. A rumbling groan rolled around in my chest.

The king and Magnus used the sturdiest of our wooden shovels to pry at the stone. Godfrey stood up the hill with his back to the rock and pressed down on his lever. Magnus stood in the dark walkway that led to the pile of stones. He hung with all his weight on the handle. Another man, who had not found enough room to tug on the rope came up behind Magnus, reached up, and also hung from the same shovel. The oak handle started to turn downward. The stone did not move.

We toiled for many moments until King Godfrey called out in frustration. "Stop!"

It took no further encouragement. The rope went limp. Men panted and wiped sweat from their foreheads, frustrated that despite their work, nothing had been accomplished. Godfrey sank down in the turf of the mound, catching his breath.

"Do we have another rope?" asked Magnus.

"Aye," said Killian. "But we've no more horses."

"There are cows in the field around this grove," said Aoife's voice from the passage. A tiny stream of light flickered out through one of the holes and lit up the king's face.

The king raised his eyebrows. "I knew there was a reason I kept you as my own when I should have sold you or sent you to the ocean's bottom for fun. Horse Ketil, make yourself useful. Brandr and Loki, help the man. Bring us a cow or two."

The king's pledged men jumped to their feet. They gathered the extra rope from Killian and dove into the trees. Horse Ketil stood and sighed before making a show of slowly moving after his fellow cattlemen. As each moment of the raid passed, his defiance of the king's wishes was becoming more open.

Killian frowned while watching him go. "I don't trust a man like that," he said.

After several long moments and countless curses echoing from the pasture, each of the three men returned leading a cow. Behind the three cows hopped three calves that appeared to be a month or so old. Godfrey's face lit with excitement. Loki said, "We caught the calves first. Their overprotective mothers came nearer and we slipped the ropes from the calves to the cows. It worked better than I expected."

"And who thought of that?" asked the king, ready to give praise.

"Horse Ketil," answered Brandr, glumly.

Surprised, Godfrey said, "And what made you think of that? I've never known you to have a way with animals." What the king meant was, "Why would you help me?"

Horse Ketil slapped his rope into the awaiting hands of another man. The Manx noble strutted toward the barrow in the clearing's center. With his back to the king, Ketil said, "I saw the cows and their engorged tits. My Edana is not much to look upon, but she has great tits. Your cousin has great tits, Godfrey."

The king clenched his jaw.

"It's King Godfrey," grumbled Killian.

Ketil nodded in a way that said, for now. "I saw the tits and thought of how much a calf yearns for milk. I thought then that the mother's instinct must be to protect her young. From there it was easy to capture the small calves. A simpleton could have come up with the plan."

"A simpleton did," murmured Killian.

Godfrey was standing again. "Shut up, priest," he said quietly. The king walked over to the Manx noble. "We have to give praise where it is due, especially if we still have hope for the truce to last on Man. We want a unified homeland, Norse and Manx. You did well, Horse Ketil. Do you see what you can accomplish with a few hours between your cups of ale? Think of what we can accomplish if we work together. You make your family on Man proud. I'll gladly convey as much to them." Then the king, in a moment of misplaced philanthropy, said, "If you still want your divorce from your woman, I'll see that Killian pushes it at the Tynwald."

Killian and several others uttered short gasps. The priest was shaking his head.

"I don't want a divorce from my fat woman, king," said Ketil, bowing sarcastically. "How else am I to have any Norse support if I get rid of her? Besides, her giant tits will be complementary to Gudruna's meek chest when I take her for a second wife after you're gone for good."

King Godfrey's face turned red with anger. His hand was tugging on the axe in his belt. Ketil stuck his chin out almost daring Godfrey to strike. The king did not kill Ketil, however. I would have, but the king was king for a reason. Occasionally, he could demonstrate restraint.

"Not yet, Godfrey," Killian was saying. "It's not worth it. Not yet."

My king swallowed his anger. "In that case, dear Ketil, since you so love your bride, I'll encourage Killian to continue to exasperate Edana's pleas." Godfrey's hand left the axe.

Ketil gave a wicked smile. "That suits me just fine."

A brief awkward silence followed. Mumbling began among the crews. Loki leaned in and whispered. "I know that I'd want to kill the Manx bastard. I know that Godfrey wants to grant a divorce and be done with both his cousin and Ketil, but we can't let it happen. For now, it's better for the king to keep them together. We don't want to create any more enemies, especially any on our own island. We've already got enough."

All I could do was shake my head. I understood nothing about alliances. I was a political idiot. I knew men and their hearts. I wore mine on my sleeve for all to see. Ketil did the same. If it were me I would take him at his word. I would believe he meant to harm the king. He just waited and waited for the right time. There was nothing to gain by keeping him alive. I would have chopped him in half on the grave under the watchful eyes of the moon. But those were my simple thoughts. Godfrey, Loki, and the others had families on Man they had to protect. They earned money from the trading that went on in the main port. They remembered how hard they had to work to take control of the island in the first place. They were willing to endure a verbal slight here and there from a man who commanded a few farmers. They were willing to listen to Ketil's blustering until the day Godfrey's army was again strong enough to deter the native Manx population from rising up against him.

The king understood the realities of his situation. It is why he was eager for treasure, for the riches in that mound would buy him his army. Godfrey turned his attention back to his grand project and began issuing orders for the cows and the ropes. Horse Ketil had more to say, however. He plopped down while untying Killian's rucksack. "I'll take my second helping of ale. And I'm not going to work on any of this treasure hunting tonight. I feel like I should be ready for whatever tomorrow might bring and I want to be fresh."

Godfrey frowned. He motioned to the priest. "Give the man ale, Killian. I really don't want to hear any more from him. Maybe he'll drink himself into a stupor. Then we can work in peace."

Displeased, but smart enough to choose his battles, the priest complied. He pushed Ketil out of the way and rummaged through the pack and gave our resident traitor a small pot of ale. The reliably unreliable drunkard leaned back on the hill and began nursing. It was clear to me, as it likely is to you, that Ketil was waiting for his moment to strike. But when? Tomorrow? If he did, would Godfrey be ready?

Magnus slapped me. He tugged on my arm and we returned to our work.

After the second rope was tied around the stone with Aoife's assistance and strung around another tree and secured to all three cows, each of our crew members found his position and heaved. This time the second rope afforded room so every man, with the exception of Leif, who stared at the sky, and Horse Ketil, who had quickly tipped over to pretend to fall asleep, had room enough to help. Even the captured farmer offered his back to the project. He was now completely curious about what would be found in the barrow that had been a part of his island's legends for generations.

The additional six or seven skippund worth of weight tugging on the ropes did the trick. The stone began scraping against the others as one end slipped upward while the other end stayed put. It quickly moved high enough that the shovels Magnus and the king used as pry bars no longer helped. Both men scrambled underneath the colossal stone, putting themselves in precarious positions should either of the ropes snap. They wedged their backs against the rock and shoved.

The stone felt lighter the higher it traveled so that once we got it moving into a nearly upright position, its weight and momentum took over. It toppled out of the pathway, crashing into the mound with a monstrous thud before slowly tumbling down into the great ring of stone, wrapping the rope around itself and jerking the cattle and horse back toward the trees we had used as pulleys.

We gave a modest cheer, but our exuberance was short-lived as Godfrey snatched his shovel and began digging out a path under the fallen stone so that the ropes could be unwound. Soon Magnus then Randulfr joined the king at tossing aside turf and dirt. Others began untying the knots and tried to tug them out from under the rock. They quickly discovered that the king was correct and a path would have to be dug.

Aoife climbed out with her torch to shed additional light where the men worked. "King Godfrey, there is nothing of worth in there." The king ignored her.

"Shut your mouth," I told the girl. We were on the hunt and would not be put off by good sense. To my astonishment, the girl did shut up. Aoife only shook her head in disgust. She stood there until the ropes were free and then crawled into her cave to repeat the process for the next stone. And the next and the next.

• • •

Dawn was upon us. The calves nursed on their mothers' teats. Horse Ketil napped. Leif had sat up, but said nothing since climbing atop the mound. The men, exhausted, dropped onto their rumps unable to mount a measurable defense against a single draugr let alone a legion of the ghosts, should they come. Randulfr tried to organize the men into something resembling a formation in case it was not the specters, but Maredubb who came. No one moved.

Godfrey crouched at the entranceway to the grave. I held Aoife by the back of her tunic, preventing her from tearing back into the passage that had become a familiar place to her throughout the night. It was the king's turn. I wanted him to lead.

Godfrey peered over his shoulder at us. "Was there another dry torch in there, girl?" asked the king.

"Aye. Up the way."

He nodded. "Let the girl go in and fetch it for me."

Aoife craned her face toward mine and gave me a mocking smile. I dropped her and like a rat in the bilge, she scurried around the king and into the tunnel. In moments she returned with the torch. I used my jasper stones to strike it and the dry-rotted fuel ignited with a poof.

"Lead the way, little miss," said Godfrey. Again the girl made a move to mock me. Before she turned, though, I smacked her miniscule rear, propelling her into the tunnel. She fell to her knees, scattering the torch. I laughed. The king scolded me. "We don't have time for games."

Aoife returned to her feet. She stood upright in the tunnel. Godfrey and I would have to crouch. We followed her down a narrow passageway made rectangular by rocks that lined its walls and great slabs of stone that acted as a ceiling as they sat on the walls and held up the earthen mound above. The walls were painted with reds and blues and yellows that had faded over the years since the original workers had interred their king or chieftain inside the chamber. I couldn't see what lay ahead since I followed Godfrey.

After just a few more paces, we entered the main chamber. It was just short of a fadmr in height. I still had to duck. To the immediate right near the wall, stood the rounded stone pillar Aoife had mentioned. The walls had spiraling serpent-like designs, not much different from the favored carvings on many stones and homes from my native lands. I wondered if they were really as old as Eyvind had said.

The king, who still stood in front of me, sighed. "You see there, Halldorr? Your little thrall lied."

My heart jumped. We had found a treasure at the cost of nothing. I was yoked to the right king. He was going to be rich. Godfrey was going to be a ring-giver. I stuck my head around Godfrey and looked down at the floor where he and Aoife stared. I saw the charred remains of a small skeleton. Next to those burned remains rested another skeleton whose clothes had turned to rags in the years since his burial. I saw the rotten shields Aoife had talked about. A bow rested on the dead man's chest. Stone-tipped arrows and spears ran along the outside edge of his body serving as a kind of fence. I saw no treasure.

"She lied?" I asked. "It looks just like she said it would."

King Godfrey kneeled down to the former chieftain of those lands and reached his hand into the ribcage. The bones crumbled apart. Godfrey brought his hand back up. It was balled into a fist. When he opened his palm I saw a single gold amulet with a broken cord attached to it. The ancient king must have worn it around his neck.

"I've got a gift of treasure for my queen. You see? The girl lied," he said with sarcasm. "The risk of this expedition was worth it." It wasn't, of course.

I scooted around him and rummaged through the rest of the burial, scattering the remains, not caring if I called down the ire of the gods. There was nothing of real value. There was no iron. I found some small sculptures of wolves and ancient auroch made of copper and bronze. The king stuffed them into a pouch along with the amulet. He sighed again and swore as he turned and felt his way out of the passage, leaving the girl and me behind.

"Is this what most strandhoggs are like?" asked Aoife. "If this is the life of a raider, I'd rather just be a bandit hiding in the woods along a highway. At least I would have a better chance of wealth and killing a man or two."

It was my turn to sigh. "I don't know what a strandhogg is usually like. This is my first."

The girl swore. "I've yoked myself to the wrong bunch."

I must say that I agreed with the slave that day. What little wealth I had was long gone and, out of drunken desperation or glory-seeking, I had vowed to follow a king who seemed to have little riches and nearly no army. Any of a hundred sad packs of brigands could wield more power than Godfrey.

We had no treasure, had fought no band of draugr, earned no glory, and yet we still had to run through the countryside, and return to our ships and Man. Once there, I was certain that if the king wasn't deposed by the weak force of the village simpleton, then his subjects' laughter would drive Godfrey to jump from the cliffs into the sea.

In a day's time I might be fleeing to yet another destination, trying to glom onto another king.

But we had to survive the coming day.

CHAPTER 4

The docile cows and their bleating calves were released to the surrounding pasture so that their owner could find them when he came out of his hovel, wherever that was. Supplies were stowed in knapsacks and the ropes rewound amidst murmurs. My fellow Greenlanders, save Leif, grumbled about the wasted expedition. Even Godfrey's core group of men wore sullen scowls. If they had been bent on throwing their lives away, why not just attack the Dal Riatans again with their limited numbers? At least then they'd die with the splendor of revenge on their souls. Godfrey did nothing to chastise either set of his small number of followers since, I think, he believed that his days as King of the Isles were numbered.

"Let's move quickly," he said somberly, his usual enthusiasm vanished. The men and the captive moved out through the alders after Godfrey. The farmer, who should have been pleased that we took him toward his home, walked with eyes staring at his boots, as dejected as the rest.

"Stay with them," I whispered to Aoife as I turned back to retrieve Leif, who now stood on the barrow lost in thought. To my astonishment the girl nodded her agreement without argument and trotted off, carrying my heavy pack for me.

Leif stroked his wispy red beard. "I mean to be a wise, moderate leader of men."

"That's fine, but you'll lead only cows and a pile of worthless rubble if you stay here."

Leif reached up and smacked my broad shoulder. He guided us down the mound. "The old stories are true. If a man finds the fortitude to remain awake on a barrow mound overnight, the gods afford him insight."

I shook my head at him. Insight! What, did Leif think he could see around all the problems the norns tossed in our way? Preposterous! Nothing in my experience demonstrated that any amount of knowledge or foresight could help a man navigate the world. Just when you had conquered the last demon and stood fixed and armed for the next beast, a simple plump woman could come to you from the side and annihilate all your plans. Her lips would call you like a siren. Her lashes would wave you into the rocks and shoals. My life had been thus. It seemed that I had strapped myself to a king who would have the same experience. His bane was to be a fairy tale told by a troublesome skald. When would I find a great, triumphant king whom I could follow?

We walked out into the waving grass of the pasture and jogged across to the next woods where Aoife had just disappeared. "Did the gods tell you where to find Godfrey a treasure and boats?"

"No," Leif answered in a manner that said that the spirits had, in fact, revealed to him an even better way forward.

"What then?"

"I can tell Godfrey only when he is ready." Leif paused just before we plunged into the woods. He cocked his ear to the wind. "While you were all toiling at the futile excavation," he began.

"Futile? It was all your idea."

"Yes, but the thrall told you what was in the grave before the lot of you had moved an ounce of rock. Godfrey spared her for something. I bought her for you for something. We ought to have listened to the girl rather than waste strength and time." He cupped his hand to his ear and closed his eyes, listening. "I heard sounds brought on the still air last night while you worked. They are the sounds of an army searching for us. And that army will be the means to victory for our king."

Leif raised his eyebrows mischievously and jumped into the woods, trotting to catch up with the rest of our raiding band. I swore about the lad. What did he know? He was the son of a murderer who was also the son of a murderer. Leif wasn't even the oldest son. He was the second son. How much more worthless could he be? He was like the fifth, dry teat on a newly freshened heifer. If the newborn calf found the dry teat as its favorite, the foolish beast would starve in a day. How much would I be like the calf if I listened to the boy's idiotic pronouncements?

I moved a step into the forest and then swore again. I cocked my ear into the wind and listened as I had seen Leif. He was crazy, I thought. There was no sound.

Until, there was a sound. In the distance, though out of my line of sight, was the faint sound of men's voices shouting and calling to one another. Their voices interrupted and pierced the constant low rumbling of another sound. Hooves, hundreds of them, growled their way over a nearby road or hard-packed meadow.

Maredubb's army was approaching. They searched for a group of Norse raiders, seen by the farmer's fellow workers.

They hunted, bent on killing us.

• • •

Yet, Leif had said that the wandering army would be our way to victory.

"Kill the farmer," Godfrey barked.

"I'll do it," called Aoife.

Everyone ignored her as the humor of her eagerness was lost on the desperate nature of our situation. "It should be me," said Killian. "It was I who helped get him into this situation and it was I who assured him of his safety."

"Make it fast. We can't have him calling to Maredubb's army," said the king. Ketil grinned while leaning against a tree. He casually picked at a hangnail. Horse Ketil appeared rested and fresh after avoiding all of last night's labor. His confidence was peaking while Godfrey's was waning.

"*If* that is his army we hear. We haven't laid eyes on it yet," said Randulfr. He stared back and forth at Leif and Ketil with accusing eyes. The hardened warrior of countless campaigns with Godfrey found that his future path was dictated by a slim, unproven young man who was on his side and, perhaps, by a slimy traitor who was decidedly against him. Randulfr was unhappy.

Killian walked to face the farmer who had heard the same ruckus from the horsemen and sensed our unease. The priest gave him a calming smile saying, "May you enter heaven at peace my son. May your sins be washed white by the perfect blood of Christ. May the same go for mine." Killian drew a long knife. The blade was thinner and narrower than a saex like the one I carried. He plunged it into the farmer's exposed throat, not stopping until his fist rammed into our captive's wind pipe. A look of wide-eyed surprise appeared at once on the dying man's face.

I could tell you it was the last time I saw such a sight, but that would be a lie. From that raid until now, I have watched all manners of men die in all manners. I've seen villains who deserved death and outstanding men who were noble and true meet their ends. To a man, each was shocked that it had come to them. You'd think they would expect it. Life is nothing but a runaway horse ride toward death's cliff. I enter every battle with the expectation I'll die. I've come close a dozen times. But if I'm honest with myself, I suppose that when those last moments come and if I find myself holding my innards in my hands and pissing in my pants, I imagine that I'll have the same look. Though every man dies, its arrival is always most unexpected.

Killian stepped to the farmer and used an amazing amount of strength given his small stature to lower the captive to last year's fallen leaves that still littered the forest floor. The priest crossed himself and rested a palm on the man's forehead as the farmer's legs jerked violently. Then the man was quiet while Killian withdrew his blade and cleaned it on his own robes.

Leif turned his attention from the dead man to answer Randulfr's charge. "You and King Godfrey have raided here before and I dare say that you know there is no wealth on this island. Neither ealdorman nor thegn could afford to pay for the number of men we heard clamoring about and making that racket. It must be King Maredubb."

Godfrey nodded and waved a hand to Randulfr. "The Greenlander is right. There is nothing here. We should never have come. Now we'll die, hemmed inland like hogs. What is a sea king doing in a forest?"

"This is perfect," giggled Ketil.

"Shut up, you conniving turd," snarled Godfrey. It was like the praise the king heaped on Horse Ketil for rounding up the cows in the middle of the night had never occurred. "I know you'd like me to fall. It's a game we all play while we say nothing of it. Shut up."

"I'm happy to discuss the game we all play," said Ketil.

"The way I figure it," interrupted Leif, seemingly unaware of the confrontation going on around him, "is that we've got until the midday meal to assemble our own army. It makes no sense to face Maredubb without one."

"My wife may find you enchanting, son of Erik, but your charms are quickly lost on me. Our best course is to skitter from woods to woods and return to our ships." The king turned to Loki, Magnus, and Brandr. "You men run to the edges of the wood. See if you can lay eyes on Maredubb. Crawl. Do whatever it takes to avoid being seen." The three ran off.

"If you depart here without treasure or other riches, you'll be forced to leave your kingdom behind within the year, or worse," surmised Leif.

"I will," agreed Godfrey. That wasn't a revelation to anyone. Ketil stood a little taller.

"And he'll be king in your place," said Leif, jerking a thumb at the Manx noble.

"Unless I kill him," said Godfrey.

"Then it will just be someone else, another Manx or maybe a Dal Riatan," continued Leif.

"Or, perhaps Maredubb will cross from here and take over," said Ketil, goading the king.

Godfrey set a hand on the hilt of his sword. "Shut up."

"So, King Godfrey, to avoid all that, we must leave here with wealth." Leif was dogged in his pursuit of the plan rattling in his head.

"There is no wealth," shouted Godfrey. "Their churches have nothing but wooden crosses and stale wine made from moldy grapes. I know because I've raided them, all of them. Other than the absent treasure there is nothing here!"

"Then why would Maredubb fight to protect it and make it his if there is nothing?" asked Leif.

It was a good question, I thought. Godfrey balled his fist and struck Leif on his cheek. Leif went down into a heap, rolled and sprang back up to his knees. He winced as he touched a quickly growing blue mark on his face. "King Godfrey, I mean no disrespect, but there must be some value on Anglesey."

"I don't know what they teach you, boy. Of course there's value. They raise crops that go to the mainland. Do you propose that the sixty of us gather sacks of barley and haul it on our backs? Will sixty sacks of grain get me back my kingdom? Dolt!" he exclaimed.

Leif was undaunted. "No. Where is Maredubb's power? Where's his capital?"

Godfrey scanned the woods for the quick return of his scouts. They didn't come. "Aberffraw!" barked the king. "It's on the southwestern side of the island, opposite where we landed yesterday."

"Then instead of fleeing toward our ships, let us move in the opposite direction of that army out there. Let's move on Aberffraw, take the village as ours and demand a ransom for her return."

Magnus ran back into the circle that surrounded the king and Leif. "There must be five hundred horsemen. They didn't spot me and they haven't caught our track. I don't know how they knew we were here."

"The farmer's lungs warned his family yesterday. Or, the trees have eyes," answered the king, bitterly. "Which direction do they move?"

"North and east," said Magnus. "Toward our ships. They move in the same direction we mean to go."

The king was shaking his head in disgust. I knew he had made a decision with which his own mind didn't agree. "No, they don't. They run east. We move west to capture a capital and an island."

• • •

Some poor traveler was going to be surprised. He would find a perfectly good horse, fit for our king, abandoned with saddle and bridle, seemingly forgotten. Perhaps even more surprising than such a fine beast, the traveler would also come across a mass of red, blonde, and brown hair tucked beneath a rotted log that sat next to a large smooth lake. The priest had insisted that we all get our long locks cut, something that, to a man, caused each of us to curse. It was mandatory, Killian said, if we were to look like helpless Welsh farmers that had fled ahead of a vicious Viking onslaught. I mumbled and grumbled while I watched the men grab a thick mat of their hair and cut it off with a saex. Just a small trim was all my hair had received in five years and now I was to lose it as part of a scheme dreamt up by Leif and an Irish priest. They were both mad as far as I was concerned. Yet, even the king sat down on the log and allowed Killian to cut off the longest portion of his hair. Godfrey stayed the priest's hand, however, when he reached to swipe off the braids in his beard. "That will be good enough to get past the guards," said the king.

"Why can't we just tuck our hair in our helmets?" I whined as I plopped down on the log, the last one to go. I couldn't bring myself to cut my own hair.

"Because it's not common for a band of Welsh refugees to come wearing armor, even armor as dented and tarnished as yours. As for your hair, you get to keep it." I immediately grinned and gave the now naked looking Magnus a mocking face. "You'll be our Norse prisoner," Killian said. My shoulders sunk.

They stood me up and bound my hands. Killian stepped back and studied my appearance. "We don't have to do anything to your mail," he said absent-mindedly. "It's seen better days." He ran to the edge of the lake and gathered a handful of mud and smeared it in my hair and face. My eyes flashed with anger and I stepped down hard on his foot. He withdrew it, yelping. "Would you rather I had Randulfr or Brandr beat you senseless so that it looked like you were captured in battle?"

"Try it," I said.

"Shut up, you two," scolded the king. He turned to address the men. "Keep your mail on under your cloaks. Helmets and even swords go into your packs. We have to look like we've just fled. As we draw closer, I want most of you to stagger and limp as if you've just barely escaped with your lives. And you," Godfrey said to Ketil, "do this right or I will personally run you through before you utter even one word of treachery." Godfrey turned to Killian, "Lead the way."

Killian called, "Aoife! You'll walk in plain sight next to me. Do nothing. Say nothing. Just walk. Cry if you like."

The girl scurried next to the priest, who followed around the north side of the lake with the rest of us in tow. Leif, behind the priest, held a long rope that was tied loosely around my neck and led me like livestock to slaughter. Further back were the king and the rest of our bedraggled bunch. Godfrey was careful to keep Ketil within the reach of one quick sword stroke.

Killian found the River Ffraw. The lake emptied into the winding creek and if we followed its course, we would soon find ourselves at Aberffraw, the seat of power in Gwynedd, Maredubb's capital city and port. Though we were all anxious, the priest and Aoife set a slow pace as we ambled out in the open along the north side of the river. He peered back and scolded us for not limping enough. Aoife repeated the priest's scorn, but Killian cuffed the side of her head as a reminder that unless she cried, she was to stay silent.

After a short time, Killian dug through the pack at his waist and pulled out a large silver cross. He held it aloft and began chanting words in Latin that would somehow see us, the refugees, safely through the dangerous lands. Above his cross I could see the sky opening up wide and blue. The scent of the air changed from tilled earth and lush green growth to the freshness of salt. We approached the sea and Castle Aberffraw.

• • •

Despite the threat of our raid and subsequent dispatch of King Maredubb and his army, the inland gate remained yawning wide open. It was almost welcoming. "If a raid ever hit their fortress, they'd expect it from the sea," whispered Killian between his Latin words. He crossed himself and murmured, "May their defenses be like clay."

A lazy sentinel stood up on the watch platform surveying our approach. It was only when the priest's voice rose to a new level that the guard was shaken from his brain-numbed slumber. He barked down to unseen men behind him. Soon those men approached the gate and stood at its center. Three wore helmets and mail in fit condition. Another three were less well-equipped. They still assembled their gear, tossing helmets atop their heads and cinching belts about their waists.

"Wait here," muttered Killian. "Sit. You're exhausted, remember," he said as he shoved Aoife forward. The men, even King Godfrey, crumpled to the earth and panted. They put on a terrific show. Horse Ketil copied what the rest of the men did, but he also studied the guards on the wall as if he looked for someone familiar. He turned away, frowning.

I stood tall and proud, for I felt like I represented my entire race to these Welsh guards. A proper Norseman wouldn't let a handful of peasants wear him out. Leif tugged down on the rope around my neck to get me off my feet. I kicked him. He cowered away, which was against his nature, but likely set the hook better than anything Killian would say.

"What have you caught yourself there, priest?" asked the leader of the Welsh soldiers. He had stepped out onto the short wooden bridge that crossed a man-made channel cut outside the fort's earthen mound and wooden palisade. "He looks like a proud one."

Killian brought the silver cross down to his side and rested a gentle hand on Aoife's head. "He's the worst creature I've ever seen." The priest ran his hand down to the girl's neck and pinched it so that she cried. "Do you see this dear one? As of last night, she and her mother were models of perfection; God's bounty was in them. That beast raped and killed the mother and did the same to the father, I think. They took every woman of our village with them, but he stayed behind for his insatiable lust. That is the only way we were able to capture him."

"Why not string him up in your village? Why have your brought him here?" asked the guard. He peeked around the priest to study our worn out band.

Killian crossed himself. "Because the entire island is covered with them! King Maredubb came to rescue us, but I'm afraid he was nearly routed. Hundreds, no thousands, of the pirates control the coasts and even inland. You must let us in and accept whatever other refugees come. King Maredubb may return and will need all able-bodied men to take back his kingdom."

The soldiers behind the main sentinel crossed themselves and breathed out audibly. "So what do you want us to do with the Norseman?" asked the sentinel.

"We don't have time for dallying. Let us in and close the gates. After that, allow one of my poor parishioners to put the first arrow into the heathen as a form of retribution. Then, do what you will."

"Retribution?" asked the soldier. "I thought priests teach that is the work of God."

"'Tis. 'Tis. But I'm afraid we are a fallen lot," answered Killian solemnly. "And everyone in this fort will be dead unless you close up these gates and await the king's help."

The soldier thought about the priest's words for just a heartbeat before he began barking orders and waving us in.

We had breached the walls of a fortress, the capital of a kingdom, with nary a drop of blood spilt.

Now, the work would begin.

• • •

The nice thing about being perceived as Welsh peasants is that no one paid our men any mind as we slunk into the fort. It is the same the world over. Unarmed, weak men are disdained, nay, loathed, by other men with spear and sword. And rightfully so. A man who allows himself to be deprived of his own defense, granting that right to others, is offering up his manhood for castration. Our band was viewed thus. In twos and threes we limped and dragged feigned bum legs across the bridge and through the inland gate. And even if they had ventured a glance in our disguised men's direction, what the soldiers who let us in would have seen were the mostly unhealed wounds from our rough and tumble game of knattleikr some days earlier, likely confirming in their eyes that the men Killian led had been attacked by Viking raiders.

I, not dressed as someone I was not, was the only one with whom the Welsh soldiers locked eyes. The leader in particular furrowed his brow at me. I met his stare and even barked like a dog, finishing with a rumbling growl. One of the man's comrades swung a wooden club at me. It was only a harsh tug from Leif on the rope around my neck that spared me from receiving the blow. He jerked me on my leash deeper into the muddy streets of the town.

"I'd bring what soldiers the king didn't take with him to the inland wall," suggested Killian as the gates slammed shut.

"Priest, don't pretend to tell me how to do my business and I'll not tell you how to run your flock," said the soldier. Killian shrugged and fell back in line with us as we moved down the main road. It ran from the inland gate, across the village, past the castle keep, and down to the river that dumped into the bay. As we moved away, the same soldier whispered to his men, "It sounds like the threat is from the island itself. Move half the men from the river and sea side to this wall." His young charge rambled off to convey his orders. "Priest, take your sad lot down to the river. You can piss there and get a drink. Don't go stinking up the king's city."

"Bless you, my son," said Killian.

"And keep your pet with you for now. We'll have some sport with him once Maredubb returns. He might have some information to give the king."

"It's a good thought. The king was wise when he made you responsible for his great citadel." The soldier stuck his chin a bit higher in the air and turned to shove some of his men and bark orders.

• • •

I was pulled behind a shop and unbound. The others dropped their hudfats in the muddy alley and strapped on every weapon they had, only to hide them again under their soiled cloaks.

"Work in twos," instructed Leif. "Move to separate parts of the village, most of you to the inland wall." Leif glanced at Killian. "Thank you for that bit about moving the soldiers inland. Getting most of the armed men where we know they'll be – spread out on a wall – will make our work that much quicker." Young Leif then addressed the rest of the crowd again. "Lay eyes on four soldiers and see them killed as soon as the bloodletting starts. Don't waste time on individual warriors until the groups are dead. Do that and we own this town in moments."

"How will we know when to start?" asked Brandr.

"When the women begin shrieking," answered Killian which was good enough for Brandr.

In an instant of increased piousness, Godfrey dropped to one knee and mumbled a prayer. Killian, I thought, would be proud, but instead he hoisted the king back up to his feet. "We can't waste time. Each moment gives King Maredubb a chance to return. The citadel must be ours before he gets tired of beating the bushes for us."

With that, the group dispersed. Godfrey grabbed Horse Ketil by a sleeve. "You'll stay right beside me and this beast," said my king as he pointed at me. Ketil whitened his grip on the shaft of his spear. I did the same on my sword as a warning.

"Is it wise to allow him a weapon?" I asked.

Godfrey shrugged. "He'll be in front of me. I'd bet my swordplay wins any contest over his use of a spear. Besides, what if the drunken fool does something good for us all? Then we both win." Horse Ketil nodded at this.

"I'm not so sure he's a drunkard," I grumbled.

"Nor am I, but he tolerates walking around with a lot of piss on his pants if he's not," answered Godfrey with a wave of his hand.

Ketil looked down at his trousers. A day old urine stain had dried in a crusty mess. Blotches from his vomiting on the sea voyage over covered one leg. "I do like to drink, King Godfrey. You'll find I also like to fight. I like to get things without much effort. And once I get the throne on the Isle of Man, I'll enjoy hanging your cousin and taking Gudruna as mine."

Godfrey wasn't about to be goaded to a verbal war just before the true bleeding was set to begin. He laughed. "Oh, it might be worth dying just to see what my Gudruna would do to your manhood if you ever tried to come to her bed."

A chicken squawked somewhere in the capital. It sounded like a butcher chased it around his shop. I didn't understand his words, but I knew cursing when I heard it. Godfrey, Ketil, and I smiled at the scene that played itself out in each of our minds' eyes. We gave up arguing with one another.

"I don't believe I'll follow the advice of that Leif of yours ever again," muttered Godfrey while the waiting dragged on. A cat hissed and chased a diseased rat behind some broken crates.

"I think you're right, king. We probably won't survive the day to have the chance to follow Leif again," I answered with gallows humor. The cat gingerly pawed at the cornered beast, not sure if he would win a fight with the sizable rat. Godfrey pinned the feline to the ground with his boot and with a single, quick stab, pierced the rat from above. It was his first kill of the raid. He released the cat which ignored the two of us and sniffed at what moments earlier had been its prey. The cat lost interest. I swear I saw it shrug as it padded off back the way it had come.

The king chuckled at the two beasts and at our situation. "We're not much different than the cat, Halldorr. Take away our quarry and we lose more than what would have been our treasure. We lose heart. And that, I'm afraid, can kill a man surer than any blade or coup."

"So if we live through this, then you will follow Leif's advice again?" I asked. "For the hunt and excitement?"

The king didn't have time to answer. Aoife's powerful little screams were the first sounds we heard. Then we heard Killian running through the town screaming about how invaders from the sea had penetrated the defenses. A moment later he yelled about a breach in the inland walls. I heard the sudden, guttural sounds of Welshmen dying at the end of sharp spears and sword edges at the nearest wall. Our raid had finally begun in earnest.

Chaos and confusion were what we needed. Like the struck coins of the English and Saracens, they were our accepted currency. The Welshmen gave us their disordered commotion by the bucketful. They heaped it on us. Before we even stepped out of the alleyway, I saw the terrified look on men's faces as they skittered past. They gathered up children and ran for what they thought might be safety in the castle keep. I'm not ashamed to say that the sight of their fear was beautiful. In return for the panic etched on their faces, in order to strike a fair bargain, we gave them something else entirely.

Those fearsome Norseman raiders, those pirates of the sea, Godfrey's men, were like wraiths. We were everywhere at once. We were like the draugr that we thought we'd meet at the barrow. And we brought a rain of death onto the bewildered men of Anglesey.

Horse Ketil, without a word from the sometimes-king, jumped into the muddy street with his spear drawn. A woman, old, perhaps fifty, halted in her tracks. She posed him no threat. Horse Ketil didn't give her a chance to flee in the opposite direction. He rammed the weapon into her soft belly, driving it and her entire body to the ground. He gave a bloodthirsty scream that sent shivers down my back. Ketil was not only hungry for power and lazy, he was cruel.

Godfrey whacked the back of my head. "Don't go limp on me. Now's the time to move, lad! Even though I hate him, you act like that bastard when you fight."

We followed Horse Ketil into the streets. Men and women ran in all directions. King Godfrey laughed as we ran, hacking down a man who carried a chicken under each arm; or, kicking a boy square in the chest who tried to resist us with a wooden hammer.

I killed three men that day. I had killed before. I've told you as much. But each time before, it had been for brute survival. Had I not killed those previous men, they would have killed me. I suppose that is just as simple as it was that day in Aberffraw. Had we not killed over a hundred soldiers and a few dozen villagers, they would have gathered heart and strength, realizing that we were few and they were many. They would have killed us. So I killed three men. One man, brave, but foolish, jumped out of an open door from his home. The king had told us all to stay out of the homes for now, plunder could be had later. I was running past the door and the foolish Welshman slashed at me with his eating knife. It raked across one of my mail sleeves, caught the flesh of my forearm, and danced away. I used my wounded arm to seize the man by his neck and launch him against the outside wall of his house. His head cracked against the rock wall with a pop, leaving a bloody spray and path as he slid down. The other two men, I dispatched with blows from my sword.

King Godfrey killed four men that day, though as the tales go since then, he killed fifty if it was one. It was Horse Ketil who surprised me, though. Not only was he eager to get the slaughter going at the start, but the man whom I thought was nothing but a traitor found the will to carry himself from one kill to another. I can personally attest that I saw him eliminate a dozen souls, as the Christians would call them. His spear, his fists, his knees, his feet were all used as weapons in Aberffraw as his actions helped bring about a victory for his rival Godfrey. I guess I didn't understand politics.

Then just as quickly as it had begun, the streets were silent. We had fought our way to the front gate and there met Killian and Aoife. The priest's robes were splattered with blood. His sword, too, was dripping with crimson. Aoife, the little monster, carried a knife evidently given her by Killian. It shone crimson as she pulled it from a soldier's ribcage; though I do not know if she killed the man or if she had driven the blade into someone killed earlier. In either case, the girl smiled broadly. We stood staring at one another, panting and grinning.

Leif slid down a ladder from the watch platform that snaked behind the palisade. "Just in time!" he huffed. "I see a large force coming to the city now."

"Maredubb?" asked Godfrey, though he knew the answer. He didn't wait for confirmation. "Gather the men and send them up to the walls. Make a show of it!"

Leif nodded his understanding and ran off through the now empty streets to swat our men toward the walls. First Randulfr, then Loki, then others began scurrying their way back and filing up the ladders to put on a show of force.

Godfrey jerked a hollowed cow's horn from around his shoulders and slapped it into Aoife's ribs. "Go deeper into the town. Play a long single note periodically." The king turned to

Magnus who had just run in. "Go back to our gear and find another horn. Blow it in answer to hers." Man and girl ran off to perform the tasks prescribed by their king.

By now the walls were filling up. As I looked at the backs of our men from below, I counted. We'd lost none. Some men had a gash here or there or a swollen eye where a Welshman or woman had gotten in a lucky swing. But the fact was that we sixty raiders had taken a town of over two thousand inhabitants and our band was still intact. It had been a bold plan – insane, but bold.

Leif trotted back and began moving to climb a ladder. Godfrey grabbed his leg. "You and Halldorr will serve as my negotiators. I don't want to give Maredubb the respect that comes with talking directly to me. Go find the finest horses this town has to offer and prepare to ride out." With that the king, showing a sparkle that was probably reminiscent of his most successful days, scampered up to the platform in order to lie and bluster.

• • •

Leif and I had found suitable horses in the stables. They were not the choicest since those were already out and mounted with the main force of Maredubb's army. We were just splashing up to the gate when we heard Aoife's horn blare. A short moment later, Magnus' horn answered somewhere else in the city. Then Aoife. Then Magnus.

"So you hear our armies coordinating movements within the city," Killian was shouting over the walls. "The king will send his emissaries out with his terms before the slaughter and rape gets quite out of hand."

The priest gave a wave with his hand. Leif jumped from his saddle, hefted the heavy timber that served as a bar, and opened the gate. He noticed three Welsh boys cowering in a nearby guardhouse behind the bodies of two dead soldiers. Leif barked at the boys to close up after we went out. I don't know that they understood his tongue, but they caught his meaning and complied well enough. The strong oak doors creaked and then slammed shut before we had even crossed the narrow bridge.

Leif set our horses' pace. Slow. We weren't nervous. At least we were not to appear concerned. I craned back to look at our men lining the walls. Nearly sixty angry, red-splattered faces glowered back at me. They were my people and yet I felt disconcerted looking at them.

I looked ahead to Maredubb. What must he be thinking? He could only assume that his city had been sacked from the sea side by a tremendous army of raiders. The men on the wall would be a small detachment from the rest.

I spun back around to again face the wall, for I had seen but did not immediately register the presence of another man. Horse Ketil had snuck out as the Welsh boys closed the gate. He jogged toward us with a smile on his face.

"This is your last chance," he said. "In a moment I'll have Maredubb's army crawling over the walls to kill those sixty pathetic Norsemen. I'll have Gudruna and I'll have the Isle of Man. I will need real warriors, though. Are you in for profit?"

"But you just helped us win in there," I said, dumbly.

"That was for survival, fool. If I didn't, Godfrey or a Welshman would have killed me."

He was running alongside my horse. I didn't have time to think anymore or debate. I did what came naturally. I tugged my boot from the stirrup and kicked the side of his head. He crashed into the mud. Ketil climbed up to his knees and shouted, "Maredubb!" I leapt from my saddle and muffled whatever else Horse Ketil was going to say. His face was smashed back into the muck. I punched his ears with a balled fist. He struggled at first, nearly shoving me off his back. I grew tired of the fight and removed my dented helmet. Soon there were a few more dimples. I pounded Ketil's head with it once, then twice, and then three times. He stopped moving. A trickle of bright red oozed from his hairline.

When I crawled up out of the soggy dirt, I saw that no one else had moved. Thankfully, the army stretched out before us had remained still. Leif, too, had waited while I finished my task.

"Is he dead?" my friend asked.

"No," I said.

"Then toss him across your horse's withers," said Leif. I obeyed and remounted my stolen beast. Leif squeezed his heels into his horse's belly and began our short trek again. In his hands, the leather reins creaked under the weight of his firm grip. His face showed steady calm.

I glanced back to Godfrey. The king's face was etched with determination.

• • •

Leif led us toward the man who sat on a stout warhorse at the front and center of the small army. Had the black beast not been specifically bred and trained for battle, it appeared as if it were strong enough to plow in the fields day and night without rest. The long black hair that grew from its fetlocks to the ground gave it the appearance of having enormous hooves. It was a pretty animal – quite the opposite of its rider.

Maredubb, like the beast and its black coat was adorned kingly enough. The man wore linen trousers that had been tucked into tall, black hard leather boots. I had never seen such boots. Our men wore simple brown boots that were cinched up the ankles. The trousers were red. Hanging to his knees was a heavily padded, sky blue silk coat with amber-colored trim at the sleeves and bottom hemline. His thighs and waist were protected by a skirt of brown leather strips. Maredubb wore scale armor that resembled the hide of a snake. His helmet was an iron bowl made of several separate pieces. Iron cheek guards hung loosely from their hinges at the sides as the king had not tied them under his chin. The nape of his neck was protected by a curtain of looped mail that dangled from the helm.

Had that been the last of it, I would have said that Maredubb and his beast were perfectly matched – two flawless specimens. But the destrier carried and the armor protected an unattractive man. Maredubb's eyes were set too close to one another so that the innermost corners were hidden behind the helmet's nose plate. One of his eyes was blue, the other brown. His nose was fat. He wore a moustache that was shaved to the same width as his nose. Below the narrow moustache was a narrow mouth with bulging lips and downturned corners. The portion of his forehead that showed beneath his armor was speckled with red that appeared like a rash.

"Which one of you is Horse Ketil?" Maredubb asked in my native tongue. "This is not how we said this invasion and ambush would happen. You were supposed to land on the north side of Anglesey. We've been everywhere looking for you."

Leif offered a pleasant smile. Out of the corner of his eye, he glanced down at Ketil. "I'm afraid none of us is Horse Ketil. King Godfrey uncovered your plot. Ketil was drowned on the voyage over. It was a terrible mishap."

Maredubb's red face turned redder. "Get out of my kingdom," Maredubb whined through gritted teeth. "I'll burn the city to the ground before I see a Norseman live there."

Leif answered. "King Godfrey of the Isles has no desire to torch the town. I think that neither do you. Two thousand of your citizenry captured or killed would make it difficult to maintain your already tenuous grip."

"I don't talk to a red-haired pup that can push nary a whisker on his chin," said Maredubb. He then waved a careless hand in the air. "There might be one thousand in the village. My army is here. What do I care of peasants?"

"There are two thousand or more in the village and you know it," charged Leif. "Many of them are the wives and daughters of the men you have here. Most of them are getting raped now. We can stop it and be gone if you stop bristling and lying. Two thousand bodies are a lot to bury. That's a lot of barley that is not harvested, a lot of bread not made, a lot of hides not tanned."

"I get your meaning," interrupted Maredubb. He scanned our men on the walls who held their spears pointed upwards. The blood that dripped from the tips was only now beginning to coagulate in thick rivers down the wooden shafts and in thick pools around their tightly gripping hands. The king rolled his narrow-set eyes. One of his pledged men returned the gesture. "What are these terms that the wretch Godfrey offers?" The horns blared in the background.

"I'll test your honesty again," began Leif.

"I won't be tested by the likes of you!" Maredubb blustered. A fat drop of Ketil's blood smacked the earth. "I should kill both of you heathens right now!" He pointed to Horse Ketil. "You've attacked one of my citizens right in front of my face. He was calling for his king when this savage beat him."

"Honesty and upright negotiations are valued even among what you call pagans, I'm afraid," Leif answered. "They're not just a Christian concern. You see, had we let this Welshman go to his king early," lied Leif as he pointed to Ketil's flaccid body, "that would have ruined the trust we've worked so hard to build between both our sides. You may have thought that we'd release more of your people before you've met a single demand. We can't allow such a misguided notion to enter your mind."

"Trust!" said ugly Maredubb with amazement. His large horse's tack rattled as the beast angrily shook its head in agreement with its master. Maredubb sighed. "So what are these terms of this Godfrey you call King of the Isles? I heard he lost to a bunch of monks in Dal Riata last year."

"And he chopped up those monks on Christmas night. Now, don't lie to me," warned Leif. "If you accurately tell us where and how much silver and gold is in your treasury, we'll simply return through those gates and take half. We'll be gone in our ships by morning. If you lie and make it difficult on us, we'll take all we find, haul away slaves to be sold in Dyflin, and burn the town anyway."

I hadn't heard these parts of the plan. It was elegant enough, simple enough. It had Leif's tracks all over it. He had inherited his good sense from his mother, whom I missed, his sense of adventure from his father, whom I missed more. Together, they blended to make a formidable combination in Leif. He gave the Welsh king a tempting choice. His army, his capital, and much of Maredubb's treasury would be intact should he take the chance that we told the truth and agree.

Nonetheless, Maredubb stewed. He curved his narrow mouth into a frown, the downturned corners drawn even closer together than usual. His face flushed with anger so that his cheeks were now redder than the rash on his forehead. Another of Magnus' or Aoife's horns blew.

"You'd best decide quickly," encouraged Leif. "The ringing of the notes tells me that our army is in place and ready to begin a massacre, a slaughter that you can prevent by cooperating and trotting away for a single night."

"I'll slit your two throats right here and assault my own walls. I'll burn the place down myself before I leave it to the likes of you! I'll burn it, burn it, burn it," shouted Maredubb. The Welsh king stood tall in his stirrups and called up to Godfrey. "You bastard! This affront will not go unpaid!" He settled back to his rump and chewed on his chubby lips.

We sat in relative silence for a long moment, the nearby sea with its constant rolling the only sound. I gave Leif a nervous sideways glance that, thankfully, Maredubb did not notice. Leif looked as paradoxically relaxed as he had the day we left for our exile. Then, he had had an experienced, pendulous-titted woman in his bed to help settle his tension. Today, he had only his own secure confidence in both his plan and the place the gods had made for him during his life in Midgard.

Leif incrementally sweetened the pot for Maredubb. "Agree now and I'll have Halldorr here leave behind your townsman. He'll stay with you tonight as a token of our appreciation that you've already agreed to our terms. Of course, you'll interrogate this man when he wakes up. What you'll find is that he tells you there is no way you'll succeed in taking the citadel by force. Remember, without another drop of blood, we'll be gone by morning."

"I'd take the offer if I were you," I said. I felt like I should add something to the negotiations.

Maredubb's next in command, who must have understood most of what was said, was nodding in agreement with our offer. He whispered some words into his king's ear. The king sat up in his saddle nodding. "Agreed. I'll take my peasant. If you are not gone by sunrise, we'll slaughter the lot of you. But know this," Maredubb said wagging a crooked finger.

"I did not lie when I said that there would be an answer to this. Godfrey will pay."

Leif was grinning. "I'm sure he'd have it no other way."

And the game continued.

• • •

As Leif and Maredubb finished up their verbal volley, I rapped Horse Ketil in his face a few more times. While no one was paying me or the supposed peasant any mind, I wanted to be sure that Ketil would be long unconscious. Otherwise, if he was able to talk too soon, Maredubb would know the ruse, attack, and slaughter us all. "Wake up from that!" I whispered to the unconscious lump. When my knuckles were bloody and Ketil's face properly tenderized, I threw him down face first into the mud by the side of the main road leading into Aberffraw. Maredubb noticed the thump, looked over, saw his peasant released, and went back to spilling his information.

After Maredubb delineated the location and amount of the treasure stored in his keep, Leif and I nodded and walked our horses back the way we had come. It took a few moments for the same terrified Welsh boys to open the gates for us. We stared straight ahead at the oaken doors, confidently showing Maredubb our backs. Leif was ebullient when the scurrying boys let us in. He tossed each a small penny for their trouble as we passed back into the fortress.

The gates slammed shut. Killian bounded his way down a ladder and helped Leif shove the timber in place. Godfrey stayed at his post with the rest of his army. The two kings, one Welsh, one Norman-Manx, eyed one another, continuing their war in silence.

"What was all that about?" asked Killian.

"We temporarily eliminated a traitor," muttered Leif.

"I knew it! He'd let everyone know his feelings. We just couldn't do anything about it. I knew Ketil was no good," said the priest. "We'll have to deal with the repercussions back home."

"I guess it was good that we kept him close," I said. "Otherwise, he could have already taken over Man."

Leif held up a hand. "We don't have time for this. We've got to move quickly before Maredubb gets suspicious and probes the walls and the sea," said Leif. "We've got to run before Ketil wakes up and is able to talk."

"That will be a while," I said, showing the bruises and cuts on my hand.

Leif was already beginning to stride toward the main citadel where the treasure was to be found. Half the citizenry was probably hidden there too. They would have to be dealt with. The other half was concealed in lofts, barns, storehouses, cabinets, or anything in which a curled human could wedge himself.

Snorts from horses and jingling reins announced that Maredubb had at last finished his duel with Godfrey. My king then slid his way down the nearest ladder, barking orders as he came. "Twenty men! That's all I want on the wall. Walk and rotate patrols so that their watchers think we've got hundreds guarding the palisade." Godfrey was grinning from ear to ear as he walked up to Leif and me. Still he barked orders over his shoulders as his small army began pouring down ladders. "Randulfr, Loki, Brandr – gather three men each and select Maredubb's best ships for our own. We might as well take three!" He was laughing now.

"I never should have doubted the two of you." The king shook his head in pleased disbelief. "Let us get some treasure and use it to build an army! I can already taste the revenge. First Anglesey, then Lismore."

CHAPTER 5

We moved through the town toward the Welsh king's castle. I feared that we would be forever in breaching or climbing or in some other way entering the curtain wall surrounding his keep. We would spend the night without success, and in the morning King Maredubb would uncover our trickery and see us killed. But, when we turned the last corner past a bakery where some of the morning's bread was still sitting warm on shelves, I saw that we had nothing to worry about and began to breathe easy.

I took the opportunity to run into the bakery and snatch all the bread I could press between my arms and chest. There was a boy aged about ten who hid under a table in the corner of the shop. He slowly tried to pull a sack of flour in front of him. I paid him no more attention and pushed my way out into the streets. When I again caught up with the rest, I doled the bread out to Godfrey first, then Killian, and then the men, holding back the warmest loaf for myself. For my troubles the men all gave me an approving grunt as they tore large hunks off with their teeth while they walked. Only a few bothered to brush off the dried, red flakes of blood that dusted the loaves from where they rubbed against my chainmail.

As I was saying, the thick stone wall would have been a problem. We would have had to send men down to the boatyard below the fortress to retrieve grappling hooks along with more long ropes. Since our ships were on the other side of Anglesey we would have had to pilfer the hooks from Maredubb's own navy's ships. Then, once we had torn apart the docks to find the iron talons we would have had to launch them high up into the crenels or over the merlons of the curtain wall. Time would have been wasted. We would have died. You know, however, that none of that was necessary because here I am scratching out my tales. Yawning wide, each on four sturdy iron hinges, rested the curtain wall's two doors. Whoever had fled into the castle had done so in such a hurry that they never took the time to slam the gates closed. We marched right in.

In truth, Maredubb's castle was more of a keep that sat in the middle of the southwest side of the town, near the widening river and bay. Toward the rear of the yard, a narrow set of stone steps had been cut into the steep slope that led down to the quayside.

Sensing danger, our men became keenly aware. Some crammed uneaten bread into their jerkins; others, like me, stuffed the last bits into our mouths and gripped our swords as we passed into the bailey. As if the gods had spite for our readiness, nothing jumped out at us. We again relaxed. Brandr chuckled at his own nerves.

Godfrey and Killian nearly bound toward the central structures. The keep consisted of two buildings that were clearly built by two different peoples. One had clean lines and near perfect uniformity, it was of lower profile. The other had two walls that appeared plumb, but two more that could have done with a better mason and a straighter string. The odd thing to me was that the better built part of the keep was weathered and worn, much older, hundreds of years older. The newer one had rocks that appeared as if they'd been pulled out of the earth that very morning. Those same fresh looking stones were bound by clean, though flaking, mortar. A short passage way with a single, squat wooden door in the center connected the two disparate buildings.

The door, which had been held open a crack, slammed shut as King Godfrey moved toward it. A heavy iron bar was loudly slid into place on the other side. "Damn!" barked Godfrey as his shoulder rammed into the immovable tree. "Leif, take a group of men around north. Randulfr, take a group around south. Find me a way in!" The king said it like he didn't expect their search to prove fruitful.

As soon as the two groups peeled away in opposite directions, we heard a hoarsely whispered shout from behind the door. At once, the door popped back open and armed men poured out into the bailey. One of Godfrey's Norsemen, who had his back to the door, fell with a spear jutting from the back of his knee.

Killian reacted in a flash, closing the distance between himself and the attackers while simultaneously drawing his long blade. The sight of a Christian priest with blood splattered all over his robes, startled one of the Welshmen, for the man's spear went from being aimed directly at Killian's unarmored chest, to angling to the side and being held almost limply. Killian did not allow his life to fall into the hands of the norns or his Providence. With his two small hands, the priest sliced the blade upward, halving the warrior's thigh.

Others teemed through the doorway, engaging us one at a time before we would have a chance to assemble into our impenetrable shield wall. Our cohesion was broken. I saw a Greenlander fall. Another of Godfrey's men had a spear jammed into the top of his boot. A second Welshman used his sword to hack down with force enough to dislodge most of our man's head from his blood spurting neck.

Two attackers saw me and approached. I had my sword at the ready. They did the same with theirs. My blade struck the sword of one of them so that the two of us came together chest to chest. He grasped my beard with one of his hands and jerked at it. I held firm and howled as I saw him come away holding a fistful of my blonde whiskers. His comrade was swinging around to my side and was a heartbeat away from slicing at my dilapidated mail. The blade might not cut me on the first or second stroke, but anything more and I knew I'd be feeding my blood into the turf.

While holding the first attacker at bay, I reached down to seize my father's saex. I felt it lifted away before I could grip the handle. Its sole edge cut my awaiting fingers as it danced.

My future was to end. My present was to be short. The thread of my life had found its end and the norns were cackling under the Yggdrasil tree. They had gotten their fun and were done sporting with me. They'd move onto someone else. I pushed myself closer into the first attacker, trying to use him as a partial shield for the blow that would come.

It didn't come in the slightest. A confused look appeared on the second Welshman's face. His sword leapt from his hand

and bounced relatively harmlessly off my shoulder. He toppled over sideways.

The first attacker's eyes went wide in horror as the slight Aoife twisted and then withdrew my saex from the second man's groin. She scrambled onto the prone guard's chest. Aoife raised the blade in order to ram it into his face, but the man wouldn't give up so easily. He swatted at her with a balled paw and she rolled off. The saex fell onto his chest.

I don't know if it was the potential loss of the only thing of sentimental value that I had left from my real father, or if it was the second time in as many days that I saw someone harm the dirty nymph. One of the two inspired me. After the battle that day I said only that my entire motivation was the former. But closer to the truth – and I can admit it now that I've raised a fearsome daughter of my own – is that it was the latter that sent lightning through my muscles.

With the howl of a wolf I drove my face into the face of the man with whom I still grappled. I bit his nose and pumped my legs so that I propelled him backward. He slammed into one of his countrymen and still I continued on. We abruptly halted when his back was crushed against the stone passageway. I heard him gasp as his breath was taken away. I dropped my sword and clutched his leather coat at his shoulders and, like a woman repeatedly rubs laundry across a river rock, I rapidly pounded him again and again against the stone wall. He grew heavy and limp and still I pounded. My anger swelled.

I cast him aside and saw that Leif and Randulfr had at last returned from their unsuccessful tour of the bailey. Their numbers were welcome and they, with interlocking shields, edged into the fray. They stabbed with efficient bursts, then inched forward. There was nothing glamorous about it. There was no swashbuckling. Those dancing motions were the things of fanciful tales from skalds who had never once found themselves knee deep in the shit and blood of the shield wall. Slash, stab, hide behind your shield. Pray to Thor, heave on the timber that you gripped and that rested against your forearm, pray to Thor, and inch forward. It was grisly. It worked.

The Welshmen began falling.

I saw the man that Aoife had stabbed was crawling with my saex in one hand. He had just been able to catch the wild Irish girl by her heel. She kicked madly, but his grip, despite the blood that seeped from his groin, remained firm. He slashed and cut the sack she wore for a dress. I barreled toward them. He swung the blade again and caught her shin. The girl screamed and cried. I dove onto his back, gripped his face with my hands from behind, and dug my fingers into anything I could find.

The bleeding Welshman bit my finger. No, he gnawed and tore at it. Instead of withdrawing, I squeezed harder. One of his eyes burst and the pressure on my finger abated. Three more of my fingers found their way into his cheek and I used his flesh like the rope handle on a pail to jerk him over. His one eye fixated on me with pure hatred which told me he still didn't know that he was a dead man. And, like I've said before, in that denial he was like all men, not quite sure it was possible that one day his body would be empty of his warrior spirit.

He swung the saex at my side. It glanced off my mail. With all my might and all my weight I leaned on his throat with my forearm. He gurgled and grunted, but I believe I rumbled even more. I spat into his face. I clenched my teeth. Air raced into and out of my flaring nostrils. I roared while he weakly hammered me with one of his knees. He wriggled his chest beneath me. With each passing moment, his strength was sapped further. His convulsions slowed. At the same time I gained strength. I felt my muscles bulge and tense. It was like what left him was entering me.

Then my opponent stopped moving. I gave one last shove into his windpipe and rolled off to grab my saex and meet another warrior.

There were no more challengers. The only men still standing were Godfrey's, his men of Man and his Greenlanders. We panted. Some rested hands on their knees, still fighting, but for air and not their lives. Leif, splattered with fresh crimson, sat on his rump and wiped his blade across a random body next to him. Aoife clutched the long cut on her leg with a grimy palm. Her tears were already drying, but the girl still shook and whimpered. I could see in her eyes that for all her talk, she was still just a frightened creature who had no idea what the norns had in store for her.

She was like me in that regard.

Godfrey clumsily walked over the scattered dead and rested a hand on my shoulder. He gripped it tightly. "Up," he gasped to catch his breath. "We've lost a fine batch of our men. Defending ourselves for the rest of the night will be even more difficult now." He paused to pant and survey the scene. "Send runners to the sentinels at the city gate. Tell them to pull back here when night falls. We need to take whatever we can and be gone."

And so Aberffraw and the Welshmen it held had not fallen without a fight.

Twelve of our men lay dead. Two more would be dead in hours so gaping were their wounds.

• • •

We wore a new, smooth path into the carved, stone steps that led down to the docks and Godfrey's newly commandeered ships. The gloaming was long past and all but one of the sentries at the town's palisade quietly withdrew, leaving our backs nearly totally unguarded. It could not be helped as we had much work to do. Out of the dozen boats docked in the river's mouth, Maredubb had three suitable warships. I say suitable because though the shipwright who built them had clearly been inspired by the boats of my people, he had failed at truly approaching their low, sleek greatness. These would be lumbering in the seas compared to ours, even the substandard *Charging Boar*. They would also prove to have a deeper draft, preventing them from entering smaller, shallower channels, or effectively sliding into beaches. But Godfrey wanted them, or at least to deprive Maredubb from having them.

Who was going to effectively row the beasts should the winds prove unfavorable had not yet been uncovered. Even if the forty-something of us were equally divided between the crafts and our backs proved strong, six or seven men rowing on a side for those particular ships would propel them like slugs in the garden.

Up and down the steps we ran while Magnus and the others finished preparing the boats. We carried a few chests of treasure. Most of the Welsh king's riches were cumbersome sundries that defied efficient packing. We stuffed them in fiber sacks or grabbed handfuls of crosses or gold-plated staffs or jewel encrusted brooches. Time was not on our side. Godfrey reminded us of this with each pass.

King Godfrey and Killian had made a survey of the twin, though different, keeps. Godfrey found Maredubb's wife, four children, and servants cowering in their chambers. He let them tremble, heaping coals on them by walking around their rooms and rummaging through their belongings as if he owned the castle. In the end he decided to stick with the terms of Leif's bargain with Maredubb and take nothing more than half the treasury. Well, he took one more thing. He couldn't resist. The monstrous hide of a brown bear covered Maredubb's bed. "Take it," Godfrey ordered when I came in to tell him we were nearly ready to flee.

I obeyed, of course. As I rolled the pelt up in my arms, Maredubb's woman ceased her shrinking, grew courage, and latched onto the other side. She leaned back and pulled. I let the prize go. The woman fell backward onto her servants and children, letting go of the hide in the process. I quickly reached out and gathered it all up in my arms. Godfrey chuckled at the scene.

"Godfrey," said Killian as he reentered the room with Leif. Leif had something to say, that much I could tell.

"What is it? Where were you?"

"Young Leif and I found a document hoard in a set of shelves," began Killian.

"Yes, I saw it. We are not here to find out what this so-called king says to that so-called king in his personal letters. We are here to get treasure! We've got it and must skim out of here before Maredubb probes our lack of defenses or before Horse Ketil tells him!" Godfrey glanced in my direction. "Damn, but you should have killed the traitor."

"Everyone says he holds sway over parts of Man," countered Leif. "We didn't want to complicate things for you."

Godfrey waved it off. "You did well, I suppose. Couldn't be helped." He put a hand to his mouth as he thought. "But if you had killed him, I could have blamed it on you and then executed you for the deed. His fellow Manx would have seen how just I am and come to my side."

Leif and I looked warily at our king before Godfrey burst out laughing. "I'm kidding. Truly, you've done well."

"The documents, Godfrey," insisted Killian.

"Listen, priest you serve your purpose and nothing more! Don't pretend to command this strandhogg or anything else beyond the four walls of your church for which I pay! We are here for treasure!" I hadn't seen the normally good-natured Godfrey this agitated, this volatile. He felt the threat of Maredubb closing in.

But the small, dark priest wouldn't be cowed. "And that is why I am telling you about the documents. They appear authentic. They bear the king's seal, King Aethelred, that is. Maredubb must have had a spy intercept them or maybe he is in league with someone in England. I read the documents and they speak of a mint, nearly unguarded."

"Like the unguarded barrow mound we spent all night excavating," countered Godfrey.

Randulfr ran in. The experienced man was worried, which set me on edge. "The runner came from the palisade. Maredubb's army is slinking toward it. Whether or not he knows anything of our ruse doesn't matter. In moments some of them will be over and let the rest in right through the main gate."

"We're off," said Godfrey, physically pushing us out of the room. Maredubb's family still cowered at the back of the room.

Killian pushed back on the king.

"Are you mad? Has the insanity of Leif touched your mind?" boomed Godfrey. Maredubb's children screamed at the outburst. They buried their heads into their mother's bosom.

"The unguarded mint," said Killian waving a rolled up parchment in the king's face.

Randulfr snatched the vellum. "We've raided Chester before. As a result it's hardly unguarded now."

Leif stepped into the fray. "There's another mint that has gone into a town that is too small to support even the tiniest of garrisons."

"That is fine," said Godfrey, shoving again. "Can we talk about this when we are back on Man?"

"No," said Leif. "King Aethelred of the English will have a full regiment there by the end of this week, with more set to arrive during the summer. For a few more days, there is a working mint in Watchet that is essentially waiting for the taking. We must decide now."

Godfrey stopped his shoving. I knew that his mind, the mind of a king reaching for more, had clasped on the idea of a naked mint, hammering out coins just for him. I clutched the bear hide and found myself wishing for the safety of the open seas outside. Otherwise, inside would quickly be our prison should Maredubb rush in.

"Where's Watchet?" asked Godfrey.

"Odin's eye!" cursed Randulfr. "We must go now!"

"Be still," said Godfrey, calmly now. "Answer me, priest."

"It's in Devon."

"That's at the south end of my usual range." King Godfrey sighed and then gently stepped around the priest and others who had barred his way. "I've heard of the earl there. Strenwald is his name. He's strong, but not insurmountable. I'm afraid the biggest challenge we'd face is that we don't have enough men left. I don't think we should chance taking another town with so few men, do you? What? Are there forty-five of us still on our feet?"

"More or less," agreed Killian. "We can loop around the island and gather up your two ships. We can send the three we steal and the *Charging Boar* limping back north to Man with just a handful of men. *Raven's Cross* and its king will then attack Watchet in Devon."

"Attack with twenty-five men?" frowned Godfrey. I could tell he wanted to do it. It's the type of raid a true sea king would make. Bold. But he hadn't become ruler by being reckless, all the time. "I'm afraid we just can't. Now let's go."

I breathed a sigh of relief.

"Why not recruit some of the Welshmen from the town to come with us?" asked Leif. "Offer them a share. You tell me the Welsh hate the English as much as you. Well then, offer them a chance at retribution while working with a proper warrior king. You!"

Godfrey halted in his path. I sighed again. This time it was not relief. The king tugged his beard, asking, "Can you arrange all this in the last few moments that we have?"

It was Killian's turn to push the king out the door. He wore a mischievous grin as he grabbed the parchment from Randulfr. "Come, sire. We have to go. You'll see that Leif and I have already assembled another fifty men for your crews. They have strong backs and are armed. We've split them among the three ships and keep their weapons locked up for now – until we are away from here and can trust them."

"Why didn't you just say so?" asked Godfrey, feigning anger. Behind his scowl he was laughing again. The king was enjoying all the events of his future raid on Watchet in his mind's eye.

"I tried to tell you. But then I saw that you'd have to come to the decision on your own."

Godfrey shrugged as we went down the narrow set of stairs to the main floor of the keep. Our footsteps echoed against the bare stone walls. "I suppose you're right. And so, if you've got this Welsh army built for me, we won't have to go limping around with just one boat and twenty-five men?"

"No, King Godfrey," said Leif. "You'll attack the mint at Watchet with over ninety men and five ships."

Godfrey was pleased. He grinned in the dim light provided by the sputtering torches along the stairwell. "Twenty men per ship is not many, but it will be enough." We didn't have an army. We had a start, though.

Loki burst through the door. "Time to go! Maredubb is in the town."

• • •

"We've lit the other boats!" called Loki.

We ran into the bailey on his tail. I still carried the bear pelt. Long ago we had taken the time to close the twin doors of the curtain wall. Nonetheless, we all glanced in that direction as if Maredubb's men would come pouring through or over at that exact moment. They did not, but we heard shouts. We heard the footfalls of horse. They were just outside. If they didn't attack the fortress, which they ought not, they would clamber down to the docks and attack us there.

Godfrey led us down the steep steps carved into the cliff. They were slippery from the night sea air and the king slipped onto his rump, skidding partway down. He got up swearing. We ran down after him, Killian hoisting his robes as he went.

"Push away! Push away!" Godfrey was waving his arms frantically. We could see that the boats were no longer moored, but sat just off the rickety wooden docks. The force of the sea coming in and the strength of the river going out reached a kind of détente and thereby allowed the boats to bob, nearly stationary.

Magnus acknowledged the order with a wave. He barked to the men and they drove the blades of their oars into the docks, leaning into them. The boats slowly came to life.

I looked left at the main path that led from the town down to the docks. It was packed with fast approaching riders. Maredubb! Next to the path, the boats that we left behind were turning into a conflagration. Loki had been wise to set fire to the only means Maredubb would have to pursue us.

Godfrey hit the short flat area of land at the bottom of the cliff and sprinted toward his would-be boats. He jumped, launching over the waters. He whacked his chest into the gunwale, and dug his fingers like claws in order to hang on. The strong hands of strangers, his Welsh volunteers, pulled him aboard. Leif jumped. Randulfr leapt. Both made it in similar fashion to the king. Loki careened forward and used one of the oars that jutted from an oar hole as a footfall. He jumped his way up it, and the next oar, until he sprang into the ship.

Killian had the presence of mind to throw the rolled letter describing the location of the mint onto the nearest craft. The short priest jumped with all his might as the boats eased further away, but did not make it over the chasm. He bounced off the bulwark and splashed into the river. It was deep there and his heavy robes became heavier with water. Killian struggled. His arms flailed. The water churned. His head snuck beneath the surface.

I cursed. Instead of leaping to save myself, I thundered to a halt. I again peered left. Maredubb was perhaps twenty yards away, his angry, red face illuminated by the growing blaze. I returned my eyes to the departing ship, saw Aoife, and launched the balled hide at her. She was surprised and its force slammed her down to the planking. "Throw us a rope!" I shouted and jumped into the river after Killian.

I realized then that I still wore my chainmail. I plunged down just as had the priest. But I was young. I frantically kicked my feet and pumped my arms until I rammed into Killian from beneath. I pushed us up out of the water just when a rope splashed down next to us. Each of us grabbed on and felt the welcoming tug from our comrades and the pilfered boat's progress.

A spear splashed into the water next to my head. Then a second whirred by. I turned to see that Maredubb's army was fanning out along the shore. An arrow, tipped with fire skipped into the air and rammed into the hull of one of Maredubb's boats, but Brandr leaned over and batted the flames out with his bare palm.

King Maredubb walked over to the man who had launched the flaming arrow and punched him. "Those are my boats! They contain my treasure! I'll not have them at the bottom of the Irish Sea." The archer remained on his feet and gave his king an impudent stare. Maredubb bristled, cowing the man to more properly avert his gaze.

Godfrey leaned on the gunwale with one arm. In the other he held up Maredubb's bear hide. "And we have a bit of your personal effects."

"You are a liar!" shouted Maredubb.

"All men are liars," laughed Godfrey. "You probably tell yourself you are handsome!" I heard a raucous round of laughter from the ships. Even our new Welshmen guffawed when

Godfrey's words were translated for them. I clung to the rope, choking on salt water. Killian, in turn, clutched onto my mail. We pulled further and further away. Maredubb slowly walked along the shore parallel to us. Godfrey continued, "But I kept my word. You'll find that your family is in fine condition. Your treasury is half full. I am no liar."

Horse Ketil limped up from the crowd of soldiers. He stopped at the end of the narrowing beach where the king had been forced to do the same. "You lie about your strength, Godfrey!" shouted Ketil. It sounded like it was painful for him to talk. With the inferno behind us at the docks, I could see that my beatings had left him with serious wounds. Black, dried blood caked his forehead. His nose was the consistency of minced flesh. "Now it is not only I who know about your weakness. A rival king, an enemy, now knows just how anemic you are. Maredubb knows just how tenuous is your grip on Man."

"I'll get my ships back. I'll get my treasure back. You will repay this debt with usury, Godfrey! With usury," called Maredubb.

Then the winds caught our sails and we danced into the sea.

PART II –Watchet!

CHAPTER 6

It took us less than a day to swing north around the island and retrieve *Raven's Cross* and *Charging Boar*. Tyrkr had seen the approach of our foreign ships from the sea and was prepared for a proper fight against our men. That is, until he saw the grinning face of Leif.

"Not a peep," Tyrkr said in his accented Norse as we came in close. We did not slide our commandeered boats into the shore. Instead, we rowed backward to slow our progress and tossed out the anchor. There was no sense in grounding, then tipping over, our less agile prizes. Even if they weren't fine warships, Godfrey would be able to peddle them in Dyflin, which was the most bustling of Norse centers in the Irish Sea.

"I heard horseman above. Turf Ear and I went up to investigate. The riders scoured the larger beach nearby, but missed this altogether. Do you have the treasure? Where did you get the army? Did the draugr come to life?" asked Tyrkr when he saw all the strangers who populated our ships.

"Something like that," said Leif as we began to transfer men to *Raven's Cross* and *Charging Boar*. King Godfrey returned to his flagship, relieving Turf Ear from his watchman's post. Leif and I climbed to our tub. The new Welsh volunteers were dispersed evenly among the ships so none could overpower us should they try.

The entire operation took mere moments after which we were once again pulling out to sea. This time we needed the oars and felt fortunate – Killian had called it a blessing – to have our Welsh sailors with us. They sat on the rowing benches next to our men and tugged at the oaken blades. There were some fits and starts as the inexperienced Welshmen began. Leif shouted at a few. I heard Godfrey do the same aboard his boat. Randulfr had taken his boot off and was swatting a man with the sole in order to teach him the rhythm.

"The treasure must have been great. Was the ancient king there?" asked Tyrkr.

"King was there," I muttered.

Aoife finished my thought. "Treasure like a dried turd."

"Then where do the boats come from? And the army? And why does the King Godfrey look so pleased to be heading home with no treasure?" asked Tyrkr. He cranked his oar as if it were a part of him. The novices were beginning to pull in time. The familiar grate-slap began. I loved the grate-slap. The oar would creak ever so slightly where it laced through the oar hole. The fat blades would slap the sea water as the rowers finished leaning forward and brought their hands up to their chests. It was a motion and sound that would repeat itself over the next two hundred fifty miles until we sailed around a couple major headlands, into the Mor Hafren, and into Watchet for more riches.

"While you ladies were lounging on the beach," began Aoife, "we men were capturing an entire city."

Tyrkr looked at me incredulously. "Sixty men capture a city?"

I merely nodded.

"You might be surprised what motivated men can accomplish," answered Aoife. "We took two thousand captives and demanded ransom from some pock-faced Welsh king. We took his boats. We took his hungriest of men. They now serve a real sea king. Godfrey is only just beginning." The little beast was like us all. She'd follow a winner as long as the winds were fair. Aoife no longer blamed Godfrey for the empty barrow. She had forgotten about the horrors of the brief battle in the castle bailey less than a day before. Her confidence had returned.

"And we go back to Man to build his army?" asked Tyrkr.

"Someday," said Leif.

Magnus leaned on the steering oar, pushing it to starboard. *Charging Boar* veered to port so that Tyrkr tipped toward the gunwale. Aoife scoffed at him as if she were now an experienced seaman.

"We go to take a mint and bring home even more treasure," I said.

Godfrey's longboat had pulled ahead. *Charging Boar* followed close behind, to starboard. The three stolen ships followed in a third line, more or less abreast of one another.

"I thought Godfrey wanted an army and revenge," said Tyrkr. "He's got his army. Now all we have to do is scurry to wherever this Dal Riata is and kill a few of them for revenge."

I shrugged. "I guess kings always want more coins. It will make gathering up men and arms easier." I justified Godfrey's actions as if I understood affairs of state. In truth, I knew nothing and was along for adventure and a treasure of my own. I hoped to survive long enough to spend my small share from Anglesey and what would come from Watchet. If I managed that, I thought I would retire to Man and find a fat woman to hump. Perhaps I could buy the rocky farm from the blind farmer who had presented his case at the Tynwald. I thought I could count on both Godfrey and Killian to speak a fair word for me.

Then I remembered that we had to not only run to Watchet, but that Tyrkr was right. If I made it through the raid on the mint, I had to survive our retribution on the Dal Riatans. I sighed, deciding then and there to give up my dreams of a farm and family. I would be a raider, dead or alive. I would be like a ship on the sea. I would put up my sail and catch the wind, allowing it to blow me where it would. The norns wove my fate. That's what I decided.

I've made many such 'decisions' in my life. They were steel in my heart at the moment I made them. They were stone and iron. I've abandoned all of them as if they were but thin parchment. As the years went by, I abandoned this decision, too. But that day I was a raider.

I looked up at the flag on the mainmast. It hung limp. There was no wind. Still, the backs of strong men propelled us on to a mint. I had no idea what a mint looked like. My people had yet to mint a single coin. We used money. All of it, however, came from foreign shores. We'd dump ourselves onto one of those shores and I'd seize my next chance for glory.

• • •

The daylight was lasting longer which made for more time to travel – a good thing for eager King Godfrey. It made the men rowing grow ever more exhausted, however. I took my turn at the rower's bench, my youthful back heaving against the heavy seas. I and my fellow Greenlanders fared well enough. Godfrey's more experienced raiders performed ably, of course. They never complained, except where experienced soldiers were expected to whine. Their backs rippled. Their hands clenched. The grate-slap wore on.

The Welshmen, new to the world of professional seamanship, coped with less success. After the first full day of rowing, we sidled the small flotilla into a cove. Killian and Godfrey assured me we were still in Wales. The Welshmen could not have cared if we had rowed all the way to the icy fjords of Hel or the fiery depths of the Christian Hell. As soon as the boats skidded or the anchors dropped, they collapsed to the decks, moaning. They weren't a fat or lazy lot. They were fine at whatever their vocations had been thus far, I'm sure. But they weren't seamen – not yet anyway. Their sore backs and shaking arms would make their shields and spears feel heavy when the raid began.

Godfrey took pity and allowed them to bypass watch that first night. This made his experienced men hate him, but his new Welsh crews love him. I suppose that is forever the lot of a ruler. Even a parent of more than one child, I imagine, will always anger one with a decision in favor of the other. And what was Godfrey but our father, our patron?

In the quiet of that night, the only sound was the crashing of waves elsewhere along the shore or the small lapping of the sea against our hulls. I wondered about my father – my first father. How would life have been different had he survived? Had he, Olef, raised me? Would I have even remembered that my first, true father ever ran with a man called Erik? Erik was exiled along with his own father from Norway. Erik was, in turn, exiled from Iceland. Both banishments for the same reason – murder. Would I have ever had an occasion to cross paths with a king, let alone serve one? Or, would I have been rutting with a fine woman under the hides of animals that I had taken? Would

I, aged twenty-one winters, already have two or three children of my own?

I was still wondering about the past when I heard Killian's voice echo across the waters. "Wake yourselves, the king wishes to depart with the tide before the sun arrives. Move! Slough off the joy of your dreams."

Several men from the surrounding boats grumbled, to which Killian replied, "Oh, my brothers, you know what the friend of Job says, 'The mirth of the wicked is brief.' What are we but wicked, Christian or pagan alike? Now, you may complain, but then with your lips flapping you may miss time for a morning meal."

The mumbling halted and men stirred to life. I ate some of the stores of bread from Man. It was dark and I didn't bother to see if it was moldy. I'm sure it was. Bite after bite crawled down my gullet. I washed it down with a pot of ale.

We rowed nearly straight southward for most of the day.

We saw a fishing boat. When its crew saw us approaching, they promptly turned and raced back toward the protection offered by shore and civilization. We laughed at them, for had we wanted to, Godfrey's ship alone could have overtaken the fishermen in moments, put them all to the sword, and taken their catch. It seemed like a lot of trouble, though, especially when the true prize of our sea romp would be worth so much more.

We turned to starboard when we saw a large promontory of land, the last large peninsula of Wales, the Welshmen said. It took many long hours to navigate around it as we kept the land to our port.

Godfrey drove us long into the night, something that again caused grumbling, but I understood. He shouted over the waves that tomorrow would bring us to Devon, Watchet specifically, if the maps were to be believed. He wanted us there early and fresh. Better to work hard today and rest for the night rather than work at the oars all day before immediately sliding into a beach and battle. Eventually, even the king was tired. He had spent time at the rowing bench to goad his followers into working harder. By the faint moonlight we found a broad, sandy beach for the night's camp. So tired were we that none of us bothered to see if we ran straight into a village. Godfrey had such distaste for the defensive abilities of Welsh settlements that he would have still blindly slid into shore even if we weren't exhausted. Afterward, he did have the sense to place several watchmen around the hills that led down to the beach.

Night passed uneventfully. Morning came. We covered ourselves in armor and belted on our weapons. We gave the Welshmen their weapons, a gesture that immediately improved their morale. Our rowers went to work, facing aft. It would be our last glimpse of Wales as we again struck a southerly course. Soon, I would lay eyes on England for the first time in my life.

It would be a strandhogg, not at all like my first ever raid on Anglesey. There, we went ashore, hoping for stealth in order to steal a hidden treasure. We ended up with treasure in a wholly different manner, of course. But Watchet, I'd soon learn, would be more like every other raid that I've experienced.

It was to be rapid, loud, and deadly.

• • •

We rowed on to Watchet through thick fog. I cursed and heard other men cursing the weather, for though we knew that the town and mint were just a short distance south, the fog might find us coming ashore ten English miles or ten English feet from our target.

For his part, Killian spent the time shouting encouragement over the rhythms of our oars. "What a blessing is this mist," he'd say. "God gave the Egyptian pharaoh a plague of frogs. He gives the English a plague of fog." And then he added, "And raiders!" I think he said it more to keep the tired Welshmen rowing, but his booming voice did serve a more immediate purpose. Since we could not see a fadmr in front of our noses, we could certainly not lay eyes on the other boats. As long as we could still hear the priest's wailing to port, those of us on *Charging Boar* knew our small fleet was together. There was no guarantee that, though we remained near one another, we sailed a true course.

I had just settled my back at rest against one of the T-shaped oar racks in the ship's center. Aoife, my slave who had yet to perform more than the most modest of tasks for me, sat next to me. I had given her the remainder of ale from the bottom of my pot. She sipped at the meager ration and licked her teeth to clean the film of sleep from their surface. "You know, Halldorr," she began.

"You ought to call me master or sir or even lord," I said unconvincingly.

To my surprise the girl paused and gave my suggestion some thought. She drained the last of what was now her ale and blew out a large breath through puffed lips. "I think not, Halldorr. If we are to be fellow warriors, at least I as your skjoldmo for a short while, then we ought to speak as equals." I chuckled at her being a shield girl, which is what skjoldmo meant. But I suppose that her use of the word at least partially explains why many years later, in a land not yet discovered by my people, I would call my own little daughter Skjoldmo.

"Then call me what you will," I said, resigned.

"I shall," she chuckled precociously. "You know, you never thanked me for saving your life in the battle at the keep."

"My life?" I asked. I remembered how I had slowly drained the life from Aoife's attacker with my forearm pressing into his throat. "I saved yours."

Killian continued his calling out. "My Welsh cousins, carry on! We go to invade and harry the English. We give them blood, for blood begets blood. They've drained yours. It is your day to drain theirs."

Godfrey shouted in response. "That's quite enough, priest." He sounded disgusted with Killian. I laughed when I thought of the bickering pair. "You'll ruin whatever advantage the fog cover has given us."

Killian, in typical fashion, would not back down so easily. "And King Godfrey, is it better to sneak into shore and find out that yours is the only longboat in an area surrounded by prickling spears? Or, would you rather come to Watchet with your entire armada intact?"

Godfrey swore to the norns for putting the priest in his path. Then he answered, defeated, "Carry on, priest."

He did.

Aoife slapped my mailed chest with the back of her hand. "So you are under the mistaken impression that because you killed the man with your hands that you saved my life?" She didn't pause for my answer. It was just as well. "Yet you forget that you wouldn't be sitting here today had I not rammed your saex into his groin. He would have chopped you in half. Pierce and twist, that's what I did."

I wasn't going to argue with the sure-minded creature. With an overdramatized bow of my head, I said, "Young Aoife, I thank you for your gallantry. Without you I would be dead."

"I know," Aoife answered plainly. She scratched at a louse in her hair. "Do you think that man would have died even without your strangling?"

"In time. He would have bled to death. You cut a man in the groin and there's almost no stopping the flow."

"So, I'll count him as my first kill. I told Godfrey, and then you, that I intended to kill a man, or two."

"Docks!" Killian screamed from port.

I rolled to my feet and was promptly sent back to the deck when *Charging Boar* hammered into a firmly placed dock piling. We didn't strike it head on, but careened starboard, the port side bouncing along the post. The first three rowers on the port side received a swift smack of the oar handle into their noses as the blades snapped to the unflinching will of the stationary dock pillar.

"Ropes!" called Leif. "Get us moored here!"

I knocked down a Welsh rower as I seized the coiled rope aft. After forming a kind of large lasso, I tossed it to the post that would otherwise quickly fade into the distance. I allowed the cord to snake overboard as I tied it off to a cleat. At once the excess length was used up. It snapped taut as fast as a feral dog's nip, sending many of us to the deck planking again.

"Pull us in!" Leif yelled. He held a separate rope and was throwing a loop toward another post that had come into view through the morning mist. Godfrey was relaying similar orders.

The calls from *Raven's Cross* sounded nearby, but I could see neither them nor the other boats.

Shouts from ahead echoed as well. Later, Killian told me it was English, a bastardized tongue formed from the words of Jutes, Angles, Saxons, Britons, Danes, and Celts. When he told me this, I remember thinking that I would do my part to add some trusty Norse words to their thieving language. That morning though, I understood little of it. I could only tell that the calls that raced over the waters carried a fair amount of agitation. Our noisy entrance into England did not go unnoticed. The alarm had sounded.

The rowers, even those with misshapen noses, fished their oars out through the oar holes and stowed them on the T-shaped racks while Leif and I hauled us ever closer to the dock. Behind me, I heard the familiar rap of shields being hauled up to the arms of their owners. I heard spears and swords clattering as men pushed for position on the rocking longboat. Aoife wedged next to me and without asking what to do recoiled the excess rope that was accumulating at my feet. She was a smart beast.

As soon as the port side strakes were an ell away from the dock, men began leaping over *Charging Boar*'s gunwale. They landed with thuds and without orders began forming a shield wall, inching their way further onto the dock and the unknown dangers that lurked ahead toward land. The hull crunched into the pier. Leif and I retied her off to the cleats. Aoife jumped over and then Leif and then me.

Leif and I pressed through our men to assess the situation. I snatched a Welshman by his hair and tugged him so that his shield was held more tightly to the next man's in the shield wall. We had clearly made it to England, hence the English. We had obviously made it to a town, hence the docks. What was less clear was whether or not we had even landed at Watchet.

To my left, I could just make out Godfrey's ship. They were now moored to a separate rickety dock that jutted out parallel to ours. To my right, past *Charging Boar*, I could see nothing but dark water and more fog. Ahead I could see the dock on which we stood disappear into the mist. The general, dark, looming form of a hillside or town lay beyond.

"Are we all here?" shouted Godfrey.

"*Charging Boar* is here!" answered Leif. "Where is here?"

Godfrey ignored the question. Brandr's voice rang out from the other side of Godfrey. "*Dancing Stag* is here!" *Dancing Stag* was the makeshift name Brandr had given one of our newly stolen boats.

"*Snake's Revenge* is here!" called Loki, who had transferred to that boat to be her captain.

Several moments went by. "By Hel, where is Randulfr and his crew?"

"We've no time to find out," Killian shouted. "We're here, wherever that is. We must move quickly and use what surprise we have left."

"Move up the docks to the shingle. We assemble there and sweep in," Godfrey called.

We jogged forward, holding our shields high to prevent a lucky archer from making an improbable kill from out of the mist. Our feet thundered across the docks until we rattled out onto a rock strewn beach. As soon as our small shield wall met that of Godfrey, I leaned down to Aoife who had remained at my heel. "Find that other ship and lead Randulfr back to us."

The girl was a fine addition to our raid. Of course, I didn't think so at the start. Of course, I protested her presence. But after I gave her my order that morning on the shingle in England, without the least bit of questioning or wavering, the dirty Irish girl grabbed my nose and cranked it. "I'll bring those men, but don't go killing all the Englishmen before I get my shot." Aoife finished by shoving my nose back into my face and tearing off down the shore.

Godfrey had stepped in front of our assembled army. He gave no speech though I had wanted one. Instead the King of the Isles did what was expected of a wicked Norse warrior. He drew his lightweight war axe from his belt, hefted his shield, and turned his back to us.

"Let us take what we will." He spoke in an almost hushed tone. It was quiet, but grave, determined. Without waiting for any answer, Godfrey stepped forward and disappeared into the fog. The army behind him exchanged glances and then followed their king into the mist and into the growing din of the unknown.

• • •

We moved forward slowly, our leather boots slipping over the smooth, rounded stones and crunching the remains of the dead shellfish that littered the shingle. It took longer than I had expected to cross the shoreline, for it was deep when measured from the docks to wherever the town began.

And there was most certainly a town. It was most certainly a garrisoned town because in the fog I heard a growing number of shouts from whomever we would oppose. They were not the terrified screams of simple villagers, though those could be heard farther on. No, these were the disciplined calls of men with military experience. They were quick clips, shouts, and growls. And, unlike most raids on civilian targets in which I have since participated, these voices drew closer, rather than farther. They grew louder rather than softer.

Then the noise became like a roiling nest of serpents.

A spear smashed into the face of a fellow Greenlander. His blood spattered my neck before his body toppled backward. A host of grunts from the fog brought dozens more spears. Most were not well aimed, but still, Welshmen, Norsemen, Manx, and Greenlanders all fell with missiles jutting from legs, arms, or worse.

Godfrey continued marching forward and so the rest of us moved on behind him.

I will now share with you a secret. I was more than a little frightened of what we would see in the heretofore unseen enemy. Though I had fear, I was experienced enough to show none while in the shield wall. I was intelligent enough to mention nothing about it later. What type of raider would I have been had I whined about my anxieties in the thick of battle or even in its aftermath? I'll answer that. I would have been a festering wound on a useless limb, good for nothing but amputation, deserving nothing but scorn.

All at once I saw vague forms, blobs of dark masses, really.

We crashed into that mass like a slow moving wave tumbles over the rocks on the shore. They stood firm with their shields raised. They were the solid earth. We flowed, or perhaps, melted, acting as the water. Our momentum fled. We were halted.

There were several moments when no one swung a weapon, be it a spear or a sword or an axe. We shoved one another, shield against shield. My old piece of timber was pressed against an Englishman's bark. The man was a head shorter than me. Everyone was shorter than me back then, though I think a shriveled woman aged fifty is probably larger than me today. I know that I held my spear at bay. My tarnished sword hung harmlessly at my waist, my father's saex securely next to it. What I did that morning in the fog was push.

I rammed my shield again and again into my opponent. He repeated the favor, staring up angrily through wide green eyes. The Englishman spat curses. I didn't know what he said, but they were curses, probably the same as the ones I hurled in his face. "You filthy stinking shit! I'll wipe you from this beach like I scrape a dog's waste from my boot."

It was as if the morning fog had made both sides tepid. The English had been willing to launch projectiles into the mist, but once our faces were a nose's distance from their own, they lost their will. In fairness, we seemed to have experienced the same. Godfrey pressed his shield against the shields of two men. The king was not a man of great size, but his zeal more than made up for it. Smaller yet was Killian. The priest held a shield just like the rest of us. He swore a string of curses in his native tongue for which I'm sure he would have to beg forgiveness from his One True God. Turf Ear screamed. He could probably only hear the loudest of the Englishmen's jeering. The Welshmen shouted and pushed. It was an entirely impotent struggle.

The king was jostling with an Englishman who was as stout as a bear. Then Godfrey lost his footing on the slick, loose stones of the shingle. His feet slid backward and he fell to his knees. Godfrey used the edge of his great round shield to stop his progress before his chest slapped into the ground. The big Englishman tipped forward onto the king and began fumbling with his spear in order to ram it into the Godfrey's exposed back.

The time for nervous posturing had ended. It was like when the drums hummed at a celebration around the bonfire during Winternights. As soon as the jarl strode to the speaking rock, the musicians all understood that it was time for their riotous noise to cease. They would halt their pounding at once so that a solid two heartbeats of dead silence passed before the jarl's powerful words rang true.

Both sides of the contest on the shingle that morning halted all movement when the king and large enemy warrior toppled together. For two lumbering heartbeats we turned our attention to the only spot that showed action. The king and the Englishman grappled. Even men at the end of the line, far out of sight of the king, sensed a change and stayed their hands. They stopped their thrusting as they peered toward the center.

The pressure against my shield ebbed. My mind calculated a hundred possibilities of what to do, but truly only one viable idea came to mind. I knew only that the shield wall and its cohesion were all important. The shield wall, intact, meant life. The shield wall, with a gap, meant certain death. Ours had a gap in it that morning, a crack that could allow the flood waters of growling Englishmen to pour through and hack us from the rear. Our knees would buckle. Our heads would be lost.

With quick ferociousness, I clutched the shaft of my spear, turned, and plunged the head into the stout Englishman's neck. Blood ran down onto the king's back. The English warrior clawed and kicked at the stones for a moment before he became still, moaning. I jerked the spear back out and was rewarded with a spray of the man's crimson. Still holding my spear, I slapped my hand on his back and lifted him off my king.

I threw his large body back to its place in their line. Godfrey jumped to his feet, instantly ready.

Only one heartbeat of silence passed this time. It was not lumbering.

The English saw their fallen comrade and reacted as all men would. They hefted their spears, stepped forward, and stabbed over the tops of their shields. More blood. This time it was ours. Cheeks were scraped. Eyes were lost, mouths left with permanent gaping holes.

We answered back with interlocking shields.

I felt a sudden breeze blow in from the sea behind me. It was an omen to be sure. We were fearsome warriors who emerged from the depths, to come ashore and wreak whatever havoc we would. Behind us, in proof that ours was a just cause, the eagle that perched itself on the topmost branches of the Yggdrasil tree was beating his wings, sending wind into the billowing sails of our hearts, of our side of the battle. Figurative, perhaps, but that's the way I felt that morning when my long blonde hair was lifted off my back by the rush of air. The fog, too, was pushed, inch by creeping inch, away from the sea.

A spear glanced off my helmet, ringing my head. I was suddenly angry and indignant. I crouched low under my shield and heaved upward sending the enemy scrambling back on his feet as he fought to retain his balance. I reached into the gap and cut a man's sword-hand badly. He recoiled.

How easy life is in the shield wall. You lock with your fellow raiders. You fight with discipline in short quick stabs and, in time, you pry the enemy apart. They fall by ones as more fissures form. They fall by twos as your men lever their way in. Then the enemy dies, all of them. It's as sure as the morning sun.

If you believe all that, you know nothing. You've experienced nothing of worth. And that saddens me.

Perhaps you are a woman, a nun, instructed in the art of reading. It would make sense that you have no knowledge of life and mostly death in the shield wall. I was married to a former nun for a rather brilliant time. She had a tenacious mind, understanding concepts of kings and queens for which I cared nothing. So my wife, the former nun, wasn't foolish or daft or stupid. She was quick-witted and intelligent. Yet with all her experience in the harsh, cruel world, with all her reading of the words of the One God, she understood nothing about the shield wall.

Of more concern to me is that you are a man, so-called, and do not understand the shield wall. A part of me applauds your chance to grow to a mature age and be so fortunate to have lived in a grand time of peace that you never had to stand in the thick line. However, I know the minds of man. He is completely serene when the harvests are good, when his wife is fertile, when his children live. Bring the rot to his barley, bring a few stillborn children from his wife's womb, or kill some of his already living children with a pestilence or a surly horse's hoof and that same calm man's thoughts change. Consolidate power into that same man's hands as in a king, jarl, or raider and that quiet, nonviolent man becomes a terror, forcing his beneficial will onto all in his path with the utmost vigor. What I am saying is that your peaceful time is an illusion. You may not have had to stand in the shield wall, but your sons will. And your sons will vomit blood and shit their trousers if you've taught them nothing of the shield wall.

Let me explain that the shield wall is not glamorous. It is not complicated. It is insanity and madness. It is brute strength, nothing more. It is unrelenting pounding. I've smelled more human waste in the shield wall than in all the times I had to empty the longhouse dung bucket as a youth. The shield wall will allow the side that understands it and employs it victory in an even contest. The shield wall can assure triumph if the side that uses it is greater in numbers. The shield wall can even tip the scales when the side that uses it is outnumbered by as much as two to one. It is effective, not elegant. Men on both sides are filleted open. The side that properly utilizes the wall should lose fewer of its precious soldiers. It is as simple as that.

The fog was quickly being dispersed by that breeze that I had thought was a sign from the old gods. I was a fool. What was revealed by the faint sunlight that was trying ever so hard to burn its way through was that the English lines were growing.

They already outnumbered us. I didn't care to hazard a guess, but theirs was some multiple of our force. The last of their stragglers were running down a sweeping slope from the town's garrison to join in the fray.

There was no doubt in my mind at that point. We had found Watchet. And the English troops that were to reinforce the mint in the coming days had already arrived.

• • •

"Shove them back into the dung hole from which they came!" called Godfrey. The king used his sword to cut a man across his knuckles. It wasn't life threatening. However, it did cause his opponent to drop his weapon and bend to retrieve it. Godfrey kicked the man's awkwardly hoisted shield with the bottom of his foot. It danced upward just long enough for the king to flick the tip of his sword into the man's exposed armpit. The Englishman fell sideways. Leif finished him with a swift kick in the face and hack at his neck with a sword.

Two English nobles rode behind the enemy's lines. One of them, who appeared to be a thegn, was reorganizing his troops now that we could see more of each other. He rode a spirited charger that eagerly danced on the rolling stones of the beach. The beast's hooves stomped and padded back and forth while its rider stood tall in the saddle screaming in his native tongue.

I cocked my arm and launched my spear over the burgeoning English line. It cracked the thegn square on his helmet so that his head flapped over. The helm toppled off to the ground while the rider fought to stay on his horse. He gripped the horse's barrel with his legs and pulled himself upright with the reins. The horse whipped its snout, blowing out bursts of air into the fading mist.

The thegn scanned his enemy – us – and saw me towering above the rest, staring back. I must give him his credit. He didn't scamper down to recover his armor. No, his lips curled like an angry she-wolf and he kicked his already agitated charger. He came up behind the line that was increasingly filling with fallen bodies and spattering blood. Then the thegn commenced shouting and pointing at me. I, of course, didn't know what he said at the time. Since that day I've learned many languages, English among them. I can relay his words to you now only because Killian laughed and laughed about them later.

The English thegn stabbed a sword in my direction, shouting, "I am Goda, a mighty lord of Devon, servant of Aethelred who is King of England. You," and this part made even Godfrey laugh because despite my tarnished armor and tarnished sword, this Goda mistook me for the leader of our band, "and your miscreants may wash ashore like weeds from the sea left behind by the tide. We'll do what we always do to the refuse that lines our beaches. We'll chop you up and cook you. I myself will hew you and baste you and serve you to my whelps." Now before you believe that the English were cannibals, let me assure you that this man, Goda, was sufficiently lathered with anger that I believe he could have said anything. I don't believe he meant to eat us, though.

His words were enough to further encourage his men, not that they needed any. We had already retreated nearly back to the docks. Several dozen of our number had fallen. Turf Ear's entire left side was limp. It was drenched in his blood which poured from twin gashes near his neck. His left arm was dangling straight down, holding his shield that dragged a path through the rocks. Still Turf Ear guarded the far left of our line. He clumsily swung his great sword at any of the score of English who tried to turn our flank. It was frightening to think that an old, wounded, near deaf man was all that prevented our line being turned. But looking back I think it was the best we could have hoped for at the time. Turf Ear cut another man down. He inched back. Turf Ear stabbed a man. He inched toward the docks.

Goda was still frothing with anger. His rage boiled so, that he needed to share it. He turned it on other men. Then Goda returned to me, directing all manners of vitriol like one well-aimed arrow after another.

The other noble, of higher rank, maybe even Strenwald, the earl of whom Godfrey had heard, rode back and forth holding his reins and nothing else. He hoisted no shield. The earl held no spear, no sword. He seemed confident as if victory was a foregone conclusion.

And it was. Or, I should say that it would have been had the One God not been with the two chief participants from our side of the battle. It would bring my heart pleasure to say that it was Thor, then my god of thunder, who propelled us to victory. It wasn't. It wasn't the eagle's wings bringing the wind. It wasn't Thor pounding out rolling thunder with his mjolnir. I knew this then as I know it now. It was the One God, for it was two of his followers who led us to victory.

The first, at least partial, follower was King Godfrey. The One God must have been ever forgiving of Godfrey's attempts to divine the future by casting lots rather than praying to Him. The True God forgave the king for sometimes falling back to the old gods. Maybe it was the king's frequent and usually generous donations to Killian's church on Man. Maybe Godfrey knew how to pray for that forgiveness with enough confidence to deserve it. Or, maybe Killian and the other priests I've met over the years are right and the One True God wants nothing more than to forgive all of us our transgressions. I hope that is the case, for mine are many. God was with King Godfrey as he hacked Englishmen that morning.

The second person with whom the One God was with at Watchet was Aoife. I had nearly forgotten about her and the mission on which I sent her. My mind was in the battle, my tongue was thirsty for English blood, my limbs worked on their own volition to parry blows and slice opponents before being directed by my head to the next threat. Goda was screaming. He grew louder as our band grew smaller, huddling more tightly behind an ever-shrinking shield wall. We were going to be pushed back to the docks. We were going to lose the ships we had just stolen and the treasure they carried. In spite of the chaos and my confusion, Aoife didn't forget her duty.

I felt a sharp pain in my back and spun to chop down whoever had just poked me. Aoife stood back there holding a bundle of spears. She'd used the butt of one of them to ram my back and get my attention. "I should cut you!" I spat as I turned around to face the menacing English.

Aoife rammed harder. Without looking back, I swatted at the spear shaft with an elbow.

"Damn you, Halldorr!" Aoife cried as she held up an arm to stop my swing. "Use these spears until you kill that screaming fool on the horse. I retrieved them from Leif's ship."

We were going to be dead soon. The English were tightening the noose. The girl had a point. I decided to take a dead thegn as a prize as my little Valkyrie led me to Valhalla. I slid my bloody sword into its cracked scabbard. Bubbling crimson spurt out the sheath's mouth. "Spear," I commanded, holding out an open palm toward Aoife. "You didn't find the other ship?"

I turned to face the battle. Godfrey and Leif had slid together to cover the hole in the shield wall I had left. They stabbed and cut the numerous English who were bent on killing them. I let loose the spear at Goda who had again moved away. It tore at the strong mail that covered his back. The chain was sturdy and held as the spear bounced away, but Goda was pushed forward in his saddle from the force of the blow. He turned to face me at the same time I turned to get another spear.

"No, I found the ship and her crew," Aoife said as she handed me another spear.

"Then where in Thor's beard are they?" I asked.

"They are where they are needed," she began.

"They're needed here!"

"Shut up and kill that noble. We'll see if the hearts of the English melt when they see a leader fall."

I cursed the nymph and spun to see that Goda was still on his horse, closing in. Earl Strenwald had ridden next to him and now both were freely calling to their men, sensing impending victory. I cocked my arm for the third time that day and launched the spear at Goda.

All at once his shouting stopped. My spear tore into his upraised chin. The steel head was driven so deep that only the wooden shaft could be seen. It was quickly covered in a river of blood. Goda's charger sensed its master's trouble. It felt the easing of the reins and weakening of Goda's knees. The beast smelled his owner's blood. The horse panicked and reared so that Goda's dead body fell with a thud to the shingle, dashing sea-worn stones to the side.

Strenwald, who I guessed was a competent commander, took the death of his second in stride. He reached for the bucking horse's reins. I heard Strenwald call soothing words to the energetic charger, trusting that his soldiers would wipe up the rest of our pathetic lot without his constant vigilance.

Bells, large, deep, peeling bells severed the mist. Strenwald furrowed his brow and spun in his saddle to look back to the town and the source of the noise. He'd instantly forgotten about Goda's wild horse.

I looked up at the town, too. The breeze had been blowing. The sun had begun its baking of the vapor. What was a moment ago beginning to form into visible images of a few homes, shops, and even a small stone garrison had receded into a black fog. The mist was enshrouding it again, darker.

Then I smelled it. Goda's beast smelled it an instant before. And it was too much for the animal's heightened awareness to take. It kicked its rear hooves into the air a half dozen times, landing each time on Goda, tearing his flesh. Then the warhorse reared, pawing at the air with its shod feet. Each time it crashed back down it crushed one of the Englishmen fighting in the line. At last, the beast ran away down the beach, kicking and scattering any English in its path.

It wasn't the fog that was rolling back in. The beast knew it before the men. It was smoke. The entire town was burning and the churches were ringing their bells in warning.

"I'd shout 'attack' if I were you, Godfrey," called Aoife.

The surprised king and the rest of us on the beach looked up toward the blazing town. It puked smoke. Coming down out of the black vomit was the missing crew, fresh, unharmed. They carried shields high and tight. They bristled with spears. Randulfr stood strong at the center. Aoife had been right. They were just where they needed to be.

"Crush them between us!" Godfrey screamed. His eyes appeared like white, burning beacons amidst his blood strewn face. "Push! Push again!"

I saw fear in the Englishmen's faces. Though they still outnumbered us, those faces blanched. Strenwald saw it too. He kicked his feet from his stirrups and jumped down to fight with his men, his now terrified men. They looked back to their homes and thought of their wives and children burning. They looked at the beaten, trounced form of Goda. The English watched the crazed charger fleeing and wished to trade places. They looked at all the bodies littering the shingle and their minds told them that all those dead were their own countrymen. I know this is what they thought because of what happened next. When a battle shifts mightily against you, you begin to see everything as a loss. Or, when you *believe* the battle has shifted, even though it has not, you see only destruction. Those soldiers that day, at that time, thought they would lose. Their hearts fled. They melted like the last icicle hanging from the longhouse eave on a sunny day.

    We pushed them. We crushed them.

    We were victorious.

CHAPTER 7

Spurred by the confusion in the English lines and with renewed vigor, we stepped on the bodies of our fallen comrades and those of the defenders. We pushed and stabbed at them. Our men who emerged from the smoke did likewise. The enemy fought hard, but with little soul. When Godfrey's sword chopped off, first, Earl Strenwald's fingers then his hand and finally his arm, the weary soldiers fell to their knees. Their hands went up as their weapons went down. They pled with us that we cease. They babbled. They sought our compassion.

"Kill one in ten of the remaining," offered Randulfr.

"Use the rest to fight the fire so we don't have to wait for a week for the embers to cool. I'd hate to have to retrieve a heavy mountain of melted, unwieldy gold from this mint," added Leif.

Killian wiped a small hand against his forehead which was wet with sweat and the splattered brains of an Englishman. "They make sense, King Godfrey."

Godfrey looked up at the growing fire. The smoke swirled and climbed into the sky. The north wind pushed it south over more of England. The king nodded in agreement, for which I was pleased because every man added would mean one less bucket of sea water to haul. However, like a zigzagging hare changing directions while darting from a fox, Godfrey changed his mind. "No, kill them all. Make it fast. I don't want to have to look over my shoulder while we take Aethelred's coins. Any one of these men would happily stab me in my back."

"The whirlwind," mumbled Killian, "you'll reap it."

"But Godfrey you accepted the Welsh as fellow raiders," I said. "What is wrong with sparing these men if they work for us just today?" At the time I didn't know of which whirlwind Killian spoke. I wasn't fond of the idea of leaving enemies alive. I say again that I didn't want to lug any more water than I had to.

"You'll kill them, Greenlander," said Godfrey. "And you'll remember to call me king." Godfrey was feeling strong again. That was a good thing. His temporary despondency while on Anglesey was becoming a distant memory now that he had two rapid triumphs in his recent history. Godfrey was also feeling arrogant. That, too, was a good thing, for of all the kinds of people who ought to be arrogant, shouldn't one be a king?

I cursed and unsheathed my sword. With two hands I brought the edge down on the shoulder of a surrendered Englishman. I swore. I felt like a murderer. The blade was tired and so were my muscles. It dug one-third of the way through and halted. When the whining soldier toppled over and writhed in pain, he jerked the hilt from my hand. The sword's guard scratched a path in the stones while he convulsed.

The rest of our band stabbed and killed the unarmed soldiers. For their part, the English didn't go without a fight. They scraped at us. They snarled like cornered rats. It was a dirty, grisly business. Even zealous Aoife and Killian lingered back and watched their feet rather than us as we tore into them. The Welsh, however, were more fervent than any of the others. It wasn't that different from how I, from Rogaland in Norway, would have treated a Dane in similar circumstances. If that Dane had wronged me or my family – as far back as two generations ago – I would have ardently chopped him to pieces. I think the Welsh felt that way about the English – and to be fair, vice versa.

"Now what?" asked Leif as the final Englishman exhaled his last. "Buckets from the boats? Scrounge what containers we can from other boats and buildings? Form a fire brigade?" He finished by saying, "We could have used those men." Leif was just as disgusted with his king as the rest of us.

"Aethelred's coins aren't in the town. Let the stinking mess, burn." Godfrey pointed with his nose to my right, the west. "We go there."

Properly confused, his army peered along the shore to the west. There, perhaps one hundred fadmr in distance, where earlier thick fog clung, stood a tall bluff that dropped straight into the sea. Sitting atop that bluff, precariously close to the eroding cliff's edge, was an earthen and stone fort. The outermost wall was strong, mortared stone that abutted the cliff's edge. I could see the top of a tall, narrow keep, like the newer one in Aberffraw, tucked inside the fort. From down there on the shingle the stronghold at Watchet looked huge, towering, and formidable.

I didn't think we could take it.

"Eat and drink," called Randulfr, anticipating his king's next order. "Only one pot of ale! We don't need thick-tongued, wobbly kneed drunkards around when we assault that dung castle."

"And piss and shit, men," added Godfrey. "We reassemble here shortly. We're not done sticking the English pigs yet."

• • •

I wanted a fitting meal, eggs in a pan for instance. I craved meat. My body cried for energy. We had no time for a cooking fire. I reached into the cage of two of the hens we carried on *Charging Boar* and stole their eggs. The hens themselves came from Maredubb's personal coop. I cracked each of the shells on my lower teeth and poured their contents into my mouth. The flavor wasn't correct for what I craved, but after just a moment of near nausea, my belly thanked me. I gulped a pot of ale before dropping my trousers and pissing over the gunwale into the lapping sea. My frothy waste mixed with the churning waves and the oozing blood that seeped and leached its way down from the battle site.

Aoife stuck her miniature rear over the same edge and relieved herself. She gnawed on a piece of salted fish and used it to wave in my direction as she spoke. "That Turf Ear was a tough critter! I think he still swore at them when he was lying in the stones."

"He was," I agreed. I looked over to where his mangled body lay heaped with the rest. It was difficult to tell whose arm or leg went with whose body. He was one of twenty-six of our number who lay dead. Another batch of wounded rolled about moaning. There was nothing that we could do for them at the moment if we wanted to survive. We had to get our quarry before the smoke from the town's fire called in more English soldiers down one of their herepaths, originally built by Alfred.

Killian nursed our wounded as best he could. He helped them to the boats and gave them a cup of ale.

"If I die on a strandhogg, I'll go that same way," Aoife blustered. "I'll fight to the end."

I cinched the cord that held up my trousers and replaced my leather belt with its scabbards dangling. I had left fingerprints made red with the blood of the English behind. "I'm sure you will." The girl made me smile. I had certainly not wished for her to come, but if I am truthful with myself, and even you, I liked the little creature. Perhaps, I decided, I'd share some of my portion of the treasure with her. She could use it to buy her freedom. Thoughts like that were for another time.

"Move!" called Godfrey. "All this smoke will eventually bring more soldiers."

Aoife hadn't finished her business. "Stay with the ships," I said.

The fiery beast began issuing a string of curses at me. When she took a moment to breathe, I answered, "Listen, you runt, I don't tell you to remain here because I'm fond of you or because I want to protect you or because I think you'll be in the way. No, I tell you to stay here because I don't want an enterprising villager to skulk over here with some of those burning embers and torch our escape route." I slapped my father's saex into her hand that held the fish. "Kill them with that if they try."

She jumped off the gunwale and wiggled so that her rag dress slipped back down to her dirty thighs. "What says I won't use this against you?" she asked.

"You won't. You're a warrior and warriors follow orders."

Her lips pursed as Aoife gave my answer some thought. She shrugged in agreement and ran across the ship, bound onto the dock, and found a place from which to stand guard. She stabbed at a dead Englishman to practice her craft.

"Halldorr!" barked Godfrey, looking perturbed.

I scurried back to the shore with my clattering gear. The king was right to be anxious. We had a mint to take.

• • •

The town burned. The northerly wind that had blown in behind us allowed the smoke to climb very little before it shoved the black mountain southward to where the residents had fled. Occasionally, I caught a glimpse of flocks of the terrified villagers staring at what had been their homes from a safe distance away among healthy green fields. At least they would be able to harvest and eat, I thought.

Godfrey led us along the shingle toward the tall bluff. With the town receding on our left, we came to the mouth of small creek. Its contents quietly dumped out into the shingle, lazily mingling with the damp stones and lapping surf. It appeared as if the brook angled to the south and west. A road, the herepath, crossed the creek and wound its way up to the mint. The king stopped there to study our goal.

"Maybe the creek curves around the fort?" I offered. "We could follow it and cover at least some of our approach."

Randulfr examined the mouth of the brook, then the tall cliffs and their tumbling rocks. "It's worth a try, King Godfrey," he said. "At least it's not one of Leif's crazy ideas." The king's lieutenant pointed up the hill. "We'll not be getting up there very easily." Several helmeted heads poked up over the mortared, stone wall. They studied us as we studied them.

Godfrey veered left and splashed into the creek. His rattling band followed him down the deep path the old waterway had cut through the soils and rocks of the landscape. We quickly lost sight of the fort as a few spindly willows and thorn bushes closed in at the tops of the banks.

"This was a wise idea, Halldorr," said Godfrey as we splashed along. "They know we're coming, but at least – if the creek goes in the right direction – they won't know where we are." He shrugged. "That's something."

"You've got fortune on your side, King Godfrey." The creek's water was cool. My submerged feet were getting cold.

"I've got nothing yet," Godfrey corrected. "We've killed some Englishmen, which is fine work if you can get it, I suppose.

But I don't do it lightly. We need to have something to show for all the blood we lost on the beach."

"Twenty-six dead on the rocks," answered Killian. He splashed along behind me. He had tied the skirts of his priestly vestments into a large knot around his waist so that only his boots and trousers were soaked. "Another sixteen wounded and stowed on the ships." The Irishman sighed. "Half of those will be dead by tomorrow. May the Almighty console them and save their souls." Killian crossed himself. I found comfort from his words and even the action of the cross. Strange, I thought.

Godfrey grunted. "So once again, we are only about fifty men and we think we will assault a castle." He didn't say it in a frustrated or defeated voice. It was almost said with confident madness. We all must have been mad, however, because when he spoke the words, they seemed as natural to me as a fish living in water. "You were also wise to leave that little thrall of yours with the boats. As dirty and filthy as she is now, maybe she'll grow into a beautiful woman one day. If you take her as your wife, I know one thing. You'll never be in want of adventure."

Tyrkr, some three men behind, laughed. "A thrall takes revenge at once. A fool never takes revenge." The rest of us laughed, not with him, but rather at him. The old adage was true, of course, as we all knew. But just as obvious to us all was that it didn't fit the conversation. Tyrkr knew only that we spoke of thralls. The maxim was one of our native Norse sayings he had picked up as his favorite. It made him, as a thrall, feel a rank above a fool, though he sometimes played both roles. But didn't we all play the fool?

"In truth, king, I left her there to protect our way out and the wounded."

"She's spirited, but what can she do if those villagers get curious and want a bit of revenge?" asked Godfrey.

"A thrall takes revenge at once," Tyrkr began.

"We heard that," barked Leif.

"The girl's surprised me. I imagine she surprised you over the past year since you took her. She did well today. I believe she'll surprise us again. As much as it drives me to madness, Leif knows how things will work out. He bought the girl for me, so I should trust him." I looked over to my young friend. He grinned behind his red, sprouting whiskers. Leif raised his eyebrows and wrinkled his forehead as if he knew more secrets that he wouldn't share. He stayed silent.

"Perhaps we should have left some able men behind to protect the ships," said Randulfr. "We've always left a guard before."

"You're right," said Godfrey. He hopped to the bank. His feet sank in the soft mud as he crawled up where there was an opening in the foliage. Godfrey peeked over the edge while we waited. "But we'll need every single man we have to take the mint."

Curious to see the fort from this vantage point, we all mimicked the king, crawling up the slippery bank to peep through the thorns and bushes. A slithering copse of trees had followed the path of the creek. It ended two or three fadmr away from the bank. Beginning at the trees' end was a long, sloping rise – wide open – that ran all the way up to the fortress's stone walls. A gate stood on this side facing the English countryside. The thick wooden doors were tightly bolted. A gaping ditch was traversed by a narrow bridge that the garrison had already torched. It lay in smoldering ruins. A wide, dirt road ran in either direction. The eastern path ran down toward the town we had burned. It was the one that wound up the hill from the beach. The western path continued on along the seaside cliffs and disappeared in the distance. The road was most definitely the herepath that more Englishmen would use to come to the aid of their countrymen at Watchet.

If we wanted Aethelred's coins, we had to act fast before they came.

Fast. But there would be no surprise.

• • •

"Hel's frozen crotch!" exclaimed Godfrey. He spun and sank on his rump into the muck. The king bit his lip and bit at the inside of his cheek. His icy confidence from just moments earlier was thawing.

"Burn the doors?" I asked. Don't judge me too harshly for my idiotic suggestion. Recall that this entire endeavor was my first strandhogg, my initiation into raiding. I knew nothing of the subject other than I was young, virile, and strong. If a man came at me with a weapon and if he didn't kill me in the first few moments, he'd soon find his entrails sloshing through his fingers. I understood that if I survived, I'd earn an allotment of the takings.

"Do you think they'll just let us march up there and kindle a fire next to the doors?" Brandr huffed.

"And if they did," Loki began, "a few arrows from the ramparts and a bucket of water would end the assault before it started. You're talking about part of a siege. Sieges can last days, weeks, or months. We don't have that kind of time. We don't have the manpower or the tools to build siege engines."

Killian laughed sardonically at Loki. "It's not a matter of tools or the number of men, fool. None of us knows the first thing of building engines." The priest gave Loki a frown then crouched and walked along the slowly moving creek to face the king. He knelt, half in the water, half in the mud. "Any guess as to how many men in the fortress?"

Godfrey glowered. "No. What did the parchment that you found at Maredubb's keep say?" The king didn't wait for any answer. "Oh, that's right. You said that the mint was to be unguarded. That was the word you used, correct? Unguarded?"

Killian shrugged, but took the jab in stride. "That is what the parchment said. Clearly that's not the case. It said only that reinforcements for an unguarded garrison were going to arrive shortly. Perhaps those reinforcements are who we fought at the shingle? Perhaps the fort is now nearly vacant."

"We won't know until we run across that open field like a deer, fly across the trench like a raven, and successfully scale the wall like a marten," said Godfrey. He closed his eyes as he thought of a way through the problem.

Leif crawled back to his feet and peeped over the bank again. "Halldorr, how tall is that wall?"

Without opening his eyes, Godfrey shoved me toward Leif. "See what the red-haired diviner has to say. Maybe he can find a way to have the soldiers invite us in like he did in Aberffraw." I, wary, joined my friend.

"From here it looks like two, or maybe just two and then a bit more, fadmr." I reached an arm over the rim of the bank and pointed through the thicket. "See that sentry's head? Would it take about fifteen of his skulls stacked to run from the bottom to the top? Why do you ask?"

Leif had already turned around. He slid down the mud into the creek and splashed through to the other side. Leif scrambled up into the thin line of forest that snaked along that bank. He planted his feet on the floor of the woods, set his hands on his hips, and looked skyward. He was nodding.

"Oh, what is it?" asked Killian. "You like to act as if you've found the master plan long before the rest of us."

"I have," said Leif. His head now scanned up and down several long, narrow trees. Situated away from the forest edge and not growing in the center of a field, they were nearly branchless, except for the very tops. Leif counted, nearly under his breath. "One, two . . ."

Killian was mumbling about Leif's frustrating condescension. I could understand the priest's anger. More than once before that day and many times since that day, Leif had done the same to me. It was maddening. His confidence, his seeming knowledge of events before they happened could make even his friends find fault. But Leif was wise. He was mostly moderate and level-headed. Furthermore, Leif was usually right.

He spun to face us. "King Godfrey, you still want the coins? And you want them now?"

Godfrey spat a wad of phlegm into the brook. "Of course, I do." He stood and walked over to the opposite bank. "What do you have in mind?"

Leif received the answer he expected and, therefore, ignored the king's petition. Leif pointed to all the men who lounged in the mud. "Anyone with a war axe, prepare to dull it. Come. Come!" He waved both hands, encouraging them up. They obeyed the young fool. We were all fools, but I've said as much.

"Cut down all the straight trees you can. Make sure they are no larger in diameter than your balled fist. We don't want to waste time chopping." He was pacing now. "We need sixteen or eighteen that are between two and a half and three fadmr in length."

Brandr protested, "It took me most of the day to make a good sturdy ladder to use around my long home. We don't have that time."

"And how many years do you expect to use it? You built it by yourself?" asked Godfrey, immediately enthusiastic about Leif's plan.

"What?" Brandr began. "Yes, I built it myself, King Godfrey. It had better last the rest of my life."

"Good. These ladders have to last less than one day. You'll have dozens of hands helping. We'll be done before midday," answered Godfrey, hauling out his short war axe and taking the first swing at a thin oak. The blade left smeared, black blood from the morning's carnage emblazoned in the cut near the tree's base.

"We'll be done by then if Halldorr runs back to the ships and brings all the cord he can find," said Leif. He marched through the trees and pointed out to the men which ones he wanted brought down. They fanned out into the small woods. Soon the sound of a dozen axes sang.

"Why me?" I asked, immediately regretting I had bothered.

"You're the fastest," he said. "Besides, you'll want to check on your thrall."

Aoife? Something about the way Leif said it made me think that there may be trouble at the boats. Without further protest, I splashed my way back down the creek toward the shingle.

"Bring some sailcloth!" Leif called after me. Only I didn't hear him. I know today that he told me such a thing because Godfrey scolded me later. I suppose it matters little that I didn't bring the cloth. It should be quite obvious to you that I survived the day. I won't be ruining my tale if I tell you that Leif lived. Many others lived, too.

Some did not. And only some of those who did not survive could be said to have died because I did not bring the sailcloth.

That is what I tell myself to keep my chin high.

• • •

The singing of the axes quickly faded as I approached the shore. The town's fire still blazed. It audibly roared as I ran along the shingle toward the boats. Though the nearest burning house was fifteen fadmr away, I could feel the inferno's heat. Based upon the works, the sluice, and the stench, that building was a tanner's shop as well as his home. No longer.

I saw activity at the ships. More than I had hoped.

Perhaps a half score of villagers – all of them angry men – had come to the shingle seeking retribution. They carried no true weapons, though what they did hold – fishermen's gaffs, scythes, hoes, wooden rods – could kill most men easily enough if given the opportunity. Our wounded fought valiantly to prevent them the chance.

One of our Welshmen already lay dead. If I remember correctly, he had an arm wound from the first fight. It would have healed in a short while if he avoided infection with the stinking pus. He was not so fortunate. His body lay sprawled out half on the dock, half on the shingle. He was the most ambulatory and, therefore, the first man to intercept the villagers. Eight more of a mixed bag of Welshmen, Manx, and Norsemen held off the crazed men from Watchet to varying degrees of success. These defenders limped and swung a sword if they could. If they were unable to heft steel, they swung fists or threw the errant stone.

I had quickened my pace, running over scattering seaside rocks. That was when I realized that I hadn't seen Aoife. She should have been in the thick of the fight. Even after her scare at Aberffraw, she had demonstrated a willingness to take risks that very morning. She would not hide away with the baggage on one of our ships.

A flash of movement further up the shingle, closer to the blaze caught my eye. It was Aoife. She struggled under the firm grasp of an Englishman who had clenched his fingers into the tawny rat's nest that sat atop her head. He was a blacksmith. I could tell, for he still wore a long leather apron that flapped with each step. His forearms would be like the iron on which he pounded all day, every day. Aoife would not soon escape.

"Bitch tits," I muttered. In the smith's other hand he carried a long board. It was charred black along most of its length. The flames on the burning end fluttered as he waved it in the air. He meant to torch our ships and compel us to face whatever English force came down the herepath. Even just a single fire successfully kindled on one or two of our ships would spread to the rest, leaving only Randulfr's boat – where that was I still did not know – as our last chance at escape.

The blacksmith closed on the boats and his comrades. I closed on the entire party.

As I have done many times since, when confronted with the poetic insanity that is battle, I screamed. It was the call of the Berserkers of time eternal. If I had the time, I felt like I would have stripped my clothes off and ferociously howled at the bastards who dared make their sortie. That's what the ancients, my ancestors, had done. The tales said as much. Had I done so, I would truly have been like the battle-mad Berserkers of yore, their heir, their kin. I didn't strip. I simultaneously drew my sword and jerked my small axe from my belt. I wailed with a rumbling, phlegm-filled madness.

The Englishman on the left of their so-called line was closest to me. Even though he spun to meet my attack, he tumbled to the earth moments later in wide-eyed terror. He thrashed about on the ground trying to stuff his innards back where they belonged. I placed a heavy boot on his chest and jumped over him.

Now, I must explain to you that this was an utterly foolish action. It was something that a skald would say a warrior did in battle because skalds, who are mostly cowards, tell tales and sing songs like the greatest of the heroes they portray, but never find themselves in the thick of the clash. The victories won by kings, jarls, and free men are enough to supply the skalds with warm broth and mead in exchange for their yarns. Dozens of things could have gone wrong with my leap. My boot could have slipped off his chest. Had I fallen, the next Englishman in line could have killed me with one swing of his staff crushing my temple. Or, the dying man on the ground could have found the presence of mind to ram his sickle into my shin. I would have fallen and again the man with the staff could have ended my life. Or, my death could have been the result of my landing on the outstretched gaff of a fisherman. Just because none of those things happened, does not mean that the act wasn't foolhardy. It was.

While flying through the air I shrieked again. The second man in the English line drove his staff up. It connected with my thigh before sliding into my groin. It hurt mightily. I felt at once nauseous, but had no time for such nonsense. My path was set. Down I toppled onto the second man. He clutched the staff that had fallen between us. He should have let it go and proceeded to grapple or bludgeon my face with his fists. His mistake cost him his life. My axe hammered its way between his ribs. By the time one of his hands seized my face, the grip was weak and waning.

I rolled off and saw the other simple townsmen already fleeing. The blacksmith had tossed Aoife over his shoulder. The little thing roiled like a captured snake. I heard her hissing. She clawed like a feral cat cornered in an alley. I clambered to my feet. The smith had stolen my father's saex from Aoife.

"Thor's beard!" I swore. I meant to chase after my quickly receding property, but the blacksmith had the sense to throw his flaming board on one of our ships. Already the baggage and stowed sails had ignited. The badly wounded who could move, crawled and hurled themselves over the gunwale and onto the hard dock or into the shallow surf. Aoife and my father's blade would have to wait. At least I knew she'd make it difficult on her captors. That is, until they made it difficult on her.

I clasped the arm of the nearest wounded, yet ambulatory, Welshman and dragged him the short distance down the dock toward the fire. We didn't attempt to communicate verbally. I tossed him into the shallow waves while I leapt over the gunwale. Feverishly, I hurled the baggage overboard to the waiting Welshman who guided it toward the shore if it was of value or let it float away or sink if not. Alight with flame or not, it went over. I was indiscriminant. My hands were singed.

Two of the terribly wounded men who were resting on the ship's decking and unable to flee the miniature blaze were already burning. Their trousers went first. The one who could still move his legs kicked madly. The other just bawled with a quivering lower lip as he watched what just that morning had been his strong fighting legs turn into taut crisps. I found an empty hudfat and threw it onto the nearest man, following behind with my body's weight. My hands smacked at the sack.

Three more of the slow moving wounded who had defended the dock from the villagers finally struggled their way onto the boat. One began throwing buckets down to the Welshman standing in the water, which had been my plan all along. The other two found a blanket, wet from the morning mist and covered the second burning man. They stamped at the blaze as best they could. When the flames that sprang from that man were finally out, the pair pulled back the wet blanket. Entire sheets of the burnt man's skin came up with the cloth, stuck in its fibers. We all cringed. In a way the norns spared the man the worst. He was already dead.

The fight went on. After many long moments and several score of buckets we discovered that the worst was avoided. The ship was saved, as were the rest. This one, which was a vessel pilfered from Maredubb days earlier, would only require a spare sail from another vessel, a new yard, and several fadmr of rope.

"Rope!" I said out loud.

The others looked at me, confused.

"I'm here for cord, lots of it." I scanned the shore to see if I could lay my eyes on the blacksmith who carried Aoife. Only a glimmer of his motley band's clothing flashed as they disappeared into a distant forest to the south and east. It is embarrassing to admit. I certainly didn't own up to my thoughts back then, for I was young and proud. But, in truth, I hesitated for a few moments. I considered abandoning my quest for the cord in order to pursue the thrall thief. In the end I decided that

Leif, with his keen mind, would better help me retrieve my little wretch than if I went headlong into an unknown forest alone.

To the hobbling wounded I shouted, "Go to the ships. Bag up every length of leather cord you can find." None of them complained for I think they realized that my mere presence had saved their lives. They did, however, moan from the gashes in their sides that reopened as they bent to fill sacks with cord.

At last it was time to return to Godfrey, whose impatience would outstrip everyone's combined. "Will you tell the king to send just a few warriors to guard us and the ships?" asked a nervous Norseman.

"No," I answered plainly. "If you had a good look at what we've got to assault in that fort on the hill, then you'd know the king needs every able man he can muster."

"But he has treasure already loaded on these ships. Another lucky toss from a villager will have it all underwater," the man protested.

He made sense. We should have had more guards. Well, we should have had just some guards where we had none. We also should have landed at Watchet and met no resistance as the parchment found by Leif and Killian had said. I should not have been cast out from my own people in Greenland for a basket of horse dung. As I've said in another writing at a different place and time, should is meaningless. *Is* is all that matters. The reality of daily life is what determines whether a man lives or dies. Freeze from fear one day while the spears are flying? Dead. Freeze another day in the same situation? Live. Should? That is just the wishful thinking of senseless dreamers. Admittedly, I'm one of those senseless dreamers, guilty of pondering how this man or that woman should act or how I should respond.

Every man has the norns weaving him a crooked, harsh path. He must do what he will. Most men try to seize control and steer the path with a firm hand on the oak rudder. Leif did it. His father did it. By Hel, I did it. And now King Godfrey steered. Godfrey, though, not only attempted to maneuver, he was reaching. His arm was growing longer by the day and he was stretching it further. The king was trying to build his treasury and his army, but I think along the way and during those weeks of raiding he began to believe that he could build a truly respectable kingdom from his hodgepodge of islands that dotted the Irish Sea.

Life was about what a man could do and would do. Godfrey would seize what he could.

"No," I repeated and ran off lugging bags bulging with cord.

• • •

Godfrey cursed up a thunderous storm at my tardiness. There is no sense in repeating his already repetitious words. It should suffice to say that I was some version of an ox or turd or a worn-out whore's sagging tits. At one point I was a combination of all three. When I explained to him that I nearly single-handedly fought off a mess of villagers and put out a fire on a treasure-laden ship, the king's anger waned. Only for a few moments, for then he found out that I had not brought sailcloth. He resumed his swearing. Neither I nor anyone else was again sent back. Godfrey was eager to move before real trouble arrived.

Leif and the others worked feverishly. They pulled out the tangle of cords from the sacks and began lashing together the narrow logs into ladders. Leif had efficiently directed his workers to lay out the rails in parallel with the rungs placed across them with an ell of spacing between. The work quickly drew to a close. It doesn't take long for a few dozen sailors to tie off as many knots.

"Are we ready?" asked Godfrey, surveying the crew when the last cord was cinched.

Killian examined the crowd and answered for them. "By God's strength, power, and grace, we are ready." The priest crossed himself. His Christian brethren did the same.

Godfrey signaled that we should prepare. I grabbed a ladder by myself. Most of the ladders would be carried by two men just because they were so awkwardly long. Hauling them between one another enabled our attackers to carry their shields in their other hands for protection as we neared the mint. Brandr tried to take up the other end of my ladder. I curled my lip at him like a surly dog. He returned the gesture, but backed off. Tyrkr would carry my shield and his own until I set the ladder in place.

We crossed the narrow brook and foisted our newly constructed equipment on the bank that faced the fortress. Thorns and briars hooked men's clothing and tore skin as we pushed through to the edge of the long clearing. It took many moments, complete with grumbling, for us to assemble. We were in plain view of the sentinels, a far, safe distance, but obvious nonetheless. We could hear their loud calls of warning to their comrades behind the stone wall. A tiny sliver of smoke curled up from the torched timbers of the bridge that led to the mint's gate.

Godfrey stepped in front of us. I loved a leader that went into harm's way before his men. Of course, it was foolish for a king to stand at the front. Yet, it made his men work for him and bleed for him and die for him, if they must. Godfrey, though partially Christian, was from a line of Norseman from old. It would have been wrong for him to command from the rear. He was a Viking from when the word meant something. If he wanted respect at the gloaming, he better earn it at dawn, every morning. Such was the fickleness of followers. I saw his confidence etched in every wrinkle of his taut, weathered face. I saw the tension in the muscles of his arm as he clutched his shield. The sight of the warrior king made me forget all about the harsh words he sent in my direction only moments before.

"Let us kill some more Englishmen," said King Godfrey in a calm tone as he marched forward.

The Welshmen erupted in cheers, for the meaning was clear enough. They thought we were going to rush ahead. They ran a few paces before realizing their error. Killian told them, "Slow now, lads. Save your energy. We don't hurry until we're nearly at the ditch."

We walked up the hill at such a relaxed pace it was as if we ambled hand-in-hand with our secret lovers to our favorite spot in the forest. Godfrey, showing his poise or covering his nerves, chatted with Randulfr about a hunt they had a few years earlier. It was in Normandy, they said. Neither could remember many of the details, for both had been inebriated to silliness at the time. They did recall that they had killed a few wolves that day.

"Why did we want sailcloth?" Tyrkr asked of Leif. I was glad he asked because I didn't know and wasn't about to appear the fool. For Tyrkr, it was a fine part.

"As I looked up the hill at the fort, I saw that trail of smoke where the entrance bridge once stood. They burned it to make us struggle through the ditch. It's what I would have done if I sat behind those walls and watched what our force did to their army on the beach. If I commanded the garrison, I would have sent a rider for help and penned myself in until assistance arrived." Leif picked a catchfly. He lazily tapped the rim of his shield with the wildflower. Its pale violet petals sprinkled down the front. A few came to rest on the iron boss, a fine example of the beauty of the meadow next to the harshness of what was to come.

"And the sailcloth?" asked Tyrkr.

Almost as if he'd forgotten what the question was, Leif answered, "Oh, I was going to stretch it around three or four of the ladders so that if we had to use them as bridges, the men wouldn't have to tiptoe across the rungs." He threw the splattered flower over his shoulder. The petals that had briefly rested on his shield fell away as well. "Too late now, though. Where's your thrall, my gift to you, Halldorr?"

The little bastard, I thought. Leif and his divining! It was like Leif knew that I had lost the girl and he was goading me. "I left her to guard the ships," I answered.

We were climbing the last part of the hill, approaching the ditch. We could see close-up that the fort's soldiers had burned the bridge sometime that morning after the defeat of their army on the shingle. What was left of the timbers smoldered. It would hold no one's weight. Godfrey extended his arms, telling us to spread out and cross the ditch at several places. In this way the defenders could not concentrate their spears and arrows on one area.

I walked behind Tyrkr, who raised both shields to protect us. Leif, Loki, and Magnus, whose leather armor creaked as he slid through the grasses, followed behind. I reached a hand down to absentmindedly clutch the grip of my father's saex. It wasn't there, I remembered. It was in the hands of a blacksmith along with . . .

"And does she guard the ships?" asked Leif as the first arrow smacked into the shield Tyrkr held. The missile's force tipped the top of the shield back so that it just kissed Tyrkr's helm. A second arrow glanced off the iron rim of the other shield and flew harmlessly over our heads. Without those bits of tree going before me, I would have already fallen into the grass. I would have been like most young men who died on the battlefield, calling for my long-dead mother.

"You must already know, if you ask," I barked. "Shouldn't we focus on getting into the fort?" I snuck a peek back to see Leif's response.

Leif gave a lazy, maddening shrug. "I suppose," he said. Then he sniggered. "It's a shame, you know. How careless a man can be with a gift. It cost him nothing so he feels free to lose it or, worse yet, discard it."

"Green-eyed snot," I began. Our brotherly argument was cut short by the screams of our fellow raiders.

• • •

The king's small group of raiders had reached their section of the ditch a few moments before did ours. Rather than struggle through the stagnant slurry of the trench, they heaved the ladder across. One of them was struck on his exposed rump while he bent to sling the make-shift bridge. His was the first wailing I had heard.

Godfrey slid his sword home. He used his shield to protect the fallen man while clamping a firm hand on the leather armor on his shoulder. "Over the trough," he encouraged his men. "Huddle under shields at the foot of the wall until enough of us cross to tilt up the ladder." Godfrey dragged the wounded man some distance away, propped a shield in front of him, and raced back up the hill to cross with the rest.

Our team's ladder was across. My shield was back in my strong hand. Leif snuck across, hoisting his shield with two hands, balancing on the rungs with nimble feet. Tyrkr followed. Then the rest of us went. Just two, perhaps three, arrows and a spear rained down on us. Godfrey's tack of spreading us was working. The garrison, made thin by our victory in the morning, was unable to defend evenly along the wall.

Killian's Welshmen were not faring so well. The English had enough numbers at that location of the wall to put up a proper fight. It did not help our cause that the first man across Killian's ladder lost his footing. He slipped down, straddling a rung, bringing the full weight of his person, shield, and weapons on his most sensitive of areas. The Welshman winced and doubled over only to be rewarded with a bevy of arrows. The easily pierced his back, which was naked of armor.

The priest held up a shield and ventured out on the ladder to move the body. Killian was strong for a little man. He was certainly muscular for a priest. However, given the awkward footing and rain of death from above, Killian couldn't disentangle the heavy corpse. He tried stepping over him, but couldn't do so. Killian backed his way off the ladder all while he prayed for the dead man's soul.

We clustered under our shields at the base of the wall, waiting for others to cross their ladders so that we could all go up at once and overwhelm the defenders. The going was slow. Nearly half of the bridges had a dead man wedged in them, preventing others from crossing. Leif's sailcloth, if stretched tightly enough, would have made for a lightweight bridge that was not a death trap. Only a dozen and a half men had been able to cross. It wouldn't take the English long to redirect their storm and finish our raid off once and for all.

I knew it the same time Godfrey knew it. His raid was a boy's whisker away from losing it all. I stared across at the king's face. It was etched in worry as he scrambled under the hale to shift men from an encumbered ladder to one that remained open.

I have come to accept it today, but did not understand it then, that a warrior's vision becomes narrow while the contest is on. You see your opponent, his spear, your target, and not much else. Normally, when a warrior is at peace and home playing his part as a farmer in the field broadcasting seed, a flash or blur in the corner of his vision startles him. He ducks and prepares to meet the sudden threat. It could be a bear, a bandit, or a leaf blowing by in the breeze. The point is that the farmer is ready for anything. Put the same man on the battlefield and he is called a warrior. You would think that he sees everything, that his senses are heightened.

When chaos is the norm, when flashes of spears and running men are everywhere, your mind focuses in on the narrow. It is a simplistic mechanism of survival. Kill what is in front of you. Move forward or flee. Those Manx, Norse, and Welsh men, who had yet to cross over, could not see the open ladders. They knew only one way forward. Some of them jumped over their dead friends. When they landed, even if in balance, their shields were down. It was an invitation to spears. They splashed down into the stinking black of the ditch, adding to the tally of our dead.

Godfrey shoved some of them and they moved over to his crossing. He smacked others and they did too. Killian could not get his inexperienced Welshmen to budge. They huddled on the far side of the ditch, massing together. Every few moments another missile found a gap and hit one. They would not last long.

"Tyrkr, follow me!" I shouted as I thrust my shield back at him. He understood and for the second time raised his and my trees above our heads. We crouched and ran toward where the priest struggled.

The English did not immediately notice us – remember what I said about the narrow vision of battle. We came to the fort side of Killian's ladder. The priest was again on the ladder trying to inspire or will his men across. The body was still stretched out in his path. Its blood still ran down its arms underneath its coat. Crimson rivers coursed over the dead man's hands and flowed down into the murky water just three ells below.

"Off the bridge, priest," I shouted. The English heard me and sent Tyrkr and me their welcome.

"I've got to get them across," Killian protested. He shouted over the one-sided battle's din.

I put my hands under the rail ends and gave it a jiggle. "Off or you'll be in the drink."

Killian carefully skipped the few steps to the other side.

Godfrey was having success getting men across open ladders. The garrison had shifted their defense with the king and continued to harry him. I could hear the enemy calling to one another from above. We might be able to make the assault without the Welshmen Killian commanded, but their numbers might be the difference between victory and defeat.

I rammed a boot on the end of one rail of the ladder. With both hands, I heaved on the other rail. Slowly at first, but with increasing speed it began to turn. Tyrkr's arm was driven into my back from a particularly heavy spear sent from the wall. We each swore, I in Norse, he in his native German. The ladder rolled over. The dead man splashed down into the ditch, bobbing. Killian didn't wait any longer. He foisted his small shield and gingerly stepped on the rungs. Halfway across, where the dead man's blood had made the footing slick, Killian slipped down to one knee. I held my breath as an English arrow pinned the priest's garment to the ladder. Killian recovered, though. He drew his knife, cut the skirt, and finished the trek.

Reluctantly, his Welshmen followed. They inched across. A full third of them died, being struck by missiles since they provided the English such slow-moving targets. None of them was hemmed into and amongst the rungs, though. Instead, the projectiles shoved them off their feet and into the trench.

What was left of our force was assembled.

It was time for the hard tasks to be done.

• • •

Since our numbers had so dwindled, Godfrey called to us, "Raise four ladders. Abandon the rest."

I ran to what I now considered my ladder since it was I who lugged it across the field, up the hill, and set it in place. A quick tug untied the slipknot of a cord that ran from the first rung to the last rung across the ditch. It took only a moment to wrap the cord's end around my wide palm. I planted both feet on the end of the rails and leaned back. A heavy rock clattered off Tyrkr's shield and cracked my cheek. The English were throwing large stones. Still I leaned.

Slowly the far end of the ladder rose. Three others did likewise. I believe all of the garrison's soldiers now converged on our narrow front. More rocks fell. Spears rained. Even several buckets of burning embers splashed down among us. Orange coals snuck down a man's back. He roared in pain and without thinking leapt into the stagnant waters of the ditch. He came up screaming. Just when his shouting began to wane, a large stone rapped his skull, making a splat. He slipped beneath the black.

Tyrkr took an arrow to the elbow. It wasn't fatal, yet when the shields he held jumped from his pain, a large rock came down and smashed my toes. Half of them on one foot were broken. I clenched my teeth. The top of my ladder rattled to a stop against the curtain wall.

Godfrey pushed past me, too anxious to wait for his ladder to reach the top. He tucked himself under his brightly striped shield and climbed while clutching a sword. His specific words, I've forgotten. Whatever he said, I remember that he spat them. His lips turned into an angry snarl. Spittle popped with the start of each phrase. Magnus followed with a spear.

Killian's ladder clattered against the battlements. The priest made sure he thrust himself in line first to ascend. He cranked his legs and arms rapidly, willing himself forward. Killian used his native tongue, his Irish, to call the One God's wrath down on the English.

I stole my shield back from Tyrkr who appeared glad to get rid of the extra weight. He inspected his elbow wound. His filthy hand brushed away a patch of blood that looked worse than what the wound actually was. I stepped back and shook out the pain in my foot. I rubbed my cheek where the rock had struck. "English," I said as if it were a curse. Why I already hated them, I know not. But have another set of men throw rocks on you and you'll soon find that you develop a pointed distaste for them. Ignore the fact, just like I did when I was young and hungry for food, riches, and glory, that I was raiding their precious, fertile lands in the first place.

Leif ran up the ladder. I craned my head back. Godfrey had just jumped over the wall. The hail storm of carnage falling on those of us remaining below paused as the English defenders addressed the king. Magnus followed. Other men did as well. I was missing the thick of it. I felt left out and angry.

I made a place in line by pushing Randulfr out of the way. Normally, the two of us would have grappled or argued, but not that time. He let me pass. Well, he allowed me to go before him because I sent my forearm into his mouth. I scaled the rungs, favoring my foot with the broken toes that had swelled up inside my tough leather boot. To my right, what had been Godfrey's bridge, his original ladder, was finally up. Loki was the first to climb it. He carried two spears in one hand and used the other to hang on. He did not carry a shield. Over him, an English bowman drew back. Loki was going to die.

Until the knot on the cord that tied one of the rungs gave way and Loki, the ladder, and the men behind him fell to the side. The English arrow harmlessly whizzed through where Loki's body had been a heartbeat sooner. The tangled mess of men crashed to the ground and rolled into the wall or the ditch.

So we had only three small rivers of men flowing into the garrison. It wouldn't be enough. They would choke us.

Only it was more than enough.

I leapt over the battlement to meet the enemy. I saw sparkling stars when my injured foot landed on the hard-packed earthen wall that sat behind the stone curtain wall of the fortress. No enemy came to meet me. They were already in full retreat down the bank and across the bailey. Our men, led by Godfrey and Killian, cut them down from behind. Just one of the English soldiers laid a hand on the thick wooden door of their keep. He died with his hand turning the latch.

Stunned, I panted and scanned the sight before me. Brandr jostled me from behind as he jumped into the fort. I drove the meat of my palm into his chest. He growled and continued on. Again, I scanned the scene. We'd won.

The bodies of the fort's defenders seemed few. I counted them. As near as I could tell twenty-four of them were all that had held us off so valiantly. We'd killed most of the garrison on the shingle that morning, a fortunate thing for us. Had more men occupied that fortress, sending spear point after arrowhead down our backs, we would not have made it. Godfrey's quest for greatness would have ended on a batch of rickety, sloppily built ladders. Our blood would have brought forth generations of grasses and wildflowers on that English hillside.

We'd won. We'd taken the mint from the English. Her coins were ours.

Godfrey meant to become a rich king in the vein of Aethelred of England or Louis of the Franks. He now had those means.

I meant to retrieve my saex and my thrall.

• • •

Brandr came running out of the garrison commander's quarters carrying the man's personal stash of ale. Godfrey had it and many more casks tapped so that our tired men lounged while guzzling the brew. A few of the Welshmen still had enough energy to revel. They danced and laughed, taking turns throwing rocks at the dead Englishmen. It was no way to treat a soldier who had died in battle, but they did and Godfrey allowed it. The men tossing the rocks became quite good at it, backing away farther and farther and hitting proscribed parts of the men's bodies from a distance. All the while, they gambled away their share of the treasure which had not yet been counted and they'd certainly not yet received. If a hastily assembled army of nuns arrived to counter us during those moments, we would have been swept from the fort.

None came, which doesn't excuse the king's unpreparedness.

The king finally began making more responsible decisions after many pots of ale had been consumed by his men. Godfrey commandeered two pairs of oxen and two carts. He loaded them first with buckets upon buckets of already-stamped silver pennies. His hard-won treasure took precedence. Our fallen brothers would have to wait for their cart rides until after the plunder was fully released.

I've said that Godfrey was reaching and he was. His priority was obviously the treasure with which he would build his great kingdom that centered on the piratical Isle of Man. With each passing bucket of coins I saw his mind swirl as the king conjured new ways to fashion his current lands into an empire.

The men who assisted him in taking the booty? Well, they'd share in his wealth and glory, but they'd have to be prepared to take a distant second to the riches. It was a fact that made me grumble.

He was not the best leader I've followed before or since. Godfrey was a good fighter. He inspired his men in battle by doing that which he commanded them. He sometimes listened to Killian's counsel. Other times he ignored the wise priest. This was one of those latter times so that Killian was left comforting the wounded in and around the fort while we loaded the treasure.

"What am I doing?" the priest asked himself over and over. "I help a sometimes Christian who is sometimes a king slaughter forever Christians so that I may pay for the ministry on Man." Killian shook his head in disgust.

I set the last tub of coins in a cart and walked to the mint's well. Tyrkr and Leif came over, their rucksacks bulging with fresh morning bread from the fortress's kitchens. England seemed like a land of plenty to me. We drew water and rinsed off the blood and grime from the two battles. I even pulled out my walrus-tooth comb and ran it through my hair and beard.

The three of us turned to walk out the now-open gates and across the planks that served as a temporary bridge. Godfrey trotted over on a stolen horse. "Where do you think you are going?"

I opened my mouth to answer, but Leif stepped in front of me. "We go to the east side of the town. We'll hide there in the woods and send word if reinforcements come down the English herepath." It was a lie. In truth we went to retrieve Aoife and my saex.

Godfrey was not the most brilliant of kings. His wife, Gudruna, and Killian had fooled him into taking on this entire expedition in the first place. He was not stupid, however. "A little late for that don't you think? We're nearly done with the work. The last of the pennies are on that cart now." The rickety cart rattled over the uneven bridge. "We've just the wounded to transport and then we're off." King Godfrey flashed a bright smile. "And Leif, you've proven your worth – first Anglesey, then here. You've a brilliant mind."

"I'm glad you feel that way, King Godfrey, because I'm about to ask again for your trust."

Though Leif's prodding and suggestions had helped Godfrey this far, the king sighed. "I think we've pressed our luck enough for one adventure."

Leif frowned. After a time of reflection, he nodded his head. "You're right. You're right, lord king. We've taken enough treasure. Who could ever want more? Even if to get more would take such little risk." Leif was baiting a hook. To what end, I knew not.

When a reaching king was Leif's quarry, the baiting worked. Godfrey peered up at the sun and mumbled to himself about how much time was left in the day. "Tell me what you're talking about."

"You are correct, King Godfrey. We don't need to run into the woods to watch for an approaching army. I've used my ability to divine that there is another treasure in the east woods. We go there to gather it for you and will present it upon our departure." I furrowed my brow as I waited for Leif to let on what was really going on. "It is a gift that will give you great pleasure."

"Well, why didn't you say so?" asked Godfrey. Then he wagged a finger. "Know that we'll not wait for you if you're delayed. We've risked much. We're heavy laden with plunder. We're short on crewmen. We must go as soon as possible."

"Understood," answered Leif. We left Godfrey to his work.

I led us down the way we'd come when we assaulted the citadel. My plan was to cross the creek, circumvent the still-burning village around the southern, landward side, and surprise the blacksmith and his allies. I planned on killing the smith. I hoped the other townsfolk just ran away.

"What was all that about more treasure?" I muttered while pushing through the thicket.

"There's none," said Leif.

"So I gathered," I said.

"I thought that the treasure was that little rascal of a thrall," said Tyrkr. He'd wrapped a cloth around his elbow and therefore carried his arm awkwardly. Leif's slave was serious about Aoife being the treasure. I thought she was, too. Perhaps even Godfrey would admit it if forced to do so. However, it made no sense to risk three warriors for a thrall worth just a penny. Forgetting Tyrkr's ability to wage war, even he was worth at least twelve times what Aoife would fetch on the auction block. It made no sense to tell Godfrey we went to rescue the girl, even though she brought laughter to his hall. So Leif had lied.

"If we make it back, then what will you give Godfrey as the treasure you just promised?" I asked.

We slunk across a narrow field and back into the cover of a copse of trees. It wrapped around in a curving arc toward the forest into which the blacksmith and Aoife had disappeared.

"These," said Leif. He had fished into his well-worn pouch and pulled out a cylindrical piece of iron that was just over a hand's width in length. The rest of the contents of his pack showed. Inside was another five of the short rods. Leif held it admiringly.

"Will you hit him over the head with it? The king's head is hard. That iron appears soft," said Tyrkr. The thrall crouched low at the sound of voices coming from a ravine.

Leif set the rod back into the rucksack with a clinging sound. Up ahead, the voices in the woods abruptly stopped – except one. Aoife rambled on rather loudly to her captors.

"I'll tell you this," the girl was saying. I don't have any idea if they understood her words or not. "If you want a proper fight, it's best if you set me free. I mean to kill a few men in battle. I thought it would be more of you English. But if you set me loose, I'm sure I can arrange to chop up some Norsemen if you prefer." A harsh shushing sound, followed by a slap, shut Aoife up.

Leif giggled. "Do you still want to save the wretch?" he whispered. "It sounds like she'll happily gut you if given the chance."

I ignored his goading. "How do we do this?" he asked.

"You're the one with all the ideas," I countered.

"Not this time," Leif said as he carefully set his pack on the ground. Tyrkr and I followed his lead, getting rid of anything that we wouldn't need in a fight.

"Then we rush in, yelling like Berserkers. They're frightened townsfolk. They'll think they're under attack and run. We kill the smith and take my saex and slave." I expected a smart retort from young Leif. Instead, he nodded and stood. He drew his sword. Tyrkr whitened his grip on his sturdy spear's shaft.

They allowed me to lead. I spent a long time sneaking for the first dozen steps. But I continued to make a racket by cracking the sticks that lay hidden under a bed of generations of fallen leaves. I gave up any thought of surprise and ran toward the lip of narrow rift. I drew my sword while I gained speed. My long-time, ill-fitting helmet fell off behind me. I jumped, broken toes and all, into the unknown.

Two hundred villagers gaped in horror while I flew through the air. My long blonde hair trailed behind me like flames on a swinging torch. "Godfrey!" I called. I don't know why. He wasn't even there. But he was my king and shouting the name of the man you served was a common enough call when entering battle. At the periphery I could see that some of the townspeople were already plunging into the deeper stretches of the forest. Others were running back toward the main herepath that followed the coastline.

I landed on the slopping hill that was made soft with eroded, silty dirt and brown and orange oak leaves. If you've ever fought in war and lived, you know that the mind can run ahead of your body. That's what mine did that day. Just as my heels touched the ground, my head was beginning to tell my body to run to where I saw Aoife tied to a sapling. If the smith or anyone else stepped into my path I would fell them like a nuisance tree.

That is not exactly what happened. My feet slapped onto the downward sloping earth. My broken toes rattled like loose dice in a coin purse, shooting pain all the way up my leg. My knees buckled so that I rolled forward, cutting my arm with my own sword. It was not an impressive display of agility. My fall ended as I skidded to a halt in slag next to a miniscule creek.

I popped back up, willing my mind to ignore the fire of pain that raged in my boot. Not knowing what else to do, I growled. The collective spread out before me gasped then broke, shoving one another to get away. Women shrieked. Babies and children cried. I'm not so foolish as to think my entrance alone had been enough to drive them all away. No, just a heartbeat after I fell from the heavens, Tyrkr bound into view. Then Leif came howling like me. Each of them landed in a more controlled manner than I.

The clearing was quickly vacating. I saw the blacksmith. He saw me. The large man thought for a moment about seizing his prize, Aoife, but decided that he would not successfully get away with her on his shoulder if an entire Viking army was chasing him. Instead, he balled one of his great smithing fists and cracked the precocious little thing on the eye. He tucked my saex into his belt. Then he ran with the others.

I think it was because Aoife was my property. Just like a farmer would show red with anger if a neighbor whipped his ox, I became enraged. I've told some of these tales about my life as a raider to my daughter, my Skjoldmo, and she just laughs. She never says it, but I know she believes that I had a warm place in my heart for that Irish thrall. When my Skjoldmo laughs, I scoff. It goes the same way every time.

"Get Aoife back to the ships," I called over my shoulder, bounding after the smith. I winced with each step. "I go after my father's saex," I said, though you know the truth.

• • •

The blacksmith was a beast, brawny and strong. The fact that he was not swift of foot was the only thing that allowed me to slowly gain on him as he darted this way and that through the woods. Soon his path cut north, toward the herepath that stretched from the fortress on the hill, through the village, and beyond in both directions. He paused, leaning against an alder with his burly forearm. The smith saw me coming out of the corner of his eye and felt in his apron, probably wishing for a hammer, the tool of his trade. It wasn't there. His hands wrapped around my saex. He sucked in a chest full of air and ran on. I limped and howled after him.

My shouting blended with the frightened calls of the villagers. They dispersed every which direction in the woods, thinking that our entire force pursued them in order to carry the women and children off to the Dyflin thrall auction.

I have done such a thing – sold off others into slavery – during my time as a raider. It's not that I am so calloused as to have no guilt because of it, even more so since I've become a Christian. Yet, I've never pondered any of the captives' eventual whereabouts. Why should I? The strong enslave the weak, the powerful the meek. If they did not, then the weak would grow strong and enslave the one-time mighty nation. Danes have enslaved the English. The English have enslaved the Danes. Irish chieftains have enslaved Norseman. Norseman kings have bought Irish thralls. I've even heard of men from the south, men called Berbers who found their way north and enslaved Danes. Killian and other priests have told me that this infamous and great Rome enslaved its enemies and her enemies enslaved her citizens. How much more reasoning should I offer? Enslave or be enslaved. At the least, be strong and thump the would-be slaver.

Of course, we were in Watchet for treasure. Besides, captives are expensive and hard to keep. An English silver penny never once becomes ill. It eats none of my food. The worst I've ever gotten was a condescending smirk from Aethelred's likeness on the face of the coin.

It was just the smith and me now. The townsfolk had scattered, each trying his best to preserve his family's lives by separating to their own hiding places. He burst out onto the herepath. The smith panted with his hands on his knees. He clutched my saex. The beast scanned the area. The town to his left was mostly black, smoking ruins with only pockets of flame. The man looked right and appeared immediately buoyant. He stood upright again and took the first two steps to run east. From his profile, I saw that he wore a relieved smile.

I meant to wipe it off. With the last of my strength, I tackled him. Our heads knocked together and we toppled across the hard-packed dirt road. We came to rest about two ells apart and he could have gotten away, for I stared up at large white clouds. My foot felt like it was the size of a hog's belly. I sucked in buckets of air. He didn't get away, though, for the big man was just as exhausted as I.

The smith rolled to all fours. He spoke to me, but I understood none of what he said. His tone was enough for me to catch his meaning. The blacksmith planted a foot on the road to push up and try again. I huffed a curse to Thor and rolled onto his other leg that pointed backward. I whacked his arm, sending the saex into the dirt.

What ensued was an all out scrap between two fatigued, yet big, men. I could give you the details, but suffice it to say that we spent many moments thumping, thrashing, and tearing at one another. He bit my hand. I twisted his groin. It ended with me on my knees astride his back. With one hand, I held both of his hands behind him. I pressed all my weight down on my other hand which ground his face into the herepath.

Now what? I asked myself the same question. If I let him go so that I could snatch the saex from the ground or a blade from my belt, the smith could reverse the situation. He was strong. We sat there panting. He groaned. I frothed.

I heard hooves approaching, more than a single horse. I lifted my head to look east to where the noise came. My skull felt heavy like a great ballast stone wedged between two ribs of a longboat. Even my neck was tired. I felt my muscles withering.

We'd fought and run all day. We'd been running since Anglesey.

I was to do more running.

Cantering directly toward me were the scouts of an army. Whether it was the reinforcements mentioned in the correspondence stolen from Maredubb or a normal patrol or specially dispatched troopers from a nearby garrison, I knew not. I understood nothing of how or why Aethelred organized his military forces. Some distance behind the horseman marched neat lines of infantry. They carried spears and shields. Behind the common soldiers trailed a short baggage train. There must have been three hundred men, small for an army, but ample to crush the few remaining men of Godfrey's invasion force who could still wield a weapon.

The scouts slowed to a trot as they approached the smith and me. Their eyes darted from the path to the nearby woods to scan for an ambush. There were three of them, two with swords, one with a spear.

My heart raced. I can say I was panicking. I craned my neck to look toward the village and the ships obscured by the smoke. There would be no outrunning the horses on foot to reach my comrades. I was stuck.

So I did what any sane Norseman would do. I gave a great shove to the blacksmith's face. I heard his nose break and saw the proof in the blood that blew to the side. The back of his head, I used as a lever, propelling myself to my feet. My knees wanted to buckle, but I willed them straight. Both my sword and my saex were immediately gathered in my hands. The weapons felt better to me than even Freydis' lovely tits had ever felt. I hunched over, ready to receive their attack.

The scouts laughed out loud at me. Laughed! But as much as they scoffed at my appearance, they were not so brash as to close. They kept their distance.

The blacksmith crawled to his feet. I let him, for he was no threat to me now that my weapons were drawn. He began conversing with the riders. After a few rounds of back and forth, the cavalrymen nodded their understanding, again checked the tree line, and moved to surround me with their weapons lowered.

I was to be their prisoner.

Behind me a young girl burst from the woods screaming. The scouts instinctively turned to face the racket. Two of them received a spear to the face for their troubles and they toppled off the sides of their chargers. The beasts, well-trained, hardly reacted to the shock. Instead, they ambled sideways, dragging each dead rider by his right foot which was tangled in the stirrup.

I reacted to the opportunity and with my saex pushed away the spear the last man was pointing at me. I swung sideways and down with my old blade, striking the warhorse just below the knee. The blade stuck in the bone and the beast's rearing jerked it from my hand. The rider struggled to regain control while Leif and Tyrkr jumped from the woods and pulled him down. His life ended soon thereafter. I pulled my saex free.

"You ruined the horse I had my eye on," scolded Leif.

"And I thought I told you to get her," I said pointing to Aoife who had ceased her mock screaming and come to my side, "to Godfrey."

"Fortunate for you they didn't take your advice," said Aoife, beaming behind a black and blue eye. She handed me my helmet that had fallen off.

The smith had sidled toward the woods, hoping we had forgotten him. I hadn't and took a step to finish my wrath. Tyrkr led the remaining two horses in my way, however. He had loosed the dead men from the stirrups and now pointed to their saddles. "You may argue with the kidnapper later."

The thrall was right. The army was approaching. More scouts had ridden in from the sides of the path. They would soon be upon us. I would have to be happy with the thorough beating I had given the man who attempted to take my property. I tossed Aoife up on the nearest beast's withers and awkwardly climbed on behind her. Leif and Tyrkr shared the second beast.

Off we rode, leaving the blacksmith breathing a sigh of relief.

However, the norns, for once, were on my side. When we'd ridden two hundred ells down the herepath, I peered back to see the army reach the smith. Without halting to ask questions, the lead element assumed that he had been a part of the ambush that they had just watched kill their scouts. The smith tipped over with two English spears jutting from his side.

I had my revenge, my saex, and my thrall.

● ● ●

I had my thrall for just a short while.

We trampled across the shingle which was shrouded with smoke. Our men's coughing, more than anything, led us to them.

"You bring me the girl as a treasure," said Godfrey, smiling broadly. "You pay me good money for her, then you turn around and give her as a gift."

"They may yet become Christian," said Killian.

"Where did the little thing get off to?" asked Godfrey.

Leif, as always, was too fast for me. I opened my mouth, first to correct the king that I had no intention of giving away the Irish girl. She was insubordinate and rarely listened, but she brought me joy. I felt entertained and light-hearted when she was around. The king could have his kingdom, his church, and his riches. I wanted a slave worth but a single silver penny. Leif cut me off. "The girl was taken by the English and Halldorr wanted to retrieve her for you. She is a gift."

"I thank you, Halldorr. The girl is a terrible servant, but she will bring my court much in the way of laughter. You've given from your little," said Godfrey with a sincere bow of his head. I scowled.

"The widow's might," Killian gushed. I knew nothing of what he said back then. By now, I've read the Christ's words about the old, poor woman many times.

"Where's Randulfr and his boat?" asked Leif, peering through the dense smoke.

"They've launched. They float just out to sea waiting for us to load the last of the wounded," said Godfrey.

"You mean we aren't ready to push off?" asked Leif as he slid from the saddle.

"Soon," answered Killian. "Patience, young warrior."

"How soon?" I barked, too loudly.

"The last cart just left to go up the hill," began Killian.

Leif turned to Tyrkr, "Go retrieve the drivers. We'll have to abandon the last of the wounded."

"I think not!" yelled Godfrey. "Those men have bled for me and I'll not have them fall into the enemy's hands. And what makes you believe you can speak for me?" Tyrkr had frozen at the king's tone.

"Fly!" shouted Leif. He smacked Tyrkr's horse's rump. Tyrkr, trustworthy and obedient to a fault, raced off. "King Godfrey, if you wish to lose all these men and the plunder for which they fought, then stay and wait. If you want to abandon your kingdom back home and dreams of dominating the Irish Sea, then stay and wait. Down that herepath," said Leif pointing eastward, "comes a great army of bristling spears. There are perhaps one thousand, no, three thousand men."

Godfrey appeared incredulous, but a series of shouts from the English army behind the veil of smoke – which was nowhere near one thousand men – seemed to confirm Leif's tale. Godfrey looked at Killian who looked back at his king, his patriarch. They agreed without a word.

The king spun on his heel and marched down the old dock. "Throw the lines. We're off."

Tyrkr came back with the confused drivers just as Aoife and I jumped about *Charging Boar*. I watched the English army begin to form up over and around the dead bodies of the soldiers we'd slaughtered that very morning. They stood impotently watching us row out to sea through thick smoke which was not unlike the dense fog in which we'd arrived.

We'd gone to Wales and gained men and treasure from King Maredubb. We'd come to England and took life from the nobles Goda and Strenwald as well as coins from Aethelred.

But as I'd done when I was a mere baby and lost my mother, as I'd done twice when Freydis publically abandoned my advances for marriage, as I'd done when I was banished and had to leave behind Thjordhildr, my second mother, I'd lost yet another woman. Well, this one wasn't yet a woman, but she was as spirited as any fine woman ought to be. Aoife was just a nasty thrall, angry and precocious. But she had been mine for just a few moments. And I'd lost her to a greedy, reaching king.

PART III – *Dal Riata!*

CHAPTER 8

Godfrey Haraldsson was indeed blessed. I didn't know if it was from his ancestors such as his father, Harald of Bayeux, and all the work they'd done or the seed they spilled into broad-hipped women. I wasn't certain if his blessings came from Thor. Thor was the most human of gods. He was one of us. He fought for us. I wondered if King Godfrey, with his somewhat reckless ways and headlong approach, engendered Thor's compassion. Perhaps it was Thor who plucked us from grim situations and made them magnificent. A turn of a blade here, a shift of a man's foot there could sometimes be the difference between victory and defeat. Thor could and would do that for a man. The oral tales said that our god of thunder had sympathy on the young lad who'd sucked the marrow from his goat's bones so that when Thor resurrected the beast, it had a malformed leg. Instead of hammering the boy and his family to death with his mjolnir, Thor took the boy on as a servant. The two went on together and had many adventures. Perhaps Godfrey was that modern-day boy.

Or, I did not know if the king was blessed by this One God, so in vogue. Killian called it Providence when God's all-powerful hand came down and presented a way out of a situation or gave a man a gift as fundamental as his life or as basic as a loaf for his supper.

Whether it was quality breeding stock of the generations that came before him, or because of habits learned at the foot of a famously strong father, or because of favor with Thor, or from God's graceful Providence mattered little to me in those days. Now I know that all goodness comes from the hand of the One True God of Abraham, Isaac, and Jacob, and me. I've read it on the vellum pages of a book and experienced it in my life. Back on the Isle of Man, after our twin successful raids in a span of less than three weeks, what mattered and what was sure in my mind was that Godfrey carried heaps of blessings on his back and walked on the high seas of luck. He danced on the outstretched oars of a longboat, extended like a shelf and parallel to the sea. He skipped from one oar to the next, never fearing of a misstep, never worrying that he'd fall into the deep.

King Godfrey was blessed.

I now understood what the life of a hero could be like. Since easing into the docks of Man, celebrations had carried on and on. They began on the shingle before many of us had even exited the longboats. Parties with ale-swilling men erupted all the way up the hillside to the walled town. The constantly muddy streets were tilled by the jubilant dancing feet of her residents. A parade spontaneously started when the king crossed into the gates. Broad-shouldered young men hefted Godfrey into the air. He sat across two of them waving to his joyful subjects. And make no mistake about it; they were now truly *his* subjects. In most men's minds, the name Ketil was forgotten. Such were the benefits of quick victory. By the time the jolly men had carried Godfrey into his great hall at the parade's terminus, musicians had appeared, eligible maidens sprung from the earth eager for a now-wealthy warrior to choose them over rivals, and men, even those who had decidedly wished to stay home and avoid Godfrey's fights just weeks earlier, rushed from their work to cheer the king. Ketil who?

My mind's eye could see no end to Godfrey's growing power. I was intoxicated without taking a sip from the ale barrels. Determination, divine intervention, good breeding, ambition, wealth, and power were in Godfrey's grasp. He'd reached his outstretched arm for just one more penny and came back with a host of them. The king would build his army and his kingdom. Today the Isles were his. Tomorrow he could claim Wales. Next month he could take the small Norse community in Ireland and take over the entire land. Next summer Scotland would ally with us. By the following year, mighty and rich England would pledge fealty to my king. In three years time, even all of Midgard would be too limiting for our power. Godfrey would find himself in league with Thor himself. They'd fight Hel and her frost giants as equals.

I had found my path to happiness, I thought. Temporarily, I gave up all ideas of a normal life raising stock and breeding a strong woman. My new way to delight wound through strandhoggs where we would take livestock, food, and women. The road was traveled by an omnipotent Godfrey. It ended at riches and splendor. My mind waxed fat.

It's all the shit of goats, of course. It's the runny utterings of a young dung-beardling to believe any of what I've just said. Yet, I trusted that fame and fortune would be mine through Godfrey. It is true that his was my first set of raids. It is true that all of what I know about the subject began in those days. So in many ways I owe all of what followed in my life to King Godfrey – successes and failures.

None of it played out as I expected it would in those heady days.

I should have guarded myself against optimism. Huh! Optimism is just a manner of thinking that brings one grief. A friend tells you he has the perfect maid for you. She'll be plump with a dress that tugs at all the right places. She'll be smart, but not too smart. The maid will make a fine woman and she'll manufacture finer children. He tells you all this and you begin to think about the subject. You turn it in your mind. Soon, before you've ever laid your orbs on her, you're convinced her hair is as red as the blood of a newly killed doe. It cascades down from her head like the water lazily bounds down a rocky ledge. The locks just cover her ample tits. She's comely and ready to wed. Her father is rich and ready to pay you huge sums to take her off his hands. The maid is perfect.

Then you see her and she has plain brown hair with a nose that is longer than her arms and a neck as skinny as a spear shaft. Her teeth, rather than two pretty rows of newly shorn sheep, more closely resemble the crooked path cut by a fence constructed on an eroding hillside. Do you see what optimistic expectations bring? I'll answer in case you do not, nothing but grief. Pessimism seems to be the way that a man ought to live. It is certainly my experience in life that what I want or hope for does not happen. That which I don't want, happens.

I should have known with absolute certainty that we'd all die by following after King Godfrey. Had I held that belief, no matter the outcome, I'd be pleased. If we did not perish, what a blessing that would be! If we did breathe our lasts, I suppose that my expectations would be met. There would be no unhappy surprises.

The norns were twisting the cords of my life, tighter and tighter. All the while they coiled, my prospects appeared bright. I followed a king who carried fortune in a pouch on his belt. Whenever he needed some luck he could apply it like salt to a meal. Thor was in his pocket. Odin was on his shoulder. The One God walked around with him in the person of Killian. But one day, the norn of what is, Verdandi, or the norn of what will be, Skuld, would let the twisted twines of my path go. The threads would burst free, unwinding in a rapid, uncontrollable manner.

In the process I'd be tossed like a rudderless ship lost at sea.

• • •

The party waned. It was dark outside the hall. Inside, the central hearth burned down to embers. Its light was diminishing so that our eyes, made heavy from lack of sleep and too much ale, drooped.

A skald told the familiar story of one of Thor's many adventures. It was the one about the famous race, I think. My eyes were closed and my mind was foggy. I heard the man's words, perhaps every other word. In the endless space between the words I could understand, I inserted those of my own making so that the tale he told became a mixture of my life story and Thor's, of cleaning up the manure of a horse and of valiant battle.

The king's hand shook me awake. In my confusion I reached for my saex. Godfrey's curiously strong grip held the weapon in place. "This is all you'll need," the king whispered. In his other hand he held a wooden shovel. It had a small steel tip, the likes of which I'd never seen. Godfrey hauled me to my feet and placed the tool into my hand. He picked his way over his followers, clingers, friends, and a few enemies to the main doors at the hall's end. That was when I realized that I had been asleep long after the last poem from the skald.

Leif and the rest of our company rested next to the thrones. Gudruna slept with her arms wrapped around my young friend. She wore the small gold amulet we'd taken from the king's skeleton on Anglesey and nothing else. Leif curled up under the bear hide we'd stolen from Maredubb's bed. It had been a blistering celebration. It was like those of old. My head ached.

I traipsed after the king, falling onto Tyrkr. The thrall ignored the assault with a snort and rolled over. The king was waving me forward as he held the door. What was he up to?

Going into the dark street provided no further answer. The square was empty. Even the fire ring in its center was silent. A lone lamp light illuminated a tiny window in the church on my left where Killian worked late into the night on his studies. When Killian wasn't raiding with his king, he studied his Lord's word and when he wasn't reading, Killian held services in his church or roamed the countryside looking for souls to save and mouths to feed. I thought of the churchman as a good one.

Godfrey walked around the side of the hall opposite the church. We passed the stone with the carved symbols of Odin and Christianity. Once we were through the small grove of trees we came to two carts that were hooked to two sets of oxen. The beasts looked at us through half-open eyes. Even they wished they were sleeping.

"What are we doing?" I asked. The contents of the carts were covered in large sheets of coarse cloth.

"Bring that," said Godfrey, referring to the second cart. He took a thin switch and lightly flicked the rumps of the first pair of oxen. If oxen could sigh, they did. I think one yawned before they tepidly stepped forward. Godfrey clicked his tongue. The beasts woke up further and moved more lively. I followed with the other cart.

Though he led us through the streets at a leisurely pace, Godfrey clearly had a purpose. We came to the main inland gates to the walled town. There, instead of the normal set of sentries, stood Randulfr and Brandr. I peered up at the raised walkway that skirted around the entire palisade and noticed that it was left unguarded.

"Are they ready?" asked Godfrey as we passed by his trusted duo.

"Four, just as you asked. Two Welshman, a Norseman, and a Greenlander," said Randulfr. "No Manx"

Godfrey nodded, passed through the gates, and led us down the dirt path. As I could have predicted, and perhaps by now you could have predicted as well, a light rain began. It always seemed to rain on those islands. I followed Godfrey. Randulfr and Brandr walked somberly after me. I peered over my shoulder at them. When they'd fully exited the gates, someone from inside slowly pushed the doors closed. I heard the many timbers fall into place as if those inside prepared for a siege. Randulfr and Brandr followed us just so far, forty ells, stopped, and turned to guard the village. Their backs faced us as we drew away.

"What's going on?" I asked.

"Where does a king hold his treasure?" asked Godfrey.

I thought he was being clever, so I answered him as such. "A king's treasure is his sword so he holds it in his belt. Or, a king's treasure is his men, so they are in his longboats. Where else would such riches be?"

Godfrey turned and walked backward next to his cart. He studied my face, smiled, and turned to again face forward. He nodded to himself in the rain as if he was pleased with a decision he'd just made. We took a turn off the main road, climbing a hill.

"I see that I've chosen wisely in bringing you, of all people, out here. But, faithful Halldorr, I don't mean my sword or my army, or my fleet, or anything like that. I meant the question quite literally. Where does a king take the coins, the hacksilver, the gold necklaces, and fine stones he's won?"

I had never served a king. Erik, my second father, had molded himself into the jarl of Greenland. His wealth was larger than any man I'd ever known, but still paltry compared with what Godfrey had accumulated in such a short time. Erik had kept his riches buried in two places. One was under the stones of his central hearth, as if no one had ever thought of that. The other was in a hole under his sleeping platform; again, it wasn't unique. But the kings of Europe seemed to have other ideas on where to store their wealth. Maredubb kept his hacksilver and jewel-encrusted goblets in a stone keep behind a guarded curtain wall, which, itself, was behind a tall wooden palisade behind a ditch. Aethelred seemed to keep his wealth spread all over his kingdom. We'd found a mint in an isolated outpost a few days' ride from his capital. Where Godfrey had placed his or would hide it was beyond me. I shrugged. "In your hall, I suppose."

"Halldorr, that is why, though you may be brave and strong enough to lead men into the fray and stench of real battle, you'll never be wily enough to fight the war of minds between kings. You'll never be a chieftain." Little did King Godfrey know that I'd lead a most foreign people for many decades.

I wasn't sure what he was getting at, but I did not like it. Godfrey didn't know of what I was capable. He knew only that I had fought and bled for him. Even now I was still hobbling from my broken toes.

"I bet you remember from your time growing up in the fatherland of Norway, Halldorr, that your father or maybe a rich uncle buried his treasure. Well, those old ways are the best ways and that is what I mean to do. You see, a king, take Maredubb, puts his faith in a series of walls and men. In the end, though, we all know where the storehouse is and so his enemies put pressure there. Aethelred puts his mints behind earthen and stone walls, but he might as well place a sign out front in large Latin or runes. I know the wealth is there and I can take it if I am smart enough or brutal enough. Usually it takes both."

So I was right. Godfrey didn't know it, but I knew that a man should bury his wealth. The Christians among you will likely take umbrage with such a thought. Nonetheless, recall that I was not yet a member of the One True Faith. I had not yet heard Christ's talk about the talents.

I reached a hand to the tarpaulin covering my cart and peeked under. It hid most of Godfrey's spoils from our raids. The other cart would carry the same.

We descended the other side of the hill. There we found four men, bound, blindfolded, and gagged by the side of the road. The king and I helped them to their feet and, with a long rope, tied them to the back of my cart. Godfrey said many encouraging words to them while we ushered them into place. They didn't fight or moan or otherwise argue. Soon we again made our way down the path.

That night was spent turning onto ever smaller trails. When we came to just the place Godfrey had picked out, we freed our four helpers and dug a great hole. A portion of the treasure was placed inside the hole and buried. Then we rebound and blindfolded our willing accomplices and moved to the next place. Each place resembled the last. It was always out of sight, inside a small grove of trees. It was always on a hilltop that overlooked the sea as if the King of the Isles wanted to pay homage to the method of his raiding.

"Why am I not blindfolded?" I asked as we walked from one of our spots to the next.

Godfrey ignored my question which annoyed me. I thought about running ahead of my oxen and cuffing the king on the side of the head. Of course, I controlled myself. For whatever reason, Godfrey had decided that he trusted me to never reveal the locations of his treasure more than he trusted the other four helpers.

The dawn was breaking when we set the last crate of hacksilver into the final pit. "Rest," ordered the king. Not a grumble answered. We plopped down around the lip of the hole.

Then I grumbled. My head still ached from the last several days of ale. My stomach roiled for want of breakfast. "Couldn't we just fill in the dirt and be done with it before we sit? Wouldn't it be better to cover the fresh dirt with sticks and leaves like we have the previous ones? It's best to do it before the light of day comes and someone spies us?"

"Halldorr," called Godfrey from the carts.

It sounded like he scolded me. I sighed. My fellow workers sniggered.

"Come, get the men some bread. It was made from my own stores of wheat."

All four workers chattered happily. Bread made from wheat was soft. It was a near delicacy to the common man who subsisted, at best, on bread from barley, which was harder and sometimes bitter.

I pushed to my feet and went to the far side of the king's cart where he was fiddling with a few loaves of bread. There was cheese and ale, enough for all of us. I announced as much to the men. They cheered and talked loudly, poking fun at one another. The king heaped portions into wooden bowls he had brought from the village. Godfrey was a generous king.

He pinched my arm and brought me down to his level. He whispered into my ear. "The old gods need their blood. These men were told that they were blindfolded and would therefore live. They were told that you were not and would die. Quite the opposite is my plan. You are here to protect me should things get tight. You will prove your worth now or die along with them." Godfrey tucked a dagger under one of the bowls and turned to carry it toward the men.

It made sense, I suppose, to kill the men just in case they had counted steps and turns. That is why Godfrey wanted no indigenous Manx. Their knowledge of the island might betray his hiding places if they escaped. But if I declined to follow the king's orders, how would he overthrow all five of us?

It was a foolish question. I did not disobey. The king had walked up to the man from Norway. He waited for me. I walked to the Greenlander. He'd come with us when we were exiled. It felt cruel to kill a man who'd demonstrated such dedication to Leif and me that he'd left his family in order to follow us into the unknown. In a way, though, it was only right that I was the one to do it. Honor was there somewhere. Looking back on that morning, I only wish I was somehow able to put a weapon into the man's hand before he died. But I would kill him quickly so that he would not suffer. Nonetheless, you may not like me for doing it at all.

Godfrey nodded. He rammed the dagger into the Norseman's back so that the blade slipped between his ribs. He tried to scream, but no voice came. I dropped the plate, slapped a hand on the Greenlander's forehead and drew my saex across his neck. His warm blood splashed onto my hand.

The two Welshmen jumped into the hole to get away and climb out the other side. They ran atop the treasure. Rather than run along the lip and hem them in, I dove after them. They were among friends, they thought. They had worn no mail. They were told that the king would dispatch me after we'd eaten a meal. They were weaponless. With my arms spread wide I brought them down. Their faces smashed into the far wall of the pit. Their knees cracked into hard chests and scattered artifacts of gold. My father's saex found a place in one of the men's lower back. I left it there. My now free hand fell onto a green statue of a fat man with narrow eyes that had been traded around the world. I used it to bludgeon the second Welshman.

It was brutal and evil. Truly, it was evil. I knew it then, but my mind would not allow such feelings to erupt. My heart wanted to weep. My eyes remained dry. This was to be the life of a raider. Remember, I thought I was on my path to happiness. A fool, I was a fool. It is only by the free grace given by the One God that I am able to stand tall today.

I climbed from the hole. Randulfr and Brandr emerged from hiding places. They had several of the most trusted, the closest men of Godfrey with them. Godfrey handed me the bowl of bread and cheese and a pot of ale. I thought that it was now my turn to die by the hand of the king or one of his lieutenants.

"Now I can count you as my trusted man. In all things you are mine. You took an oath with words. Now the oath is sealed with blood," said Godfrey. He unclasped the elegant ring-pin that held his cloak at his shoulder. He tossed it to me. "Now you're my man." I looked at the arm-ring I wore that told the world I was Erik Thorvaldsson's sworn man. But my second father was still in Greenland. He'd banished me. I decided that I was Godfrey's oath-bound servant. I'd follow him until one of us died and was released to serve Odin.

The king turned his back to me and walked to the man he had killed at the edge of the pit. He took a finger and dabbed at the dead man's blood. He wiped two stripes down his cheeks, one from each eye. When the king again faced me he appeared as fearsome as a warrior of the old tales.

"And you'll not tell Killian anything about this," he began.

"I won't say a word to anyone about the killing or the treasure," I swore, pinning the gift in place.

"Killian would never endorse the killings, but he likely knows that they must be done, for protection of secrets, for appeasing the old gods of this island, and for my family's old gods. No, don't tell him I dabbled in the man's blood. He'll question my commitment to the One True Faith."

I nodded and ate my bread in silent thought. After I finished, I helped Randulfr and the others push the dead bodies into the pit and cover the hole.

We ambled our way back to the village, arriving by the midday meal. The town was still just as closed up as it was before. The king had made sure that only a handful of people knew where his riches were buried. If any of the wealth ever came up missing, the culprits, us, could be dispatched with a single order.

We entered after the whistle of the king alerted the men behind the gates. After going our separate ways, I went to the Odin stone outside Godfrey's hall.

I spoke to Odin there. I paid no attention to the fact that the cross was overshadowing him. I wanted no rebuke for my part in the night's affair. The cross and my reading of the One God's word have done enough of that over the years since then. Likewise, those same articles have brought forgiveness. That night I wanted to ignore my faults and sins.

I thanked the gods for sending me to a king who was a winner. I followed a victorious king who was ruthless when need be. I was devoted to a king who trusted me with his most precious secrets.

I had made it further than I had ever hoped. I was an orphan. Most orphans wound up dead or enslaved or stealing pennies enough from passersby to scratch out a pathetic existence. Because of Erik's blood oath with my true father, I was spared such a life. Yet, while maturing on Iceland and Greenland, I had only wanted a plump wife and a plot of land.

Now, with Godfrey cutting the waves and I in his wake, I saw that one day we could conquer the world.

CHAPTER 9

With the riches properly dispersed deep in the earth and the pockets of nonstop celebrations dripping to an end, the island settled into what I gathered was a more normal routine. Talk of strandhoggs and war briefly faded. Killian helped the king give the law at the Tynwald. Church services were held. I skipped them. The farmers' oats came in. A few of the enterprising, risk-taking farmers even broadcast late barley as they harvested the oats. I marveled at such a thing. Nowhere I had lived previously would have had a long enough growing season to even contemplate a year with double crops! But the cool, not cold, wet, not deluging, weather seemed perfect for such a thing. If they could duplicate that pattern year in and year out, they'd even raise enough food to sell to traders. Astonishing!

And those traders came and went. Some of these merchants traveled overland, picking up goods from the small shops in Godfrey's capital and taking them out across the island, through Rushen, Doarlish Cashen, and up to Knock y Donee. They sold farm tools, steel, ropes, nails, or anything else a homesteader would need. Sometimes English or Kufic coins were exchanged. More often than not, however, these traders had to accept a hen or her eggs for their wares from these simpler, poorer residents.

Other peddlers, the adventurous sort, tucked into Godfrey's port on their way to the booming town of Dyflin. Sometimes they carried thralls for Dyflin's Monday slave auction. These men and women and children were gathered by raids on Scotland, or England, or Wales, or even Ireland itself. I was told the Berbers or other Muslims made the journey north to Dyflin for its constant stock of thralls. The same sea merchants also brought fine finished goods from the continent, especially from the kingdom of the Germans or from the formerly great Rome. It was a Frankish man who laid out his wares on the floor before the king that had Godfrey especially excited one Thursday.

"A real +ULFBERHT+," said Godfrey with such giddiness that he sounded like a maid who'd just discovered that the man she was arranged to wed was actually something other than hideous. He giggled. He studied his reflection in the shining blade as he moved it in front of his face, stopping only when the letters +ULFBERHT+ interrupted the image. Godfrey seemed captivated by the word. I knew nothing of writing, certainly not those Latin letters or the Frankish word they formed. Clearly they assembled to make something that the king thought was special.

"It is indeed," agreed the happy merchant. The man, too, was excited, for he could sense a pending sale. The peddler stood stooped to one side so that I could see just half his grin. His age was too young to justify such a posture so I assumed that he was born with the defect. It forced him to gaze at the king through the upper corner of his eyes.

Aoife brought the king a plate of smoked fish. Godfrey picked up a slice and ate it, offering some to the merchant with a wave of his hand. The girl obeyed and walked the plate to the man. He snatched three bits and shoved them into his mouth and past his gullet before anyone could protest. The food would do him good. He appeared dangerously thin with grossly protruding cheek bones. Aoife turned up her lip into a snarl that was directed toward me as she silently walked away. The girl somehow blamed me for not rescuing her from the king and a life of housework. The king! As if it was my fault. She would just have to learn that she had her fate. I had mine.

"Do you know what this means, Halldorr?" asked Godfrey. He answered his own question. "The +ULFBERHT+ is the most renowned blade in Christendom. The king who carries such a specimen cannot be killed. He cannot be defeated." Aoife moved to the shadows, still holding her plate of food.

"Such a blade would be priceless," I said, not knowing what else to say.

My comment seemed to upset the king, but buoy the peddler even further. The crooked merchant smiled again. "Yes, king. I can see that you surround yourself with strong, able, and intelligent men. This young man knows that such a weapon –

light, flexible, sharp, strong – has nearly infinite value in the right hands. Dare I say that yours are the right hands?"

"You may dare," said Godfrey. He frowned at me as if his enthusiastic response hadn't already increased the price of the sword more than my comment ever could. The king slid the beautiful weapon into its scabbard. The sheath itself appeared poorly constructed compared with the main attraction. Yet, the blade was able to nearly silently whoosh into place. The guard made a gentle clack as it came to rest against the throat.

"King of the Isles," the peddler began his closing chatter, "will be what history says was just your beginning, Godfrey Haraldsson. King of Dyflin, King of Jorvik, King of Wales, Scotland, England, these are all in your future if you just add the fearsome weapon to the arsenal at your belt."

Queen Gudruna walked in, her long green dress fluttering. One of her braids was errant. A shock of her hair was tucked under the chain that held the Anglesey amulet around her neck. I knew she was finding more excuses and time in order to spend the latter with Leif. I suspected that the stray hairs dancing on her head were the result of one more of those occasions. "What is the cost, merchant?" she asked. "The king is a busy man and has no time for clingers or compliments from greedy peddlers. What is it worth to you to leave today without the king instituting a burdensome port tax?"

Godfrey smacked his queen's rump as she stepped past him to her throne. He smiled. They kissed when she sat. Godfrey allowed the marital flexibility of his old faith to shine through. He didn't take offense at Gudruna's indiscretions. It was a convenient position for the king to take since he wanted the same freedom for himself. I've never been comfortable with such a thing. It would be hard to know which children I should feed and which I should turn outside. I'd be jealous and want to thump any man who'd plow my woman in such a way. Also, as Killian pointed out, no respectable Christian king should do such a thing.

"Now, that is why every king needs a queen!" exclaimed Godfrey. "She cuts a man's heart surer than even this blade." He waved the sheathed sword in the air. "The woman is right. I may have forgotten to announce the port tax that was to begin today. Of course, if the price of the blade is correct, I can easily push the tax until after you've left." To my knowledge Godfrey had never thought of or discussed a port tax. He certainly never set one in place, for to do so would do nothing but drive the lifeblood of coins that the traders brought to another port.

"But the blade cost me a fair penny across the seas and across the channel," pleaded the merchant who did not know the king's mind.

"And you'll make your money on it and on all the other goods you sell in Godfrey's kingdom," said Gudruna. "We may always barter or bicker back and forth, but I warn you that I've never seen the result of such a quarrel come out in the favor of the merchant when the king is involved."

"But particularly if the queen is involved," said Godfrey with a twinkle in his eye.

If it was possible, the trader's shoulders, especially the one that tilted toward the floor, sank down even more. He was defeated by the quick thinking and quicker tongue of Gudruna. The peddler's eyes darted back and forth as he ran through the possible scenarios of bid and then offer that would ensue once he set his price. "Eight silver pounds?" he said, at last, to the floor.

Godfrey again kissed his bride, this time on her cheek. "You're much too kind, merchant. I want you happy and I want you to tell others that King Godfrey is generous to his friends. You'll take ten pounds." It was a fortune to the average man, but inexpensive if the blade was as renowned as the king had said.

The bent peddler straightened as best he could. A natural, wide grin stretched across his worn face. The teeth that showed were yellowed; a few were long since gone, leaving black gaps behind. "You are most munificent, King Godfrey. I accept your kindness with joy. It is a fair price and still a fine bargain for you. I'll spread the news from port to port that Godfrey is liberal with his coin."

Gudruna stuck a finger of caution into the air. "Not too liberal, peddler."

"No, no, of course not, Queen Gudruna. Let an evil end come to any man who says that Godfrey spends his treasury unwisely." The peddler crossed himself just as Killian shoved open the doors at the far end of the hall. The priest came bounding toward our tiny assemblage.

"Spread the word, merchant, that King Godfrey has divine Providence on his side. Say that when you slide into Christian ports. Say that King Godfrey has the crack of Thor's mjolnir hammering in his smithy when you go to the ports of the Danes or Norsemen. Tell them I want able and ferocious men to come to serve me. Do that and your ten pounds of silver will find itself multiplied from my fair hand." The peddler was nodding with excitement. The king reached a hand back and gently set it on Aoife's shoulder. "Girl, take the merchant to the steward and have him give our trader here his coins."

Aoife led the toddling trader to the back of the hall. "Foolish errands," she grumbled. "All I ever wanted was to serve a king on the high seas. I wanted to kill a man or two. I got one, but it looks like I'll get no others." On and on she mumbled as they faded into the shadows and through a door. Godfrey laughed at her. Gudruna frowned.

Killian inserted his words into the momentary silence left in the girl's wake. "Did I just hear you say that man is getting ten pounds of silver? For what?"

King Godfrey patted the scabbard as he set it next to his simple throne. "An +ULFBERHT+!"

The priest's eyes widened with wonder. "A true +ULFBERH+T? For two hundred years the master sword smiths in that family have produced some of the most admired blades. They do it all from their outpost in the land of the Franks." Godfrey beamed at the praise being heaped on his new purchase. "I'd say it would be an honor just to see the forge that produces such magnificent objects, but I suppose it looks just as sooty and dirty as our own shop here in town." Killian paused before snapping his fingers. "I've heard there are many forgeries being sold now. They are trying to capitalize on the +ULFBERH+T name. They use inferior steel and techniques. Such blades are said to be a liability in battle. Is it genuine?"

"I'm sure you didn't come to give me a lesson in trade and war," warned Godfrey.

Killian immediately forgot about the sword. "No. I've come to alert you that your cousin, Lady Edana is afoot."

It was at that moment that the thick-necked woman punched open the hall's doors. She was a different person than what I'd remembered from just weeks before. The first time I had laid eyes on her she appeared to be a fleshy creature, well-fed, and spoiled like a favorite cow. That was the night of my first Tynwald before our successful raids. Now the woman had somehow made all of her ample parts fit into a dress that pushed them in a host of directions, mostly in, but with some noticeably pronounced bulges that stretched her tailor's talents with a seam to the limit. Edana looked stronger, confident, and angry. She was almost man-like, warrior-like. Gone was her impotent frustration that had been cultivated further by both Killian and the king as they gave the law at the Thing. Edana now scowled as she pushed her way through the hall directly toward Godfrey. Like the prow of a mighty longboat, she sliced a path among the furniture, tossing benches out of her way so that the ten armed men who trailed behind her plentiful aft passed through cleanly.

The joy I'd seen on Godfrey's face for the past few weeks fled. No, it sunk as a war axe dropped into the sea by a clumsy seaman is quickly eaten by the depths.

• • •

The king's elation from his grand purchase was replaced by the cruel knowledge that despite his recent success against external foes, Godfrey still had small factions working against him on his own island and now in his own capital. The truth was that the life of a Norseman was the same whether he was a bondi living among the other free men of his status or an outright king as Godfrey fancied himself. Defending rank was a constant battle. Never could any king, especially the king of the ever-changing Isles, rest with assurance that his hoard of silver was well hidden. Never could any free man sleep soundly. A bandit would gladly slice his throat and take his farm. The law was what a man could get away with. Edana, with her few clingers, appeared all too willing to play the part of the thief, not in the night, but in broad daylight.

She wagged a regally bejeweled finger at the king. "My husband? I've been told that you allowed him to be captured by the enemy." Godfrey snuck a glance at me, but said nothing of my role in getting rid of Horse Ketil. As quick as his orbs jumped to me, they leapt back at the rotund Edana. "Can't answer for your own actions?" she asked. "Need to look to vagrants from Greenland, wherever that is, for your answers?"

Godfrey slowly mustered a stately attitude. "Lady Edana, it is not customary to burst into a king's longhouse unannounced and then compound the infraction by accusing him of things which you know nothing about."

The cow wouldn't be cowed. "You're my cousin! I knew you when you still shit your trousers. And about Horse Ketil, I know enough. His family here and his extended family in Ireland and Scotland, you recall, allow you to reign over this hunk of rock and a few others because I ask them to stay their strong hands. I am the glue that binds your operation together." Maybe at one time, I thought. Now Godfrey's glue was a monstrous hoard of treasure. "Should now be the time I change my opinion? Should I foster the natural distrust of you and take my men to the side of Ketil's family? To be clear, my intentions would involve deposing you and your Norseman followers. Will you work to retrieve my husband to get back into my good graces?"

I remember thinking that I'd stick the woman like a finished hog. We could put her on a spit and feed the poor on the island for weeks. Killian could speak a sermon on the subject. Loki's words echoed again in my mind, "Politics of the Irish Sea." The fat woman roasting over a fire might not do.

And Godfrey clearly believed in Edana's authority, for he didn't send her out in disgrace. The king calmly studied her small army and said, "I recall that you submitted to my and Killian's authority for your divorce."

"A divorce never granted by the whims of your fancy and your priest's desires. I submitted by choice. It's a choice I am reconsidering," she barked. Edana glowered at Killian.

"And what makes a man you hated and wanted to divorce so very important?" I asked rather dumbly.

"I'll answer that," interrupted Killian.

"You'll not," croaked Edana.

Gudruna chopped a hand in the air like an axe. "Stop this!" Godfrey leaned back in his throne. He reached down and studied the brilliant hilt of his new sword, preparing to let the able Gudruna handle the beast before them. He was probably dreaming of his next conquest, his eventual revenge on Dal Riata. Such thoughts constantly lapped the shores of his mind.

"We know why you want the man back. It is your best way to convince Ketil's family that you are on their side. You want power for yourself. Without him you are nothing more than an old widow. At your age a new husband would be difficult to catch and you would soon find yourself in the nunnery," said Gudruna.

"And your new sisters would quickly find themselves eaten out of the convent," mumbled the priest.

"Killian, keep your bickering mouth quiet," warned Godfrey. He whitened his grip on the sword, but left it in the scabbard. The small priest glowered, grumbling in silence.

"Just because we know your reasons for wanting your drunkard of a husband back and just because we despise your reasons, does not mean they don't have merit," began Gudruna.

Killian and I looked at the queen with furrowed brows. Godfrey gave a wry grin as he appreciated Gudruna's deft statecraft. He shrugged and waved for his woman to continue.

"We are not foolish. We value the peaceful benefits that come with the support of Horse Ketil's people, on Man and Ireland and even Scotland."

"I should say so! Despite your recent fortune – all of it lucky, from what I've heard – you command an army of, what, two hundred men in total? What do you have – five ships if you count those you've stolen?" Edana put her plump hands on her hips. She ended with a satisfied, "Humph."

Gudruna nodded. Godfrey was shaking his head. "More than that. The Manx have reconsidered. Many who were once for Ketil have found a place in their hearts for me. New ones join every day. And more will come. The peddler I just overpaid will spread the news. Within the month, men will pour in from all over the seas," said the king.

"Ha! Not enough men will be foolish enough to follow you." Edana scanned the then empty hall and pointed to me. "This idiot and more like him, perhaps. But no more."

Gudruna frowned. "King Godfrey, Lady Edana, the number of men that serve us or will serve us is not the issue. Securing the power due Edana is what we must discuss." I thought that the number of men serving someone actually was the issue, for power would determine who would rule. But I didn't understand that sometimes in the art of politics its participants say the opposite of what they believe. The queen fiddled with her gold amulet. "King Godfrey, we may do one of two things. We may send envoys to negotiate with King Maredubb for Ketil's release. I think truly that neither you nor Edana wish that. Or, we may discuss a power-sharing relationship right here on this island, granting your cousin and her men sway over local issues." The queen turned to face her husband. She winked so that only the king and I saw her, leaving Edana in the dark.

Godfrey gently set his prized sword down next to his throne. He stood, nodding, and walked to Edana. He made a show of grasping her hands in his. "Lady Edana, cousin, I've allowed much sport to be made of you and with you. I've allowed this priest too much freedom. But you and my wife here have today shown me my errors. You've reminded me of my obligations for further peace for our subjects, Manx and Norse. Come back another time when we may work out specific details on our sharing. It will be good for me to know that my own family member controls our new homeland while I concentrate abroad and expand our frontiers."

Edana jerked her hands free. "Oh, that's a brilliant speech – and extemporaneous, too!" She paced back and forth in front of her small army. "When do we meet? I'll not be put off with this like I am in the divorce."

Godfrey's face tightened. It reddened. I thought he was going to belch fire at the woman. Gudruna interrupted him before the fit could erupt. "One week. I'll personally arrange everything for a week's time."

"No, we'll meet tomorrow," clipped Edana. "That will give me just enough time to lay out my terms."

Godfrey clenched his jaw. Gudruna answered easily. "Very well. You may find lodging in the city and come by in the morning." Gudruna patted the throne next to her. Godfrey obediently sat. The queen continued. "And my warrior king has taken so much plunder in the past several weeks that he has treasure to offer."

Godfrey blanched.

Edana's eyes became fixed on the queen. She was as greedy as any man. She was as greedy as her husband, that much is sure. "A few trinkets from a poor Welsh king won't be enough!" warned Edana.

"Some," corrected Gudruna, "only some is from Maredubb. The rest is from the English and they are wealthy enough."

Edana pinched her fat lips as she thought. "What say you warrior king? Do you agree with the mind behind your throne? Will you meet in the morning? Will you pay me my due?"

Godfrey spent time grinding his teeth, obviously regretting that he had let his woman perform the negotiations. But it was clear he had no other ideas about how to recapture the peace from Edana and more importantly how to keep the peace with Horse Ketil's armed kinsmen. Through clenched teeth, Godfrey answered, "Yes, it will be as the queen says."

"Then I'll see you right here in the morning," said Edana. "If you don't keep your word on this, I will begin fomenting discontent by midday. If that happens, by tomorrow's gloaming, you'll have an armed horde outside your gates." Without warning, the corpulent woman spun on her heels and wedged her way between her twin lines of men. They splayed apart like the sides of a log split with a stout maul.

When she had gone, Godfrey seized his woman's hand. His grip was tender despite his obvious anger. "Give her my island! Share Maredubb's treasure? Spill English coins into her ample lap? I need that wealth for my own army. A vow of peace? All this for my fat cousin? Horse Ketil was caught in the act of treachery. Without Halldorr rapping him on his head, we'd all be dead. Now I've got the same thing in my own family." Godfrey looked up at the rafters and uttered a string of curses. When he finished he glanced at Killian. "Sorry for the Christian slurs, priest." He didn't apologize for threatening to crush Thor's balls in his tirade. "Horse Ketil is probably already free. He is probably a drunken member of Maredubb's court. Ketil's probably already sent representatives to his family here and in Ireland and Scotland. What we need is unity! I'll need all that wealth to protect my land and to seize more."

"Are you quite finished?" asked Gudruna, cutting off her husband.

"No!" he shouted.

I chuckled, for the queen truly meant that he was finished whether he wanted to be or not. She walked over his next several words with her own. "We are king and queen here and over several islands. We hold on with the most tenuous of grips."

"That is true," began Godfrey.

"You're finished, husband," said Gudruna as a soothing reminder. Godfrey scowled at Killian and me before we could laugh. "You have now accumulated significant riches. The only other piece we lack is men. How confident are you that men will come?"

Godfrey sat silently.

"Speak," urged his wife.

"I thought I was finished," said the king not unlike a five year old child. "Men will come. They must come or we are finished. Gold won't protect our city or this island or my ships. We need men and so they must come to us."

The queen set out her hands, palms up. "There you have it. They will come. You'll have your army. Your army will protect you from Maredubb and Ketil's family, with or without Edana."

"But what will I pay my soldiers with if I have to give my cousin a chunk of Maredubb's gold?"

Gudruna shook her head, tut-tut-ting Godfrey. "Husband, we'll see just how confident you are in your ability to build a real force of sea warriors. Arrest the fat cow in the morning. Ambush her tiny force and kill them or throw them in chains as well."

"But Ketil," said Killian. "The traitor's family."

"The king said it himself. His family might already be against us. Horse Ketil and Maredubb are likely allying with them right now, plotting our overthrow. We need only to build our forces and strengthen ties to Dyflin, the friendly Irish clans, and our Norse homeland. His cousin does have sway over her in-laws, but not that much."

"She sways the earth when she walks," growled Killian.

Godfrey was smiling at his wife. He pulled her hand to his lips and kissed it softly. Then he pulled her to him and kissed her lips. When the moments lingered and her hand went into his lap, Killian and I backed away.

The doors to the hall burst open a third time. Randulfr came in much the same way as Killian and Edana before him. His face was flushed. His skin shone with sweat. His chest heaved from a long run. I was instantly worried. Randulfr pounded to a halt in front of the twin thrones.

Godfrey, his lips on his woman's neck, peeked up at his lieutenant. The king rolled his eyes and grunted. The two royal lovers pulled away from one another but still held hands. "What is it?" asked the king.

"Ships, Godfrey. Two ships of men have arrived, one from Ireland, one from Normandy. They are full of men who wish to fight for you."

The king grinned wickedly. He slowly stood, gathered his sword and his woman, and began to walk toward his small bed chambers at the structure's rear. "I told you they'd come," he said to Gudruna.

"You did," she cooed.

"Randulfr!" barked Godfrey over his shoulder. "Talk to Halldorr and figure out how we'll best get Edana and her men arrested in the morning. Keep it quiet."

Randulfr looked to me, confused. Killian grinned. It was an impious smile for a priest. It was infectious. Soon the corners of my mouth were turning up at the thought of shackling the rotund, pompous woman.

Godfrey playfully pushed his woman through the door to their chambers. "I told you they'd come," he said again.

"And now it's our turn," laughed Gudruna as the king kicked the door closed behind them.

• • •

And come they did. The men, that is.

Hardscrabble bandits, downright brigands, pirates, fools, unlucky farmers, cast-offs, all of them came to serve the up-and-coming king. Sailors, slaves, blacksmiths who wanted to be warriors, and warriors who wanted to settle into a trade flooded the town. They came from the poorest hillsides in Wales and the windswept coasts of Man. Over the coming weeks they came from Ireland, Sudreyjar, Dyflin, old Pictland, the Faeroerne, and Norway. A smattering of Danes showed up in a rotting hulk of a boat that looked like it would soon be clogging up the sea floor of whatever port in which it finally sank. Three Englishmen, well, they were from Cornwall and Scilly, so we considered them men of the sea and not Englishmen, sailed with the Danes. Men came from all over looking for fortune, and since rapid success sires litters of triumph, they were cocksure. I was shocked at just how fast news spread of Godfrey's victories. The sword peddler's words and those of Godfrey's victims traveled far and wide.

What little wealth in terms of silver coins these new arrivals into Godfrey's court on Man brought with them was spent in the two taverns and one brothel in town. The half dozen tired whores and enthusiastic barmen quickly had all the additional riches in their pockets. But like all coins it ran away like water to the sea. The whores bought ale and clothing. The tavern owners bought whores and food. The small economy of Man underwent a momentary surge.

Mostly our new citizens, these rascals, brought the same problems that had likely stalked them through their entire lives.

Merchants and families quickly discovered the necessity of closing and barring their doors and windows at sunset. The streets were filled with drunken men, armed drunkards who were eager for action and riches. The nightly fights were, more often than not, deadly. The newcomers and some established soldiers died in the muddy avenues with knives plunged into their chests or spears jutting from their bellies. Muscular, rapid fists killed three men within the first week.

 I had grown up in the normal, coarse, harshness of life. Norway, Iceland, and Greenland had all required diligence for the mere act of survival. To make it through one single winter in any of those locations meant that a man and his family were tough and wily. My first and second families in those places had retained their sense of wonder and joy in the world despite the difficult lifestyles prescribed to them by fate. I had been a professional raider now for several months. I had seen battle, blood, and downright war. Things had gone poorly and situations had gone well. The Welshmen and Englishmen against whom I had struggled were tenacious, unbending. The men with whom I had fought were rough, but had joviality that could shine through in the bleakest of circumstances. This new batch of men was unlike any I had ever met. They were brutish. They were cruel for cruelty's sake. Though they pledged their fealty in public ceremonies to King Godfrey, they remained mercenaries. And mercenaries, everyone should know, had loyalties that shifted like riverbed silt.

 "Half of these men could be instruments of Maredubb," protested Killian. "They could be agents of the Ui Neill, Dal Riata, or Horse Ketil himself! They are sent here to usurp your authority, to kill you." Killian walked next to an oxen-drawn cart that was heavy laden with a newly carved stone. A cross relief was etched on its front side. Inside the boundaries of the Christian symbol were Norse runes, chopped in by one of Godfrey's masons.

 Godfrey looked down from the charger he rode. His fine new blade rested in its scabbard against the horse's flank. "I assume they all work for someone else. That's why I'll keep them close. When I kept Ketil at my side it worked out in the end. At best and most likely these newcomers operate for themselves well before they give any consideration to their holy oaths to me." The king gave me a compliment by looking my way. "They can't all be bound to their king by blood like Halldorr."

"So what will you do?" asked Leif. He rode a sloppy-looking bay next to my equally questionable borrowed horse. Each of the animals' backs swayed low.

"He'll die. His queen will die. His kingdom will go to another. I'll serve a new king within the year. That's what he'll do! That's what I'll do," said Killian, whipping the nearest ox to add an exclamation. "King Godfrey is getting ahead of himself in doing this thing we do."

"Don't be so dramatic," Godfrey said with a roll of his eyes. "You liked the idea yesterday." Our procession stopped just outside Kirk Braddan. Edana's incessant babbling, which had been drowned out by the clatter of hooves, feet, and wheels, invaded our ears. "Would someone please gag the woman," said the king.

Loki hopped up to the cart on which she rode and stuffed a rag into her trap. The woman fought with vigor, nipping his fingers with her bared teeth. Soon all we could hear was a low, guttural series of moans emanating from the beast of a woman. But just as she'd given up on the struggle against the cords that bound her wrists and ankles, in a short while Edana gave up fighting the cloth.

Workers came to the cart that carried the stone cross and retrieved shovels. Godfrey absentmindedly pointed to the earth with his eyes and they quickly set to work at the side of the road digging a hole to receive the monument.

King Godfrey rested his hands on his saddle's pommel, patiently waiting. "I trust none of our new men, Leif. Hell, I barely trust you and you helped bring me Aberffraw *and* Watchet! Distrust is what will save me. I'll have Randulfr, Loki, and Halldorr, and a dozen others around me when we go to war." The king put me into the list of men he trusted. It was true, for he had allowed me to see where he stashed his hoards of riches. We had killed, no murdered, our faithful soldiers over the last pit. Their blood truly shackled me to the king. Why he trusted me and not his other new men, like Leif or Tyrkr or the other Greenlanders, I do not know. Looking back, I suppose it was because I was simple. I was not simple like the village dolt, drooling down my chest. I was simple to read. I wanted a fat woman and land that produced fat crops, even though I temporarily thought otherwise. Since I had never been fortunate enough to get a wife or land, I would serve whoever was closest. Godfrey and, likely, anyone else could see that. King Godfrey meant to pull me close to himself. "No assassin will get through that mess of muscle. Besides, these newcomers want strength. Even if they came with treacherous intent, once they see their share of hacksilver and gold, their loyalties will settle where they ought." The king scratched at a flea in his beard.

"May it be as you say," whispered Killian, still not convinced.

The hole was finished. Killian skillfully guided the oxen backward toward it. When the tail of the cart hung just over the lip, he stopped. I jumped into the cart and along with ten other men shoved or pulled the slab back. Inch by inch, ell by ell, the heavy marker scraped against the worn wood. At last gravity took over and the base of the carved cross fell into the hole. Brandr was struck in the chin by the top of the cross as it flew up. He fell back into the cart, fighting instinctive tears. When Brandr moved his hand away from his chin, it was already badly swollen and red. He'd bit his tongue. When he gritted his teeth, they were outlined in blood. We laughed at him. He kicked my shin like a child. We laughed harder. King Godfrey joined in.

"Even your closest men are incapable of serious thought," scolded Killian. "Neither are you."

Godfrey shrugged. "I'd have it no other way." The king studied his closest advisor and, dare I say, friend. "I am lucky to have a good woman with a head on her shoulders. I am more fortunate to have a priest who cares about his adopted people and king."

The priest huffed, moved the oxen and their cart out of the way, and stepped to face the stone cross. "Turn it south," he said, leaving Godfrey's compliment hanging. The men obeyed.

"Good," Killian said. "Now hold it upright in the hole." He took a plumb bob made of a rock and string from his pocket while the workers did as he asked. "Left," the priest commanded. "My left, not yours," he barked. "There. Hold it there," Killian said, tapping the smooth stone. His fingers lingered for a heartbeat on the sharp chisel marks of the runes. Then he stepped back again to admire his work and with a nod from Killian, the men began refilling the small pit.

Meanwhile, others had moved Edana's cart under the boughs of a tree across the hard-packed road. The single, speckled palfrey that had struggled to lug the large woman along the path now rested one of its rear legs in a cocked manner. The horse rested its eyes while Randulfr gave the men who jumped into the cart orders.

"Over that branch there," he said, pointing.

"Won't do," said Tyrkr. "She's a fat one. Not that I'd mind her resting in my lap, mind you. But she'll break that branch as sure as her husband is a drunk. Then you'll just have to cinch her up again."

"That's fair," admitted Randulfr, taking the criticism from a slave better than he had ever taken advice from young Leif. "Over there? What about that limb?"

Tyrkr was shaking his head. "Even if that one holds, look at the rope. Do you think it will hold?"

"Oh, lad, you are a foreign one, aren't you," said Godfrey as he squeezed his heels into the belly of his horse. The creature stepped across the road toward Edana. "Everyone from these parts knows that the women on Man make the finest sailor's rope in the world. Men come from all over to buy from our rope walks."

"That's because the pagans all believe the women here are witches!" called Killian. "They think the witches give the ropes magical powers."

"That rope will need magic if it is supposed to support Edana," observed Tyrkr. "It'll take most of its length to wrap around her neck just once." Edana began struggling again. I suppose she had known what her fate was to be once we tied her up and loaded her in the cart. Hearing her captors talk about it so, reinvigorated her labor.

"We'll find out, won't we? It's the rope we have and so it must do. I want her to hang in front of the stone cross. I want her to know just what will be read by every man who passes this marker for all eternity. I want her to read it while she dangles. It will be the last thing Edana sees before she dies. Mostly, I want her to know it says nothing about her, for to scratch her name in runes would give her credit with the gods. Now Randulfr quit dallying. Get her strung up," said Godfrey. "I've got an expedition to plan."

Tyrkr threw the rope over the second bough they had seen. Randulfr caught the end and tied it off on the tree's trunk. Tyrkr laced the loop over Edana's head and tightened the noose against the back of her neck. Edana tried to flee. The men let her.

Edana's step rocked the cart. The horse awakened and skittered forward. The men in the cart rode along. So did Edana. She did, at least, until the rope smacked taut. Her cheeks bulged as the last gasp of air was caught in them. Likewise, Edana's eyes flared in horror and wonder. Women are no different than men in that regard. I've told you that all men, especially the good ones, are utterly shocked that they meet their end. Edana was too. She flung back. The branch sagged, creaking under her great weight. It sunk so low that one of her toes briefly brushed the ground. It was a shame that such a thing happened, for it gave her momentary hope. Still bound, Edana fought to stick the toes of both her feet downward. She gurgled. Edana grunted.

Godfrey rode over to the stone cross and rested his hand on it. He patted it twice. "Lady Edana, I think you see that I am king. Outright. I am King of the Isles. No threats from you or your husband or your in-law relations will change that. I want you to read this and know that the dishonor your husband has brought to you will haunt your spirits forever. He will go to neither Valhalla nor the Christian heaven. You will certainly go to only the one place that will have you."

"I hope it has a banquet table," said Loki. The men laughed.

"Hush fools," chided Killian. "This is an execution. We're not street criminals murdering for fun." Killian had been all for getting Edana out of the way. But the complicated man was decidedly angry when it came to actually performing the act.

"The priest is right," said Godfrey. "I've made my point. Let's go back and finalize our plans. It's time for our final revenge on Dal Riata."

Edana's face was red. Her entire head appeared bigger. Godfrey pushed off from the monument and rode back the way he'd come. Others, on foot, followed, carrying shovels on their shoulders. Killian whipped his oxen. Those beasts of burden sprang to action, no doubt pleased to have dropped off the great load they'd carried out.

Leif, Tyrkr, Magnus, all of them left to scheme with the monarchs. I stayed behind. I'd never seen someone hanged.

Edana spat. Dribble came down her chin. A series of veins on her broad forehead swelled to the size of fingers. They pulsed. Thin, blue veins under the skin of her cheeks burst. Snot came from her nose. Her teeth chattered. Piss ran down her legs and dropped the hair's distance to the ground from her twitching toes. Edana's eyes stared across the road to the cross we'd just erected.

I looked at it, too. I couldn't read then, not even my native Norse runes. The only way I knew what it said is because Killian had told me. Running along the horizontal member of the cross were the words, "Horse Ketil betrayed in a truce his own oath fellow." Yes, Ketil had betrayed Godfrey, the man with whom he'd helped build a peace with the Manx natives. At the end of a man's life all he could hope for was to have retained his honor. Ketil would forever be known as a man with none.

I smelled shit.

Turning, I could see that Edana had expired. Her bowels had released.

It was an awful death. I suppose that when you threaten a king, you had best expect such an ending, cousin or not. I climbed into the saddle on my sway-backed horse and trotted after Godfrey.

He had his army. He had his wealth. He had his longships. It was finally time to run to Dal Riata, the entire reason I'd agreed to follow the sometimes-king in the first place.

CHAPTER 10

There was still stinking flesh left on the bloated form of Edana when we set out from Man on our great and glorious raid. So many ravens had settled onto the limbs of her tree and so many perched on her shoulders to get just one more nibble at her eyes or her neck fat that the front and back of her gown were littered with their white droppings. I know this because I intentionally ventured out to view the macabre scene when I had no reason to go that direction. It seemed wrong to kill her that way, but was I on Godfrey's throne, I would have done the same. Cut the head off of little problems before they become immense.

The scene at the docks and on the shingle was similar to when we left for our first adventure, only busier. Hundreds of men in a dozen ships gathered sails and ropes. They packed supplies, laying hens, and weapons. Their shields rested on the gunwales. If they could afford mail, it was stowed with the baggage. If they could afford only hard leather vests for armor, they wore them.

Peddlers, all of them clever if they'd survived in that brutal business for any length of time, came down to the quay. They sold produce from the backs of wagons. Some sold trinkets so the men with families could give their women a small token or amulet before they left. The peddlers and the few men who were honest with themselves understood that even if we were successful, this might be their last trip. The merchants meant to get the last of the coins of those future dead men. The men meant to give their women something to sell in order to live.

I carried my hudfat to *Charging Boar*. It was packed with my humble belongings. I had my rich ring-pin from Godfrey and wore my arm ring from my second father, Erik. My purse jingled with extra coins given to me by the king. I appeared wealthy when compared to most men. I suppose I was, for the king was generous and gave me a healthy portion of the hacksilver for my part in his raids on Watchet and Anglesey as well as my silence as to his treasure's whereabouts. Because I looked young, foolish, and flush with coin, the peddlers targeted me with their calls.

"Hey, beast," called a brothel owner who'd come down to stand on the stones. "I've got a woman who can tame you. She'll have you purring in her lap in moments." He pointed up the hill where one of his workers plied her trade on a Welshman in a narrow alley.

That was an easy ditch to pass by. "No, friend," I answered. Of course, I craved a woman as much as any young man, perhaps more. Yet, I'd been torched by Freydis. Even a heartless encounter did not appeal to me.

The brothel man mumbled something under his breath. I turned to have him repeat the slur, when I noticed a merchant I'd seen before, on Greenland. Instead of pummeling the first, I moved to the small table the second peddler had set up on the shingle. He bent down to stack a series of rocks under one of the legs in order to steady the makeshift counter. When my large shadow fell across the side of his face, he jumped up. "Welcome!" he said as he swept his hand over his small amount of goods. His tooth-filled smile was the same one I remembered from Greenland the previous year. "You are obviously a man who appreciates fine metal work. I am an artisan. My works are famous." Then, he paused, squinting. "Do I know you from somewhere?"

"Greenland," I said.

He snapped his fingers. "The brooches!" he remembered. "Oh, now those were fine. That was a great purchase you made for your woman. And she was an equally fine specimen. Fiery red hair, I recall. The kind who makes you want to come back alive." He nodded toward our boats. "Care to give her something to remember you by?" The metal-worker picked up a silver neck ring then dropped it carelessly on his table. "That won't do for a man with your taste or for a woman like yours. You spent good money on those gold brooches. The Midgard Serpent, I put on them, and the norns!" The man bent down to dig through his pack, singing an incomprehensible tune.

"I don't need anything from you today," I said.

The peddler held up a hand to shut me up. "I won't hear of it. Your purchase in Eystribyggo enabled me to pay my way home. I'll give you this for a song." The merchant held out a set of brooches. These weren't as regal as my first purchase from him. They weren't gold. They were bronze with raised etchings of the frozen Niflheim filled with gnashing dragons. I thought about how fitting they would have been for Freydis. Like Hel's dwelling place, Leif's sister had grown blue cold to me. Instead, I had spent a fortune on gold for her. Fate, I thought.

The metal work on the bronze brooches was less than enticing. "You look disappointed," the trader said. He stroked his impeccably kept beard. "I'll grant you that they are not what you bought before." He swept an arm under the dangling chains that held the twin brooches together. "They are not what you bought before because I didn't make them. I took them as part of a trade from a Finn. He didn't make them either. He said that he too took them in trade. I do know that they are fetching, for bronze. Someday they will tarnish, but today they'll look good on the," he hesitated, "bountiful chest of your woman."

"I have no woman," I said stepping away.

"Oh, no!" the merchant said. He walked around his table to chase me. "Nonetheless, take these as a gift. I owe you that. Show them to your fellow sailors and tell them I sold the brooches to you for a few silver pennies." The man wanted me to drum him some business.

"Fine," I answered, clasping the bronze chains and slinging the large brooches over my shoulder. I thought that one day I'd give them to Aoife so that she could look like a little lady, even though she was a slave. Today though, if Aoife tried to wear them, they would topple her slight frame over. Maybe I'd buy the girl from the king and set her free. She could become a skjoldmo like she dreamed. I could act as her father and negotiate with her suitor one day over the bride-price.

The metal smith still chattered after me as I moved toward the ships. He only stopped when the king and queen began descending the hill far behind me. The artisan ran back to reorganize his wares to make them as tempting to the king as possible.

I chuckled at the peddler. All of us chase and battle. For warriors in pursuit of the enemy, it is easy to see the hunt, the killing. But I assure you we all fight. The farmer hacks at the sod, creeping his plot farther into the wilderness so that he may produce just a bushel more of barley. With more grain, perhaps more of his children will survive yet another dreaded Norwegian winter. The peddler ordered his little metal soldiers so that they could stab Gudruna's heart, thereby getting to the king and his purse. As I said, we all fight.

I bumped into something in my path. Looking down, I saw a hunched over woman in a tattered brown cloak. She leaned on a crooked cane that seemed too short. The woman peered up at me with one eye wide, the other squinting. I could not tell if the second eye was still there or had been plucked out. "It's not good. It's not a good omen," the old woman grunted.

Stepping to one side, I attempted to pass her and walk onto the dock. She took that little cane and cracked my shin. "Damn you, old fool," I said. "I didn't see you. I meant you no harm."

"And you're the one with two eyes!"

"And your one eye spends its time staring down at the horse dung on the road, you hump-backed crow," I said.

"Odin's birds know the world. I'd say it's not a bad thing to be a bird on the wing," she countered. "Sisters!" she called. "We've got a young warrior who needs our merchandise." The woman continued on the path on which she had been before we bumped into one another. To the side of the main path to the ships and among large tufts of grass were two more old hags. One of them had a cane like the sister in front of me. The third old woman leaned on the second sister with a shriveled hand sticking out from under a ragged coat. They looked like triplets.

I had tired of them. "No, I do not need whatever it is you peddle."

All three cackled in time, almost singing a familiar musical tune while they laughed. "Doesn't need, he says!" said the first.

"What we sell," said the second.

"Only, of course he does," finished the third.

"How can any Norseman not need the spirits of the norns on his side?" asked the first woman as she sidled next to her sisters.

"Especially when he goes to battle," said the second.

"With a man like Godfrey," finished the third.

Their unconventional selling tactics had me. "What kind of man is Godfrey? Are you the ones to sell me the spirits of the norns?"

They laughed again. I smiled, but did not know if they cackled at me or with me.

"It's clear he's young," the first woman said, shaking her head.

"For he asks the wrong questions," said the second sea hag, nodding.

The third woman rested her other hand on the first sister so that she was balanced between the two. "So we will give him the answers to the proper questions while awaiting his silly mind to catch up."

I turned to walk away.

"You are a lost man, sent away from three homes."

I froze.

"Now you cling to a king as you look for a third father."

"He is not the one to fill that role. Another will."

"Son of Olef, you chase and fight for things you don't understand."

"You say you want a hearth and a plump wife."

"But do you?"

"We ask it," they said in unison.

"Yes," I said with certainty. "Well, no. I seek glory and profit now."

Frowns formed on their wrinkled faces. "He is so young that he thinks he knows something, anything," said the first woman. She sounded sad.

The woman in the center waved me over. I thought she would fall into the grass and roll onto the stones because she teetered so much. I obeyed her command.

"Like the scene on the brooches," began the first woman while pointing to my shoulder, "your life shows nothing of worth. You will end up serving the cold bitch Hel in her underworld. Stay on your path and that is what you will do."

I scoffed then. I looked over to the metal smith, wondering if he and the old women had hatched an elaborate plan to make coin from superstitious Norsemen. "You want my silver and gold. You want my English pennies and Kufic coins and what you sell is fear," I accused.

One by one the old women reached their mangled hands into their coats. Each pulled out a short length of rope that had a single knot in the center. One at a time, they dropped them onto the stones of the shingle. The first woman said, "Take them. Take the ropes. When the wind is needed, it will be had. It will be all that saves you from your path."

"And the cost for your magic rope?"

"The brooches," the third one answered plainly. "The brooches give you an image in your mind's eye of your destination. Change your destination."

I snatched the ugly bronze brooches from my shoulder and dropped them to the ground. What did I really care for them, they were a gift to me for a woman I did not have. Even little Aoife couldn't use them for years. Back then I thought I would never be anyone's father, certainly not an Irish thrall's. I bent down and gathered all three of the short, knotted ropes and set them where the brooches had just rested.

"Ah, Halldorr shows wisdom!" giggled the second woman. All three again laughed.

"How do you know my name when I don't know yours?" I asked.

Their tiny bodies vibrated from laughter. Had their faces not been so etched from weather and their bodies so stooped, I would have said they were almost like adorable grandmothers. "You know us."

"You curse us because you believe we curse you," explained the second.

"I am Urdr, she is Verdandi, and she is Skuld." They sniggered again.

"Crazy witches. You claim to be the norns?" I huffed as I left them and walked to the ship without looking back.

Killian stood on the dock looking up at a tall, thin priest who was as young as me. I'd not seen the man before. "You'll need to be aggressive here while I'm gone," Killian was saying. "Many of the Manx are already Christians. They understand what it is you do. Remember, there are many inhabitants here who would just as soon cut you and hang you upside down from a tree as a sacrifice to their pagan gods." The young priest blanched.

"Oh, don't let your imagination run wild," cautioned Killian, seeing what his words had done to the young man. The older priest jabbed me in my ribs with a rigid finger. "Most of the worst, like this one here, will be away while you run the masses. Look at him, he's even found some of the magic, knotted ropes from our local witch population. I didn't think they were skulking about today." He scanned around at all the sailors and merchants. I turned to point to where I had gotten my ropes, but the place was now vacant, the sea hags gone.

"Halldorr and his ilk will be my concern," said Killian resuming his instruction before he moved to follow me. He called over his shoulder to the young man. "It's the queen you need to worry about. She'll tempt you young man. She practices some of the old gods' arts with her gifts. A skald might come by the hall. He'll tell tales of battle and love. The heart of the queen will swell. Don't forget that you've taken vows."

We left the stunned, baby-faced man standing by himself. "Who was that?" I asked.

The dark priest spat into the rocking water below. "My replacement, though I don't think he knows it yet. The bishop in Ireland has control of our parish. He has tired of how I run my flock." Killian chuckled. "I can't say that I blame them since I frequent the shield wall. Leaders ought to live out the faith. I frequently fail." He spat again. "Coddled, lad, that's what the priests in the far reaches of my homeland are. They're just as comfortable on the continent and in England. It's been too long since they've had to deal with hard, true pagans. How else am I to lead? And they go send that meek bugger. He came with a ship full of our new warriors a week ago." Killian hastily tossed his pack into *Raven's Cross*, but kept on with me. "And what do you think those ropes will get you?" He plucked one from my shoulder.

"I don't know. It can't hurt to have the local spirits on my side."

"Can't it?" asked Killian. He didn't press the point. "When I was a lad myself, there was a pocket of pagans living in the next valley. Praise God, they've since converted. But I remember that the patriarch of their family swore by the ropes twisted by the witches of Man. Those knots, you see, are supposed to house the energy of the wind. It is bound by a spell to stay close. Then when you untie the knot, the wind erupts. Your sails billow. The flags turn about and snap. Your journey flies. Your strandhogg finishes with success. Thralls are taken then sold. Coins weigh down your purse. In other words, all the things a pagan could love come trotting your way." He swung my rope and slapped me with it. "All of that is constrained in that tight, little knot." The priest struck me with each of the last three words.

I grabbed my rope back. "Then I'll keep the cords and untie them at the right time."

"There is no way you will need to unleash the power in those knots," called Godfrey from behind. Killian and I spun to see that the king now stood on a set of rickety crates that housed chickens. Beneath him, the birds flapped their wings in their tiny cages. Feathers fluttered. Leif pushed his way around the stack, carrying two hudfats, his own and one I didn't recognize.

"We are about to exact revenge on the so-called churchmen up north," Godfrey began.

"We did invade them first, after all," muttered Killian. I shushed the Irishman. He was correct, but when a king is about to give a speech about a forthcoming battle, who wants a bird chirping in his ear about the intricacies of truth?

"Dal Riata was once a real kingdom. Now it is a shadow that has stretched too long. The evening sun is setting on its place in history. The morning sun rises on a new kingdom, our Kingdom of the Isles!" We cheered for Godfrey and what he was cobbling together. I had only known victory with him and expected no less.

Godfrey moved his hands to his hips for a truly heroic pose. In so doing, his weight shifted and the wobbly crates teetered. The king crouched and spread his arms out wide to catch his balance. The crowd of onlookers gasped in the moment when it looked like their king would topple; a terrible omen. Yet, Godfrey remained standing. He rose to stand even taller, scanning his warriors who had all stopped what they were doing. They were scattered over the stones on the shingle, the docks, the ships. They stopped and listened to their new king and when they saw him nearly fall, but then thrive, they cheered again. After tucking the two bags in *Charging Boar*, Leif sat on the bulwark to listen.

"Look at this motley bunch of refuse," he called. "My father was driven from Bayeux in Normandy! I'm from a line of cast-offs. You are cast-offs." Godfrey pointed down to me. "Misfits, orphans, and hooligans who believe in the power of witchcraft." The king pointed to a gaggle of Welshmen. "Vagrants, hungry Christian vagrants who've come to find fortune with a Christian king. Like Christ you come with nothing but the offer of sacrifice. Huh! In truth, I'm a Christian king who favors Thor on many days, the red-bearded, barrel-chested, Thor." Godfrey clapped his hands and rubbed them together. The crates again teetered. He rebalanced and laughed. His men laughed with him. "The Christ has won my salvation of that I am sure. But when the sod is wet with blood as thick as dew and my feet ache from a forced march, I remember my grandfather telling me of Thor. He cracks his mjolnir. The thunder rolls from it, covering everything in its path. Let us, Christian, pagan, the found, the lost, let us roll over the Dal Riatans and form a land where men can win glory by their own hands!"

We cheered. I cheered loudly, for the words of the king made sense. My ancestors had scraped a living from the fjords of Norway. During full days' worth of darkness, icy mountains pushed at our backs. During the midnight sun, icy waters sloshed at our feet. It was on narrow strips of land and aboard the buffeting ships of the sea that my people had flourished. My mind flashed ahead many years when I would be a man of wealth, living on a farm on Man. Servants would obey my commands out of respect and just a bit of fear. My children would mostly listen, but I could see that I'd have a son who was adventurous and a little too wild to tame. Of him I would be proud. He would lead warriors. My grandchildren would worship me like a god, bearded and old, full of years, experience, and wisdom. My banishment and exile from Greenland had led me to all of it. What a blessing was this Providence!

"Behind, we Manx leave our farms, our homes, and our women." I had not heard Godfrey ever refer to himself as a Manx, but since his kingdom was housed there, I suppose it made sense to claim the heritage when the situation was right. "We go to battle knowing that our women, should they be attacked, are hardy enough to repel all of Aethelred's army! My queen will rule in my absence like she has on many occasions." Gudruna stepped forward to look up at her husband. The king looked down at her and I saw a flash of excitement and pride in his eyes. "The woman is in many ways a better leader than I. She's wise and prudent." He tapped his new sword which napped in its scabbard. "As many of you know from an evening I'd care to forget some years ago, your queen can even wield one of these with skill." The long-time crewmen of Godfrey chuckled.

Killian leaned in, "The king was overly drunk one night and challenged anyone in the hall to swordplay. She was the only one foolish enough to agree. It turns out she wasn't so foolish."

"Aoife!" barked Godfrey. "Aoife! Where is that girl?" He scanned the crowd. "Spare a dirty Irish thrall from the bitter markets elsewhere and see how you're rewarded. Aoife!"

My erstwhile thrall skipped out from among the legs of the spectators. "Here, King Godfrey."

"Take these and give them to the queen. Tie them to the belt at her waist." Godfrey took the large iron keys from his belt and handed them to the outstretched limb of Aoife. She paused and looked up at the king while he continued. "Let these keys be a symbol that I pass all authority to Gudruna while I am gone. She runs my hall. She runs my fortress within the earthworks and palisade. The queen runs my island. Gudruna runs my kingdom." Godfrey peered down at Aoife.

"Why are you not doing what I asked? Put the keys on the queen's belt."

"I'll only put the keys on her belt if you promise to take me along with you. I didn't agree to serve you in order to stay behind when the time for a-Viking came. I came to kill a man or two." Those nearest who could hear her words erupted with laughter. They, in turn spread her words to the others. Soon everyone laughed.

The king could have been one to seethe with rage. He'd already lost the battle with the precocious girl. Had he stewed and lashed out, Godfrey would have appeared weak. In a split second, he chose wisely. "I welcome you into our man's army, little lady." He bowed to her with a sweep of his hands, which continued and deepened the raucous round of mirth.

"Will I be given a weapon?" Aoife pushed.

Godfrey was having fun now. "Only the finest your tiny arms can hold."

"May I be in your personal guard?"

"I would have it no other way."

"And an arm-ring of gold?"

"Don't push your luck."

Aoife smiled and turned, tying the dangling, heavy keys to the queen's belt. I could just barely hear an Irish tune the girl hummed while she worked.

Godfrey waved his hands and in short order the roaring laughter slowed to head-shaking chuckles. "Our preparations are done. My speech is done. Our key-giving ceremony is done." He paused for what seemed a long while. Many silent heartbeats passed by, during which it seemed that Godfrey took the time to stare at each one of us. He looked into our eyes, into our souls. I felt like he was testing my mettle when the king peered at me. When he moved on to another man, I was left wondering what he'd discovered. Did I measure up? He then finished his words. With uncharacteristic softness, he said, "Let us begin our task."

• • •

Throughout the morning as we filed around the southern edge of Man in order to turn north toward Dal Riata, the settlement and monastery at Lismore to be precise, the seas were calm. The winds, though weak, were fickle, shifting this way and that, forcing us to beat to windward and frequently change tack on many a header. We had just enough wind for the men to stow the oars and rest their backs. This made us all feel easy, since a man who had just spent a day or two pulling at the oars held his spear with only wavering strength.

 We didn't waste the time we were given. I sat among the sloppily piled hudfats that belonged to our fellow Greenlanders and a few of the newcomers who'd joined our crew. Next to me, Tyrkr slid a whetstone along Leif's axe to put on a new edge. I did the same to my blades. Across the shifting hills and valleys of the sea, aboard *Raven's Cross*, I saw that our king had Aoife awkwardly putting a shine on his fine new sword. Their pilot turned at that moment, shifting the passengers as his portside slid up a swell. A small amount of crimson spurt from Aoife's hand. I heard her utter a string of curses in her strange, old tongue while dropping the whetstone and clamping on the wound. They disappeared for a few moments as their boat pitched away. When I saw them again, Aoife stood leaning over the waters with her waist against the bulwark. The little creature gripped the gunwale with a bloody hand. The other was cocked back over her shoulder. My heart nearly jumped into my throat.

 Given my obvious fondness for the wretched Irish creature, you likely think that I was afraid of what she would do or I feared for her health and safety. Yes, I've demonstrated these feelings in my tale thus fare. Not this time! She wasn't going to bleed to death. I could see that even though the hull was reddening from her cut, it was the water washing over it that spread the blood and made it appear worse than it was. She certainly wasn't about to plunge herself into the sea, intentionally or accidentally. The girl was too strong-willed for the first and too intelligent for the second. No, I nearly panicked because she held the whetstone aloft and was winding up in order to hurl it into the sea in a fit of anger!

 Growing up with the heroic tales told to me by my father or around winter hearths, I assumed that everyone knew them. Clearly, I was wrong. Every Norseman I had ever known would never have risked throwing a whetstone. And if someone became temporarily daft and felt compelled to do such a thing, he would certainly never throw one while at that very moment subject to the vagaries of the sea.

I have since lived many years worshipping the Christ. And most of my aged days have been in the presence of a people who follow the god Glooskap. Both of those experiences made me understand that I must explain the aspects of the old gods that I once took for granted.

You see, Thor is on the side of man. He is the god of thunder, yes, but he walks with us. He sups with us. The barrel-chested son of Odin laughs, drinks, races, fights, wins, and occasionally loses with us, his followers. He is hardy as well as hearty.

There was a time when Hrungnir, the giant, was challenged by Thor to a contest to the death. The giant, with his three-sided heart made of stone, his head of stone, and his shield of stone, wielded as his weapon a magnificent whetstone. But Thor had a clever peasant manservant at his side. The servant convinced Hrungnir that Thor's attack would come from beneath the earth. The dim-witted giant threw his shield down and stood on it, daring Thor to come from the ground. Thor, of course, could have attacked from the dirt, but instead hurled mjolnir at Hrungnir. The giant reacted quickly. He raised the magic whetstone over his shoulder, heaving it. Mjolnir crashed into the whetstone, smashing it to bits. The hammer continued on through and smashed the giant's stone head. Hrungnir fell dead.

But a splinter from the whetstone became forever lodged in Thor's head. The whetstones we use to this day came from the remaining shards. Whenever a man throws one, the stone lodged in Thor's head shifts. Thor feels pain. He becomes frustrated and angry. He whitens his grip on mjolnir. The seas become roiled and rough. Storms blow. Lightning crashes. Thunder rolls. Men die.

Godfrey veritably jumped across the deck and snatched Aoife's arm. I saw him shouting at the girl. It was the first time I'd seen him truly angry with the waif. He shook her and, no doubt, explained to her the nearly grave error. My heart settled back into my chest. I again began to breathe.

"Funny thing," said a familiar, feminine voice. There should have been no women aboard.

"She is," I said, referring to Aoife.

"Aren't you surprised I'm here?" asked Gudruna.

I turned toward her. She was wearing a man's armor. A great brown cloak served to masquerade her womanly features. Gudruna had a short sword on her belt. "Where are the king's keys?" I asked instead of playing whatever game she had in mind.

"Given to the new priest to hold," said Leif walking up from behind.

"Godfrey won't approve of the location of the keys or his queen," I warned.

"Neither will affect the outcome of our raiding," Leif answered.

Gudruna rested a boot on the luggage. I saw the pale skin of her leg under her dress. The fair, short hairs stood tall from the cool sea air. "Ruling the household while the king is away is a noble role. But we've got nothing to worry about at home. We'll thump Lismore. I want to be a part of my great husband's adventure."

"Huh," I said. Godfrey, Killian, Randulfr, none of them would be happy. If the lady wanted to take part then she should ride the waves on *Raven's Cross*, not the ship of her young lover. The pair waved off my indifference and sat among the baggage. My thoughts returned to our mission.

By my reckoning of the crude maps Godfrey had produced, we'd be at the shores of Dal Riata's heart sometime the next day. The very island where Godfrey had begun the deadly back-and-forth killings was our target. The monastery at Lismore would be ravaged once and for all by our sweeping force. Slaughtering men for sport was not our intent. However, and the Christians among you may not understand, our people's martial ethos demanded action. It demanded a man venture out from his fjord and strike. The gods performed glorious deeds in forming our world. The sea kings of yore achieved great fame for drawing the strongest bands of followers to their halls. These wave-pirates, wave-lovers, our ancestors, the very men who carved out the farmsteads and villages and halls from the virgin forest commanded us, their progeny, to do likewise. We were to conquer for glory. My heart warmed thinking about it.

"You're smiling," observed Leif. I looked at him with one squinting eye. The late summer sun was yet warm, but the air was changing. The nights and our shadows during the day were longer. Leif's red beard had filled in even since the start of that season. His scruff fluttered against his baby face. "You like manual labor so much?" he asked, pointing to the blades in my hands.

Huh! Manual labor was better than sitting around thinking. A man's thoughts, unchecked, could lead to all sorts of problems. I slowly moved my whetstone down the length of my sword. I should have replaced the weapon from one of Man's traders, but instead I hid my middling wealth under a rock behind the tenth tree inside the last great forest on the island. I suppose I was saving for something larger; my farm, perhaps, or a bride-price, if ever I found a woman. "I smile because I dream of taking your place inside the queen," I lied, mostly to pester Leif and his woman.

Gudruna laughed. Leif stood and leaned on the gunwale as Magnus pushed the steering oar to send us in a more favorable direction for the wind. "It's the queen's choice," Leif said. "And the king's." Leif sized me up with his eyes. "She'd not have you." Gudruna was laughing more.

"What's wrong with me?" I asked, angry, though I could not have cared less whether or not Gudruna wanted me. She was too thin a woman for me. I wanted one with meat. They're the ones who survive childbirth and have the fortitude to turn babies into men. I realized then that the king and queen had no children. I looked at Gudruna. Too thin for making children, I thought.

Leif smiled and punched my shoulder. I smiled back. The three of us laughed.

Tyrkr made some comment about the queen's rump in his native tongue. He then used the whetstone and sword in some sort of demonstration of what he said. The queen, not knowing what he said, but understanding his motions, rolled on the baggage. Her laughter, sweet like that of most women, was infectious. The crew chuckled along with us.

Soon we rambled to a halt. "I smile because we go to exact our king's revenge. The hall of Odin will be filled with more men in a matter of days." I was speaking like a true believer in the king, for I was in those days. "You and I were exiled from Greenland for an attack that was not our fault. Out of our disgrace the norns have seen fit to send us to a king who fights and wins. He'll be a great ring-giver. Godfrey will be hallowed in the halls. His queen will be known as Gudruna the Wise. Skalds will talk of us in the tales. We'll be victorious or wind up in Odin's hall. What is there not to smile about? By dusk tomorrow it may well be over."

"Tomorrow?" asked Leif.

"Or the next day," I said, shrugging.

"We go to Iona first," said Leif.

"The Christian monastery?" I asked. "Does Killian rule the king or Godfrey the priest?"

"The monastery is still there, but Godfrey says that it's been under Norse control for years. Sometimes he claims it as one of his isles."

"And other times?" I asked.

"Dyflin controls it with the help of some of the friendlier Irish."

"So, why do we go there? And why wasn't I told? I'm a commander of some of these men."

Gudruna shrugged. "You stayed behind to gawk at Edana's fat corpse while we planned. Captains were told."

"And helmsmen," called Magnus from the rudder. He pushed to change direction yet again.

I cursed at being left out, though it didn't really matter. Fate would shove us where she must. I set my stone into its pouch and stuffed my sword into its cracked scabbard. My pouting was as overdone as a rich noble's spoiled child.

"We go to gather a few more men, maybe even deepen our relationships," explained Gudruna. "Godfrey says that

Kvaran, the King of Dyflin, and occasionally the ruler of Jorvik, is there now. Our king hopes to form a quick alliance to bolster our numbers."

"Another sea king," I muttered. "Isn't one enough? Can we trust this King of Dyflin?"

"Of course not," shrugged Leif. "Godfrey's under no illusions. He trusts you, Killian, and a few others."

"We'll see," I mumbled. "More kings, huh."

• • •

Iona was a tiny, picturesque island. Small and situated as it was on the westernmost end of a much larger island, it was in no way protected from the constant winds sent from the far reaches of the ocean. From the time we made landfall to the time we put Iona on our stern, the wind steadily pulled and tore at us. Living in such a place would age a man, perhaps even more so than in the glacial fjords of my homeland. A man's face would be tugged and prodded by the breeze. It would be pecked by the sharp beaks of the rain. In response an inhabitant of Iona would wince to protect his eyes and lips. His wrinkles would be fully formed before he'd seen twenty summers. Iona with its wind and its monastery would age a man.

Five monks lived on the island in a series of buildings that obviously used to house dozens of their brethren. The wind had done its work on those five men. They were hard and wrinkled. Had they not been monks, they would have resembled our wicked-looking crews. These monks' hands were calloused and worn. Their sandals and frocks were tattered. Life on the island had not been kind to those Christians since the coming of my ancestors many years before. They walked hunched. Even their tiny gardens were populated by plants that grew at angles due to the unending breeze.

Two buildings still wore the black streaks of a former blaze set during a long-forgotten raid. Their crumbled heaps displayed the marks like badges of honor almost in the same way a mighty Norseman clings to his favorite sword in death. Providence had at least temporarily abandoned the Iona faithful.

"Peace be unto you," said one of the monks in greeting. He used my native tongue which proved just who had ruled the land for many winters. We'd left most of the men and weapons back at the ships, for it was to be a short, peaceful stay. Gudruna was among them. She had rightly said that if Godfrey found out about her now, he'd sail right back to Man and drop her off.

"You say, 'and to you,'" said Killian from behind as we walked over the sod toward the main monastery building.

"I'll say what I will," I huffed, but otherwise I ignored the monk and the priest. Soon they ignored me and began babbling in Latin.

I scanned the part of the island I could see. I saw no real settlements. I saw no one except a skinny boy aged perhaps ten years. To the monastery he carried a bucket of fish he'd caught with a small net that was draped over his shoulder. It dripped down his clothing, darkening it. The boy paid the wetness no heed as he walked. After he saw our menacing group of bristling men, he changed his course, giving us an extra wide berth. Up a small hill fifteen sheep tore at the spindly grass of late summer. Their wool was just beginning to fill for the coming months of cold. A ram mounted a ewe, assuring their kind would continue for at least another season. One ship, other than those in our armada, was beached on the shingle. Its tall mast angled lazily to one side. Its bulwark held no shields. If we could gather an additional army here in this desolate place, fortune was most surely shining upon us.

"Welcome to the Order of Saint Columba," said another weatherworn monk as we entered an ancient church. It had been built, destroyed, rebuilt, destroyed, and reconstructed many times over the years as evidenced by the different colored stones and varying quality and styles of construction. Though I still had no real understanding of their faith, seeing the obvious perseverance of the monks from one generation to the next was duly impressive.

The monk who greeted us began to rub his hands together as he scanned our men from one face to another. He looked especially nervous whenever he looked on the newcomers. I've told you they were hard men. In truth, our new brigands and mercenaries made me just as wary. Scowls, frowns, and scars covered the men. The monk added, "All our wealth has been taken to Norway or Dyflin over the years. There is nothing here for you now." He looked a second time at our mad, motley bunch. "And if you bring nothing but mayhem in your wake, know that Kvaran, King of Dyflin, is here convalescing with a retinue of his retainers. Any of our blood you wish to spill, we will gladly shed for our faith, but know this: Kvaran has become a faithful servant. He has become a friend and will not let an affront to Iona go unanswered. Many of you will die."

"Oh, Maclean!" came an exasperated, almost bored voice from a dark alcove along one of the church's long walls. "Unless they are Ui Neill dung-beardlings, we've nothing to worry about. And besides, if they aren't men who follow the One God, they'd welcome death by the sword. Your threats mean nothing."

"Kvaran?" shouted Godfrey. His voice echoed off the stone walls and saintly statues. Only one of the latter stood without a snapped limb or cracked face. My king stepped ahead, peeking into the recess that housed this second king.

"Godfrey?" said the indifferent voice.

"You don't sound excited to see me," said Godfrey, grinning while feigning distress.

Killian tugged down on my arm. "I've never met a more apathetic man than Kvaran. He sees defeat in everything."

"Yet he's a king," I whispered.

"A king who's hemmed in by the Ui Neill. The Battle of Tara saw to that. Without the support of Godfrey and the Irish Leinster clan, Kvaran's great city would be overrun in a matter of days."

"I had hoped for some peace and quiet here in the abbey," answered Kvaran plainly. "I'm not looking forward to meeting with anyone, especially clingers and overly complimentary ones like you. When you've lived as long as I, we'll see how thrilled you are to greet guests."

Maclean the monk brought Godfrey a chair. He sat. One of the legs was shorter than the other three. It clacked as it teetered back and forth against the flagstone floor. My king, for his part, waved us out in order to quell Kvaran's nerves. "What is it friend?" asked Godfrey.

The rest of the men who'd entered the church filed out after Maclean. I heard the monk begin to give lessons on the basics of Christianity and raising peas. Neither subject appealed to me at the time so I plopped down in the shadows to listen to what two kings said to one another. I'd not be left as the last one to know Godfrey's plans this time.

"A small wound," began Kvaran. His foot was soon held out into the dim light. He wore a rich-looking shoe of red felt. One step into a puddle would ruin it. I thought it foolishly impractical. Above the low boot was a small bandage that wrapped around the lower leg of Dyflin's king.

"I am sorry. How long until you recover?" Godfrey asked.

"It's nothing." The leg retreated back into the darkness. "I'm nearly well. My pride is hurt more than anything." He sighed. "Great success early in life is difficult to follow. The last few years have been a challenge in Dyflin. I leave my son, Gluniairn, in charge while I'm away."

"How is Iron Knee?"

"He's well enough. I leave him. I'm ashamed to say that I hope that Dyflin falls while I'm away. Then it can't be said that I let it fall. The weight my father's words would kill me even if the damned Irish don't. What do you want on Iona? Are you finally giving up the old gods for good? Done plowing other women and allowing other men to plow your woman?"

Godfrey disregarded Kvaran's taunt. "How is Gytha?"

"My sister is fine," Kvaran sighed again. He sounded exhausted with not only the conversation but life. "She is in need of a husband. Now why are you here?"

"And Silkbeard?" Godfrey asked.

"My youngest son is well!" Kvaran huffed. "Perhaps the fool Maclean was rightly concerned. Maybe there will be bloodshed here today. If you don't answer me, a single call from my horn will bring my oath-sworn men to my side. They'll cut long before they begin asking questions." I heard a tap, tap against the hard floor. "These stones will be red."

Godfrey chuckled at the older, frustrated man. "There is no need for such a thing. We are already aligned in purpose and for that I am grateful. The gods show their favor on our union."

"You're in a church. There is but One True God, Godfrey," chided Kvaran.

"Quite right." Godfrey remained cheery. "When I am in our church on Man, I say the same. But you remember your father's gods, no? You remember Thor's Woods, just north of Dyflin? You remember the strength from the old heroes that our ancestors' gods convey?"

There was a long pause when all I could hear was the whistling of the incessant breeze against the church's walls. Then, for the first time in the conversation, Kvaran sounded interested. "I do," he whispered.

"Let us make a tighter pact." Godfrey tugged on his beard. "Let's pool all our resources to build a kingdom that sits in the crown of the Irish Sea: Dyflin, the Kingdom of the Isles, even Jorvik far to the east. From there we step left and crush the whole of mainland Ireland. From our throne we move right and swallow the English pissers."

Again perturbed, Kvaran asked, "And who will be king? You? Am I to be your stooge? Your vassal? Maybe you'd like me to empty your dung bucket? Polish your mail?"

"Nothing like that," assured Godfrey. "I want whatever men you can spare while we move to finish off the bleeding corpse that is Dal Riata. Give me those men and you will rule our joint kingdom as the sole sovereign."

Kvaran laughed cynically. "And you will carry my shit for me? May I wed your Gudruna?"

Firmly now, Godfrey answered, "I will rule as king once you pass on the battlefield or in your bed at a ripe old age."

I remember thinking that for a king to die at a ripe age sounded awful. Such a demise would bring a man into Hel's hall quicker than any other death. Were I a king and if I made it to my good many years, I'd pick a fight with the strongest Norseman in the village just to be killed in conflict. How else would Odin populate his hall with valiant warriors? But Kvaran was a Christian.

"And my sons? You think your kingship would be peaceful with Iron Knee and Silkbeard about? They are not monks who would be happy washing another man's feet."

"I've thought of that. They'd serve me to be sure. One in Dyflin, not as king in title, but with more power and authority over the region than you, the current King of Dyflin, hold. The other would retain a similar position in Jorvik. From their strongholds we would launch our great, conquering raids."

"And if you take the rest of Dal Riata today, I rule it?"

"Until the day you die of natural causes," said Godfrey. He placed a hand on his heart after making the sign of the cross.

"What's more natural than a knife to the belly, eh?" accused Kvaran.

"Truly natural causes, Kvaran. Have I ever given you reason to doubt me? Have I not brought trade, commerce, slaves, and wealth galore to the streets within your great palisade? My raids on the Ui Neill, have they not helped add to your strength while weakening them? I am a descendant of a Norseman. I am a man made by my oaths. By Hel, I'll bring in my priest to verify all that I say and all my promises if it pleases you."

"No, I don't need your priest." A wrinkled hand came into the light and pointed to the statues that lined the walls. "The saints listen. I've got my monks here on Iona. I've got my own priests in Dyflin. That's quite enough."

"Oh, Kvaran, my priest is a fighter," countered Godfrey. "He's a good man. You'd like him."

"Oh, I'm sure I would," said Kvaran sardonically. Then his tone softened. "I'm sure I would. Priests and monks are no worse than any man. When they are good they lead men to the True Faith. When they are bad, like any man, they are prideful and greedy."

Godfrey was shaking his head. "I didn't come to talk of churchmen. Do we have an alliance?"

Kvaran was silent in his dark alcove. Godfrey let him stew. High above, a pigeon fluttered into the church through one of the gaping holes left behind by years of strife.

"And after you take Dal Riata," Kvaran chose his words carefully, "you'll send your army of miscreants to Dyflin, not as conquerors, but as liberators? Together with the Leinster clan, we'll drive the bastard Ui Neill into the thrall markets as the spent commodities they are?"

Godfrey didn't hesitate. "In the summer. It's too late to plan a new campaign this year. By the end of winter Dal Riata will be secure on my back. I will turn my front to you and my men and I will bleed with you."

"Oh, I do hope that our side is not the one that bleeds." Kvaran carefully said his words. "I give you what men I will. You give me a vast kingdom. You have an agreement." I saw a thin arm extend out into the main part of the church. Godfrey clasped the forearm. The extended hand grasped my king's forearm. They held each other's arms for a solid heartbeat.

"Now, I'll wait for you to send word to Dyflin for your men," breathed Godfrey as he stood tall in the church. "In a matter of days our vast armada will row from here and swamp Dal Riata." Kvaran chuckled.

Godfrey marched out through the door, leaving Kvaran and me behind. I could hear my king enthusiastically shouting to his men to gather for the good news.

Inside the church, Kvaran mumbled under his breath, "He should have his woman do his negotiating. Better to look at and shrewder."

Kvaran gave a low whistle. One of his men walked out from another alcove. He'd been hidden the whole time. "What is it, lord king?"

"The monster, too," said Kvaran. I couldn't see Dyflin's king, but he must have pointed in my direction. The guard looked right at me and waved me over. I stood and as I approached saw that Kvaran used an existing gap in the wall's stone carvings to peer out and see what was coming to him. He'd known I was there the entire time.

The guard patted me for weapons. I had none. When I turned to face the mysterious king, I could still only see his red shoes. His face was concealed in shadow. "You are my witnesses to the transaction that just took place. I've got a man on my side and a man on Godfrey's side."

The guard nodded. I agreed as well.

"Good, then you know that I agreed to support Godfrey," said Kvaran.

My head bobbed up and down.

"Then you also know I never told Godfrey any amount of men or supplies that I'd give. He asked for my support in his endeavor. I gave it. In return, I am king over it all."

CHAPTER 11

The guard and I were witnesses. It pained me but I agreed with the wily king of Dyflin in his telling of the accord. Kvaran didn't have to send word to Dyflin. He didn't have to supply much of anything. The men he had guarding the walls in his market town were all necessary just to keep the wild men of Ireland at bay, he said. Shrewd Kvaran had gained a renewed alliance with the potential to further acquire wealth and prestige from Godfrey's toils. All he had to give in return was a band of the ten men who had been lounging on the shores of Iona while he sulked in the dark recesses of a church. Even that was generous of him, for Godfrey and he had clasped arms on such vague terms.

Ten men! The rest of his crew, Kvaran required them be left behind on Iona so that he could safely make his way back home. We received ten men!

Godfrey moaned at his foolishness the whole way down the shore to our ships. Killian grumbled at the king's stupidity, though the diminutive priest had the sense to do it in only certain company, for our king spent the rest of that day angrily throwing dried nuggets of sheep dung at a sun-bleached piece of driftwood. In between his fits of irritation, the king challenged some of his warriors to wrestling matches. Such was his fury that Godfrey was able to throw much larger men to the ground. He won with punches, kicks, and gouging where none of those were permitted. The losers, seeing the king's mood, dared not complain about the nuances of rule infractions.

Godfrey had promised to make Kvaran king in his place. He'd sworn in a church. The rub, of course, was that Godfrey would do all the fighting. I'll grant you that Kvaran was old and his days on the throne were to be numbered, but ten men? Gudruna was not pleased when she found out what her man had done. "He took my idea and dashed it against the rocks of that church!" she said. "King Godfrey is brave. He is good in the shield wall. I should do his negotiating." The queen was right. It mattered not.

After sleeping for just one night on our beached ships, far away from Kvaran and the rest of his troop, we left Iona. The winds had shifted against their natural course and we moved eastward, directly into them. Our sails were stowed. The oars were not. I sat on a chest aboard *Charging Boar* next to the men. The oar's wood felt smooth in my hands. I pushed it down and leaned forward. I pulled the oar handle up and slowly leaned back. I hauled the blade through the glistening morning seas. The work was back-breaking and methodical. It took me no thought other than the memories housed in my young, bulging muscles. I peeked over the gunwale and watched our blades slice into the waves. They came out dripping their reflective waters back into the deep. Again they dove. Like the rhythmic, beautiful grate-slap sound, the motion repeated itself. It felt like my pumping heart beat at the same rate. I was one with our ship, which was at one with the sea. Many men would become bored or angry with the chore. I felt at home breathing in the salty smell of the sea, working as all men should. Scanning my fellow raiders, I saw that only a few felt as I did. The rest performed the job, no more.

The men aboard every other ship in our fleet fought wind and wave as they attempted to move their oars in time. Their work was not good enough and so they made poor time against the wind to Lismore. *Raven's Cross* danced poetically with oars shifting in unison. Most of the mercenaries, though tough like hogs' hides, knew nothing of the ways of the sea, however. On the ships where they outnumbered experienced men, their oars rattled and fought against one another. I heard clacks and swearing in several languages echoing over the swells.

At that moment, I recalled the ropes I had gotten from the witches. Their knots were supposed to harness the energy of the wind. Untying one of those knots was to change the wind's course. Perhaps it would alter the intensity of the breeze, too, pushing us fast on the surf rather than slapping us in the face. I briefly toyed with the notion of calling for a break at my oar so that I could test the witches' magic. The men of the fleet would welcome the respite. Once word got around that I had been the savior of their backs, I would be called a hero, minor, fleeting, but hero, nonetheless. I stayed put.

My pleasures were simple: a good woman, mead, the hunt, crops, and the sea. I had become a raider who traveled by the oceans. Wealth, I fancied it as much as the next man. Riches taken from another, my mind was fine with the thought. Others would happily take it from me if I chose to be weak. I'd rather be strong and take it from them first. So, during those times, serving Godfrey, I was a raider who went a-Viking with and for his king. But the sea, that day, was me. It beat the back of my uncovered head. It blew my long, blonde hair around into my face. I reveled in the moment. My compatriots, be damned. The ropes remained stowed. The knots stayed cinched.

Soon I questioned my decision.

We stayed in our eastward direction, with land close by on the north. As we moved farther and farther, the land from the south began drawing nearer. We entered what I would call a fjord. The Scots, I'm told, call it a loch. This loch was known as Linnhe and its tide was flowing out to sea so that we battled against the wind and the tide. The frequency and volume of muttering from the men increased. Our armada became spread out wider as *Charging Boar* and *Raven's Cross* pulled farther ahead of the others. 'The knots?' you may ask. I was too stubborn to change my mind. Though my back began to tire and ache, I chuckled to myself, especially when others groaned.

My shipmates thought me mad. I probably was. I probably am.

• • •

The time for the midday meal came and went. That is when we would have seen Lismore had we been under sail with a favorable tailwind. In shifts we took momentary breaks to eat salted fish and then piss over the gunwale. Some of the men rested their backs on the useless mast, pressing against its smooth wood in order to ease a kink.

I ran the steering oar while Magnus took my spot on the rowing bench. That's when Killian shouted from *Raven's Cross*.

"Lismore!" The sleeve of his robe fell back to his elbow as his pale arm jabbed repeatedly from the prow of the king's ship.

Godfrey shoved Aoife out of his way. He stepped over men and arms and baggage as he moved to join Killian next to the dragon's head. The king used one hand to steady himself on the forestay. The two, king and priest, conferred. Godfrey barked an order to Randulfr, who ran the rudder. *Raven's Cross* eased over toward us slowly. Gudruna plopped onto a rowing bench and turned away so that her husband wouldn't see her.

Leif brought over a ragged piece of parchment on which Killian had hastily copied Godfrey's map. We looked at it and compared it with the island that drew nearer. "Not a good representation," I said.

"He's a priest," said Leif in answer. Killian had drawn Lismore in the shape of a fat cross. In reality it was a long, slender island that ran from the southwest to the northeast.

"Where's the main settlement? Where's the monastery situated?"

Leif shrugged. "I don't know. Killian's map doesn't show." He pointed off to starboard, where there was much activity aboard the king's ship. "But it seems that Godfrey means to land soon." I followed Leif's glance. Men were slipping their heavy mail or their hard leather jerkins over their heads. Belts were strapped. Spears secured. Bows found. Even some arrows were located as men rutted through the luggage like hogs searching the forest floor. Helmets adorned heads.

"Around to the south!" shouted Godfrey over the wind. "Follow us! We're not here to sneak up on them from the rocks on the northwest like we did last time. We go directly to the monastery and town. We go in fast so that the cowardly bastards don't have time to run inland."

I peered over my shoulder to the rest of our fleet straggling far behind us. "Shouldn't we circle around or rest until they catch up?" I asked young Leif. Why I asked a babe for advice, I'll never know. But I always, for my whole life, deferred to Leif. Perhaps it was because his father was my second father. Erik took me in when he could have rapped my head against a rock as a sacrifice to Odin.

"No, Godfrey knows what he's doing," said Leif softly. He cupped his hands to his mouth and called back to Godfrey, "We'll be ready!" Godfrey nodded and went back to growling at the men aboard his ship. The king slapped Brandr on his helmet with his palm. Brandr returned the gesture. Godfrey seized his man's shoulders and shook them, laughing.

"Just like he knew what he was doing at Anglesey? What about Watchet? Without us, he would have been crushed in both situations," I grunted.

"I gave him Anglesey's capital. I'll grant you. It was Aoife who saved us at Watchet. You were a mere butcher in both cases. Gudruna gave him Edana." Leif began calmly suiting himself for the coming fight. "And Aoife and I will be at the king's side even if the rest of his army is not." Leif looked to Gudruna. "I'd say Godfrey will have all he needs."

• • •

The men, who now sang loudly while lugging *Raven's Cross* one oar bite at a time across the fjord, propelled the craft ever faster. It skipped ahead of *Charging Boar* on our starboard side. I heard Godfrey's voice boom some indecipherable command and Randulfr hauled on the steering oar. The king's ship danced across our path, making a true course for the south side of the center of Lismore. I had to quickly follow Randulfr's lead or we would have rammed the king's port and sent us both to Hel's depths.

Godfrey was eager. He raced his ship toward a low, rocky outcropping that sat like a lopsided shelf which angled out of the sea. Just based on the cliffs on either side of the shelf and the shape of the island, I suspected that there would be a more suitable beach or shingle on which to land just a bit farther east. Leif, and even Tyrkr, said as much. But Godfrey had waited for his revenge on Lismore for as long as he could. I saw him scramble up the bow of *Raven's Cross*. With one arm he clung to the brightly colored, elaborately carved dragon prow. In his right hand he drew his shining blade, his +ULFBERHT+, and stretched it out ahead just as his longship's keel began skidding to a halt on the flat rock. Killian and Aoife rolled onto the decking. Several rowers toppled backward into the man behind, or more precisely, to the fore of, them.

Godfrey splashed down. His men poured over the sides. Loki slipped on algae that had grown on the rocks in the shallow water. He went down face first. His knees struck the rock. He fought the light undertow while pawing like a hound. Loki was weighted down by the armor. His feet slid off the ledge and he began sinking. He would have been our first casualty of the day had Killian not grabbed a hold of Loki's hair and held him steady. Brandr wrapped his arms around the priest's waist and together they hauled Loki upright. Alone, Godfrey was already climbing up a narrow ravine that led up to the island's plateau.

"Stow the oars!" screamed Leif when we were just five fadmr from the shelf. It would be a tight fit, for there was just enough room for two ships there. Our rowers made quick work of lacing the oak handles out through the holes and handing them back aboard. It would do no good to lop off our oars by ramming them into the stern of *Raven's Cross*. I bit my lip then sent *Charging Boar* skidding alongside the king's ship. Our keel bit so that we came to rest with our starboard side kissing Godfrey's port.

Godfrey had disappeared above. His men followed close behind. Only Randulfr, seemingly the only responsible one, lingered. He stretched a long rope that was tied to a knee aboard the king's ship all the way to a single spire of a rock and tied it off. Randulfr knew that if the tide had been rushing out while we came in, the waters would soon rise and lift our ships free. They might still be smashed against the rocks, but at least they wouldn't drift away.

I slapped on my dented helmet and grabbed an extra spear. We jumped over our portside gunwale and chased after the reaching king.

The reaching queen chased after her own version of glory.

• • •

I made it to the top of the ravine and peeked over my shoulder. A few of the other ships would arrive in just several heartbeats. However, since the rock shelf was packed, they would have to continue on and find a more suitable place to land, a spot like the one we should have found in the first place.

The unmistakable clang of steel clashing brought my head back into the moment. Before me was stretched a short, rolling plain that led to a town. The open ground's deep green grass was buckling down for the coming winter as each blade tipped its head and faded to a sadder hue. We were arriving up ahead in piecemeal fashion to what was shaping up to be a battle. Our tactic was not a brilliant one because we never once formed the shield wall. We never once could coalesce our force into a single fist so that we could drive the unlucky souls at Lismore into the ground in one motion. That would have been merciful to the defenders. After a few moments and a few deaths they could have thrown down their weapons and surrendered. We wouldn't even have had our bloodlust up. Most of the island's defenders would have survived to sheer their sheep after the coming freeze and inevitable thaw.

Godfrey fought against a farmer who wielded a hoe. The king's sword snapped the implement and hewed the man's arm in one motion. His was a beautiful blade doing what the Franks had designed it to do. The sword killed. The +ULFBERHT+ rang and sang while it did so. The king hummed a tune that followed the melody spun by the blade. He was giddy in his piratical element.

Gudruna found a man with a narrow, rectangular shield. He held a long spear and laughed when he faced his small, female opponent. It seemed that he was right to scoff because with one shove of his shield boss, the petite woman fell backward onto her rump. No amount of skill with a blade could counteract mass and momentum.

She bent her knees and planted her feet. But her feet were walking on the back of her skirts. Gudruna fell on her back again. The man with the narrow shield carefully stepped forward. He was no fool. He hid behind the shield and held the spear pointed at Gudruna's armored heart.

Gudruna was the wiser. She flipped the front of her skirts up. The attacker's eyes dropped to the naked crux between her legs. When those eyes again locked with Gudruna's, the queen's sword had cleaved out a wedge in his leg. Two more vicious hacks from the queen tipped the man over.

Meanwhile, Killian ran up behind the king to protect his flank. The small priest faced two men who ran from the village that surrounded the towering stone monastery at the center. One of these men appeared to be a soldier. He wore mail, a helmet, and carried a spear with a sharp, steel point that had recently had a new edge drawn on. This man was younger and faster than Killian. The spear flicked. Killian fell back, clutching his arm that now ran red. Only his thick, coarse priestly robe prevented the spear from reaching the bone.

The second man, clearly a butcher, for he was already covered in blood from his head to his boots before the battle had begun, wielded a fat knife, a tool of his trade. The weapon was about the length of my saex. The butcher scurried over top the priest, clamped a hand on his neck, and raised the tool. I dimly recalled the spear in my own hand. Without worrying about who else might be running between us, I cocked my arm, stepped, and released. The butcher's side was pierced. His grip on the priest's neck and his knife relaxed. He collapsed on Killian.

Gudruna had recovered and ran in. She hauled the dying butcher off the priest while simultaneously defending against the soldier. Killian helped push the bloody butcher. He used the bottom of his war boot and kicked the soldier's knee. The man howled. His scream was answered with Gudruna's short sword in the eye. Killian kicked him again so that the soldier tipped backward, off the blade, sending what was left of his eyeball flying and a spray of crimson into the afternoon air.

More soldiers now poured from the town. Godfrey had said nothing of a garrison being stationed on Lismore. He should have known, for it was where he'd raided many times before. It was where his men had been hanged. It was where he'd killed the abbot on Christmas. Never once did he mention a fort or a quartering of infantry. Even the Dal Riatans could learn, I suppose.

One of Godfrey's crewmen died from a hurled javelin. Well, the man didn't die immediately. Rarely do men die instantly in battle. The missile pierced deeply into our comrade's thigh. He folded in half and slumped. He yet sat upright, teetering for many strange moments. The man studied the javelin's shaft as if it wasn't jutting from his bleeding leg. Then he watched the battle roil around him. He didn't show fear. That is, until he felt the pain. Once the wave of intense throbbing finally hit the surprised warrior, he threw up his salted fish and ale. His fingers feverishly tore at his ripped trousers. His hands began to shake when he tightly wrapped them around the javelin and pulled. The narrow head sprung free. The wound wasn't wide, but it was nearly through the width of his thigh. Blood pooled on the grass. He struggled to get up, just once. It was almost over. Our man fell back down, groaning. Only then did he know his fate. His eyes scanned the earth, looking for his weapon. He found the butcher's knife. It would do. The dying man clutched the handle and tipped back fully onto the grass. As I ran by him I saw the mixture of emotions on his face. Anger showed in the corners of his mouth. Defiance was expressed in the corners of his eyes. Disbelief and fear haunted his countenance, though I would never say so to a fellow warrior. He pulled the knife to his chest and passed into Odin's hall.

Aoife tugged on the bit of my mail that hung below my belt. "To the king, idiot!"

I looked in the direction she pointed. Leif and Randulfr were there. They were fighting directly into a pack of the enemy. In the center of the enemy was Godfrey. He'd cleared out a circle with his shield and sword.

I shoved Aoife to the ground in order to rush to the king, and to protect her from the melee that would follow.

With my shield raised, I ran headlong into the outskirts of the clump of enemy swordsmen. Two of their men fell over from the force of my blow. Randulfr dispatched them both before they could rejoin their brethren.

Gudruna snuck in behind me. She stabbed with that short sword with remarkable efficiency. Time and again her thin arm snuck under my raised sword and protected my side.

Godfrey smacked a man across his face with the edge of his shield. Teeth flew. One of them bounced off my check.

I spat in the face of my opponent. He did the same to me. My blood burned with fierce anger. I pulled out my father's saex. With my shoulder, I repeatedly heaved up and into my shield until one of my thrusts forced his war bark up. I rammed the small blade into his belly. He wore leather mail. It was surprisingly strong, for I felt my momentum check. It infuriated me all the more. I used the whole of my arm, body, and legs to drive the short sword through the armor and into his flesh. He melted.

More of Godfrey's crew came to our aid. They added force to our push. Slowly, methodically we slaughtered the Dal Riatans. We caught the bloodlust. We felled them like trees being harvested for the longboats. They crashed into one another. They formed a corpse street. I stepped on them. We slipped, but the might and support of the partial shield wall kept us upright. At last my shield boss met Godfrey's.

The king's eyes widened. At first they gave his characteristic sparkle. He even opened his mouth to say something sarcastic, something funny. The king was doing what the old gods had created his family to do. His new Christian God seemed to merely tolerate his actions in Midgard. "Good of you to arrive, Halldorr!" A rock smashed into his cheek.

We looked toward the village. What was left of the town's men had reorganized. They'd looted ours and the dead soldiers' weapons. Some had gathered helmets.

Gudruna pushed past me. She screamed, light shield lofted, weapon raised. Alone, the queen ran straight toward the newly assembled enemy.

The joy left Godfrey's face. He frowned, instantly recognizing her voice. "Kill them! Protect the queen!" He pointed his dripping sword. I could just see the unmistakable '+UL' near the guard. The rest of the manufacturer's name was blanketed with Dal Riatan blood.

Our hearts swelled to protect the one grown woman among us. Our bloodlust was in full lather. We allowed it to run. By now though, we'd assembled properly and didn't sprint like the wild men of Ireland's inland regions. Only a handful of the other ships' men had arrived. It was more than enough.

Gudruna was already fighting against three men, parrying their blows deftly when we arrived. Leif snatched the queen from her suicide run. She was roughly tossed behind us as we advanced. We hemmed the last of the town's defenders in between two shield walls, ours and the one from the newly arrived ships. We closed in a frighteningly controlled manner, shields locked, swords and spears bristling.

The townsmen rethought their position. Their faces showed fear, without a cut, their blood drained, their hearts sank. They looked over their shoulders at their families and monks who fled in the opposite direction. Spears and shields crashed to the ground. Metal clanged. The defenders went to their knees and held their hands up behind their heads. I heard them try to use Latin to speak to us, which Killian had said was a universal language. I understood not their words, but their meaning was plain enough. They wanted to surrender.

Next to me, Godfrey cursed. He looked back at his queen and growled. The king panted and for a moment, I swear to you, it appeared that he was coming to his senses. His mind was taking control of his body after the bloodletting. Godfrey was angry at his queen, yes, but most of us had survived.

Then King Godfrey peered through the town and saw a lone tree that sat in a vast pasture north of town. There he saw the last of his men who'd been executed a year earlier. The man's body, weather beaten and animal eaten, still rocked in the breeze at the end of a fraying rope. The rest of his crew from the previous raid was still piled high in the sheep dung heap. The king rubbed his cheek where the stone had hit earlier. He winced. His palm came away red. Godfrey's face contorted. It showed rage.

Godfrey called out to us. "Finish the defenders. If they wish to die without a sword in their hands, so be it. We'll take what's left of their families as plunder."

Killian, with his arm wrapped in a hastily applied bandage, ran in front of us. "Godfrey, don't do this. The men we slaughtered on the beach at Watchet were soldiers. And English," added the Irish priest. "These men are protecting their lives and families. They are Christian brothers like you and me.

Don't do this. You've won. You've taken the stronghold of the island. Don't let your revenge go too far."

"Halldorr," shouted King Godfrey.

"Lord!" I answered.

Godfrey scowled at the queen. He looked again at his dead men from last year. "Escort the priest out of my way."

I frowned at Killian and reached for his shoulder. The priest wasn't going to be able stop the butchering. He was stopping the battle thrill I momentarily felt, however. I suppose Godfrey was doing that too. I grabbed Killian's vestment and jerked him back through the lines and held him there. Side-by-side, we watched all that unfolded next.

When it was done I realized that I had released the priest, who stood quietly next to me. Gudruna had moved next to us. My eyes burned. I hadn't blinked all the while during Godfrey's murder of the town's would-be protectors. I squeezed them shut and open. Someone's blood oozed into them, burning them more. I wiped it away with a dirty paw.

Killian spoke softly. "Hubris and anger usually get a man killed quickly. Sometimes a king can delay such retribution, but it comes. It comes."

I met the priest's eyes, saying nothing in return. "I've broken many vows to serve King Godfrey," said Killian. "At first I thought it was best to placate him. It would allow me to come close and show him my faith, its quiet power, its justice, its mercy. He is to be a Christian, after all, so how much work would I have to do? That's what I thought. But instead of him drawing closer to Christ, I faded with him. My natural tendencies for adventure were exploited by the evil one, by Godfrey. We didn't improve in our walk. We didn't progress like the pilgrims we are to be. The king and I have both gone backwards to act more like your ancestors. I'm a Christian in faith, but a pagan in deeds." His shoulders and head slumped.

The first of the fires began to catch. All around, men looted. They pulled what they could from houses and shops and from the monastery. Most of the richest wealth had been taken in previous raids, but there was always more hidden. There wouldn't be after this strandhogg. The men were thorough.

Holes were dug in floors. Cracks were searched, crevices scoured. The booty was piled in the green grass that was temporarily colored red.

The priest silently stepped away. He bent to pick up his sword and after cleaning it off, carefully slid it home. Killian disappeared over the lip of the ravine and climbed down to the ships. I wondered if I would ever see him again.

"He'll be back," said Gudruna, reading my thoughts. "In mind and spirit, Killian loves the shield wall. The king has told me as much."

"The king also told you to mind the house while he was gone," barked Godfrey as he strode past us to pay his respects to the bodies left from last year's slaughter.

• • •

"Divide the bounty up among the crews," the king said to us.

The priest's attitude had infected me. I decided I didn't want any of the wealth taken after murdering those men for no reason. I was angry with myself for not stopping it. Yet, I was even angrier with myself for having such thoughts. Those were not the ideals of my people. My people lived for war. Our men wanted to populate the great halls of the gods. How else would we do that but with slaughter and battle? I sat stewing. It was to be the first time my soul experienced the inner turmoil that the Christian faith demanded. In so many ways it was more difficult, much more of a challenge than the simple, outright cleaving of your opponent. I kept these thoughts to myself.

Randulfr dragged a captive into the circle of light formed by the campfire. The man, his arms bound around a stick behind his back, was the abbot who had taken the place of the one Godfrey killed the previous year. His face was bruised. Two trails of blood snaked their way down in front of his ear from a wound somewhere amidst his short hair. I was struck by his lack of fear.

The chief of the monks was thrust to the ground. One of his knees struck a pebble. He winced, then closed his eyes and mumbled Latin. When his eyes reopened, the abbot was again at peace. He appeared in better mental condition than I felt.

"Why the soldiers?" snapped Godfrey. "They sounded Irish or Welsh to me."

The abbot met the king's gaze and slowly pointed with his nose at the king's chest. "Underneath that mail, my son, what do you wear? Against the skin of your chest, what rests there and feels the beat of your heart?"

"I'm asking the questions," said the king. Gudruna sat next to Godfrey. The pair certainly hadn't made up. They had more immediate matters to tackle.

"And I will answer them all, lord king." The abbot didn't mock Godfrey. His sincerity was disarming. "Help me understand a few things." The man paused as he lifted his knee off the pebble and adjusted himself into a more comfortable position. "Help me and I'll answer all your questions with the veracity of Christ."

Godfrey examined his prisoner and gave a long sigh. He reached into his collar and fished out a gold chain. From it dangled a simple golden cross. "Is this what you wanted to see?"

"That will do, yes. I met your father once."

"Many men crossed the path of my father. Many of them didn't survive the encounter," quipped Godfrey.

"Harald of Bayeux was a fighter, but was no brute. He came to the faith with earnestness. I met him around that time. You know that was part of the reason he abandoned Normandy. He didn't like the heathens in Rouen, their slave markets."

"And another part of his reason was that the Normans were getting better at cornering the markets for goods beyond thralls. He wanted something left for his son to inherit. Harald wanted his son to become a king," said Godfrey.

The abbot sniffed. "You," he said to me. "Will you scratch my forehead?"

I looked at Godfrey, who nodded. In turn, I told Aoife to scratch the man's head. She got up from where she sat next to the king and complied.

"Thank you, lass. You've fallen in with a rough bunch."

"Not rough enough," she said.

The abbot faced Godfrey. "Harald was a man of action. He was a Norseman, but not of old. He, as I say, was no monster. His raids were quick and if they could be painless, were. He avoided many of the Christian lands, for he wanted alliances with them. In a practical sense, Harald wanted trade."

Godfrey scoffed, "You're testing my patience. Haraldsson will get trade. He will get alliances. He'll get it all his way."

"I fear Harald's son will get it all and more."

King Godfrey raised himself to his feet. He walked to the crouching abbot. Godfrey rested his hands on his hips. "I have in my belt a great sword. It is the sword of a king, a conqueror. I am done reminiscing with you. Answer my questions."

The abbot frowned. He appeared genuinely disappointed. "Very well. The soldiers came just weeks ago. They began to build a fort across the island, on the northeast end. The fort is hardly begun so the soldiers all lived in what was that village." With his bruised head, he pointed to the cracking and smoking silhouette. It was the second village I'd destroyed that year.

"Were they Irish?"

The abbot slowly shook his head. "No. Most were of the native Dal Riatan. Others, though, said they came from Wales. They served a king down there called Maredubb."

Godfrey and Randulfr exchanged glances. "Why would they be here if they serve Maredubb?" asked Randulfr.

The abbot attempted to shrug, but the rope and stick behind his back pinched. "You're reaching the extent of my knowledge, I'm afraid."

Leif threw a log he'd been whittling into the fire. A small burst of sparks scattered into the sky. "I know why they were here."

"Let's stop with the mysteries," commanded Godfrey.

"Of course." Leif scratched his arm. "You've let the whole world know you meant to come to Dal Riata. You want it firmly and forever in your Kingdom of the Isles."

"So? That is a king's right."

"All men of power want more. That's how they protect what they've already got. You expand into the frontiers so that your enemies are fighting and dying there, rather than attacking and stealing from your capital. That's what my father's done in Greenland. The skraelings are forever on the run. My father's just a jarl, but a king does much the same on a grander scale."

"And your point?"

"A crafty man doesn't tell his enemies where he will attack next."

"But a strong king can afford to do so," answered Godfrey. He held his arms out and showed us all the campfires that dotted the landscape. "When a king is mighty, with a string of fortune, and a growing army, he can get away with telling the enemy exactly what he will do. The idea is that the enemy, weaker, can do nothing about it."

"Not unlike the Greek's Cassandra, huh?" asked Killian, shuffling into our midst. I smiled when I saw that he had not hurled himself onto his sword or the rocks. Gudruna was right. I believe that he was working at being true to the One God. But when Killian was knitted together in his mother's womb, a thread was woven in that craved adventure. It's a thread that never would have seen use had Godfrey not thrust himself onto Man.

Godfrey and Gudruna smiled at seeing the priest's return. Killian rested a hand on the abbot's shoulder. The abbot refused to meet eyes with our priest. The prisoner looked away. Killian's melancholy returned.

"Cassandra or the norns, whatever," Godfrey huffed. "They know the future. My enemies know the future. In it they die."

Young Leif kicked at the earth, making a furrow with his foot. "You're right, lord king," said Leif, in a way that clearly said that he thought the king was wrong. "What I mean is that since the Dal Riatans knew you were coming in force, they had to ally themselves with another. And who else has reason enough to want to fight you other than Maredubb? It makes sense. It was his treasury you used to build this army. The people here would want to ally with a man who doesn't raid their churches, someone who is a true Christian." Both the abbot and

Killian grunted their agreement. "Horse Ketil probably helped with the introductions."

Godfrey smiled. "Aethelred too. I've given him cause. Why not just say that everyone is against me?"

The king was not taking the news with the proper gravity. We all shook our heads. The queen said, "Yes, and given time, Aethelred may send a force against you. But Aethelred is safely in London. Maredubb, whom you've seen with your own eyes, is just a few days sailing from here. His army is either already in Dal Riata or preparing to invade Man while we are busy fumbling up here for your silly revenge."

Godfrey at last paused to think rather than banter. He turned to the abbot. "So is this true. Does Maredubb have an entire army in Dal Riata? Or, was it just these few men?"

The abbot peered up at the king's face which was illuminated with the flashing campfire. "At last you cut to the heart. Your questions come full circle, king." The abbot said the last word with not a little derision. "I've been instructed to give you a challenge. King Maredubb awaits you. He doesn't hide behind the walls of his Aberffraw. He will not attack your stronghold on Man."

"A great sea battle!" exclaimed Godfrey. My sea-king was excited at the prospect.

"No, none of you raiders will have the benefit of your longships if you accept the contest." The abbot straightened himself as best he could. "How fitting that you and your *priest*, falling back to your old gods as you do, will meet your true Maker in the place where the ancient kings used to be crowned. Maredubb is calling you there. The pagans that haunt it will kill you."

"Dunadd," breathed Killian.

CHAPTER 12

Godfrey left fifty men on Lismore. It was not enough to truly hold the island if someone meant to invade it, but he'd never left any presence in the wake of his previous raids. Those fifty men were to travel across the narrow middle of the island and finish the fort begun by the island's would-be defenders. The rest of us sailed for Dunadd. Gudruna, her secret clearly out, rode aboard the king's flagship.

Charging Boar was designated a thrall ship. Four other ships in our small fleet carried slaves as well. We carried eight women and three boys who stood at the precipice of manhood. These Dal Riatan prisoners, taken from the woods outside the village, were bound tightly to the ship's ribs. They were in the way of our work. It would be worth it though, for once we finished our task in Dunadd, Godfrey had said, the slaves would bring about a great profit at the thrall auction in Dyflin. The Islamic Empire often sent merchants this far north. The rich Moors or Berbers or Arabs never seemed to tire of receiving expendable labor. The men, it was told, would be neutered and turned into house servants. The female thralls, like women slaves everywhere, would be put to multiple uses.

With the extra bodies onboard we bumped into each other more than ever. Tempers flared despite having won the King of the Isles a new island, regardless of the fact that Godfrey and those serving him had a new source of wealth from which to draw. I was still a little surly.

Magnus cut across the wake left behind by *Raven's Cross* in order to find less choppy seas. Our ship was temporarily buffeted so that I brushed up against Leif. He was forced to push down onto the thin wooden bars of a cage in which we'd placed chickens we pilfered. The cages had been roughly handled during loading, turned upside down and right side up again and again. Leif withdrew his hand and looked at the palm. It was smeared with the white and brown of manure.

"Watch where you lumber," said Leif, uncharacteristically short-tempered.

"At least Brandr watches the hogs on another ship," I said. "Otherwise, all of us would smell as bad as you will."

"Oaf," said Leif, reaching over the gunwale and dragging his hands upward against the wet strakes.

"Do we have a problem?" I asked, feeling ready to fight. I had hoped we did.

"Huh! We have an enormous problem. If you can't see it, you're blind."

"Goat's ass," I said to Leif. It wasn't anything like a common curse. I believe I made it up on the spot. It fit the moment. I gave him a shove.

"Godfrey is our problem." Leif didn't shove back. I was disappointed.

"How so?" asked a cooler Magnus from the rudder.

"If Maredubb and his Dal Riatans knew we were coming to Lismore as everyone along the coastline of the Irish Sea did, why did they not lie in wait there? Why not let us land, fight a small force at the edge of town, and then swoop from the woods while we sleep like babies curled up to our treasure."

"And curled up to females," offered Tyrkr.

"Goat's ass," I said to Tyrkr. He shut his mouth and went back to sharpening Leif's sword. It had received several nicks during our skirmish on Lismore.

Leif continued, "And why tell all your plans to the abbot so that he could pass a challenge onto Godfrey?"

"You seem to know. You always know so tell us, soothsayer." I was exasperated. I wondered how I was to survive thirteen years of exile with such a man. He was normally moderate and fair, but oftentimes maddeningly condescending.

"Because they know Godfrey and his hubris." Leif sniffed his chicken shit hand. He scraped it on the salt-water-washed strakes a second time. "Our opponents have come to appreciate that Godfrey, once his interest is piqued, will not stop. He is a bear come from the cave in late winter, so hungry that the mere scent of blood inflames his mind. They tell the abbot to pass on the challenge after a small bloodletting on Lismore so that our king may be pulled into the boat. The hook has been set.

Horse Ketil probably pulls us to land! We will be on a dinner plate, feeding Maredubb and the Dal Riatans."

"Why say nothing to Godfrey, then?" I asked.

"Would it have made a difference?"

Magnus and I looked at each other. "No," we agreed.

"Gudruna. You could say something to her," I said.

Leif frowned. "The queen likes me for a romp, nothing more. You see her look at the king. You see her drive him. She's used me to drive him. It's easy to see her as the wise one, the brains. The facts are murkier. He often looks the fool, because it is Godfrey who has to work at the edge of the sword. Gudruna stays behind and pushes her man for more and more."

"Not today," I said.

"No, not today," agreed Leif. "The queen rides with the king. They make up over there under covers. When they emerge, they'll be of one body and mind. They will drive us like oxen. Gudruna and Godfrey, both, want all of Dal Riata."

"So we are stuck," said Magnus.

Leif threw his hands up. "We are oath bound to an animal and his bride who are not crafty enough to avoid the trap set in plain sight. We will die in Dunadd."

And where is Dunadd, you might ask. Dunadd sat in the middle of a narrow, jagged finger of land that jutted southwest into the northern tip of Irish Sea from Scotland. It was the ancient capital of Dal Riata, which itself was built by an Irishman hundreds of years earlier. Now Godfrey, the Scots, and the Irish all laid claim to various sections of the old kingdom.

I had never been there, but many of the men in our widely travelled crew had. They said that despite the fact that it was situated on a formidable hilltop, the capital was not insurmountable; a distantly comforting thought since there had to be a reason Maredubb and the Dal Riatans chose it as the place to meet. The reason was, of course, that the site gave our enemies some advantage. What those benefits were, I knew not at the time. I would soon enough.

Our discussion had gone on and on as we drew closer. "Then you'll have to find a way out. You did it on Anglesey.

You had us build ladders at Watchet. You'll do it again," I said, though not entirely convinced by my own words.

Leif reluctantly nodded and flopped back onto the baggage heap. His head bumped a tough leather sack and he angrily pulled it out and peered in. The bag contained the five short iron rods that Leif had stolen from the mint at Watchet. The sight of them calmed Leif. He smiled, cinched the bag neatly, and set it back under his head. This time he lowered himself slowly and used the rigid sack and its hard contents like a pillow. Leif stared up at the small pennant that snapped smartly in the wind. He was preparing to retreat into his mind. Leif could be a-Viking in his head for a long while.

I plopped down on another man's war chest with the intent to polish my saex. It was important that I try to push the fear of the coming engagement from my head, lest it take root in my heart and the souls of the entire army. Like the insane, I forced myself to laugh as I drew out my short blade. I chuckled at the thought of silly Aoife and how she had tried to throw a whetstone. I peeked over at her small head on the king's ship. At least she refrained from trying to kill us today.

"You two are unbelievable." It was faithful Tyrkr.

"You are a race of men descended from Sigurd the dragon slayer. How can you fret about a yapping Welsh king?" Tyrkr flapped Leif's sword accusingly. "While I may be a thrall here and now, I am from the line that gave the world Arminius of the wald." I didn't know who that was at the time. Since then, and with my reading of the Latin and talking with learned men, I understand that Arminius had led a set of disorganized tribes to an improbably fantastic victory over the world's greatest army, wiping every one of his enemies from the battlefield – every one.

"The legends say that Arminius never lost hope. He pushed his way through every trial. Is Maredubb the greatest king the world has ever seen?"

I thought the question rhetorical, though he waited for an answer. "No," Leif said at last.

"He is not!" agreed Tyrkr. The thrall was as clear on this topic as any he'd ever bothered to speak on. "And the Dal Riatans are they on the rise or on the fall?"

"Fall," I said quickly. I nodded and smiled, for real this time. I did not laugh like a crazy person.

The lowly thrall, simple, but utterly dedicated beyond reproach to Erik and his sons, made a speech in his accented Norse. Where he fell short of words as he translated his native German into our tongue, nothing of his vigor and heart was reduced. His passion and ferocity shined through his oration. I straightened my back as I listened.

"The thralls talk around the dung heap. We carry our master's shit to the mound and congregate there. The talk all last night was about Dunadd. What this man said about the citadel. What that man said about a time he visited the hill fort." Tyrkr pointed again, this time with a balled fist. "Know this. Godfrey is a king who fights. I'd rather follow a master who fights than one who lounges in the longhouse rubbing his hands in worry. The same goes for you. You'd rather charge after a king who reaches for more. You say he doesn't think about his actions beforehand. So what! He's led us this far. The other thralls say that Dunadd had once been among the great northern strongholds. Kingships were bestowed atop its rocky banks. Yet, King Godfrey was right to leave straight away. Dal Riata and its crumbling capital are mere vestiges of their former glory. They were grapes, fat and ripe for the harvest by our sea king and you, his Ring-Danes and Ring-Norse, are his reapers."

Those in earshot sat in stunned silence. Or, maybe it was more like shamed silence. We had doubted our victorious king and his eager queen. It took a slave to set us on the true path.

Leif slowly climbed back to his feet. He took the whetstone from Tyrkr and his sword. Leif began sharpening it himself. "And don't forget his Ring-German," said Leif with a smile.

Our concerns were gone. We were young and we would win. There was no doubt in our minds.

We were also foolish.

• • •

The tide and the winds were in our favor. The breeze smelled of victory as we slipped into the small mouth of the

River Add. The lands to the right side, or southwest, of the river were higher, populated with a forest of oak. The shores and terrain to our left, northeast, were lower and consisted mostly of swamps and bogs.

"Terrific," mumbled Magnus.

"What?" I asked.

"Where there are swamps, there are mosquitoes."

There were. After moving upriver just several fadmr, we swept through thick swarms of the pests. Magnus slapped at his neck and flapped at his ears in order to drive the bugs away. He'd remove a hand from the rudder, swat, and replace it. Maddeningly, he repeated the feat time and again. I let the critters feast. At any one time I had three mosquitoes nursing from my bloodstream. Sure, it was more than bothersome. Yet, I was confident that in just a few more weeks as the days shortened further and the nights grew colder, I would survive and the pests would die.

I had to survive the coming encounter first, however.

Raven's Cross quickly ran aground in the very center of the Add. Magnus reacted properly and slid us to shore before *Charging Boar* saw a similar fate. The boats behind us did likewise, making an open lane down the middle of the river. Our crews all began hopping out, shields ready for war.

"Thor's beard!" Godfrey swore. He and Gudruna walked next to one another. As Leif had predicted, their determined faces showed unity. They would both lead us in the coming fight. "Dunadd is inland a few of the English miles. Stop acting like nervous old women. We're not under attack."

"Who puts a capital city inland away from the sea?" I asked. "It can't be more than a dung pile."

The king splashed down into the river himself. "And if it's not, we'll make it into one before we leave. We'll also make it a pyre." His men followed, gathering their rucksacks for the trek over land. "Halldorr, name fifteen men to stay behind and guard the ships." The king and queen were already marching to the northeast, into the bog.

"Wouldn't it be best to stay on the higher ground and move on the other side of the river?" asked Leif.

"It's deceiving to look at from here," answered Killian for the king, since Godfrey was already out of earshot. "The River Add quickly curves and moves away from the heights. Once it turns, both sides will be thick swamps. The Dal Riatans call it the Moine Mhor, the Great Moss."

"Swamps and mosquitoes," mumbled Magnus.

"I'm afraid so, lad," said Killian.

I called out the names of fifteen men just as I was ordered. I left a healthy split of Norsemen, Danes, Manx, a Greenlander, Welsh, and Irish so that no one band could overpower the other. The newcomers, I believed, still needed plenty of supervision.

"And what of the king's ship?" one of them asked as I lost my boot into the bog. It was the first of several such occasions on the march to Dunadd that day.

"That's why there are fifteen of you," I shouted. I may have cursed at the man. If I did, it was out of frustration from the buzzing pests and the slop, for he asked a valid question. "Disperse five of you as an outer perimeter. Stay awake. The rest use ropes to dislodge *Raven's Cross.*"

All I heard as I plunged into the muck after the others was a fresh round of swearing and the telltale slap of a man's hand against the back of his neck.

Swamps and mosquitoes. And death.

• • •

All day we marched in the thickest, wettest shithole I've ever encountered. The equinox had come and gone, but laboring as we did under the weight of armor, supplies, and weaponry made even the lightest and fittest among us – Killian – sweat and gurgle for breath. The river was usually within sight on our right side. Godfrey sent a scout to the far side of the waterway to shadow us and warn us of any danger. He also ordered a small screen of men to run ahead of us and to our left. The king took no chances that day, even though he had a reputation for being impulsive. We even had a rearguard of a dozen men following behind and keeping the king apprised of the situation.

As you may guess, the situation was dismal. It was wet, stinking, and foul.

"The idiot Germans don't even put cities in places like this," said Leif.

Tyrkr smiled at the barb. He just nodded in agreement while reaching for a branch on a rotting tree trunk to prevent himself from falling into a sinkhole.

"Why put a capital here?" Brandr asked. He stunk of hog manure from the booty he hauled from Lismore. Combined with his sweat, the hot stench of the bog created a force so powerful that every man kept a solid five paces between the hog man and himself.

Godfrey, who'd seen Dunadd in passing while raiding, remained ebullient. "Tsk tsk. It's all the bastards have got. Don't judge them too harshly."

"But why do we want this?" I asked.

"Want this?" asked Godfrey. He swatted a mosquito on his forehead. It had been sucking his blood for a while and created a horrible mess. The king, trying anything he could to keep his men's spirits high, pinched the crushed beast off and popped it into his mouth. "Ah, the little creatures taste like iron." He slapped one on my arm and did the same. "Want this? I don't want this place. Who would put a city here? The Picts didn't even do this. It was the bastard Irishmen who founded Dal Riata ages ago. I don't want this place. I do want to keep anyone else with any power away from my lands, though. If King Maredubb is holed up with what's left of the weak Dal Riatans, we'll use this as a chance to rid ourselves of both. We'll then take Anglesey by the winter's thaw."

It made sense. Since those days, I've been a leader. I've been a chieftain of a people wholly unrelated to anyone I had ever met before. What I know is that even simple men who hunt in the forest without any steel and who have never heard of a wheel understand power. Families try to lord over other families so that their children become rulers in the next generation. Tribes fight to lord over other tribes so that the prime hunting grounds are teeming with their warriors and not someone else's. Godfrey was a king and to stay a king in the cruel world meant that he had to forever beat away the wolves that nipped at his heels. The wolf was watching the longhouse, always.

Evening had now fallen. We sat on water-soaked logs that were slick with snotty algae. Each man grimly ate whatever he had brought for himself. There were no fires. Even if we hadn't been in hostile territory, finding a square fadmr of land that wasn't covered in more than an ell of muck was impossible. I ate two boiled eggs that had become crushed in my pack from the day's walk. They dried out my palate. I washed them down with fresh water from the River Add, which was now more like a creek. My pot of ale, I vowed to save for after the battle. I was going to climb that hill fort, no matter the height, and drink my ale while relieving myself on the corpse of Maredubb. Maybe my piss would cure the rash on his face. The thought made me grin. Perhaps I'd take his fancy black boots for myself, though few men's feet were as large as mine.

"You were born for this," whispered Killian in the night. "I see it on your face that despite the conditions and the pending terror, you live for this."

I shook my head. "Now, maybe. Before and after, no. One day I want to be a raider. The next I want to raise cattle. I've wanted nothing more than a woman to rut and land to till for my entire life."

"Your entire life? Are you even eighteen?"

"I've lived twenty-one winters as best I can tell," I said defensively.

Killian patted my shoulder. "You're young, that's all I meant. You've got many years to find your dream and then live it."

Or, I wondered, did I have many years to waste following things my heart only thought it wanted?

The moon was cresting the horizon. I could see the priest's face. He was a good man trapped in a world that he would not have created had he been given the choice. Or, maybe he was living right where he wanted. It was just hard for him to accept. "Thank you," I said.

"Do you mind if I pray for you and for our king and for our mission?" asked Killian.

"Now? With me? Why not just pray out loud for the whole mess? Plenty of others are Christians. I'm what you call a pagan, remember."

"I recall well enough," Killian said. "If you'd rather I didn't, I won't force it on you."

Something about his demeanor at that moment made me say, "No, I want you to pray. Go ahead."

Pleased now, Killian began by crossing himself. Before closing his eyes and bowing his head, he physically stuck his fingers on my eyelids and closed them. He also shoved my head down so that my chin sat on my chest. Then he began his talk, first in Latin, then in his native tongue, then in Norse. It was a fine prayer. He mentioned men and deeds about which I knew nothing at the time. He spoke of a man named Gideon, especially. Killian finished by saying what I now know as a Psalm of King David. "Blessed be the Lord my strength, which teacheth my hands for war, and my fingers for battle. My goodness, and my fortress, my high tower, and my deliverer, my shield, and He in whom I trust; who subdueth my people under me."

When I repeated his word, "Amen," I looked up. All around me the men, Christian and followers of the old gods alike, had listened to Killian's words. The priest's face brightened more than I'd seen it in some time. He'd again found the Christ.

Splashing in the river caused every man to jump. Bows were drawn, spears raised, and swords pointed at the sound. "It's Loki!" called Loki in a harsh whisper. He moved into the soggy clearing. His eyes widened when he saw all of our raised weapons. "Easy, I've got nothing but news." We relaxed.

"Speak," ordered Gudruna.

"We're close. Across the river the plain gradually rises up out of this slurry as you move south. There are even some late crops still standing in the field where farmers were able to walk without sinking up to their knees. Then, Dunadd rises up out of the earth. It sits there. It's a fortress on a rock. It's got two rows of outer curtain walls made from stone. Inside each of those, I saw simple structures, small houses and the like. Higher up the hill, two more rows of curtain walls act as an open air keep."

Several men whistled in awe at the description. A harsh glance from Godfrey shut them up.

"Tell me about sentries and activity," said the king.

"Fires burned brightly throughout the fort. I heard laughter and singing. There were many men, but I have no idea about numbers. I saw sentries walking around the curtain walls. There were a few men walking down the paths of the plain, but I avoided them. We won't go in unnoticed," warned Loki.

"We were invited so I don't think that Maredubb will be surprised if we show up at his doorstep," said Killian.

"Where are all Maredubb's ships if he's here? Wouldn't he have come in the same way?" I asked.

"Likely no," said Killian. "We came from Lismore to the north. If he came directly from Anglesey, Maredubb's vessels are strewn about on the southern coast."

"If he's even here," muttered Godfrey.

"He's here," said Aoife. She was blanketed with mud and mosquito bumps from the walk in. The men ignored her. I furrowed my brow at the girl.

Godfrey agreed with her though. "He's here. The only question I have is how we take that hill without a prolonged siege. We're not equipped for the coming cold. We're not a big enough force to encircle it."

"Aye," said Killian. "There's a well on the hill. They could sit there a long while."

We looked at one another, each hoping the other would have an answer. No one did.

"When I saw Dunadd from a distance long ago, I thought I recall seeing that the River Add passed closely by the fort. But you say that we've got to cross a plain," said Godfrey, trying to find out any way to easily overcome its defenses.

"Add turns. It flows north past the hill, then turns west to wind its way to the sea. The walls of the hill fort directly face that side. The other sides of the hill aren't burdened with walls, for they don't need to be. The natural slope of the hill is, well, it's near vertical. Our heads would be shoved into a rain of steel if we tried any of the ways," answered Loki.

"Yes, I remember that, now," the king breathed. Godfrey's knuckles turned white while he pulled on his beard and thought.

"Assault on two sides," offered Randulfr. "That way if one of us fails, the other still has a chance."

Leif shook his red head. "No matter their numbers, they'll work on their interior lines and support their men wherever they are needed before we can even send word from one of our groups to the other. They'll chop us up piecemeal. Both teams, in turn, would be defeated."

Randulfr agreed quietly. He frowned at having been corrected by such a young man.

"The only way is straight on, hard and fast, like we did at Watchet," said Godfrey, resolving himself to the carnage that would follow such an order. Gudruna gripped her king's shoulder. She was nodding.

"Unless we did both," I said.

Confused and more than a little perturbed, the men looked at me in the moonlight. Before anyone could protest, I laid out my plan. Loki, the only one of us who'd seen the fort up close, agreed that it could work. Leif agreed. Killian nodded, so did Brandr and Randulfr. The king and queen furrowed their brows.

Godfrey sucked a deep breath in through his nostrils. He reached into a pouch that hung from around his neck and pulled out his bundle of smooth rune stones. Killian muttered about blasphemy. The king cupped his hands together and rattled them. "Give me a dry surface," said Godfrey. A man produced a jerkin and we stretched it between us and pulled it taut so that it became a tabletop. The king didn't hesitate. He scattered the stones. Gudruna peeked over her king's crouched form.

We had no real soothsayer of old among us so that it was up to Godfrey to read them himself. Two stones with their runes right side up rested directly in front of the king. I knew that upon seeing them, Godfrey would command us forward. We'd follow my plan and attack Dunadd. Evil grins from the king and his queen confirmed this.

The rune stones were gathered and returned to the bag that hung from Godfrey's neck. He and the others began preparations to immediately move as I suggested. I sank down with my rump in the mud.

You see, Godfrey and Gudruna saw two runes face up. The first, the Teiwaz, told him to allow things to take their course. In other words, he ought to follow my proposals. The second rune, the Fehu, said that he should share his fortune with others. Well, he'd have nothing to share if the result of the battle was anything short of victory.

I had kneeled opposite the king as we stretched the jerkin. I saw the same two runes facing the king as plain as day. From my vantage point, they were reversed. The upside down Teiwaz warned against hasty actions. The transposed Fehu instructed us to avoid premature celebrations.

Which viewpoint was correct? I knew not.

And it mattered not, for my plan was already in motion.

• • •

I suppose it is fitting that I led a group of mostly miscreants across the river that night. What other type of men could I be expected to lead? Godfrey saw my value early on. He gave me a ring-pin for it. Mellow and friendly, quick to laugh, lover of women and ale, all of it described me when peace was at hand and the night surrounded the longhouse. When the dawn broke, however, and brought with it, not its traditional blanket of moisture, but instead a dew of swords, that is when Halldorr Olefsson gained in stature. I was a hard-nosed savage in the shield wall. In those times I had true value, for I gave my actions no thought. My body knew them long before my mind. Training didn't give me this insight. Battle exercises honed my natural gifts as I aged, but practice certainly didn't bestow on me my ability to wage war. It was Odin's gift. That night as we splashed up the other side of the River Add, I asked Thor to thank his father for me.

Gone were my misgivings. What sense would it be to fret? Behind me crouched two dozen men. If I worried about the reading or misreading of the rune stones and the omens they might portend, I would do nothing but get the men killed. Oh, a raven swooped low, what does it mean? There, on the hillside, a stag proudly displayed his rack to us, will we win? Nonsense. We were fighting men, armed for war. We would take the hill fort. Or, we would not take the hill fort. The norns etched out our paths, each man's different, though that night hundreds of lives intersected beneath the cloudless sky.

We skulked through a field of beans that had lost all of its leaves. Had we passed through during the day, much of our cover was gone. The darkness would have to be enough to hide our tiny force's advance. The moon shined down on us so I made sure to tell the men to cover their mail and helmets with cloaks and hoods. The dried foliage that littered the ground crackled with each step no matter how careful we moved. The fat pods of dried beans rattled as we brushed past. We were not stealth. I could just hope that the men on the hill were blinded by their torchlight and made deaf by their singing. Even if just one of those were true, our insane plan might work.

I stopped the men. They were obedient to my raised hand and dropped lower. Three sentries passed by on the nearby path that led between two fields. The outer two argued with the first that he hogged all the ale. In answer, the middle guard tipped the pot back even further to chug as much as he could. He received a punch to the stomach, sprayed out his last mouthful, and lost the pot to the other men. They slowly ambled away.

"Why didn't we kill them?" asked one of the Manx soldiers. His warm breath brushed my ear as he drew near, whispering. It was moist and rank. I pushed him away.

"Because we don't want to raise any suspicion if they don't return. We don't want to raise any alarm from our quarter," I said. The alarm would come, to be sure. But Godfrey and the rest would force it to be raised. The king began moving out at the same time my little group left the swamp. Godfrey, however, had to stay in the Moine Mohr awhile longer, taking a circuitous route around the river until he was across from the walls of Dunadd. Once there, he would ford the brook or take a bridge if it was available. Neither Loki nor Godfrey knew what to expect. After getting the army across, with silence if possible, our king would rush the walls and gates. They'd use the ropes and grappling hooks we brought from the ships. There'd be no construction of ladders that night. There was no time. The sounds of a hundred axes felling trees would no doubt alert Maredubb exactly where we were afoot.

"Move," I groaned as loudly as I dared. Our crackling and rattling resumed.

Godfrey's was the larger force. It would be the loudest and boldest. It might fail in its attempt to storm the curtain walls. That was all taken into consideration. Our hope was that after many long moments of seeing that nothing came from the west – my small group's target – that the fort's commander would shift all but a few men to face Godfrey. My two dozen would scale the steep, rocky side of the hillock in the predawn darkness, find a way in, and create a foothold around the main gate. It seemed like an imprudent idea as I had spoken it aloud in the swamp. But Godfrey liked it. He was king. Gudruna loved it. She was queen. The rune stones guaranteed success in the monarchs' eyes. The plan would be attempted.

I again held up my hand. We stopped and sank lower amid the dry, vertical stalks. It struck me that the coming winter was turning these late bean plants into skeletons of what they'd been in their prime, just weeks earlier. Those bones now stood in final defiance to the inevitable – their harvest by man or their last demise from the heavy snows of winter. How soon would my corpse be doing the same? Would I even see the next morning's light?

I had hoped to get closer to the base of the hill, but dared not chance it. The field closest to the western side of the cliffs was long harvested. Short stubble was all that remained. Even a drunk sentry might be able to see us cross if we barreled toward our objective. Not knowing what else to do, I waited.

Patience is not a suit I wear well. Since becoming a follower of the One God, I understand it is a virtue. I truly believe it to be. I've even prayed for it on occasion. I wish it would come to me. If I could drink a cup and retain it forever, I would. Countless times, I thought to myself, you've got patience now, Halldorr. But all those times were mere fantasy. They occurred during times of plenty or peace. As soon as true patience was required, I wilted like a drought-plagued flower.

I huffed through my nose and gnawed on my cheek. I heard a few of the men chatting behind me. A stern stare shut them up. Other men shifted their weight from one foot to the other. They made a clattering sound of their armor, a crackling sound of the fallen leaves, and rattling sound from the dried beans. Though it was no more racket than we'd made for our entire journey, it was deafening to me. I jerked the Manx next to me and whispered into his ear with my fetid breath, "Tell those newcomers that if I hear one more peep from them, I'll ram this rusty sword into their bellies before we even cross that field."

The Manx hesitated, thinking that I wasn't serious. After all, I had warned them about talking time and again that night. Why would one more warning be any different or more serious than the last? I hammered the pommel of my sword into his boot. He grunted, but immediately conveyed my message. The moving, adjusting, and babbling ceased. I at last felt patient.

The hill loomed fifty fadmr in front of us. I couldn't make out the exact details of what we had to climb, so as we approached, we would just have to make quick decisions. At the top, I could see the back of a pair of the curtain walls. These would be the ones that formed the Dal Riatan's version of a keep, open air. But, roofs or not, it would play that part if Godfrey's battle pushed past the outer curtain walls. We meant to scale that cliff and jump over the walls.

Torches that were raised at intervals along the top of the walls splashed light outward. The light didn't travel far, however. The bright flames would likely also make the guards, whose heads I could just see sticking above the stone walls, truly blind to our movements. As any lad who has ever peeped into the hall of fair maiden can attest, if a roaring fire is near her, he can approach all the way to the door without being noticed. I had stolen more than a few glances at the bewitching Freydis over the years. I had even peeked a time or two at Leif's mother.

Even though Thjordhildr was nearly old, thirty-five I think, her shape alone gave reason enough to call to me as a young lad. In any event, I hoped that the idiot soldiers of Maredubb's army would be just as blind to our whereabouts.

My patience was gone again. All was quiet except for the lingering revelry from the fort. It echoed up off the walls and settled down upon us on the low plain. Was the night almost gone? How long had we waited? I looked to the sky to see where the dragon constellation sat. Instead of finding stars, I swore I saw a brightening sky. I mumbled a few curses about the king's progress and squinted to peer over the fort toward the east and the sun.

No, it was just the light of those damned torches.

A lone shout rang out. Whoever called it had booming lungs. The voice ended in a painful sounding gurgle. More voices erupted, splitting the night. I heard a thunder of hooves, the footfalls of men, warriors who meant to take a hill. Godfrey's war call wasn't distinguishable from the hundreds of others, but I could picture him. He would have his shining blade drawn. Godfrey would be screaming with spittle running down his beard. His eyes would be wide. He would be more alive than at any other time in his life, for he was entering battle. I smiled to myself as I thought about my king. Godfrey was made in the mold of Thor. He was not Odin, gifted with a love of poetry and verse. He was a trickster. He was jolly. Godfrey was quick to anger and quicker to forgive his men. I was one of his soldiers and it made me proud. Even the bastards behind me were his men. They were my men, too, and I would lead them to victory.

Only once again, I needed patience.

• • •

The key was to wait just long enough. Sit too long and Godfrey could be wiped out completely. Run too quickly and Maredubb might have too many eagle-eyed guards surveying the west for an army. Wait, I told myself.

Voices from above us called to and fro. Captains barked orders. I heard scrambling feet. The lights became brighter behind the walls. Good, I thought, the buffoons are lighting more fires, ensuring they will be so blind to our approach that victory is already in my jerkin's pocket.

Then the sky itself belched to life – and light.

Dozens of arrows, alight, sprang over those walls. They arced high up into the sky. It was a beautiful sight and I was struck dumb while I watched. We were in their range. I came to my senses just as they reached their apogee. "Shields," I grunted. "Quiet. They still may not know we're here."

We scraped and clanged. Metal bosses and rims banged against swords and spears as we brought up our bark. We were loud, but this time I had no fear of being heard. Godfrey's attack on the east was deafening.

The burning arrows began to fall. They landed well short. They clustered in just a few places as if the men had been aiming at designated targets. They were. With the help of the new source of light in the field, I could now see that in the hill's shadow, the defenders had piled dry tinder in great heaps. The arrows pierced the mounds. Some went deep between branches. Others landed with grand thuds when they struck fat logs. The fires borne by the missiles dispersed. The fodder for the coming conflagration was perfectly set. The vast bundles of wood sparked to life. The field before us would soon be as well lit as midday.

"Back," I snarled. I drew my shield under my chest and turned my ass to the hill. Under our cloaks we fled from the prying eyes of the fires' light.

We ran thirty fadmr. "Stop," I said. Each man in our group turned around. But the men had all turned around to look at me, not the growing spectacle of light. What were my orders? They didn't ask. They didn't have to. Their faces said it all.

I stuck my head up out of the beans and looked for inspiration. Trees! My homeland was a world of trees. My people were master woodworkers and shipwrights. The trees would work. They'd save us all. "Skirt the field," I rasped. "To those trees on the south." I stood and ran before I even saw if they understood.

In short order, I burst into the line of trees. It was made of old growth adders with thick thorns growing at the base. The line was thin and long. It was a boundary between two fields. It was perfect for us. The rest of my men poked through. More than one man lost his cloak to the thorns. Mine remained. It made no matter whether we had them or not. I thought they were no longer needed.

"Follow," I said. We hunched over and pounded on toward the east and the southern tip of the hill.

By now the fires blazed. Our initial field of approach was impossible if we had wanted to proceed unseen. From our new position, however, we had just a few paces from the edge of the tree line to the face of the cliffs. "Crouch and move fast. We're so close to the hill now, they won't see us. They scan the west for an army. They won't look under their noses for ants."

I don't know if my talk made any sense. I just bent forward and ran. I rolled into the base of the cliff and waited for shouts from above or a hail of missiles. None came.

My men looked at me from the tree line. I frantically waved them on. The Manx with the squalid breath took a last glance up to the walls, kissed the cross that hung from his neck, and ran. He made it safely. The rest came in ones and twos. None of us were seen.

I stole a look over a boulder. We could approach the keep walls from where we lay, but the slope was too gentle. They'd see us coming. Three archers or six men with javelins could hold us off for days. We had to crawl northward along the western edge to our original target.

My back was pressed against the jagged rocks of the cliff's base. We inched our way north. I swear that I heard Leif screaming out my name for help. I wanted to jump over those walls and cut down every last one of Maredubb's men to save my friend. Patience, I told myself. Leif would certainly die if we failed.

We stopped. I put my belly against the rocks and crawled. I didn't wait. I didn't give orders. I climbed.

The going was easier than I originally thought. The face of the cliff was not entirely sheer. It went straight up for a fadmr or two, then had a thin ledge where scrub grasses held on for dear life. Soon, I did the same. Up we climbed, I at the top followed by a few Manx and then a host of newcomers of indecipherable origins.

We were close. I could hear distinct words from the Dal Riatans. I was to help Godfrey secure a kingdom and final revenge for the humiliating hangings his Ring-Followers had endured.

I paused on the last thin outcrop before we would climb the last face and the wall. I let our men catch up and breathe. When the last one had rested his hands on his knees for several heartbeats, I nodded sternly. My hands dug into the tight crevices they could find. I climbed.

Now I tried not to grunt. I was so close. Any sound might warn the enemy. When the fingernail on the middle finger of my left hand tore off, I shuddered. I gasped, but didn't yelp. Up I went.

The men behind me began making a loud ruckus. Some yelled. Some cried. I fought to hold my awkward position at the base of the stone wall and crane my head to see what was the matter. I heard a thump. I saw a man fall, bounce off the narrow shelf and clang his way down the cliff. I saw swords drawn. They were covered in crimson. They flashed in the night.

Below me, the newcomers, the piratical mercenaries, had shown their colors. They were hacking down anyone truly loyal to Godfrey. The traitors had let the Manx climb ahead on the last leg. The traitorous bastards then cut the exposed men from behind. Legs were slashed. Groins were stabbed. It wasn't even a fight. It was over before it began.

And I was the only one left who was loyal to Godfrey.

• • •

I clung to the side of that hill just out of reach of their swords. One of the bastards threw a spear up at me. He missed. Not by much. The weapon's head made sparks as its steel grated against the rocks next to my face.

I couldn't scrabble my way down to them. They'd do to me what they did to the Manx. I couldn't hurl myself down on them. The outcrop was not wide enough. I might take a few with me, but to jump was to commit painful suicide by scraping my flesh off and bludgeoning my head against boulders all the way down. Up was my only choice.

The enemy at my back had the same idea. They didn't try to chase me, for a sword battle on the face of a wall was no way to earn glory. It might make for a great yarn if told by the right skald. Men would long to be us as they heard the tales. Women would murmur amongst themselves about how they would want such a man as the one who could cling to a cliff with one hand and kill men with the other. How much more could a man do if given the use of both hands, especially in bed, those young lasses would wonder. But neither the newcomers nor I wanted to risk it that dark morning.

The bastards began shouting to the men behind the wall. The defenders reacted instantly. I heard their heavy boots thunder toward us. I was glad I still had my cloak then. I pulled its dark hood up over my blonde hair and drew myself into the wall. My chest muscles screamed. I clutched the wall and made myself a part of her.

Whoosh! Pffft! Missiles ran past my ears. The breezes they created ruffled my coat along my back. The javelins were close, but they missed me. They did not miss the sheep dung spread out on the ledge, though. Those men screamed. The traitors bled. They said over and again how they were on the side of Maredubb. They shouted about how the conniving Welsh king and his drunken stooge, Horse Ketil, had sent them. The sentries on the wall were not in a position to decide what was true and what was not. They only knew that just a few ells below were men who should not be there. The defenders sent a hail storm of oak and steel down. In moments, except for the labored, gurgling breath of one traitor, it was again quiet.

On my side of the hill, that is.

To the east, I could hear Godfrey's battle yet raging.

The fact that it still ran on told me that he hadn't surmounted the walls. My king had tumbled against them and collapsed. He would need me on the inside to open the gates.

But I was alone. The newcomers I led betrayed me and the king.

I closed my eyes and pushed my forehead against the cool stone. There were two hundred newcomers with Godfrey, Gudruna, and Leif.

The roar I heard, the clanging of axes, and cries for mothers came not from an exchange of force between Maredubb and Godfrey. No, I now understood that it came from within Godfrey's own army.

The ranks were eating themselves.

All the while Maredubb sat inside the safety of Dunadd watching the spectacle, watching one more kingly rival in the Irish Sea disappear.

• • •

For too many moments I clung to the wall. I wasn't afraid as much as I was uncertain of just what I should do. The watchmen above had again turned their attention to the main attack. I heard their giggles. Many of them likely wagered on some aspect of the destruction taking place at their gates. Many a Norseman would have done the same. A man's humor turns morose when carnage reigns.

With no more missiles whizzing past, I knew the sentinels' attention was clearly elsewhere. I was able to move freely – but which way? Back down the way I had come? That would take time and do nothing for the cause. Up and over the wall? I would be stuck within moments, for I was but one man against an entire garrison. Instead, I chose to sidle along the wall until a better idea came to me. I went south for no good reason other than I saw a decent finger hold in the wall in that direction.

If the sentries above were showing an interest in their duties, they would have seen my struggle or heard my grunting. They weren't. I thanked Providence. Grasp after painful grasp I made it around the top curtain wall of the open keep. With every move, the finger on my left hand blossomed with a fresh pulse of blood. At last, I rounded the curved fortification. I could now see down into the next section of the wall, set lower on the hill in stair-step fashion. I was also able to look beyond, into the lower levels of walls. What I saw made my throat swell in my neck. I felt like I would choke on a growing bite of apple.

In the lowest bailey was the fancy Maredubb. He was in full regalia sitting on his smart black destrier with the enormous hooves. His linen trousers were light green this time, though like his red ones, they were tucked into tall black leather boots. I wanted those boots. Maredubb's long padded coat that showed under his scale armor was again blue, but royal, not sky.

Next to Maredubb sat Horse Ketil on a borrowed horse. He'd recovered from the beating I'd given him on Anglesey. He was tottering on his loaned horse. He was drunk or feigning drunkenness. Horse Ketil's skin was green and his countenance fearful of what their forces would encounter once Maredubb gave the order to open the gates. It looked like his hope of taking over Man without a fight was lost. Chaos was knocking outside the fort's door.

A watchman, perched on a walkway behind the lowest curtain wall, was shouting details of the battle down to the mounted king. I couldn't hear anything Maredubb said in return, but I saw him gesturing with his hands. His infantry stood proud in tight lines behind the Welsh king. They were unsullied, rested, and from their faces, I could tell they were ready for avenging the humiliation Godfrey had given their king just months before.

Beyond the gate I saw the fight going on and on. It ranged from partially up the hillside to partially along the narrow flatland next to the River Add. I realized then that it was first light. To the east, the tip of the sun was just cresting the horizon. Had I been in the arms of my bride, I would have said it was a beautiful sunrise. I would have rutted with the fictitious woman while the youngest of my brood of children prepared my morning meal. In the real world, the air was cool like those of all late summer days. The sun was red. It splashed its faint light on a dense set of clouds that had blown in before dawn. The clouds showed violet at their broad, single base and darkened to grey then black toward their multiple, wispy peaks. The red, yellow, and orange leaves of the trees that lined the river looked especially sharp that morning. I felt like I could see all the way home to Rogaland. The scene was, in fact, beautiful. But Sunna was dressed in red, blood red. It was morning and with the color of the sun the norns were hinting that beneath the roots of Yggdrasil they were weaving a day of death. Odin would have many fine men enter his hall by the time of the gloaming.

A spear sliced the air past my nose. Its point stuck between two rocks. The shaft vibrated loudly from the shock of impact. A watchman from the next lower wall had noticed me and took a chance with his weapon. Without thinking, I sprang to hang from the shaft and used it as a swing to propel me the last few ells. Thump! My feet landed on the top of the second wall. I ran along its arcing length, kicking the man in his face who'd thrown the spear. He crumpled.

Below, inside the wall, I saw a flat rock that had an old carving of a charging boar. Thinking of Leif's ship, I thought that perhaps the Dal Riatans weren't all bad. Perhaps we weren't that different. But there was no time for being introspective. In another twenty steps a second guard noticed me. I thrust a boot in his face, too. He toppled into a third watchman and like water cascading down rocks splashes further and further afield, more and more of the enemy was alerted.

I leapt into the air and fell down on the third curtain wall, stair-stepping lower. Arrows whiffed past. If I could survive the run of such a gauntlet, jumping from one wall, running, and bounding for the next wall down, my path would take me directly to the main gate and Godfrey. I write this sitting here today an aged man, a little bitter, a little tired, and sometimes forgetful. What I hoped to do there for King Godfrey, I do not know.

One more jump. I ran along the top of the lowest wall out of view from the men standing down in the previous bailey. Their spears stopped. But I was a newfound target for the eager soldiers lined up directly behind Maredubb. They certainly had pent up energy and a plethora of unused missiles. Anticipating an onslaught, I intentionally changed my pace by temporarily slowing. A hedge of spears raced in front of my chest. I pushed my speed. A spear tripped me. Another set of spears tore at my flapping cloak. Their momentum caused the coat to jerk at my neck and sent me over the curtain wall into the clash outside. Within the bailey I could hear the raucous cries of Maredubb's army, led by a chanting Horse Ketil, celebrating their first kill in the battle at Dunadd. The noise they made quickly faded. I rolled in the air and landed on my side on a tuft of grass, bounced over a weather-worn rock, and skidded across another pile of stones.

I came to rest against the legs of a newcomer who fought one of Kvaran's men. The traitorous newcomer was surprised to see me. He craned his face up toward Dunadd's wall, wondering from where I came. His shock was the only thing that saved me. After struggling for a single heartbeat to gather any of my weapons or my shield, I gave up. They were wrapped in my coat. I reached up under the dangling tails of the traitor's chainmail and latched on with an iron grip to his manhood. I used it like a handle to pull myself up. He screamed in agony, bending at the waist. Kvaran's man used a great sword to cleave the newcomer's head from his body, spreading a great blooming red mist into the morning.

"Thanks," the man said as he stepped away to engage another newcomer.

I stood and gathered my bearings. I faced east toward the Add River. Behind me and to the left was the tightly shut gate of Dunadd, the one that Maredubb would order opened when the timing was proper for his intentions. Spread everywhere were pockets of fighters. The largest of these pockets was midway up the hillside. Godfrey and Gudruna had called together a host of Greenlanders, Manx, Welsh, and even a few of the warriors from Dyflin. They'd formed a shield wall in the midst of the mayhem. The full length of King Godfrey's once-bright, new blade was caked in blood and entrails of the men he'd hewn. The mass of warriors' oak was alive. It efficiently stabbed and cleared a path, inching up the hill toward the gate. A few of the men in the middle of the round shield wall had partially unfurled their grappling hooks. By Thor, my king still thought he could take the fort!

For a fleeting moment I was caught up by the king's confidence, the luck and fate and fortune he felt were on his side.

I looked up at the walls behind me and began thinking of the best way to surmount them. I pictured all I had seen throughout the night and morning. Where should I lead the king so that he could claim victory? I studied the gate and my senses returned. Maredubb's army was still nestled behind it as safe and comfortable as a newborn next to his mother's milk-swollen breasts.

I ran toward Godfrey. I cut three newcomers from behind with my old sword. More mists of crimson colored the air before splattering against other men and the rocks at our feet. I walked on a bridge of bodies that got deeper with every new step of the shield wall. Godfrey and the others fought like maniacal demons. They were draugr, sucking life's air from their victims. It was horrifying.

One of Kvaran's men slipped in a pool of slick blood. He fell forward onto his shield, exposing his back and creating a gap in the line. The traitors did not allow the chance to pass by unanswered. The fallen man was immediately killed. So too were the men of Dyflin on either side of him. Leif screamed and sidled. The gap closed. The moving slaughterhouse resumed its climb.

I hacked at the back of our enemies' calves as I ran through. Killian saw my approach and at the right moment, tipped his shield to the side to allow my passage into the inner safety of the wall. I ran into Aoife. I'd forgotten she was even with us. She carried a skin of water that had an arrow jutting from one side. The skin was flaccid. Water trickled down the arrow shaft and flecked the red-drenched earth. On her back Aoife had slung two sheaves of arrows, although as I scanned our circle of shields, I could see that all our archers were dead.

I remember wishing at that moment that she would jerk on my beard and give me the plan that would save us. That didn't happen. The once proud, strong, defiant girl was wide-eyed with terror. She was near frozen. Tears streamed down her cheeks. "Home!" she cried. "I want home. I want my sisters and my mother!"

My knee slapped the earth and I grabbed her chin in my hand. Our eyes met. Hers were buried beneath pools of liquid. "Be strong," was all I had time to say.

"Randulfr! Take my place," shouted Godfrey. His favorite warrior stepped in just as Godfrey moved back to talk to me. He yanked me up by my hair.

"You're supposed to be inside opening the gate!" The king panted. He swiped a bloody paw across his face to clean away sweat and the remains of the enemy. He removed the old and replaced it with a new streak of mess.

"The bastards," I began, "turned on us."

Godfrey got a sarcastic look on his face and looked around the outside of the shield wall. "Oh, you must be joking, because things over here are going well."

"We can't open the gate," I said. Gudruna's sword clanged off a man's helmet. The riotous noise of the battle that surrounded us cleaved my ears.

"No matter!" answered Godfrey. "The traitors will be mopped up in just a few more steps. Then we assault the fort like men, none of your trickery."

I tugged back on Killian, pulling him into the conversation. He nearly rammed his short sword into my eye. "Tell the king that we must withdraw now! We cannot take that fort. Without the newcomers on our side our numbers are too small. And we've lost dozens of fighters here." I pointed a finger at the gate. "Maredubb lies in wait. Horse Ketil and an army, too."

Killian was shaking his head in disagreement. The norns were pulling at the Christian's adventurous thread. They must surely have been giggling. "We've got this! This fort will be ours. The king has Providence on his side. He slices the enemy with his fine blade." Killian had the bloodlust like I'd never seen. His face was not his own. He'd morphed into one of us. Killian was no longer a priest, temporarily, at least.

Godfrey ran one side of his new sword across his thigh to remove the coagulating blood. He flipped it to wipe the other side. Killian's battle-mad eyes locked on the sword. He grabbed the king's wrist. "I thought you said this was an +ULFBERH+T!"

The king slapped away the priest's hand. "It is an +ULFBERHT+. It says so right there."

Godfrey stepped to take his place back in the shield wall. Killian was suddenly the same priest I'd gotten to know. The diminutive man tugged back on the larger Godfrey. "No king. Halldorr is right. I lost my senses. We must leave now." He pointed to the king's sword. "That is counterfeit! There are reports all over Europe of men who've taken those false blades into battle and find themselves and their armies decorating the foliage."

Godfrey again shoved Killian. "Superstitious? What kind of priest are you?" A spear fell between us all.

Aoife was screaming louder now. She had moved to the back of the hollow shield wall as it progressed upward.

"Killian is right, lord king!" I called. "I don't care what his reason is at this moment, but his conclusion is correct. We'll lose if we stay."

"And if we flee, we're admitting defeat already!" The king grabbed my beard and wrenched it hard. "One chance! A man gets one chance in his life at true greatness. These odds, against me like they are, give me the chance for fame. If I lose, I join Odin." He turned to Killian. "Sorry, father." The priest nodded his understanding. "But if we win, think of it. If we somehow take this hill and gain a new kingdom, the legends, the sagas, the songs will be filled with our names for eternity. Sigurd the dragon slayer will be forgotten."

The king gritted his bared teeth. I felt truly stout of heart at that moment. I was ready to follow him, damn the costs. Godfrey turned to face the front again. He took one step forward when I saw his head snap back. An arrow glanced off his helmet and shot past me to finish its course. The king shook his head to recover his senses. He blinked to clear the spider webs.

We heard a high pitched scream from behind and we all turned to see what made the noise, though I think in our hearts we knew. Aoife was lying on her back with the arrow jutting from her belly. Her mouth was gaping as she belted a constant shriek. One hand tore at the shaft of the missile. Another was balled into a fist, beating the sloppy red earth. The men in the rear of our round shield wall stepped gingerly backward. One of them stepped on her pounding arm, pinning it to the ground. He paid no attention since he'd been stepping on bodies and their parts all morning. I ran to the girl and jerked her out by her ankle.

Pulling her writhing form into my arms, I awaited her malicious slap for treating her so roughly. It came not.

"Sword," she rasped, holding up a trembling arm. I could see the print of the man's boot on her skin. "Sword," Aoife coughed.

I screamed at her. "You're not so close to death that you need a blade. Valhalla is closed to you right now."

Despite my protest, I complied with her wishes. I reached to the dirt and grabbed a dead man's blade. I set the grip into her small hand which firmed at the mere touch. Aoife smiled with eyes closed. The grin fled as she began coughing blood. My lower lip quivered. Tears came and began washing away the crimson splattered across my cheeks. Aoife's hand tightened on the sword even while she convulsed. She gave two grunts and then exhaled for one long, last time.

The girl I cradled was dead.

My confidence ebbed.

• • •

More arrows slapped the shields of the leading edge of our mass of men. Spears, too, danced in the morning air. Both types of missiles leapt over our front ranks. They killed the unfortunate men who advanced blindly backward up the hill as they themselves did their best to chop down the last of the newcomers. While cradling Aoife's lifeless form, I peered ahead to see from where the new deadly menace came.

The morning became more dreadful. Maredubb had found the right moment. The gate clattered open. He and his men poured through and down the hill, sending their rain of steel as envoys ahead of them. The negotiations were short as the sharp tips pierced our rugged diplomats.

Godfrey and Killian were already at their places in the front of the shield wall. All talk of retreat was forgotten. It was time to avenge our newly fallen. I think both men were inspired by Aoife's sacrifice. The courage she demonstrated in life didn't flee with her death. No. It sprang from her soul into all of us. It rejuvenated us. The time had come for action. The king called, "Charge! Keep tight and run up the hill! Stay strong. Cut them!" He pushed forward, Gudruna at his side. The rest of the men surged behind them. Even the men at the back of the circular shield wall turned and ran, abandoning the few newcomers who yet lived. The greater threat was Maredubb's army. It was up, not down.

I joined them, for I had no choice. I would have preferred to carry Aoife's body to the river. There I would have spent a full day constructing a small longboat for the girl. Such vessels were fit only for warriors. She was one. I would have liked to set her in the ship with weapons. I would have shoved it from the shore already alight. The flames would have consumed her craft and body even before I stopped crying. All of that would have been a fitting way for her to be sent to Valhalla. I could do none of it.

Before going to my place in the line, I gently set Aoife's body across the back of a large dead man. There was no time for more tears, though I had them and they flowed mightily. They clouded my vision. I wiped them away. Snot clogged the moustache of my beard. Aoife's straw-like hair was more disheveled than usual. I pinched a lock and set it behind her ear. Even a few of the newcomer brigands stopped their fighting and watched. They had known the precocious girl, too. They'd liked her. Everyone did, except those she meant to kill. I simultaneously laughed and cried at the thought of the little beast acting as a ravaging pirate. My throat swelled so that I felt like I was trying to swallow an entire apple. I gave Aoife a soft pat to her forehead. It was still warm. More tears came.

"She's gone, Halldorr," said one of the newcomers with surprising tenderness. He was nothing but a dishonorable traitor. In a flash I slipped my saex out and into his thigh. I quickly killed the other two onlookers. They fell like flower petals decorating Aoife's resting place. After one last look at the little demon who had been more alive than any of us, I hoisted my shield and ran to my rightful place.

• • •

The last man from Dyflin fell choking on his own blood. Our Welsh soldiers were dying. The Manx toppled. Yet, we pushed with all our might up that hill. We actually made headway, for not all of Maredubb's men could force their way through the narrow gate. Our tiny army's progress had checked theirs. The men in the rear ranks of the enemy helplessly watched our two sides meld together into a writhing mass of flesh and steel.

Horse Ketil pushed the chest of his charger into my shield. He swung down at me with intense vitriol lurking in each stroke. "I'll repay you, fool! You used your fists. I'll use this steel," Ketil called. I leaned into the horse's neck, using it as protection from his blows. It would only be a moment, I thought, before the frightened ass would run out of hate-fueled energy. I'd stab his leg then.

Only he didn't tire. Horse Ketil skillfully moved his horse from side to side, exposing me again and again. It was a repeat of the madness he'd unleashed when we took over the city of Aberffraw. Ketil used his sword as would a practiced warrior. He saw the surprise on my face. "A drunkard is what you see in me. Or, you see a man who pretends badly. I've found that being underestimated brings benefits." His blade removed the last of my tattered cloak. "Kings say things in front of you they ought not, when they think you are drunk or just blustering power. In the process, I gain treasure for myself and my clan. I gain alliances. Man will be free." He swung again. I dodged it, but fell backward into a bloody mess. "Maredubb thinks me a drunk, too! Soon Anglesey will be under my control."

Ketil prodded his horse forward to crush me with its marching hooves. Killian swung his sword. It severed Ketil's leg and buried itself in the beast's ribs. Out of instinct, Ketil made a broad retaliatory stroke with his blade. The tip splayed through Killian's face. The priest, my first true Christian friend, fell into the heap of our men's bodies. Ketil's horse sensed his master's distress, felt the steel lodged in its side, and bolted back toward the gate. It trampled dozens of the enemy.

Godfrey looked down at Killian, his trusted advisor, friend, and priest. Killian peered back with death's blank stare. The king suddenly had a renewed vigor, an otherworldly energy. Out of sheer will, Godfrey pushed ahead. He killed one, two, then three more of the enemy. The rest of us saw him. We were inspired. I know I was heartened by his prowess. I climbed to my feet and howled like Fenrir, the wolf of legend. Our shrinking band came together. We hacked and stepped. We cut and walked on a blanket of death. The corpses made us a path. We moved closer to the gate.

"Thor's beard!" screamed Godfrey as he cleaved another man.

Maredubb was there now. He sat on his beautiful destrier. Its black coat was marred with red blood and brown dirt even though they'd been in the fight a short while. King Maredubb's fancy leather boots were likewise covered. The ugly king was killing as efficiently as was ours. With two hands he brought a long handled war axe down at the head of Godfrey. The king held his blade aloft to block it. That would be the test of whether or not it was a true work of the famous Frankish craftsmen.

The axe was halted in midair. The two kings shouted strings of curses at one another. Neither heard what the other said. They stood there, Maredubb's different colored eyes angrily burning at Godfrey.

I again took heart. My king was nearly single-handedly climbing the hill. His blade was better than a work of art, it was magic. I knew it. Gudruna knew it. And Godfrey knew it.

Maredubb didn't know it. He simply picked up his giant axe again. He raised it with both hands above his head. King Maredubb leaned into his swing bringing every ounce of his strength, weight, and leverage with him. He could have split a bull in half with the force he put behind that blow. Godfrey defiantly stuck the sword in the axe's path.

The blade snapped in two. The +ULFBERHT+, as false as a made-up whore, shattered. It splintered like the massive whetstone of Hrungnir. The war axe continued falling as if it had felt no resistance. It crushed into the helmet of my king, creating a vast chasm on the crown. Godfrey's arms went limp. He teetered. Some unnamed man in Maredubb's army shoved a short sword into my king's neck. Godfrey collapsed.

Gudruna belched out a terrified wail. Her face, always beautiful and confident, bent into the faces of all her husband's victims. She stopped fighting. It got her killed. A club beat her shoulder. Gudruna fell to a knee. The same club came down on the back of her helmeted head. Her neck snapped. The Queen of the Isles toppled dead onto her husband. The hand of her killer clasped on the gold amulet from Anglesey that Godfrey had given her. He tore it away and melted into the throng.

Both armies paused. It was just a moment, I know. Maybe it was less than a heartbeat. It seemed to go on for hours as only the truly outrageous surprises in the middle of a battle can. Our hearts melted in that moment. My brothers – Danes, Norsemen, Greenlanders, Manx, and even Irish and Welsh – and I lost our will. The combined souls of the Dal Riatan and Maredubb's armies swelled.

"Slaughter them!" called Maredubb.

They did.

• • •

We broke. Our asses faced the fort's defenders and we ran down the hill. As any of you who have had the fortune to participate in a great war know, turning your back to flee invites even more carnage than what you were trying to escape in the first place. But for a fleeting pulse, it feels like you are doing something to remedy the situation.

Until the pursuers lock in their aim.

The rear ranks of Maredubb's army forced their way out. They wanted a part in the victory. They knocked down the front ranks and heaved spears into the sky. One after another arced over the killing field. They slammed into the backs of terrified warriors.

I thundered to a halt at Aoife's body. My comrades ran into and around me. I looked at their faces. Gone was all bravado. Fled was all valor. They were replaced with the wide-eyed, vacant stare of fear. Seeing my friends thus made me ashamed for a heartbeat. Then I remembered that I would look the same to them. I bent down and scooped Aoife into my arms. An arrow grazed my shoulder, but I held on.

I wanted to hug the little creature and forget the horrors of the day. I didn't care if I would die with her, with Godfrey and the rest. You know I didn't, however, for I lived to pen this tale. It wasn't me who got me moving. Her peaceful face slapped me back to reality. From her next life, Aoife shouted at me. She tugged on my finger and kicked my shin. "Run, you fool! Run!"

I did.

We burst into the trees and down into the River Add. A few men went straight through into the unknown wilderness of Dal Riata. Several more turned right and ran into the thinning waters upstream. Calm-headed Leif gathered the rest of us together. "Lose your weight," he said as he stripped himself of anything that wasn't needed. His helmet, his mail, his jerkin, all of it splashed into the water. "You should leave her, Halldorr."

"I'll not!" I yelled as I and the others dropped everything of excess weight into the flowing water.

"He won't," said Randulfr. Godfrey's lieutenant looked at me and gave a nod. He understood. Randulfr turned with a defiant gaze to Leif. "He won't. I've had enough of your plans."

Leif threw up his hands in surrender. "Fine. Drop everything else. Hurry." We finished the task. Each man kept a single weapon, mostly swords. I held onto my father's saex. Aoife was balanced on my shoulder.

We splashed downstream as fast as our lungs and legs would propel us. I looked around to see who made it that far. Tyrkr ran, drenched in blood, stone faced. Randulfr, Loki, and Brandr had survived that long. And there was Leif, of course, and Magnus. Four other Greenlanders trailed behind.

The river went on a maniacally curving course. We made terrible time if we expected to ever make it to our ships, but after running at least an English mile we gave up. We fell to a halt. Each man except for me crashed into the Add, exhausted. I teetered on my feet, holding Aoife. We caught our breath and slowly gathered together. The others climbed to all fours. I rested one hand on my knee and for the first time felt the soothing coolness of the water rolling past my shins. We, survivors of the previous slaughter, locked eyes and knew that we were going to die.

One-by-one we stood upright with weapons at the ready to meet whatever would come down the river or whatever might come pounding over the bank. We remained planted in the undulating waters for a long while.

The shrill, wailing cry of a lapwing broke the silence.

"They aren't coming?" asked Brandr.

None of us believed it so we waited.

We again looked at one another. Without uttering a word we turned and slowly walked down the river toward our fleet.

• • •

"Do you smell that?" asked Leif.

"What?" I asked.

"Smoke," said Tyrkr. He pointed high up through the treetops that extended up from the soggy banks of the Add.

"The fleet," gasped Randulfr, plunging forward.

Leif grabbed him by the shoulder. "If they've taken the main road and beaten us there, they'll be watching the river. We'll be ambushed from the side. We've no armor."

"So we let the fleet burn? How do we escape?" accused Brandr.

"And I said I was tired of listening to you," said Randulfr. He stuck a weak finger into Leif's chest.

"No," said Leif, answering Brandr, but ignoring Randulfr. "Back into the swamps. It's not far now." He climbed out of the water on the northern bank, expecting us to follow.

"I should command," said Randulfr.

"You're right, you should," I said, following after Leif. The Greenlanders and Tyrkr came along.

Loki gave Randulfr an encouraging slap on his shoulder. "You should, but you don't today. Leif's got a way with planning. I suppose we ought to follow." There was no time for further grumbling. The rest came – Randulfr, too.

Soon we crouched in the thicket downstream from our boats. *Raven's Cross* was ablaze. It sat right in the middle of the River Add where it had run aground. The men I'd left behind to free the ship were dead. That is, except the newcomers who now lounged along the river next to the captives we meant to sell in Dyflin. They were freed from their shackles. Maredubb and a score of mounted warriors were just riding up.

"I've posted some men to intercept the bastards running down the river. They might already be dead," bragged King Maredubb.

The mast on Godfrey's flagship crunched as it fell into the waters. Maredubb took note. "Ah, the upstart's been paid back. It feels so good." The Welsh king studied the rest of our armada that rested peacefully between us and him. A cool wind from the north shook our thicket. It also made the open portion of a hastily lowered sail snap on *Charging Boar*. Maredubb pointed. "Why does the rest of the fleet not burn?"

The lead newcomer appeared confused, but did not move. His hands were securely fastened behind his head as he reclined. "I knew you'd want to burn Godfrey's ship, but why burn a fine fleet that you can put to use, or sell?"

Maredubb's face flushed red. He spoke through clenched teeth. "Because a true king, one who is not a scoundrel like the Norsemen or Danes, isn't a thief! I'll not be called Maredubb the Scavenger! If I want an armada, I'll build it myself. Now burn the floating logs of shit!"

The lounging men slowly sat up. It wasn't fast enough for the king.

"Burn it now! Move, or you'll be strapped to their masts and it will be your pyre." If it was possible, the king's face became redder. He pointed to the would-be slaves. "You, too!"

All of them scrambled. Someone found a few suitable torches from the nearby woods. They walked them to *Raven's Cross* to capture flames. They had to use their hands to shield their faces from the heat. The torches popped to life before their ends even touched the fire.

"Leif?" asked Randulfr. "If I don't hear a plan right now, I'm going to run out there and attack the goat turds."

The odds were fairly even, but we had no shields and no mail. Leif nodded. "My plan is simple. We edge toward this last ship in the line nearest us. We hope that we can get it pushed off and get enough rowing power to get away downstream."

"And abandon *Charging Boar*?" I asked stupidly. One of Aoife's arms touched mine. Her body was already cool to the touch.

Leif rightly didn't bother to answer. He crouched and quietly shuffled toward the nearest ship. It was a tub-like knarr, not much different from *Charging Boar*, but it didn't have a sail made by my loin's desire, Freydis. I'd miss that ship and all she represented.

"Not there," barked Maredubb. "Can you not feel the wind? You'll fight it all day and still the rest of the Viking fleet will sit there safely. Start with the northernmost boats and let the wind do the work." The men who carried the burning limbs allowed their shoulders to slump and trudged along the river's edge. They came directly to the ship we'd picked out.

Leif held up a hand, paused, and changed directions. Like roped cows, we followed without objection. He snaked back into the swamp only briefly. Leif led us over fallen logs and under limbs until we looked through another set of thorns. We were directly adjacent to *Charging Boar*. Downriver the ship we'd just left already had flames lapping up the prow. Its baggage burned brightly. The wind was pushing sheets of flame toward the other ships. In moments every single ship of Godfrey's short-term fleet would be on fire.

"How will we get past that?" asked Randulfr, pointing to the people with torches and the growing blaze.

"I don't know. We will or we won't," said Leif with maddening indifference. "Move fast. I'll jump aboard and haul the sail. You all push."

"The wind is against us!" Brandr protested.

"If it stays that way, we die," said Leif. He burst from our hiding place, ending all chance for argument. He was over the gunwale before anyone on the opposite bank even noticed. The roar of the fires covered any noise he made. Leif pulled on the fat rope with his hands and strong forearms, lifting the sail higher and higher.

We followed him, ramming our shoulders into the strakes and prow. My head was tucked between the ship and Aoife. We grunted and worked. The shallow-keeled vessel slipped back easily. The men began scrambling up the strakes. Randulfr reached down for Aoife. He gently lifted her and set her among the baggage. I stayed in the water and easily guided the ship to face the proper direction.

The movement at the side of his vision finally caught Maredubb's attention. He looked once, then twice. The king screamed at his horsemen. "Get them!"

His riders hadn't yet seen us. They hesitated a moment to see what the king was shouting about. We would need every heartbeat they gave us. We used them. Brandr found a bow, strung it and began sending poorly aimed arrows toward shore. The rest found oars. Leif tied off the tall red and white striped sail. Magnus took his place at the rudder.

"Leif, the damn sail is pushing us back," shouted Magnus. "The wind is against us. The oars and current are barely enough to move us forward. Drop the cloth or you'll get us killed."

"We're dead anyway," answered Leif.

Brandr's arrows took down two riders as they splashed into the river. Leif sent spears in their direction. Three horses went scrambling when he buried steel head into the necks. I pulled myself up into the ship. "Take an oar," commanded Magnus. "We need force. If the soldiers don't get us, the fire will." I stood looking at Magnus. Something was tugging on my mind, trying to be remembered. "Unless you can control the wind with your thoughts, grab some oak, idiot!"

The wind! I plunged into the baggage, tossing men's packs out of the way. One of Aoife's hands fell onto my hudfat. The girl was again saving us. I unlaced the sinew cord of the sack, found my quarry, said a prayer, to whom I don't recall, and tugged.

Tyrkr used an oar to strike a rider. The rest of our oarsmen stayed put. They pulled. Every muscle on their naked backs bulged. Slowly we moved downstream. Then the smoke that was beginning to choke us cleared. It ran away north, ahead of us instead of into our faces. The pennant snapped. Our sail billowed – in the right direction. The winds had shifted. We skipped forward, propelled by the triple power of men, current, and wind.

The riders were left in our wake. They tried to pursue in the stream's center, but their horses would soon be swimming instead of running. They halted, sending a few impotent spears after us. We squeaked through the narrow channel created by our burning fleet. I found a bucket and leaned over the gunwale. I used the river water to quickly put out any fires that started from the flying ash.

When we sailed out of the mouth of the River Add I looked to port. There on the far bank was Maredubb. He alone had raced his horse to the shoreline. The king sat there watching us go. He could do nothing else.

We had survived. Some of us survived, I mean.

Maredubb was victorious. Godfrey and his hopes for kingdom were dashed.

CHAPTER 13

The river had become Loch Crinan. The wind I'd unleashed from the knotted ropes given me by the witches on Man stayed with us for the remainder of the day. We were thankful for the wind and stowed every oar. Except for Magnus at the helm, we fell on top of the baggage and stared at the sky.

I say that I changed the course of the wind, because in the midst of our flight, when the riders were upon us and the breeze blew us backward, I laid my hands on those ropes given to me by the crazed sisters. I pulled. To this day I still wonder about that moment. Was it my fate all along that the wind would change in that instant? Perhaps the norns would think it funny and they wove my thread in such a way. Was it the ropes? I don't know. Or, was it Providence? I'd prayed to the Christian God once that day. Maybe that is how he answered.

Very quickly the loch turned into a long, narrow finger of the Irish Sea. Magnus leaned on the rudder and turned us on a southwest tack. Loki didn't like that direction. "We should return to Lismore and warn the men we left behind. Maredubb or the Dal Riatans could sack them before they finish the palisade Godfrey wanted built."

Randulfr sat up on a sea chest. He was picking at an old, stray piece of leather he'd found. Randulfr slapped it against his hand and threw it into the sea. "Or, the traitors among the men we left on Lismore have already slaughtered our side." Randulfr swallowed his spittle. It appeared as if it was a real chore. And it was an unpleasant task, for he was in the process of swallowing much more. His pride went down in that gulp. He'd served a king who went from victorious to ruin on a crisp morning. Now he was agreeing to serve a kid. "What do you think, Leif?"

Leif rolled off the hudfat on which he'd been resting. "Randulfr is more than right. Our men may already be dead. If they are not, what will an exhausted band of rubble be able to do if Maredubb lands?"

"We can warn them!" protested Loki. We could have I suppose. No one really wanted to, however.

"Well, where do we go?" I asked. "Man will be crawling with Maredubb's soldiers in a week or two or now! By Hel, Killian's replacement priest may run the island already. We can't return to Greenland, we haven't even been gone a year."

"We have to abandon the tiny hoards of treasure we all probably buried on Man. We must find a king to follow, a new ring-giver," answered Leif. He studied Randulfr, who nodded in agreement.

"Rogaland?" I asked. "Should we return to the land of our fathers and grandfathers?"

"No," answered Leif. "None of us will be satisfied with serving some jarl who is vassal to a king's vassal. As I said, we need a real king."

"To where? To whom?" Loki asked. "And what about our brothers on Lismore?"

Randulfr and Leif exchanged knowing glances. Randulfr, in those moments, had accepted Leif's command. He waved for his captain to answer.

"I'd say we know only one king who is wily and has proven he is capable through a long reign. We go to Dyflin and offer our services to King Kvaran and his sons."

"Sitric Silkbeard and Iron Knee," I whispered. I had heard Godfrey and Kvaran mention those names in the church on Iona. They were the best names I could think of for warriors. I hoped they lived up to the monikers.

"And what will make Kvaran want to send help to the outpost on Lismore?" asked Loki.

Leif grinned, "I don't know. Maybe we tell him that is where his ten men are held captive." Leif rattled around in his bags. He pulled out those cylindrical pieces of iron he'd stolen from Watchet's mint. "And if that doesn't work, we'll sell him these coin dies. With them the Viking King Kvaran of Dyflin will soon be minting his own English pennies with Aethelred's smirking face looking back at him."

Like Aethelred's image, we smiled. It felt wrong to grin after such a grim day. We'd all lost men with whom we'd drunk ale. Dead were men with whom we'd bled. Gone was a priest, small in stature, large in personality. Evaporated was the erstwhile sea king, Godfrey. He'd died the way he would have wanted, leading his men in a great battle. It was even as though the lovely and sharp Gudruna never was. They were carrion.

And vanished was the lively Irish thrall, Aoife. We moved toward the setting sun and I thought of her and all she'd done in order to find herself a bit of freedom and adventure. The girl had belittled me. She'd poked and prodded. She talked back to a king. I stirred.

The rest of the survivors watched silently as I tore a long section of extra sail. I set Aoife's body crossways on the cloth. Among the baggage of dead men I found heavy war axes and swords. None of my compatriots complained when I set the valuable items onto the girl and wrapped the fabric tightly around her, tying it so that the weights would stay secure. Leif lowered the sail so that we slowed.

Randulfr helped me pick Aoife's cloaked body up. I know that Christians say things when a loved one dies. They recite words from the One God, from the Word. I didn't know any such details then. I bent and kissed the cloth that covered her nose. I straightened and nodded to Randulfr. The two of us leaned over so that we set her on the top of the sea. When we let her go, Aoife's white grave wrappings dropped into the depths. I could see her for only a single heartbeat until the darkness swallowed her whole.

The sound of rope rubbing on timber meant that Leif was already pulling up the sail. The others wanted to be far away from Dunadd. I leaned on the gunwale and stared at the murky sea. It began slipping past my view faster and faster as the sail gathered the strength of the wind. The rest of the men went about their business in respectful silence.

My time of sadness had passed. I no longer mourned the girl, not because I hadn't grown to love her. No. I stopped whimpering because I did love the little imp. With my chin resting on my forearm, I smiled when I thought of Aoife, for I knew that of all the women I've ever met, she, along with the daughter that I have yet to tell you about, would meet me in Valhalla.

THE END

(Dear Reader-See Historical Remarks to separate fact from fiction.)

HISTORICAL REMARKS

Godfrey Haraldsson and his brother Magnus pillaged their way around the Irish Sea and even around the entire island of Ireland itself for much of the second half of the Tenth Century. For clarity, I've eliminated brother Magnus so that he was not confused with my character, the helmsman, who bore the same name. Godfrey's brother is thought to have spent time attacking the west coast of Ireland – which is where Godfrey in my story gathered up Aoife – while Godfrey battered the Irish Sea.

There are some who say the brothers' base of operations was the Isle of Man. Other historians say no, Godfrey more likely operated out of the Hebrides, further north. There is, of course, a correct answer that is as of yet unknown with certainty. A new document find or a new archaeological study may one day give us the right answer. I chose Man simply because it was central to the places that Godfrey and Magnus raided and has a rich history all its own.

The Isle of Man has had more Viking hacksilver hoards discovered on its lands than all of Ireland – astonishing when you think of the size differences. But, the finds demonstrate the economic power and gravity that this weigh-station on so many northern trade routes wielded. Man has many interesting Norse graves, constructed of stones arranged in the shape of a ship's hull. Some of these can be found at Balladoole and Ballateare. The stone I described with the mixture of Christian and Norse theologies is real and exists to this day. Similarly, the stone dedicated to the traitor named Horse Ketil still sits on Man, though no one knows who Horse Ketil was or what he did to be so maligned for eternity.

The Norse peoples in Norway and abroad in Iceland and Greenland and Man were free compared to their English or other medieval counterparts. It took much longer for kings to consolidate their power over the large stretches of difficult terrain in the mountains and fjords and independent peoples. Under these conditions one of the governing mechanisms that evolved was the Thing, or local assembly. The Thing was called occasionally to settle disputes between participants in the open. The Thing on the Isle of Man has become known as the Tynwald. Its roots go back to the Viking sea kings over 1,000 years ago. Tynwald is still what the island's parliament is called, allowing the small island to claim to have the oldest parliament in the world with an unbroken existence. I am certain that the proud descendents of Iceland's first settlers may want to argue the claim when it comes to their Althing. But that is another story.

Exactly who was Godfrey Haraldsson's father is not known with certainty. Many believe it was Harald Bluetooth, famous son of Gorm the Old from Denmark and the man for whom we've named Bluetooth communication technology today. Others say, as have I, that Godfrey's father was Harald of Bayeux, a Norman Viking. For an in depth discussion of this topic and much of the history in *Norseman Raider*, read *Viking Pirates and Christian Princes* by Benjamin Hudson. It contains a wealth of information.

Godfrey was known as a King of the Isles. Exactly which islands were among those Isles was something that was in constant flux. It ebbed and flowed with the despairs and fortunes of its kings and the strength of the peoples that surrounded the islands kingdom – Irish, Welsh, and the Scots.

Dal Riata was founded by an Irishman back when Scotland was known as Pictland during the Dark Ages. Like the Kingdom of the Isles, its borders expanded and contracted many times over the years. Generally speaking, Dal Riata included a smidgen of northern Ireland in the Ulster region and the western reaches of Scotland, Argyll today.

Our hero, Halldorr, is fictional. Leif Eriksson is not. Tyrkr, the German thrall is not. Both were very real men who lived extraordinary lives, but it is unlikely that they were involved with Godfrey in any way. You may want to read the original three of *The Norseman Chronicles: The Norseman, Paths of the Norseman, and Norseman Chief* if you wish to have a better understanding as to why they wound up where they did in my tale.

The incidents that set Godfrey's actions in motion were real. In 986 A.D. Godfrey attacked Dal Riata; we're not sure where, but I assumed Lismore and its monastery. During the raid, 140 of his warriors were caught and hanged. Godfrey went away, but came back in the dark of Christmas night. He and his company killed the bishop, the abbot, and 13 monks who prayed in the monastery's church before his army scurried away. In my mind he got ample revenge, but I figured Godfrey, an up-and-coming Viking king, would want more.

Godfrey is thought to have raided the Welsh island of Anglesey many times during his career. The raid I highlighted actually did take place in 987 A.D. In that raid his band of unknown numbers took 2,000 captives while soundly defeating the Welsh ruler Maredubb ab Owain. Maredubb had to flee from the island to the heart of Wales. He didn't return to pay the ransom of treasure for his people until 989 A.D.

The barrow grave I used as my model for the one on Anglesey, the one told of by Eyvind in my story, is called Bryn Celli Ddu. It rests to this day on the southeastern edge of Anglesey Island. The mound is in an open field, but it is thought to have been surrounded by trees at some time in its history. The grave was robbed long ago. It was built for a man of importance in the Stone Age. Different phases of its construction are thought to have taken place as far back as 4,000 B.C.

In 988 A.D. Godfrey's army is thought to have raided the mint at Watchet. This is conjecture, sound perhaps, but still a guess. Godfrey was one of the most active Vikings in those waters during that time. Since the *Anglo-Saxon Chronicle* is silent on exactly who wreaked the devastation on Watchet that year, scholars assume it was King Godfrey. Devon nobles, Goda and Strenwald, were killed during the attack. You can still see remains, albeit meager, of the mint on the cliffs west of the modern day town of Watchet in what is today Somerset. At the time our story takes place it was considered part of Devon. The mint on the hill was active from 979 to 1050 A.D. It was abandoned for a time due to the erosion on the cliffs. Its location moved westward and it again began producing coins in 1080.

Immediately after the raid in Watchet and across the Irish Sea in Dyflin (today's Dublin) English coins began to circulate. Obviously, many coins were stolen from the mint. However, at the same time, the first coins to be minted in all of Ireland began to appear. They were English pennies stamped by dies taken from Watchet.

Godfrey was actually killed in a raid in Dal Riata in 989 A.D. The exact circumstances are unknown, but I thought it a nice yarn to spin to have him still hunting for his revenge. The climactic battle at the ancient fort of Dunadd is pure, made-up fun. But the fort did exist and it was the capital of Dal Riata for centuries. At the time our tale took place, it would have been surrounded by swamps known as the Moine Mohr, making it difficult to reach by anything other than the main road. You can visit the ruins today.

I spent some time in the story talking about strange Frankish blades. I intentionally spelled the names with slight variation. Modern science has proven that the blades marked with +ULFBERH+T are of a quality of steel superior to any steel in Europe until the Twentieth Century. Those blades are strong, durable, light, and flexible. They were perfect for battle. Blades marked with +ULFBERHT+ are thought to be weak copies. Their steel is of a typical low grade for the times. They were brittle. Just like manufacturers must contend with intellectual and trademark piracy today, so did the Frankish sword smiths. In 2013 Nova and National Geographic produced a fine documentary called *The Viking Sword* which lays out a strong case for the two types of blades.

The readings I used to prepare for *Norseman Raider* included the previously mentioned work by Mr. Hudson as well as the *Poetic Edda* and *Prose Edda*, which are Icelandic writings from the Thirteenth Century. The latter two works were penned by Snorri Sturluson, but included oral tales carried down through the ages by the poets of the day, skalds. The stories written by Snorri would have been familiar to all of the broader Scandinavian culture. As in my previous Halldorr novels, I utilized *Vikings: The North Atlantic Saga*, edited by Fitzhugh and Ward. *Viking Poetry of Love and War* by Judith Jesch gave great ideas for the types of things the people of my tale held dear. The two verses recited by Eyvind the Troublesome in our story are translations from Icelandic poems. The first was originally recited on the night Porir Jokull died, August 21, 1238. I found the verse in a paper by Professor Anthony Faulkes who is at the University of Birmingham. For the Kormakr poem I used a combination of translations from Rory McTurk, Emeritus Professor at the University of Leeds and Lee M. Hollander. Finally, Aoife's speech near the beginning of the novel was based upon a Tenth Century poem by Egil Skallgrimsson. In it a young boy dreams of going a-Viking and killing a man or two.

It is likely that Halldorr has more life in him. As a rule, if Halldorr breathes, then adventure follows. I encourage you to read more of his tales. The first three of *The Norseman Chronicles* may be found on Amazon and Barnes & Noble. In his next work he will come face-to-face with famous historical figures such a Kvaran, Gytha, Silkbeard, Iron Knee, Mael Sechnaill, Olaf Tryggvason, and many more.

Lastly, if you desire a change of pace from the rampaging Norsemen, check out my three-book series entitled *The Wald Chronicles*. It follows the struggle of a rag-tag group of Germanic tribesmen against mighty Rome under Augustus.

ABOUT THE AUTHOR

Jason Born is the author of *The Norseman Chronicles*, a multi-volume work of historical fiction detailing the adventures of the Viking, Halldorr, who lived during the time of Erik the Red and Sweyn Forkbeard. *The Wald Chronicles* series of historical novels centers on the conflict in Germania between the Roman legionaries and their tribal adversaries over 2,000 years ago. He is an analyst and portfolio manager for a Registered Investment Advisory firm. Jason lives in the Midwest with his wife and three children. If you enjoyed this work and would like to see more, Jason asks you to consider doing the following:

1. Please encourage your friends to buy a copy – and read it!
2. Go to his author page (Jason Born – Author) on Facebook and click "Like" so that you may follow information on GIVEAWAYS or his next book.
3. If you think the book deserves praise, please post a five star review on Amazon and/or a five star review on Goodreads.com.
4. Follow him on Twitter, handle - @authorjasonborn
5. Visit his website, www.authorjasonborn.com, for the most complete information.

Made in the USA
Lexington, KY
30 April 2015